D0090179

# WALKAWAY

## also by cory doctorow

*The Complete Idiot's Guide to Publishing Science Fiction*
(with Karl Schroeder)

*Essential Blogging*
(with Rael Dornfest, J. Scott Johnson, Shelley Powers,
Benjamin Trott, and Mena G. Trott)

*Down and Out in the Magic Kingdom*

*A Place So Foreign and Eight More*

*Eastern Standard Tribe*

*Someone Comes to Town, Someone Leaves Town*

*Overclocked: Stories of the Future Present*

*Little Brother*

*Content: Selected Essays on Technology, Creativity, Copyright,
and the Future of the Future*

*Makers*

*For the Win*

*With a Little Help*

*Context: Further Selected Essays on Productivity, Creativity, Parenting,
and Politics in the 21st Century*

*The Great Big Beautiful Tomorrow*

*The Rapture of the Nerds* (with Charles Stross)

*Pirate Cinema*

*Homeland*

cory doctorow

# WALKAWAY

A Tom Doherty Associates Book
New York

This is a work of fiction. All of the characters, organizations, and events portrayed in this novel are either products of the author's imagination or are used fictitiously.

WALKAWAY



Designed by Mary A. Wirth



Edited by Patrick Nielsen Hayden

A Tor Book
Published by Tom Doherty Associates
175 Fifth Avenue
New York, NY 10010

www.tor-forge.com



The Library of Congress Cataloging-in-Publication Data is available upon request

ISBN 978-0-7653-9276-3 (hardcover)
ISBN 978-0-7653-9417-0 (signed edition)
ISBN 978-0-7653-9278-7 (e-book)



First Edition: April 2017

Printed in the United States of America

0 9 8 7 6 5 4 3 2 1

*For Erik Stewart and Aaron Swartz.*

*First days, better nations.*

*We fight on.*

# WALKAWAY

# 1

# communist party

## [i]

Hubert Vernon Rudolph Clayton Irving Wilson Alva Anton Jeff Harley Timothy Curtis Cleveland Cecil Ollie Edmund Eli Wiley Marvin Ellis Espinoza was too old to be at a Communist party. At twenty-seven, he had seven years on the next oldest partier. He felt the demographic void. He wanted to hide behind one of the enormous filthy machines that dotted the floor of the derelict factory. Anything to escape the frank, flat looks from the beautiful children of every shade and size who couldn't understand why an old man was creepering around.

"Let's go," he said to Seth, who'd dragged him to the party. Seth was terrified of aging out of the beautiful children demographic and entering the world of non-work. He had an instinct for finding the most outré, cutting edge, transgressive goings-on among the children who'd been receding in their rearview mirrors. Hubert, Etc, Espinoza only hung out with Seth because part of his thing about not letting go of his childhood was also not letting go of childhood friends. He was insistent on the subject, and Hubert, Etc was a pushover.

"This is about to get *real*," Seth said. "Why don't you get us beers?"

That was exactly what Hubert, Etc didn't want to do. The beer was where the most insouciant adolescents congregated, merry and weird as tropical fishes. Each more elfin and tragic than the last. Hubert, Etc remembered that age, the certainty that the world was so broken that only an idiot would deign to acknowledge it or its inevitability. Hubert, Etc often confronted his reflection in his bathroom screen, stared into his eyes in their nest of bruisey bags, and remembered being someone who spent every minute denying the world's legitimacy, and now he was enmeshed in it. Hubert, Etc couldn't self-delude the knowledge away. Anyone under twenty would spot it in a second.

"Go *on,* man, come on. I got you into this party. Least you can do."

Hubert, Etc didn't say any obvious things about not wanting to come in the first place and not wanting beer in the second place. There were lots of pointless places an argument with Seth could go. He had his Peter Pan face on, prepared to be ha-ha-only-serious until you wore down, and Hubert, Etc started the night worn.

"I don't have any money," Hubert, Etc said.

Seth gave him a look.

"Oh, yeah," Hubert, Etc said. "Communist party."

Seth passed him two red party cups, their color surely no accident.

As Hubert, Etc drew up to the taps—spoodged onto a vertical piece of structural steel that shot out of the floor and up to the rafters, skinned with checkered safety-yellow bar codes and smudges of entropy and dancing lights of the DJ—and tried to figure out which of the beautiful children was bartender, factum factotum, or commissar. No one moved to help him or block him as he edged closer, though three of the children stopped to watch with intense expressions.

All three wore Marx glasses with the huge, bushy beards hanging, like in the vocoder videos, full of surreal menace. These ones were dyed bright colors, and one had something in it—memory wire?—that made it crawl like tentacles.

Hubert, Etc clumsily filled a cup, and the girl held it while he filled the other. The beer was incandescent, or bioluminescent, and Hubert, Etc worried about what might be in the transgenic jesus microbes that could turn water into beer, but the girl was looking at him from behind those glasses, her eyes unreadable in the flickering dance-lights. He drank.

"Not bad." He burped, burped again. "Fizzy, though?"

"Because it's fast-acting. It was ditch water an hour ago. We sieved it, brought it up to room temp, dumped in the culture. It's live, too—add some precursor, it'll come back. Survives in your urine. Just save some, you want to make more."

"Communist beer?" Hubert, Etc said. The best bon mot he could scrounge. He was better when he had time to think.

"*Nazdarovya.*" She clicked her cup against his and drained it, loosing a bone-rattling belch when she finished. She gave her chest a thump and scared out smaller burps, refilled the glass.

"If it comes out in pee," Hubert, Etc said, "what happens if someone adds the precursor to the sewers? Will it turn to beer?"

She gave him a look of adolescent scorn. "That would be stupid. Once it's diluted it can't metabolize precursor. Flush and it's just pee. The critters die in an hour or two, so a latrine won't turn into a reservoir of long-lived existential threats to the water supply. It's just beer." Burp. "Fizzy beer."

Hubert, Etc sipped. It was really good. Didn't taste like piss at all. "All beer is rented, right?" he said.

"Most beer is rented. This is free. You know: 'free as in free beer.'" She drank half the cup, spilling into her beard. It beaded on the crinkly refugee stuff. "You don't come to a lot of Communist parties."

Hubert, Etc shrugged. "I don't," he said. "I'm old and boring. Eight years ago, we weren't doing this."

"What were you doing, Gramps?" Not in a mean way, but her two friends—a girl the same shade as Seth and a guy with beautiful cat-eyes—sniggered.

"Hoping to get jobs on the zeppelins!" Seth said, slinging an arm around Hubert, Etc's neck. "I'm Seth, by the way. This is Hubert, Etc."

"Etcetera?" the girl said. Just a little smile. Hubert, Etc liked her. He thought that she was probably secretly nice, probably didn't think he was a dork just because he was a few years older, and hadn't heard of her favorite kind of synthetic beer. He recognized this belief was driven by a theory of humanity that most people were good, but also by a horrible, oppressive loneliness and nonspecific horniness. Hubert, Etc was bright, which wasn't always easy, and had a moderate handle on his psyche that made it hard to bullshit himself.

"Tell her, dude," Seth said. "Come on, it's a great story."

"It's not a great story," Hubert, Etc said. "My parents gave me a lot of middle names is all."

"How many is a lot?"

"Twenty," he said. "The top twenty names from the 1890 census."

"That's only nineteen," she said, quickly. "And one first name."

Seth laughed like this was the funniest thing he'd ever heard. Even Hubert, Etc smiled. "Most people don't get that. Technically, I have nineteen middle names and one first name."

"Why did your parents give you nineteen middle names and one first name?" she asked. "And are you sure it's nineteen middle names? Maybe you have ten first names and ten middle names."

"I think that it's hard to claim to have more than one first name, because first has a specificity that middle lacks. Notwithstanding your Mary Anns and Jean Marcs and such, which are hyphenated by convention."

"Fair point," she said. "Though, come on, if Mary Ann is a first name, why isn't Mary Ann Tanya Jessie Banana Pants Monkey Vomit etc?"

"My parents would agree. They were making a statement about names, after

Anonymous brought in its Real Name Policy. They'd both been active, worked to make it a political party, so they were really fucked off. Thought it was obvious that if you were 'Anonymous' you couldn't have a 'Real Name Policy.' They decided to give their kid a unique name that never fit into any database and would give him the right to legally use a whole bunch of sub-names.

"By the time I got all this, I was used to 'Hubert,' and I stuck to it."

Seth took Hubert's beer cup, swilled from it, burped. "I've always called you Hubert, Etc, though. It's cool, and it's easier to say."

"I don't mind."

"Do it, though, okay?"

"What?" Hubert, Etc knew the answer.

"The names. You've got to hear this."

"You don't have to," she said.

"I do, probably, or you'll wonder." He'd made peace with it. It was part of growing up. "Hubert Vernon Rudolph Clayton Irving Wilson Alva Anton Jeff Harley Timothy Curtis Cleveland Cecil Ollie Edmund Eli Wiley Marvin Ellis Espinoza."

She cocked her head, nodded. "Needs more Banana Pants."

"Bet you got teased like hell at school though, right?" Seth said.

This pissed Hubert, Etc off. It was stupid, and it was a recurring stupidity. "Come on, really? You think that *names* are why kids get teased? The causal arrow points the other way. If the kids are making fun of your name, it's because you're unpopular—you're not unpopular because of your name. If the coolest kid in school was called 'Harry Balls' they'd call him Harold. If the school goat was called 'Lisa Brown,' they'd call her 'Shitstain.'" He nearly said, *Seriously,* don't be an asshole, but didn't. He was invested in being an adult. Seth paid no attention to the possibility that he was being an asshole.

"What's *your* name?" Seth said to the girl.

"Lisa Brown," she replied.

Hubert, Etc snickered.

"Seriously?"

"No."

He waited to see if she'd offer her name, shrugged. "I'm Seth." He went to her friends, who'd inched closer. One of them did a fancy handshake, which he faked with totally unselfconscious enthusiasm that Hubert, Etc envied and was embarrassed by.

The dance music got louder. Seth refilled Hubert, Etc's cup and took it to the dance floor. Hubert was the only one without a cup. The girl refilled hers and passed it.

"Good stuff," she shouted, her breath tickling his cheek. The music was really loud, an automated mix, tied into DJ stuff that used lidar and heat-mapping to characterize crowd-responses to musical mixes and optimized them to get everyone on the floor. They'd had it back when Hubert, Etc was young enough to go clubbing, called it Rule 34 for all the different mixes, but it had been cheesy then. Now it was the business.

"Kinda hoppy, though."

"Not the taste. The enzymes. Stuff in it helps you break it down, stops it from turning into formaldehyde in your blood. Good for reducing hangovers. It's Turkish."

"Turkish?"

"Well, Turkish-ish. Came out of refus in Syria. They've got a lab. It's called Gezi. If you're interested, I can send you stuff about it."

Was she hitting on him? Eight years ago, giving someone your contact details was an invitation. Maybe they'd swung into a time of more promiscuous name-space management and less promiscuous socio-sexual norms. Hubert, Etc wished he'd skimmed a précis of current sociology of twenty-year-olds. He rubbed the interface strip on his ring finger and muttered "contact details," held out his hand. Her hand was warm, rough, and small. She touched a strip she wore as a choker and whispered, and he felt a confirming buzz from his system, then a double-buzz that meant that she'd reciprocated.

"So you can white-list me."

Hubert, Etc wondered if she was used to sharing contacts so widely that she had to worry about spam or—

"You've never been to one of these," she said, her face right up to his ear again.

"No," he shouted. Her hair smelled like burning tires and licorice.

"You'll love this, come on, let's get in close, they're going to start soon."

She took his hand again, and as her calluses rasped over his skin, he felt another buzz. It was endogenous and hadn't originated with his interface stuff.

---

They skirted the dancers, kicking through leaves and puffs of dust that swirled in the lights. There were glittering motes in the dust that made the air seem laden with fairy-glitter. Hubert, Etc caught sight of Seth. Seth looked back and clocked the scene—the girl, the hands, the scramble through dark spaces for private vantage, and his face creased with passing envy before turning into a fratty leer to which he added a thumbs-up. The automatic music thudded, Cantopop and rumba that Rule 34 tumbled out of its directed random-walk through music-space.

"Here's good," she said, as they yanked themselves onto a catwalk. The gritty service-ladder left rust streaks on Hubert, Etc's palms. Out of the music's blast, they could hear each other, and Hubert, Etc was aware of his breath and pulse.

"Keep your eye on that." She pointed at a machine to one side. Hubert, Etc squinted and saw her friends from before moving around it. "They do furniture, mostly shelving. There was a ton of feedstock in the storeroom."

"Did you help put this"—a sweep of his arm to take in the factory, the dancers—"together?"

She laid one finger alongside the rubber nose, winked slowly. "Supreme Soviet," she said. She tapped the temple of her glasses, and he caught a shimmer as their magnification kicked in with false color and stabilization. "They've got it." The music cut off mid-note.

A rumble in the bones of the factory vibrated the catwalk. The dancers looked around for its source, then a wave of attention propagated through them as gaze followed gaze and they focused on the machine, which moved, dust shaking down, dance-lights skewering it, lighting more motes. A new smell now, woodsy, full of dangerous volatiles that boiled off the machine's elements as they glowed to life. The hush in the room broke when the first composite plank dropped onto the assembly bed, nudged by thousands of infinitesimal fingers that corrected its alignment just as the next plank dropped. Now they fell at regular intervals, a ladder of thin, strong, supple cellulosic boards, swiftly joined by crosspieces, also swept into position, lining up the prefabricated joinery elements that clicked together with a snick. The fingers lifted the grid, moved it down the line, and a new grid was assembled just as quickly, then they mated and clicked together.

More of them, then a loop of fastening fabric thrown, caught, and cinched around the framework, and the completed piece was tossed to one side. Another was a minute behind it on the line. A dancer sauntered over to the output file and lifted the finished piece easily, brought it one-handed onto the dance floor, sliced through the fastening with a knife that gleamed in the dance-lights. The bed—that's what it was—click-clacked into place, yawning back, ready for a mattress. The dancer climbed up onto the bed's grid of slats and started jumping up and down. It was as springy as a trampoline, and in moments she was doing midair splits, butt drops, even a somersault.

The girl sat back and ran a finger around her beard. "Good stuff." Hubert, Etc was sure she was smiling.

"That's a cool bed frame," Hubert, Etc said, for lack of something better to say.

"One of the best," she said. "They had a ton of profitable lines, but bed frames were the best. Big with hotels, because they're practically indestructible and they're featherlight."

"Why aren't they making them anymore?"

"Oh, they are. Muji shut down the plant and moved to Alberta six months ago. Got a huge subsidy to relocate—Ontario couldn't match the deal. They'd only been here for a couple of years, only employed twenty people all told, their two-year tax holiday was ending. Place has been empty since then. We can do the whole line from here, all Muji's furniture, including white-label stuff they do for Nestlé and Standard & Poors & Möet & Chandon. Chairs, tables, bookcases, shelving. There's an empty feedstock plant in Orangeville we're hitting for the next party, raw material for the supply chain. If we don't get caught, we can do enough furnishings for a couple thousand families."

"You don't charge for them or anything?"

A long look. "Communist party, remember?"

"Yeah, but, how do you eat and stuff?"

She shrugged. "Here and there. This and that. Kindness of strangers."

"So people bring you food and you give them this stuff?"

"No," she said. "We don't do barter. This is gifts, the gift economy. Everything freely given, nothing sought in return."

It was Hubert, Etc's turn. "How often do you get a gift around the same time as you're giving one of these away? Who doesn't show up with something to leave behind when they take something?"

"Of course. It's hard to get people out of the scarcity quid-pro-quo habit. But we know they don't *have* to bring anything. Did *you* bring anything tonight?"

He patted his pockets. "I've got a couple million bucks, nothing much."

"Keep it. Money is the one thing we don't take. My mom always said money was the crappiest present. Anyone trying to give or get money around here, we sling 'em out on their butts, no second chances."

"I'll keep my wallet in my pants."

"Good idea." She was kind enough not to notice the double entendre that made Hubert, Etc blush. "I'm Pranksterella, by the way."

"And I thought my parents were screwed up."

The beard wiggled inscrutably: "My parents didn't give me that one," she said. "It's my party name."

"Like Trotsky," he said. "He was Lev Davidovich. Did an independent history unit on Bolshevism in the eleventh grade. This is much more interesting."

"They say Old Karl had the right diagnosis and the wrong prescription." She shrugged. "Putting the 'party' back into Communist party makes a difference. Jury's still out. We'll probably implode. You guys did, right? The zeppelins?"

"Zeppelins *explode,*" he said.

"Har. De. Har."

"Sorry." He stuck his legs out and rested against a guardrail that creaked, then held. He realized that he could have gone over and fallen ten meters to the concrete floor. "But yeah, the zepps didn't work out." They'd made perfect sense on paper. All these time-rich, cash-poor people with friends all over the world. Zepps were cheap as hell to run, if you didn't care where or how fast you went. There'd been hundreds of startups, talking big about climate-appropriate transport and the "new age of aviation." Despite all that, there was the inescapable sense that they were in a gold rush, a game of musical chairs that would end with a few lucky souls sitting on enough money to stop pretending to give a shit about any kind of aviation except for the kind that came with champagne and a warm eye mask after takeoff. A lot of money sloshed around, a lot of talk from governments about nurturing local talent and new industrial reality. The talk came with huge R&D tax credits and more investment money.

Three years into it—during which Hubert, Etc and everyone he knew gave up everything to scramble to put huge, floating cigars into the sky—the thing imploded. Just a few years on, it was retro-chic. Hubert, Etc had seen a "genuine Mark II zeppelin comfort suite" in a clip on super-fashionable decor. A painstakingly restored set of flying dormitory furniture was refitted for two rich, stationary people, not dozens of itinerant flying hobos. Hubert, Etc once spent three months in a co-op that was building the prefab suites, ready to slot into airship platforms. His sweat-equity was supposed to entitle him to a certain amount of time every year in the sky on board any ship carrying a co-op unit, bumbling through the world's prevailing winds to wherever.

"Wasn't your fault. It's the nature of the beast to believe in bubbles and think you can just entrepreneur your way out." She unclipped her beard and her glasses. She had a fox face, lots of points, grooved where the heavy glasses had rested, sheened with sweat. She wiped the sweat with her shirttail, giving him a glimpse of her pale stomach, a mole by her navel.

"And your people here?" He wished for more beer, realized he needed a piss, wondered if he should hold it in to make more.

"We're not going to entrepreneur our way out of anything. This isn't entrepreneurship."

"Anti-entrepreneurship's been tried, too—slacking doesn't get you anywhere."

"We're not anti-entrepreneur, either. We're not entrepreneurial in the way that baseball isn't tic-tac-toe. We're playing a different game."

"What's that?"

"Post-scarcity," said with near-religious solemnity.

He didn't succeed at keeping his face still, because she looked pissed off. "Sorry." Hubert, Etc was one of nature's apologizers. A housemate once made a set of cardboard tombstones for Halloween, hung like bunting across the kitchen cabinets. Hubert, Etc's read "Sorry."

"Don't sorry me. Look, Etcetera, at all this. On paper, this place is useless, the stuff coming off that line has to be destroyed. It's a trademark violation; even though it came off an official Muji line, using Muji's feedstock, it doesn't have Muji's license, so that configuration of cellulose and glue is a crime. That's so manifestly fucked up and shit that anyone who pays attention to it is playing the wrong game and doesn't deserve consideration. Anyone who says the world is a better place with this building left to rot—"

"I don't think that's the argument," Hubert, Etc said. He'd once had this kind of discussion a lot. He wasn't young and avant-garde, but he understood this. "It's that telling people what they can do with their stuff produces worse outcomes than letting them do stupid things and letting the market sort out the good ideas from—"

"You think anyone believes that anymore? You know why people who need furniture don't just break down the door of this place? It's not market orthodoxy."

"Of course not. It's fear."

"They're right to be afraid. This world, if you aren't a success, you're a failure. If you're not on top, you're on the bottom. If you're in between, you're hanging on by your fingernails, hoping you can get a better grip before your strength gives out. Everyone holding on is too scared to let go. Everyone on the bottom is too worn down to try. The people on the top? They're the ones who depend on things staying the way they are."

"So what do you call your philosophy then? Post-fear?"

She shrugged. "Don't care. Lots of names for it. None of that matters. *That's* what I care about." She pointed to the dancers and the beds. Another line of machines was online and folding-table-and-chair sets were piling up.

"What about 'communist'?"

"What about it?"

"That's a label with a lot of history. You could be communists."

She waved her beard at him. "Communist *party*. That doesn't make us 'communists' any more than throwing a birthday party makes us 'birthdayists.' Communism is an interesting thing to do, nothing I ever want to be."

The ladder clanged and the catwalk vibrated like a tuning fork. They looked over the edge just as Seth's head came into view. "Hello, lovebirds!" he said. He was sloppy and jittery, high on something interesting. Hubert, Etc grabbed him before he could reel over the guardrail. Another person popped over the edge, one of the bearded threesome that had been by the beer.

"Hey-hey!" He seemed stoned, too, but it was hard for Hubert, Etc to tell.

"This is the guy," Seth said. "The guy with the names."

"You're Etcetera!" the new guy said, arms wide like he was greeting a lost brother. "I'm Billiam." He gave Hubert, Etc a lingering drunkard's embrace. Hubert, Etc had dated guys, was open to the idea, but Billiam, beautiful tilted eyes aside, was not his type and too high to consider in any event. Hubert, Etc firmly peeled him off, and the girl helped.

"Billiam," she said, "what have you two been up to?"

Billiam and Seth locked eyes and dissolved into hysterical giggles.

She gave Billiam a playful shove that sent him sprawling, one foot dangling over the catwalk.

"Meta," she said. "Or something like it."

He'd heard of it. It gave you ironic distance—a very now kind of high. Conspiracy people thought it was too zeitgeisty to be a coincidence, claimed it was spread to soften the population for its miserable lot. In his day—eight years before—the scourge had been called "Now," something they gave to source-code auditors and drone pilots to give them robotic focus. He'd eaten a shit-ton of it while working on zepps. It made him feel like a happy android. The conspiracy people had said the same thing about Now that they said about Meta. End of the day, anything that made you discount objective reality and assign a premium to some kind of internal mental state was going to be both pro-survival and pro–status-quo.

"What's your name?" Hubert, Etc said.

"Does it matter?" she said.

"It's driving me nuts," he admitted.

"You've got it in your address book," she said.

He rolled his eyes. Of course he did. He rubbed the interface patch on his cuff and fingered it for a moment. "Natalie Redwater?" he said. "As in *the* Redwaters?"

"There are a lot of Redwaters," she said. "We're some of them. Not the ones you're thinking of, though."

"Close to them," Billiam said from his stoned, prone, ironic world. "Cousins?"

"Cousins," she said.

Hubert, Etc tried hard not to let phrases like "trustafarian" and "fauxhemian" cross his mind. He probably failed. She didn't look happy about having her name out.

"Cousins as in 'poor country relations,'" Seth said, from his fetal position, "or cousins as in 'get to use the small airplane?'"

Hubert, Etc felt bad, not just because he was crushing on her. He'd known people born to privilege, plenty in the zepp scene, and they could be nice people whose salient facts extended beyond unearned privilege. Seth wouldn't have normally been a dick about this kind of thing—it was precisely the sort of thing he wasn't normally a dick about—but he was high.

"Cousins as in 'enough to worry about kidnapping' and 'not enough to pay the ransom,' she said, with the air of someone repeating a timeworn phrase.

The arrival of the two stoned boys sucked the magic out of the night. Below, the machines found a steady rhythm, and Rule 34 spun again, blending witch house and New Romantic, automatically syncing with the machines' beat. It wasn't pulling a lot of dancers, but a few diehards were out, being beautiful and in motion. Hubert, Etc stared at them.

Three things happened: the music changed (psychobilly and dubstep), he opened his mouth to say something, and Billiam said, in a tittering singsong: "Buuuu-sted!" and pointed at the ceiling.

They followed his finger and saw the flock of drones detach from the ceiling, fold back their wings, and plunge into a screaming drop. Natalie pulled her beard back on and Billiam made sure his was on, too.

"Seth, masks!" Hubert, Etc shook his friend. There had been a good reason for Seth to carry both of their masks, but he couldn't remember it. Seth sat up with his eyebrows raised and a smirk on his face. Tucking chin to chest, Hubert, Etc swarmed over Seth and roughly turned out his pockets. He slapped his mask to his face and felt the fabric adhere in bunches and whorls as his breath teased it out and the oils in his skin were wicked through its weave. He did Seth.

"You don't need to do this," Seth said.

"Right," said Hubert, Etc. "It's out of the goodness of my heart."

"You're worried they'll walk my social graph and find you in the one-hop/high-intensity zone." Seth's smile, glowing in the darkness of his face, was infuriatingly calm. It vanished behind the mask. That was the stupid Meta. "You'd be screwed then. They'll run your data going back years, dude, until they find something. They always find something. They'll put the screws to you, threaten you with every horrible unless you turn narc. Room 101 all the way, baby—"

Hubert, Etc gave Seth a harder-than-necessary slap upside the head. Seth said "Ow," mildly, stopped talking. The drones flew a coverage pattern, like pigeons on crank. Hubert, Etc's interface surfaces shivered as they detected attempted incursions and shut down. Hubert, Etc downloaded countermeasures regularly, if only to fight off drive-by identity thief creeps, but he shivered back, wondering if he was more up-to-date than the cop-bots.

The party had broken up. Dancers fled, some holding furniture. The music leapt to offensive-capability volume, a sound so loud it made your eyes hurt. Hubert, Etc clapped his hands over his ears just as one of the drones clipped an I-beam and spun out, smashing to the ground. A drone dive-bombed the sound-system's control unit, knocked it to the ground. The sound went on.

Hubert, Etc pulled Seth to sit, pointed at the ladder. They let go of their ears to climb down. It was torture: the brutal sound, the painful vibrations of the metal under their hands and feet. Natalie came down, pointed at a doorway.

Something heavy and painful clipped Hubert, Etc in the head and shoulder, knocking him to his knees. He got to all fours, then to his feet, seeing stars behind the mask.

He looked for whatever had hit him. It took him a second to make sense of what he saw. Billiam lay on the floor, limbs in a strange swastika, head visibly misshapen, an inky pool of blood spread around it in the dimness. Fighting dizziness and pain from the sound, he bent over Billiam and gingerly peeled the beard. It was saturated with blood. Billiam's face was smashed into a parody of human features; his forehead had an ugly dent encompassing one eye. Hubert, Etc tried for a pulse at Billiam's wrist and then his throat, but all he felt was the thunder of the music. He put his hand on Billiam's chest to feel for the rise and fall of breath, but couldn't tell.

He looked up, but Seth and Natalie had already reached the door. They must not have seen Billiam fall, must not have seen him crash into Hubert, Etc. A drone ruffled Hubert, Etc's hair. Hubert, Etc wanted to cry. He pushed the feeling down, remembering first aid. He shouldn't move Billiam. But if he stayed, he'd be nabbed. It might be too late. The part of his brain in charge of cowardly self-justification chattered: Why not just go? It's not like you can do anything. He might even be dead. He looks dead.

Hubert, Etc had made a concerted study of that voice and had concluded that it was an asshole. He tried to think past the self-serving rationalizations. He grabbed a bag someone left behind and, working gently, rolled Billiam into recovery position and put the bag under his head. He was propping Billiam up with a broken chair and a length of pipe, eyes squinted, head hammering, when someone grabbed him by his sore shoulder. He almost vomited. This was the day he'd known was coming all his life, when he ended up in prison.

But it wasn't a cop—it was Natalie. She said something inaudible over the music. He pointed at Billiam. She knelt down and made a light. She threw up, having the presence of mind to do so in her purse. Hubert, Etc noted distantly that she was thinking of esophageal cells and DNA. That distant part admired her foresight. She got to her feet, grabbed him again by his bad arm, yanked hard. He screamed in pain, the sound lost in the roar, and went, leaving Billiam behind.

## [ii]

Seth came off of Meta hard, around 4:00 A.M., as they sat in a ravine, listening to their ears ring and water below them burble, listening to the efficient whooshing of passing law enforcement vehicles on the road above. He sat on a log with that superior grin, then he was weeping, head in hands, bent between his knees, with the unselfconscious bray of a toddler.

Hubert, Etc and Natalie looked at him from their spots against tree trunks, braced against the ravine's slope. They went to him. Hubert, Etc awkwardly embraced him, and Seth buried his face in Hubert, Etc's chest. Natalie stroked his arm, murmured things that Hubert, Etc thought of as *feminine* in some comforting sense. Hubert, Etc was conscious of Seth's crying and the possibility it might be detected by law-enforcement apparatus. This interfered with his empathy, which wasn't so extensive to begin with, because Seth was fucked up because he'd taken a stupid drug at a trendy party they'd had no business attending, and now Hubert, Etc was covered in dried blood he hadn't been able to wipe away on dew-dampened leaves and rocks.

Hubert, Etc squashed Seth's face harder against his chest, partly to muffle him. Hubert, Etc's ears still rang, his head throbbed with his pulse, his fingertips tingled with the soft wreck of Billiam's face. He was sure Billiam was dead when they left. And because he was Hubert, Etc, he was suspicious of that certainty because if Billiam had already been dead, then they hadn't left him to die alone on the floor.

Natalie patted Seth's arm.

"Come on, buddy," she said. "That's the comedown. Think it out with me, you can do that with a Meta comedown, it's part of the package. Come on, Steve."

"Seth," Hubert, Etc said.

"Seth," she said. She was just as impatient with Seth as he was. "Come on. Think it out. It's terrible, it's awful, but this isn't your real reaction, it's just dope. Come on, Seth, think it out." She kept on repeating "think it out." This must be what you said to people who had a hard time with Meta. He said it, too, and Seth's sobs subsided. He was quiet for a time, then snored softly.

Natalie and Hubert, Etc looked at each other. "What now?" Natalie said.

Hubert, Etc shrugged. "Seth had the car-tokens to get home. We could wake him up."

Natalie squeezed her eyes tight. "I don't want to do any messaging from here. You came in lockdown, right?"

Hubert, Etc didn't roll his eyes. His generation perfected lockdown, getting their systems to go fully dark on their way to parties. It hadn't been easy, but everyone too lazy to bother ended up in jail, sometimes with their friends, so it became widespread.

"We came in lockdown," he said. They'd carred to a place with a thousand statistically probable destinations within a short walk, walked a long way to the party. They weren't stupid.

"Well, do you think it's safe to light up?"

"Safe for what?"

He could see her suppressing an eye roll. "To be an acceptable risk. And if you say, 'acceptable in what way,' I'll slug you. Do you think it's a good idea to light up?"

"I want to say, 'good compared to what?' I don't know, Natalie. I think—" He swallowed. "I'm pretty sure Billiam is—" He swallowed. "I think he's dead." Neither of them looked at the other. Such a stupid accident. "Whatever else, I think it means that the cops'll be brutal, because a dead person puts the thing in a different category. On the other hand, our DNA is all over that place, and with the deal they'll make, they'll come after us no matter what. On the other hand, I mean, in addition to that, or with that in mind, if we light up now, we're adding corroboration to any inference that says that we were there, which means that—"

"Enough paranoid rat-holing. We can't light up."

"How did you get here?"

"A friend," she said. "I'm sure she got herself home; she's warm and cozy under a blanket with a cup of tea waiting for her when she gets up." Natalie sounded bitter for the first time. Hubert, Etc realized he was half frozen and half starving, so thirsty it was like the inside of his mouth had been painted with starch.

"We've got to go." He looked at himself. In the gray dawn light, the dried blood looked like mud. "Do you think I could get onto the subway like this?"

She craned her neck, shoving stray elements of Seth off her lap. "Not like that. Maybe in Steve's jacket, though."

"Seth," he said.

"Whatever." She shook Seth by the shoulder, a little roughly. "Come on, Seth, time to go."

---

They arrived at the station at 5:30, Hubert, Etc wearing Seth's jacket, which was big on him, carrying his jacket under his arm. The first train rolled in and they shuffled in with bleary morning-shifters and wincing partiers. The people with jobs glared at the partiers. The people with jobs smelled good; the partiers did not, not even to Hubert, Etc's deadened nose. During the zeppelin bubble, he'd had early mornings as they crunched on meaningless deadlines with the urgency of a car crash for no discernible reason. He'd ridden the first train into work. Hell, he'd slept in the office.

Seth's comedown had plateaued. He was a perfect oil painting of *Man with Drug Hangover,* in grubby colors, a lot of shadow and cross-hatching. The cold air had turned his bare arms the color of corned beef, but Hubert, Etc didn't feel bad about having commandeered his jacket. "Look at 'em," Seth said in a stagey whisper. "So well-behaved." They were Desi, Persian, white-bread, but all the same, all in their working peoples' uniforms of respectability. A couple of the employed gave them shitty looks. Seth noticed, getting ready to pick a fight.

"Don't," Hubert, Etc said, as Seth said, "It's the ultimate self-deception. Like they're going to be able to change anything with a paycheck. If a paycheck could change your life, do you think they'd let you have one?"

It was a good line. Seth had used it before. "Seth," he said, in a firmer tone.

"What?" Seth sat up straighter, looked belligerent. Toronto's subways, like most subways, were places of civil inattention. It took a lot to get other people to overtly acknowledge you. Seth had done it. People stared.

Natalie leaned over and cupped her hand to Seth's ear, hissed something. He clamped his mouth shut and glared, then looked at his feet. She gave Hubert, Etc a half smile.

"Where are we going?" she said. Hubert, Etc was cheered by that "we." They'd been comrades-in-arms for the night and he had her contact details, but he'd been half expecting her to say that she was going home and leaving him with Seth.

"Fran's?" he said.

She made a face.

"Come on," he said. "It's twenty-four hours, it's warm, they don't throw you out—"

"Yeah," she said. "It's a pit, though."

He shrugged. He remembered when the last Fran's had shut, when he was a teenager, and when the chain was rebooted as a hobby business by a lesser Weston, amid fanfare about the family and its connection to the city's institutions. The new Fran's felt haunted, and the feeling was, ironically, most intense during special events with live servers instead of automats. Live humans bearing trays of food highlighted the fact that the restaurant was designed for free-ranging, dumb robots and a minimum of human oversight. But it was cheap, and you could sit there a long time.

He wished he'd suggested somewhere cool. When he'd cared about this stuff, he'd had a continuous list of places where he would go if he had the money and someone to go with. Seth had that kind of list on tap, but he didn't want to talk to Seth. He wished Seth would volunteer to go home and sleep off his trauma and drug residue. Which wasn't going to happen, because this was Seth.

"Fine," she said.

Her eyes glazed over and she looked at her lap, cupped her hand over the interaction surface on her thigh, checking her messages. This reminded Hubert, Etc to light up, and his own interface surfaces buzzed, letting him know about the things he should be doing. He dewormed his inboxes, flushing the junk and spum. He snooze-barred messages to bug him again later—something from his parents, an old girlfriend, some work he'd chased at a caterer's.

They were almost at St Clair station now, and as they stood, one of the morning-shift people got into Seth's space. He was a big guy, fair-skinned, freckled with a large, beaky nose and a conservative collar-length haircut. He wore a cheap overcoat with some kind of uniform under it, maybe medical. "You," he said, leaning in, "are a mouthy little fuck, for someone who's sponging welfare and partying all night. Why don't you go get a fucking job?"

Seth leaned away, but the guy followed him, everyone swaying with the motion of the slowing train. Hubert, Etc's adrenals found an unsuspected reservoir and goosed. His heart thundered. Someone was going to get hit. The guy was big, smelled of soap. There were cameras on the people and on the train, but he didn't look like he gave a shit.

Natalie put a hand on the guy's chest and pushed. He looked down in surprise at the slim, female hand on his chest, clamped his huge hand over her wrist. She whipped her free hand around, bashing him in the chest with her purse, which sprang open and sloshed cold vomit down his chest. She looked as disgusted as he did, but when he let go and stumbled back, she leaped through the closing subway doors, Hubert, Etc and Seth on her heels. They turned in time to see the guy sniffing his hand incredulously, his body language telegraphing *I can't believe you dumped a bag full of barf on me*—

"Natalie," Seth said on the escalators—the other passengers who'd gotten off gave them a wide berth. "Why was your purse full of sick?"

She shook her head. "I'd forgotten about it. I got sick when I saw—" She closed her eyes. "When I saw Billiam."

"I'd forgotten it, too," Hubert, Etc said.

"I hope nothing important fell out when I hit the guy," she said. Her purse—medium-sized with a gitchy abstract pattern printed on its exterior vinyl—was slung across her body. She gingerly opened it, made a face, peered at its revolting depths. "I don't know how the hell you start to clean this up. I'd throw it away except it's got some stuff that should be washable."

Seth wrinkled his nose. "Gloves and a mask. And someone else's sink. Dude, what did you *eat*?"

She glared at him, but a little grin played at her lips. "Came in handy, didn't it? Steve, we've had a shitty night. Do you think you could keep it low-key? Not picking fights?"

He had the grace to look ashamed. Hubert, Etc felt a spurt of jealousy jet from asshole to appetite, wanted to shove Seth down the escalator. He said, "None of us're in the best shape. Some food will help. And coffium."

Seth and Natalie both jolted at the mention of coffium. "Yesss," Natalie said. "Come on." She vaulted up, two big steps at a time. They cleared the turnstiles, stepped out into a blinking-bright morning, bustling with turned-out people doing Saturday morning shopping in turned-out showrooms. The rebuilt Fran's had a narrow glass frontage between a bathroom remodeler's salon and a place that sold giant concrete sculptures.

"Remember the Fran's neon?" Hubert, Etc said. "It was such an amazing color, wild red." He pointed to the LED-lit tube. "Never looks right to me. Makes me want to tweak reality's gamma slider."

Natalie gave him a funny look. They found a booth, the table lighting up with menus as they sat. The menus in front of each of them grew speech-bubbles as the automat's biometrics recognized them and highlit their last orders, welcoming them back. Hubert, Etc saw Natalie had ordered lasagna with double garlic bread the last time, and it had been four years since she'd placed that order. "You don't eat here often?"

"Just once," she said. "Opening day." She tapped the menu for a while, ordering a double chocolate malt, corned beef hash, hash browns, extra HP Sauce and mayo, and a half grapefruit with brown sugar. "I was a guest of the Weston's. It was a family thing." She looked him square in the eye, daring him to make a deal out of her privilege. "The neon sign? My dad bought it. It's hanging in our cottage in the Muskokas."

Hubert, Etc kept his face still. "I'd like to see it someday," he said, evenly. He waited for Seth to say something.

"My name's Seth, not Steve." The shit-eating grin was unmistakable. He reached across the table and twiddled Natalie's order, dragging a copy of it over to his place setting.

"What the hell." Hubert, Etc grabbed Seth's order and copied it to his place setting, too. He tapped the large-sized coffium-pot, and Natalie smacked her palm down on the submit.

"Come on," Natalie said. "Say it."

Hubert, Etc said, "Nothing to say. Your family knows the Westons."

"Yeah," she said. "We do. We're foofs."

Hubert, Etc nodded as if he knew what that meant, but Seth had no shame. "What's a foof?"

"Fine old Ontario family," she said.

"Never heard the term," Seth said.

"Me either."

She shrugged. "You probably have to be a foof to know what a foof is. I got a lot of it at summer camp."

The food arrived then, atop a trundling robot that docked with their table. They cleared its top layer, and it rotated its carousel for the next tray, then a third. The fourth had the coffium. Natalie set it on their table, and Hubert, Etc couldn't help but admire her arm muscles as she set it down. He noticed she didn't shave her armpits and felt unaccountably intimate in that knowledge. They sorted out the dishes and poured the coffee.

He plucked the nuclear-red cherry from the top of the whipped-cream mountain on his shake and ate it stem and all. Natalie did the same. Seth scalded his tongue on the coffium and spilled ice water in his haste.

Natalie used the edge of her plate as a palette and swirled together a beige mixture of HP Sauce and mayo. She forked up small mouthfuls of food swirled in the mixture.

"That looks *vile*." Seth said it, not him, because he didn't want to be a jerk. Seth was a portable, external id. Not always comfortable or appropriate, but handy nevertheless.

"It's called the brown love." She dabbed with a red-and-white striped napkin, waited for Seth to make an innuendo, which didn't come. "Invented it in high school. You don't want to try it, your loss." She forked up more hash and pointed it at them. On impulse, Hubert, Etc let her feed it to him. It was surprisingly good, and the clink of the fork on his tooth made him shiver like an amazing piss.

"Fantastic." He meant it. He prepared his own smear, using Natalie's for color reference.

Seth refused to try, to Hubert, Etc's secret delight. The food was better than he remembered, and more expensive. He hadn't budgeted for the meal and it was going to hurt.

He pondered this, standing at the urinal and smelling his asparagus-y active-culture piss. Thinking of money, smelling the smell, he almost clamped down and ran out to get a cup to save some. Free beer was free beer, even if it did start out as used beer. All water was used beer. But it was down the drain before the thought was complete.

When he got back to the table, an older man sat next to Natalie.

He had shaggy hair, well cut, and skin with the luster of good leather. He wore a fabric-dyed cement-colored knit cardigan, with mottled horn buttons sewn on with hot pink thread. Beneath it, a tight black t-shirt revealed his muscular chest and flat stomach. He wore a simple wedding band and had short, clean, even fingernails, a kind of ostentatious no-manicure.

"Hi there," he said. Hubert, Etc sat down opposite him. He extended a hand. "I'm Jacob. Natalie's father."

They shook. "I'm Hubert," he said, as Seth said, "Call him 'Etcetera.'"

"Call me Hubert," he said, again. His external id was a pain in the ass.

"Nice to meet you, Hubert."

"My father spies on me," Natalie said. "That's why he's here."

Jacob shrugged. "It could be worse. It's not like I have your phone tapped. It's just public sources."

Natalie put her fork down and pushed her plate away. "He buys cam-feeds, real-time credit reports, market analytics. Like a background check on a new hire. But all the time."

Seth said, "That's creepy. And expensive."

"Not so expensive. I can afford it."

"Dad's made the transition to old rich," Natalie said. "He isn't embarrassed by money. Not like my grandparents were. He knows he's practically a member of a different species and can't see why he should hide it."

"My daughter is making a game of trying to embarrass me in public, something she's been working on since she was ten. I don't embarrass easy."

"Why should you be embarrassed? You'd have to care what other people think of you in order to be embarrassed. You don't, so you aren't."

Hubert, Etc felt embarrassed for them, felt like he should say something, if only so that Seth didn't get all the mindshare. "I bet he cares what you think of him," he risked.

They both grinned and the family resemblance was uncanny, down to the identical double dimple on the right side. "That's why I do it. I'm proxy for every human beneath his notice. It's not fun, either, despite what he thinks."

"I don't see you rejecting the privilege, Natty," he said, putting an arm around her shoulders. She let him keep it there for a measured moment, then shrugged it off.

"Not yet," she said.

His silence was eloquently skeptical. He moved her plate over to his place setting, tapped the table's NO SHARING message and waved a contact on his sleeve over it, tapped out a pattern with his thumb and forefinger. He polished off the last of the corned beef hash and then reached for her shake. She stopped him and said, "Mine." He settled for the dregs of her coffium.

"Are you going to invite your little friends over for a playdate, then?" He wiped his mouth and loaded the plates on the robot that re-docked with the table.

"You guys want a shower?"

Seth pounded the table, making the menu dance as it tried to interpret his instructions. "Come on, brother, we eat tonight!"

Hubert, Etc gave him an elbow jab. "Better count the spoons," he said.

"They count themselves," Jacob said. He did something with his sleeve and said, "The car'll be around in a sec."

## [iii]

It wasn't a carshare car, of course. The Redwaters were one of the big names—there'd been a Redwater mayor, Redwater MPs, a Redwater Finance Minister, any number of Redwater CEOs. The car was still small, not a stretch, but it was indefinably solid, skirted with matte rubber that covered the wheels. Hubert, Etc thought that there was something interesting underneath it. There were intriguing somethings about this car, and an inconspicuous Longines logo worked into the corner of the window glass. The suspension did something clever to compensate for his weight, actively dampening it, not like stone-age springs. He sat in a rear-facing jump seat, saw the windows weren't windows at all. They were thick armor, coated with hi-rez screens. Jacob took the other jump seat and said, "Home." The car waited until they were all seated securely and buckled in before it leapt into traffic. From his vantage the cars around them were melting out of their way.

"I don't think I've ever traveled this fast in city traffic," he said.

Jacob gave him a fatherly wink.

Natalie reached across the large internal compartment and gave her dad a sock in the thigh. "He's showing off. There's custom firmware in these, lets them cut the clearance envelope in half, which makes the other cars back off because we're driving like unpredictable assholes."

"Is that legal?" Hubert, Etc said.

"It's a civil offense," Jacob said. "The fines are paid by direct-debit."

"What if you kill someone?" Seth got to the point.

"That's a criminal matter, more serious. Won't happen, though. There's a lot of game theory stuff going on in the car's lookahead, modeling likely outs and defectors and injecting a huge margin of safety. Really, we're playing it safer than the stock firmware, but only because the car itself has got much better braking and acceleration and handling characteristics than a stock car."

"And because you're terrifying other cars' systems into getting out of your way," Seth said.

"Right," Natalie said, before her dad could object. He shrugged and Hubert, Etc remembered what she'd said about his being "old rich," unconcerned by the idea that anyone would resent his buying his way through traffic.

They raced through city streets. Natalie closed her eyes and reclined. There were dark circles under her eyes and she was tense, had been since her dad turned up. Hubert, Etc tried not to stare.

"Where do you live?" Seth asked.

"Eglinton Ravine, by the Parkway," Jacob said. "I had it built about ten years ago."

Hubert, Etc remembered school trips to the Ontario Science Centre, tried to remember the ravine, but could only recall a deep forested zone glimpsed from the window of a speeding school bus.

The food he'd had from Fran's weighed in his gut like a cannonball. He thought about the blood on his clothes and under his fingernails, mud on his shoes, crumbling to the upholstery. The car surged, his guts complained. They braked hard, and then merged with another lane of traffic, a whisper between them and the car behind, a tiny carshare whose passenger, an elegant Arabic-looking woman in office makeup, looked at them with alarm before they skipped to the next lane.

## [iv]

The house was one of three in a row overlooking the ravine's edge, at the end of a winding, rutted road overhung with leafy trees. The garage door slid aside as they pulled into the rightmost house. It shut and locked into place with huge, shining round rods sunk deep into the floor and ceiling and walls. The car doors gasped open and he was in a vast space beneath all three houses, brightly lit and dotted with vehicles. Jacob held his hand out to Natalie and she ignored him, then stumbled a little as she twisted to avoid him taking her elbow.

"Come on," she said to Hubert, Etc and Seth and set off for the garage's other end.

"Thanks for the ride," Hubert, Etc called as he quickstepped after her. Jacob leaned against the car, watching them go. Hubert, Etc couldn't make out his expression.

She took them up a narrow staircase to a large, messy room with sofas and a panoramic window overlooking the ravine—a green, steep drop-off with the Don River below, white and frothing as it cascaded to Lake Ontario. It smelled funky, old laundry and unwashed dishes, an overlay of scented candles. One wall was finger-painted from floor to ceiling and scribbled on with Sharpies and glitter and ballpoint.

"The kids' wing," she said. "My sister's away at university in Rio, so it's mine for now. I don't think my parents have been in here five times since the house was built."

"The whole thing is one house?" Hubert, Etc said.

"Yeah," she said.

"Doesn't seem like the way you'd build a house if you didn't care about how rich you seemed to other people," he said.

She shook her head. "It was a zoning thing. The people on the other side of the ravine"—she gestured at the picture window—"didn't want to have to look at a 'monster house' over breakfast. They're rich people, we're rich people, the zoning board didn't know what to do. Dad settled for building a giant house that looked like three houses." She swept a sofa free of clutter. "Food's in the pantry. I'm gonna use the upstairs bathroom. The downstairs one is there, help yourself to toiletries." She went up the stairs and disappeared around a corner.

Seth grinned at Hubert, Etc meaningfully, a silent comment on his romantic feelings for Natalie. He wasn't in the mood. He'd held a dead man in his arms. He was bloody, tired, and nauseated.

"I'm going to stand under the shower for an hour," he said. "So you'd better go first."

"How do you know I won't stand under the shower for an hour?" Seth's maddening grin.

"Don't." He'd spotted towels on the ground by the stone fireplace. He passed one to Seth and shook the other one out and put it on the mantel.

There was kindling and newspaper and split logs. He built a fire. He found a large t-shirt that didn't smell bad, with fake burn-holes all over it, a pair of track-bottoms he thought would fit. He stripped off his shirt, pants, and jacket and threw them in the fire. He didn't know what forensics could do about identifying blood on clothing after laundering but he was sure they could do less with ash. The woven interaction surfaces melted and released acrid smoke. He padded around in a stranger's clothes, wondering whose they'd been. Maybe Billiam's.

Natalie came around the corner and stood on the landing, contemplating him and the mess. "Steve in the bathroom?"

"Seth. Yeah."

"You can use mine, come on." Just like that, he was in a strange girl's bedroom.

It was the bedroom of someone who'd been a student until recently: framed certificates, shelves full of books and trophies, thumbtacked posters for bands and causes, but overlaid with political posters, desk piled with broken interaction surfaces, elaborate homemade vapers that could turn titanium into inhalable smoke. A scattering of paper money, bespeaking illicit transactions, and clunky, semi-functional caging around the walls, floors, and ceiling—a kid's attempt to block parental spyware. It was better opsec than Hubert, Etc practiced, but he wasn't sure it'd work.

Natalie wore loose pajamas, black-and-white striped, and no bra, and he did not stare or even peek. She ran her hand down the bathroom door's edge, a spot smeared with years of hand prints beyond any ever-clean surface, and it sighed open. "All yours."

He passed through the door and turned to close it. She stared at him. "Keep the clothes," she said. There were tears in her eyes.

"I'm—" He faltered. "I'm very sorry about Billiam."

"Me too." A tear slipped down her cheek. "He was an asshole, but he was our asshole. He got fucked up too early at the parties. It was his fault. I miss him." Another tear.

"Do you want a hug?"

"No thank you. Just go shower."

The bathroom was the kind you saw in showrooms. Active noise-cancellation ate the sound of the water; smart jets' algorithms increased and decreased the pressure, predicting what he wanted sprayed and how hard; interactive surfaces turned anything into a mirror at a double-tap, giving him an unnerving look at his ass and the back of his head; air-circulators bathed him in warm breezes after he turned down the water, simultaneously drying the bathroom's surfaces of condensate.

She was waiting in the doorway. "Sorry," she said. Her eyes were dry. He held out his towel and made a questioning face. She took it from him and threw it on the floor.

"Let's see what Steve's up to."

"Seth."

"Who cares."

Seth had found the pantry and cleared a coffee table, done a neat job of it, folding and organizing things, piling them in a clear patch of floor. He'd cleared three chairs. On the table: a platter of fruit, teapot and cups, croissants. They smelled good.

"Snack?"

"Good work, Steve." Natalie sounded like she meant it.

"Any time." Seth didn't correct her.

They snacked in silence. Hubert, Etc wanted to ask about the house, about the food. About Billiam, the party, the third person with a beard, the other girl who'd been their partner-in-crime. But sleep was heavy in his limbs. His eyelids drooped. Natalie looked from him to Seth—who also looked like he could nod off in his chair—and said, "Okay, boys, hit the couches. I'm going to bed."

She staggered upstairs and Hubert, Etc stretched out on the least-cluttered sofa, eyes closing as he pressed his face into the cushions' seam. In the brief moment before sleep, he saw the twisted body of Billiam, felt a phantom sensation of the pulp of Billiam's skull in his fingers. He had a toe-to-scalp shiver, up and down twice before it subsided and he mercifully slept.

---

He woke to muttered voices. He looked blearily, trying to orient himself: Seth's back on the sofa opposite him, the finger-painted wall. He lifted his head—a hungover throb—and located the voices. Natalie, standing in a doorway at the far end, arguing through a crack in the door in a hushed voice. The answer was male, older, maddeningly calm. Jacob. His head slumped. He was going to have to get up. His bladder was painfully full.

As awkward as ever in his life, dressed in a stranger's clothes, hungover, in a strange room where a strange—attractive—girl argued with her rich father, he padded as inconspicuously as he could to the toilet. Natalie looked at him, made an unreadable face, turned to her argument.

When Hubert, Etc came back, drying his hands on the ass of his borrowed track-bottoms, Natalie and her father sat stone-faced across from each other. Jacob sat on the sofa that Hubert, Etc had vacated and she in a chair. Seth slept.

Hubert, Etc went to the pantry—soft lights within came on and he saw a door on the other side, understood that some *servant* refilled it during the day—brought out carrot sticks, celery, and hummus on a tray and set it down between the two Redwaters. They glared at each other.

"Thank you, Hubert," Jacob Redwater said. He dipped a carrot in hummus, didn't eat.

Hubert, Etc sat down next to him, because there was nowhere else.

Natalie said, "Hubert, what's more important, human rights or property rights?"

Hubert, Etc turned the question over. It was loaded. "Are property rights a human right?"

Jacob smiled and crunched his carrot stick, and Hubert, Etc sensed he'd said the wrong thing.

Natalie looked grim. "You tell me. That factory we switched on last night. It was worth more as a write-off than it was as a going concern. Some entity that owned it demanded that it sit rotting and useless, even though there were people who wanted what it could make."

"If they wanted the factory, they could buy the factory," Jacob said. "Then make things and sell them."

"I don't think those people could afford to buy a factory," Hubert, Etc said, glancing at Natalie for approval. She nodded minutely.

"That's what capital markets are for," Jacob said. "If you've got a plan for profitably using an asset someone else isn't using, then you draw up a business plan and take it to investors. If you're right, one of them will fund you—maybe more than one. Then you sell what you make."

"What if no one invests?" Hubert, Etc said. "I know a ton of zepp startups that died because they couldn't get money, even though they were making amazing stuff."

Jacob took on the air of someone explaining a complex subject to a child. "If no one wants to invest, that means that you don't have an idea worth investing in, or you aren't the right person to execute that idea because you don't know how to convince people to invest."

"Don't you see the circularity there?" Natalie said. "If you can't convince someone to pay to turn on the factory to make things that people need, then the factory shouldn't be turned on?"

"As opposed to what? A free-for-all? Just smash down the doors, walk in and take over?"

"Why not, if no one else is doing anything with it?"

The talking-to-a-toddler look: "Because it's not yours."

"So what?"

"You wouldn't be happy if a mob busted in here and carried all your precious things out, would you, Natty?"

With less than a day's experience, Hubert, Etc could tell that Natalie didn't want to be called "Natty." Jacob knew it, was baiting his daughter. It was cheating.

"I wouldn't mind," Hubert, Etc said. "I don't have much, most of what matters is backed up. I mean, so long as I could find a bed and some clothes the next day, it wouldn't make a difference."

"Natty's got plenty more than a change of clothes and a bed here in her nest," Jacob said. "Natty likes nice things."

"I do. I want everyone else to have them." Her look could have sliced steel.

"Let them work for it, the way we have."

Natalie snorted.

Jacob looked at Hubert, Etc. "You were at the party last night?"

It was dusk outside the picture window, pinky-orange light sweeping down the ravine, staining the river's rippling surface.

"I was."

"What do you think about breaking into private property and stealing what you find there?"

Hubert, Etc wished that he'd pretended to be asleep. He was pretty sure Seth was faking it.

"No one was using it." He looked at Natalie. "The hydrogen cells'd filled up, so the windmills were going to waste. The feedstock was worth practically nothing."

Natalie said, "What's the point of having private property if all does is rot?"

"Oh, please. Private property is the most productive property. Temporary inefficiencies don't change that. Only kooks and crooks think that stealing other property is a valid form of political action."

"Only kleptocrats use terms like 'temporary inefficiencies' for wasteful abominations like that Muji factory."

"It's easy to talk about kleptocrats when Daddy pulls strings to keep the cops off your lazy ass. They'll arrest a hell of a lot of people today, Natty, but not you or your friends."

"Don't pretend your political embarrassment is generosity. Let 'em put me away."

"Maybe I will. Maybe a couple of years of hard work in prison will make you appreciate what you've got."

She looked at Hubert, Etc. "He's been threatening to send me to a prison since I was ten. It used to be those scared-straight places on private islands, until they were all busted for 'corrective rape.' Now it's adult prison. Why the fuck not, Dad? You're a major shareholder in most of 'em—they'd give you a discount. I could get inside perspective on the family business."

Jacob gave a showy laugh. "Like I'd trust you to run anything. Business is a meritocracy, child. You think you're going to walk into some fat job just because you're my kid—"

"I don't. Because there aren't any 'jobs' left. Just financial engineering and politics. I'm not qualified for either. For one thing, I can't say 'meritocracy' with a straight face."

Hubert, Etc saw that one land. It emboldened him. "It's the height of self-serving circular bullshit, isn't it? 'We're the best people we know, we're on top, therefore we have a meritocracy. How do we know we're the best? Because we're on top. QED.' The most amazing thing about 'meritocracy' is that so many brilliant captains of industry haven't noticed that it's made of such radioactively obvious bullshit you could spot it orbit." He snuck another look at Natalie. She gave him a minute nod that thrilled him.

Jacob looked more pissed. Distantly, Hubert, Etc wondered how such a powerful man could be so thin-skinned. Jacob stood and glared. "Easy to say, but last time I looked, you two hadn't done a fucking thing that mattered to anyone, and were depending on 'bullshit' to keep your asses out of jail."

"There he goes with the jail stuff again. I suppose prison is one way to win an argument if you can't think of a better one."

"It's traditional," Seth said, lifting his face from the pillows. "Spanish Inquisition. USSR. Saudi Arabia. Gitmo."

Jacob walked out, closing the connecting door with a dignified click. It was more pissed than a slam. Hubert, Etc felt victorious.

"This hotel is goddamned noisy." Seth rolled onto his back, stretching to expose his hairy stomach, gone soft since the last time Hubert, Etc saw it.

"The room service is awesome, though," Hubert, Etc said. "And you can't beat the price."

Seth sat up. "That's your dad, huh?"

"I know that it's a cliché to hate your old man when you're twenty, but he's such an asshole," Natalie said. "He really believes that meritocracy stuff. Seriously believes in it. He's one step away from talking about having the blood of kings in his veins."

"The thing I've never understood," Hubert, Etc said, "is how someone can be delusional and still manage to own half the planet? I get how having some delusions would be useful when you're bossing people around and ripping everyone off, but doesn't that break down eventually? It's still capitalism out there. If your competitor brings in some person who isn't delusional, wouldn't that person end up bankrupting you?"

Natalie said, "There's more than one way to be smart. People like my dad assume that because they're smart about being evil bastards, they're smart about everything—"

"And because they're smart at everything," Seth said, "that makes it okay for them to be evil bastards?"

"Exactly," she said. "So people like my dad are good at figuring out how to take your company with its 'smart people' and get it declared illegal, poach its best ideas, or just buy it and leverage it and financialize it until it doesn't make anything except for exotic derivatives and tax credits. And the thing is, that's not good enough for him! He *wants* to be the one percent of the one percent of the one percent because of his inherent virtue, not because the system is rigged. His whole identity rests on the idea that the system is legit and that he earned his position into it fair and square and everyone else is a whiner."

"If they didn't want to be poor, they shoulda had the sense to be born rich," Seth said.

"No offense," Hubert, Etc added.

"None taken." She picked through a pile of laundry, producing a loose-knit eggplant colored cardigan, a pair of twisted underwear hanging off a sleeve. She slingshotted them toward the stairs. "I know my family is richer than Scrooge McDuck, but I don't pretend we got that way by doing anything except getting lucky a long time ago and using graft, corruption, and sleaze to build that luck up to this tacky place and a dozen more like it."

"And what about last night?" Hubert, Etc asked, emboldened by her frankness. "What about that party and all?"

"What about it?" she said, her tone playful and challenging.

"What about being richer than Scrooge McDuck and staging a Communist party?"

"Why shouldn't I?"

"It's not like you need to—"

"But I can. Remember, it's not just 'to each according to her need,' it's 'from each according to her ability.' I know how to find factories that are perfect for direct action. I know how to get into them. I know how to pwnify their machines. I know how to throw a hell of a party. I have all this unearned, undeserved privilege. Apart from killing myself as an enemy of the human species, can you think of anything better for me to do with it?"

"You could give money to—"

She froze him with a look. "Haven't you figured it out? Giving money away doesn't solve anything. Asking the zottarich to redeem themselves by giving money away acknowledges that they deserve it all, should be in charge of deciding where it goes. It's pretending that you can get rich without being a bandit. Letting them decide what gets funded declares the planet to be a giant corporation that the major shareholders get to direct. It says that government is just middle-management, hired or fired on the whim of the directors."

"Plus, if you believe all that, you don't have to give all your money away," Seth said. She didn't seem pissed.

"What the fuck do we need money for? So long as you keep on pretending that money is anything but a consensus hallucination induced by the ruling elite to convince you to let them hoard the best stuff, you're never going to make a difference. Steve, the problem isn't that people spend their money the wrong way, or that the wrong people have money. The problem *is* money. Money only works if there isn't enough to go around—if you're convinced scarce things are fairly allocated—but it's the same circular meritocratic argument that Etcetera annihilated for my dad: markets are the fairest way to figure out who should get what, and the markets have produced the current terrible allocation, therefore the current terrible allocation is the best solution to a hard problem."

"Every time I hear someone saying that money is bullshit, I check to see how much money they have. No offense, Natty, but it's a lot easier to talk about money being bullshit when you have it." Seth sat up and rubbed vigorously at his legs. Dried mud flaked off his jeans.

She snorted. "Is that all you've got? 'Champagne socialist?' You think the fact that I was born into a lot of money—a *lot* of money, more money than you'll ever see or even imagine—disqualifies me from having an opinion about it?"

Seth wandered over to the larder and pulled out food—fresh fruit, royal jelly rehydration drink, pizza in a M.R.E. box whose tab he pulled and pitched. The silence stretched. Hubert, Etc was about to speak, then Seth said, "I've met a lot of cops with bullshit theories about crime and human nature. Generals clearly have batshit opinions about the gravity of ending human life. Every priest, rabbi, and imam seems to know a lot about an invisible, all-powerful being who appears be a fairy tale. So yeah, having a lot of money probably does disqualify you from knowing a single fucking thing about it." He unboxed the pizza, avoided the rising steam. "Slice?" he said, the smell of garlic, tomato, corn niblets, and anchovies swirled like an oregano dust devil.

Hubert, Etc hunkered down for Natalie's eruption. Seth was a master of provocation. But it didn't come.

"That's not entirely stupid. Let's say that we've got different perspectives on money. Tell me, Steve, do you think you can spend and redistribute your way to a better world?"

"Damned if I know."

Hubert, Etc took the pizza box and had a slice. It was good for flash-baked M.R.E. The sauce was tangy and spicy and might be addictive as crack.

When he realized that there were as many pizzas as he could eat lurking in potentia in the Redwater estate, he took two more.

"I'm suspicious of any plan to fix unfairness that starts with 'step one, dismantle the entire system and replace it with a better one,' especially if you can't do anything else until step one is done. Of all the ways that people kid themselves into doing nothing, that one is the most self-serving."

"What about walkaways?" Hubert, Etc said. "Seems to me that they're doing something that makes a difference. No money, no pretending money matters, and they're doing it right now."

Natalie and Seth looked at him. He finished his third slice. "They're weird and sketchy, but that goes with the territory whenever you're talking destroying the world as we know it and putting another one in its place."

"He's kidding, right?" Natalie said.

"Damned if I know," Seth said. "He's strange. Etcetera, you're kidding, right?"

Hubert, Etc warmed to being the center of attention. "I'm totally serious. Look, I've heard the stories, too, I don't know if they're true, and if you two are serious about all this change-the-world stuff, I don't think you can pretend that a couple million weirdos who have exactly that mission don't exist because you're uncomfortable with their lifestyle. It's not like self-heating pizzas are an innate human institution we've enjoyed as a species for thousands of years."

"What are you proposing?"

"Not proposing, exactly. But if you wanted, you could have all the info you needed to go walkaway in about ten minutes' time, could be on the road tomorrow, living like it was the first days of a better nation—or a weirder one."

Natalie looked at the darkening sky for a long time. "Billiam used to joke about walkaways. There'd always be a couple who'd show up at the Communist parties the next day and tweak this and that to make it run better. Didn't talk to us at all, wouldn't make eye contact, but they always left stuff running better than they found it. Billiam said we were all going to end up as walkaways."

"He was a good friend of yours, huh?" Hubert, Etc felt stupid.

"I'd known him off and on for three years. He wasn't my best friend, but we'd had fun together. He was a good person, though I'd seen him be a flaming asshole."

Seth surprised Hubert, Etc by saying, "That's not very nice."

She made an impatient noise. "Bullshit. I've got zero tolerance for not speaking ill of the dead. Billiam was sixty percent good guy, forty percent utter prick.

That puts him in the middle of humanity's bell curve. He hated bullshit with heat from the center of the sun. He was my friend, not yours."

Hubert, Etc felt tears, didn't know why. He went into the bathroom, sat on the toilet lid with his eyes closed, then stared into the mirror screen, letting it cycle through his profiles and the back and top of his head. He looked like shit. His second thought, which came in a bolt of clarity, was that he looked like a normal human, among billions of humans, no more or less good or bad than anyone. He thought about Natalie's talk of the bell curve and thought that he was within a sigma or two of normal on every axis.

He splashed cold water on his face and stepped out, trailing his hands along the finger-painted wall. Natalie and Seth looked at him with guilt or concern.

"You okay, buddy?" Seth said.

"Natalie," he said, "I don't think that the average person is sixty percent good and forty percent prick. I think that the average person sometimes kids himself that he's the center of the universe, and it's okay if he does something that he'd be pissed about if someone else did it to him, and tries not to think about it too hard."

"Uh, okay—" Natalie said.

"And I think that the tragedy of human existence is our world is run by people who are really good at kidding themselves, like your father. Your dad manages to kid himself that he's rich and powerful because he's the cream and has risen to the top. But he's not stupid. He *knows* he's kidding himself. So underneath that top layer of bullshit is another, more aware belief system: the belief that everyone else would kid themselves the same way he does, if they had the chance."

"That's exactly right," she said.

"His beliefs don't start with the idea that it's okay to kid yourself you're a special snowflake who deserves more cookies than all the other kids. It starts with the idea that it's *human nature* to kid yourself and take the last cookie, so if he doesn't, someone else will, so he had better be the most lavishly self-deluded of all, the most prolific taker of cookies, lest someone more horrible, immoral, and greedy than he gets there first and eats all the cookies, takes the plate, and charges rent to drink the milk."

Seth said: "Insert tragedy of the commons here."

Natalie put her hands up. "You know, I've heard the term 'tragedy of the commons' like a thousand times and I've never actually looked it up. What is it? Something to do with poor people being tragic?"

"That's commoners," Hubert, Etc said. Something was awake and loose inside him now. He wanted to kick the pizza off the coffee table and use it for a stage. "Commons. Common land that belongs to no one. Villages had commons where anyone could bring their livestock for a day's grazing. The tragedy part is that if the land isn't anyone's, then someone will come along and let their sheep eat until there's nothing but mud. Everyone knows that that bastard is on the way, so they might as well *be* that bastard. Better that sheep belonging to a nice guy like you should fill their bellies than the grass going to some selfish dickhead's sheep."

"Sounds like bullshit to me."

"Oh, it is," Hubert, Etc said. The thing was moving in his guts, setting his balls and face tingling. "It's more than mere bullshit. It's searing, evil, world-changing bullshit. The solution to the tragedy of the commons isn't to get a cop to make sure sociopaths aren't overgrazing the land, or shunning anyone who does it, turning him into a pariah. The solution is to let a robber-baron own the land that used to be everyone's, because once he's running it for profit, he'll take exquisite care to generate profit forever."

"That's the tragedy of the commons? A fairy tale about giving public assets to rich people to run as personal empires because that way they'll make sure they're better managed than they would be if we just made up some rules? God, my dad must *love* that story."

"It's the origin story of people like your dad," Hubert, Etc said. "It's obvious bullshit for anyone whose sweet deal doesn't depend on it not being obvious."

"Hear that, Dad?" she said, looking around the room. "Obvious to anyone whose sweet deal doesn't depend on it not being obvious, you deluded sociopathic fuck."

"He's got you bugged?" Seth said.

"I've got an individual privacy filter on the house network. But of course the cameras are rolling, because if I get kidnapped or murdered, he'd review them. Of course that's bullshit and he's always been able to spoof the locks. He learned it from me, when he went through some audit logs and saw I was doing it. Now he's locked me out but I'm goddamned certain there are times he's gone through my footage." She looked into the air in front of her face. "Yes, Dad, I know you're listening. It's pathetic."

Hubert, Etc remembered looking at his reflection in the bathroom and wondered if there was long-term archiving of its feed. He knew plenty of people with bugged homes, but you couldn't live as though you were being observed. When your infographics said you were fully patched, you had to trust them. That's what made the panics about huge zero-day security ruptures such a fright: the sudden knowledge that everything might have been auto-pwned by a random crim or asshole who used a skin-detection algorithm to catch you masturbating, keywords to flag your embarrassing conversations, harvesting your biometrics for playback attacks on your finances and social nets.

Living with the knowledge that there were creeps inside your perimeter was *creepy*. Of all the weird things about being zottarich, this was the weirdest. So far.

"Sorry," Hubert, Etc said. "Just getting my head around this. How often does he spy on you?"

"Who knows? I go somewhere else any time I want to have a real conversation, usually." She looked around the huge, airy, filthy room. "I don't come back here much."

Hubert, Etc had assumed that the place was a dump because Natalie was a rich slob who didn't know how good she had it, but he understood that it was a calculated gesture of contempt. This wasn't her home, it was a perch. Hubert, Etc didn't always have the best relationship with his parents, but this was a different level.

"What about your mom?" he said. "Does she know he spies on you?"

"Sure," she said. "Mom doesn't come by often, either—she's in GMT minus eight or minus nine." She cocked her head. "Oh, you mean is this a sex thing? No, I'm sure it isn't. My dad gets his flesh through specialists. He's never been that kind of perv." She addressed the air. "See, Dad? I stuck up for you. Whatever you are, you're not kinked for your own daughters. Bravo."

The hair on the back of his neck rose. The thing that had come alive in him had done a slow roll in his guts.

She looked at them. "You look like you've seen a ghost. Don't worry, get used to it. It's no different from being out in reality, sensed and recorded all the time. What's the worst that can happen? Dad's not going to have you rubbed out or send mercs on your trail after we drop out."

"After we drop out?"

"Isn't that what we were talking about? Going walkaway? That's where this thing was headed—some kind of prince-and-pauper thing: 'I'll wager I can put on vagabond's rags and go unnoticed among the lower classes, what-ho?' "

"Don't make me join the walkaways, Etcetera," Seth said.

The thing inside Hubert, Etc's guts roiled. "Was that where I was headed?"

Natalie caught his eye. Her face shone. She was beautiful. She had zits, a sprinkle of freckles, the sclerae of her eyes were pink and her lids were red-rimmed. She was brimming with life, sorrow, and whatever he'd felt when he realized that the whispered conversations about money and jobs that all the grown-ups had all the time were the outward reflection of deep, unending terror. A fear that gnawed at every grown person. A primordial terror of the tiger outside the cave.

"Sure as shit sounded like it to me," she said.

"Seth," he said. "What is it that keeps you from going walkaway, exactly?"

To his surprise, Seth looked genuinely distressed. "You're joking. Those people are bananas. They're *homeless people,* Hubert—" Hubert, Etc noted that Seth had called him 'Hubert,' always a sign that they'd tapped into a rich seam of Seth's psyche. "They're bums. They eat garbage—"

"Not exactly garbage," Hubert, Etc said. "No more than the beer we were drinking last night was piss. Give me a good reason. Loyalty to your employer? Prospects of a rich and fulfilled life?" Like Hubert, Etc, the longest Seth had been employed was six months, and the first month had been classed as "training"—not paid. Neither of them had had anything like real work in months.

"How about fear of prison?"

"How about it? You dragged me to an illegal party last night. That's more likely to get us busted than anything we'd do out in the abandoned territories—"

"The territories? Be serious, you'd be dead inside of a month."

"It's not the surface of the moon. It's places where no one wants to bother arresting the population for vagrancy."

"Yeah, they don't arrest 'em, they incinerate 'em for being squatter-terrorists," Seth said. "And then there's the friendly fire. It's a fucking gladiator pit for excess humans."

"He's got a point," Natalie said. "We'd have to arm up if we went. Dad's panic room's full of toys, though—stuff designed to slip millimeter wave. If we brought enough matériel, we'd be the kings of the badlands. Could be fun."

Hubert, Etc boggled. "Haven't you two ever seen a walkaway? They're practically Zen monks. They're not out mowing down their rivals with resin AK-3DPs. You've seen too many movies."

"I've seen walkaways, the people who'd visit the liberations, but who knows what they're like in their native habitat? There's no sense in being naïve. You've got to be insane if you think we're going to stroll into Mordor with packs full of delicious M.R.E.s and be welcomed as spiritual brothers."

Hubert, Etc was now as upset as Seth. "Have you two ever killed someone? Are you prepared to do so? Would you point a gun at another human being and gun him down?"

Natalie shrugged. "If it was me or him, fuck yeah." Seth nodded.

"You're both full of shit."

He and Seth glared. Natalie was more amused than ever.

The standoff might have continued if Hubert, Etc hadn't looked up the FAQ. They had a brief argument about which anonymizer to trust—if you were Natalie's age, all of the proxies that Hubert and Seth used were considered false-flag ops for harvesting intel on dissidents. Natalie, meanwhile, liked an anonymizer that Seth and Hubert, Etc had heard was junk-science wishful-thinking voodoo. It turned out the two systems could be daisy chained, and so they all grudgingly set them up and started searching.

There were as many walkaway FAQs as walkaways. The impulse to walk away was bound up with the urge to write Thoreauvian memoirs about societal malaise and the tradecraft of going off-grid in the age of total information awareness. They included appendices summing things up for the tldr crowd, with videos, darknet links, shapefiles, and wetjet formulas for making your own crucial frontier enzymes and GMOs. Some of this was radioactively hot, the kind of thing that'd get you watchlisted so hard you'd have to fight through the clouds of drones to go out for milk, but there was nothing in it about weapons.

Hubert, Etc pointed this out to Natalie and Seth, trying not to be smug. Seth said, "Of course no one talks about peacemakers where spooks could see it. It'll all be deep darknet."

"You're saying the fact that we can't find anything about weapons is proof that there must be weapons because if there were weapons no one would talk about weapons?" Hubert, Etc had experience winning arguments with Seth. He noted with pleasure that Natalie agreed and basked in a moment of admiration.

Seth gave him a belligerent look, couldn't keep it up. "Fine. No weapons."

It dawned on Hubert, Etc that this wasn't a thought experiment—somewhere on the way, reading FAQs and watching videos, they'd shaded from playing let's-pretend to planning. He had screens of notes and a huge wad of cached stuff.

"Are we going to actually do this? Actually for real?"

Natalie looked around the room pointedly. Hubert, Etc thought of the parties and the fooling around that must have taken place here, weird zottarich kids who'd played whatever decadent games they favored over the years. He thought of the cameras, spooling up their planning session from different angles, dropping it into long-term archiving.

"Fuck yeah," she whispered. "Let's do it."

# 2

## you all meet in a tavern

### [i]

Sundays at the Belt and Braces were the busiest, and there was always competition for the best jobs. The first person through the door hit the lights and checked the infographics. These were easy enough to read that anyone could make sense of them, even noobs. But Limpopo was no noob. She had more commits into the Belt and Braces' firmware than anyone, an order of magnitude lead over the rest. It was technically in poor taste for her to count her commits, let alone keep a tally. In a gift economy, you gave without keeping score, because keeping score implied an expectation of reward. If you're doing something for reward, it's an investment, not a gift.

In theory, Limpopo agreed. In practice, it was so easy to keep score, the leaderboard was so satisfying that she couldn't help herself. She wasn't proud of this. Mostly. But this Sunday, first through the door of the Belt and Braces, alone in the big common room with its aligned rows of tables and chairs, all the infographics showing nominal, she felt proud. She patted the wall with a perverse, unacceptable proprietary air. She helped build the Belt and Braces, scavenging badlands for the parts its drone outriders had identified for its construction. It was the project she'd found her walkaway with, the thing uppermost in her mind when she'd looked around the badlands, set down her pack, emptied her pockets of anything worth stealing, put extra underwear in a bag, and walked out onto the Niagara escarpment, past the invisible line that separated civilization from no-man's-land, out of the world as it was and into the world as it could be.

The codebase originated with the UN High Commission on Refugees, had been field-trialled a *lot*. You told it the kind of building you wanted, gave it a scavenging range, and it directed its drones to inventory anything nearby, scanning multi-band, doing deep database scrapes against urban planning and building-code sources to identify usable blocks for whatever you were making. This turned into a scavenger hunt inventory, and the refugees or aid workers (or, in shameful incidents, the trafficked juvenile slaves) fanned out to retrieve the pieces the building needed to conjure itself into existence.

These flowed into the job site. The building tracked and configured them, a continuously refactored critical path for its build plan that factored in the skill levels of workers or robots on-site at any moment. The effect was something like magic and something like ritual humiliation. If you installed something wrong, the system tried to find a way to work around your stupid mistake. Failing that, the system buzzed your haptics with rising intensity. If you ignored them, it tried optical and even audible. If you squelched that, it started telling the other humans that something was amiss, instructed them to fix it. There'd been a lot of A/B splitting of this—it was there in the codebase and its unit-tests for anyone to review—and the most successful strategy the buildings had found for correcting humans was to pretend they didn't exist.

If you planted a piece of structural steel in a way that the building really couldn't work with and ignored the rising chorus of warnings, someone else would be told that there was a piece of "misaligned" material and tasked to it, with high urgency. It was the same error that the buildings generated if something slipped. The error didn't assume that a human being had fucked up through malice or incompetence. The initial theory had been that an error without a responsible party would be more socially graceful. People doubled down on their mistakes, especially when embarrassed in front of peers. The name-and-shame alternate versions had shown hot-cheeked fierce denial was the biggest impediment to standing up a building.

So if you fucked up, soon someone would turn up with a mecha or a forklift or a screwdriver and a job ticket to unfuck the thing you were percussively maintaining into submission. You could pretend you were doing the same job as the new guy, part of the solution instead of the problem's cause. This let you save face, so you wouldn't insist you were doing it right and the building's stupid instructions (and everything else in the universe) was wrong.

Reality was chewily weirder in a way that Limpopo loved. It turned out that if you were dispatched to defubar something and found someone who was obviously the source of the enfubarage, you could completely tell the structural steel wasn't three degrees off true because of slippage: it was three degrees off true because some dipshit flubbed it. What's more, Señor Dipshit knew that you knew he was at fault. But the fact that the ticket read URGENT RETRUE STRUCTURAL MEMBER-3' AT 120° NNE not URGENT RETRUE STRUCTURAL MEMBER-3' AT 120° NNE BECAUSE SOME DIPSHIT CAN'T FOLLOW INSTRUCTIONS let both of you do this mannered kabuki in which you operated in the third person passive voice: "The beam has become off-true" not "You fucked up the beam."

That pretense—researchers called it "networked social disattention" but everyone else called it the "How'd that get there?" effect—was a vital shift in the UNHCR's distributed shelter initiative. Prior to that, it had all been gamified to fuckery, with leaderboards for the most correct installs and best looters. Test builds were marred by angry confrontations and fistfights. Even this was a virtue, since every build would fissure into two or three subgroups, each putting up their own buildings. Three for the price of one! Inevitably, these forked-off projects would be less ambitious than the original plan.

Early sites had a characteristic look: a wide, flat, low building, the first three stories of something that had been planned for ten before half the workers quit. A hundred meters away, three more buildings, each half the size of the first, representing forked and re-forked buildings revenge-built by alienated splitters. Some sites had Fibonacci spirals of ever-smaller forks, terminating in a hostility-radiating Wendy House.

The buildings made the leap from the UNHCR repo to the walkaways and mutated into innumerable variations beyond the clinic/school/shelter refugee pantheon. The Belt and Braces was the first tavern ever attempted. Layouts for restaurant kitchens weren't far off from the camp kitchens, and big common spaces were easy enough, but the actual zeitgeist of the thing was substantially different, tweaked in a thousand ways so that you'd never walk into it and say, "This is a refugee residence that's been converted to a restaurant."

But you'd never mistake the Belt and Braces for a normal restaurant. Its major feature was the projection-mapped lighting that painted surfaces and items throughout its interior with subtle red/green tones telling you where something needed human attention. This was the UNHCR playbook, but again, there was a world of difference between dishing up M.R.E.s to climate refus and serving fancy dry-ice cocktails made from wet-printers and powdered alcohol. No refugee camp ever went through quite so many cocktail parasols and perfect-knot swizzle sticks.

On an average day, the Belt and Braces served a couple hundred people. On Sundays, it was more like five hundred. The influx of noobs brought scouts for talent, sexual partners, bandmates, playmates, and, of course, victims. Being the first one through the door meant that Limpopo would get to play maître d'.

The assays showed last night's beer had come up well. The hydrogen cells were running 45 percent, which would run the Belt and Braces for two weeks flat out—the eggbeaters on the roof had been running hard, electrolyzing waste water and pumping cracked hydrogen into the cells. There were fifty cells in the basement, harvested out of abandoned jets the drones had spotted. The jets hadn't been airworthy in a long time, but had yielded quantities of matériel for the Belt and Braces, including dozens of benches made from their seats. The hard-wearing upholstery came clean, its dirt-shedding surfaces revealing designs with each wipe of their rags like reappearing disappearing ink.

But the hydrogen cells had been the biggest find of all; without them, the Belt and Braces would have been very different, prone to shortages and brownouts. Limpopo fretted that they'd be stolen; it took all her self-control not to install surveillanceware all around the utility hatches.

The pre-prep stuff on the larders showed green, but she still made a point of personally sniffing the cheese cultures and prodding the dough through its kneading-film. The sauce precursors smelled tasty, and the ice-cream maker hummed as it lazily aerated the frozen cream. She called for coffium and sat skewered on a beam of light in the middle of the commons as the delicious, fruity, musky aroma wafted into the room.

The first cup of coffium danced hot in her mouth and its early-onset ingredients percolated into her bloodstream through the mucous membranes under her tongue. Her fingertips and scalp tingled and she closed her eyes to enjoy the effects the second-wave substances brought on as her gut started to work. Her hearing became preternatural, the big muscles in her quads and pecs and shoulders got a fiery feeling like dancing while standing still.

She took another deep draught and closed her eyes, and when she opened them again, she had company.

They were such obvious noobs they could have come from central casting. Worse, they were shleppers, their heavy outsized packs, many-pocketed trekking coats, and cargo pants stuffed to bulging. They looked overinflated. Shleppers were neurotic and probably destined to walkback within weeks, leaving behind lingering interpersonal upfuckednesses. Limpopo had gone walkaway the right way, with nothing more than clean underwear, which turned out to be superfluous. She tried not to prejudge these three, especially in that giddy first five minutes of her coffium buzz. She didn't want to harsh her mellow.

"Welcome to the B and B!" she shouted, louder than intended. They flinched, then rallied.

"Hi there," the girl said, and walked forward. Her clothes were beautiful, bias-cut and contrast stitched. Limpopo immediately coveted them. She'd pull the girl's image from the archives later and decompose the patterns and run a set for herself. She'd be the envy of all who saw her, until the design propagated and became old news. "Sorry to just walk in, but we heard—"

"You heard right." Limpopo's voice was quieter but still too shouty. Either the coffium had to burn down so she could control her affect, or she needed to drink a lot more so she could stop giving a shit. She thumped the refill zone and put her cup under the nozzle. "Open to everyone, all day, every day, but Sundays are special, our way of saying hello to our new neighbors and getting to know them. I'm Limpopo. What do you want to be called?"

The phrasing was particular to the walkaways, an explicit invitation to remake yourself. It was the height of walkaway sophistication to greet people with it, and Limpopo used it deliberately on these three because she could tell they were tightly wound.

The shorter of the two guys, with a scruffy kinked beard and a stubbly shaved head stuck his hand out. "I'm Gizmo von Puddleducks. This is Zombie McDingleberry and Etcetera." The other two rolled their eyes.

"Thank you, 'Gizmo,' but actually, you can call me Stable Strategies," the girl said.

The other guy, tall but hunched over with an owlish expression and exhaustion lines on his face, sighed. "You might as well call me Etcetera. Thanks, 'Herr von Puddleducks.' "

"Very pleased to meet," Limpopo said. "Why don't you put your stuff down and grab a seat and I'll get you some coffium, yeah?"

The three looked at each other and Gizmo shrugged and said, "Hell yeah." He shrugged out of his pack and let it fall to the floor with a thump that made Limpopo jump. Jesus fuck, what *were* these noobs hauling over hill and dale? Bricks?

The other two followed suit. The girl took off her shoes and rubbed her feet. Then they all did it. Limpopo wrinkled her nose at the smell of sweaty feet and made a note to show them the sock exchange. She squeezed off three coffiums, using the paper-thin ceramic cups printed with twining, grippy texture strips. She set the cups down onto saucers and added small carrot biscuits and pickled radishes and carried them to the noobs' table on a tray that clicked into a squared-off dock. She got her jumbo mug and brandished it: "To the first days of a better world," she said, another cornball walkaway thing, but Sundays were the day for cornball walkaway things.

"The first days," Etcetera said, with surprising (dismaying) sincerity.

"First days," the other two said and clinked. They drank and were quiet while it kicked off for them. The girl got a cat-with-canary grin and took short, loud breaths, each making her taller. The others were less demonstrative, but their eyes shone. Limpopo's own dose was optimal now, and she suddenly wanted these noobs to be as welcome as possible. She wanted them to feel awesome and confident.

"You guys want brunch? There's waffles with real maple syrup, eggs as you like 'em, some pork belly and chicken ribs, and I'm pretty sure croissants, too."

"Can we help?" Etcetera said.

"Don't sweat that. Sit there and soak it in, let the Belt and Braces take care of you. Later on, we'll see if we can get you a job." She didn't say they were too noob to have earned the right to pitch in at the B&B, that walkaways for fifty clicks would love to humblebrag on helping at the Belt and Braces. The B&B's kitchen took care of everything, anyway. It had taken Limpopo a while to get the idea that food was applied chemistry and humans were shitty lab techs, but after John Henry splits with automat systems, even she agreed that the B&B produced the best food with minimum human intervention. And there were croissants, which was exciting!

She *did* squeeze the oranges herself, but only because when she peaked she liked to squeeze her hands and work the muscles in her shoulders and arms, and could get the orange hulls nearly as clean as the machine. They were blue oranges anyway, optimized for northern greenhouse cultivation, and yielded their juice eagerly. She plated everything—that, at least, was something humans could rock—and delivered it.

By the time she came out of the kitchen, there were more noobs, and one of them needed medical attention for heat exhaustion. She was just getting to grips with that—coffium was great for keeping your cool when multitasking—when more old hands came in and efficiently settled and fed everyone else. Before long, there was a steady rocking rhythm to the B&B that Limpopo fucking *loved*, the hum of a complex adaptive system where humans and software coexisted in a state that could be called *dancing*.

The menu evolved through the day, depending on the feedstocks visitors brought. Limpopo nibbled around the edges, moving from one red light to the next, till they went green, developing a kind of sixth sense about the next red zone, logging more than her share of work units. If there had been a leaderboard for the B&B that day, she'd have been embarrassingly off the charts. She pretended as hard as she could that her friends weren't noticing her bustling activity. The gift economy was not supposed to be a karmic ledger with your good deeds down one column and the ways you'd benefited from others down the other. The point of walkaways was living for abundance, and in abundance, why worry if you were putting in as much as you took out? But freeloaders were freeloaders, and there was no shortage of assholes who'd take all the best stuff or ruin things through thoughtlessness. People noticed. Assholes didn't get invited to parties. No one went out of their way to look out for them. Even without a ledger, there was still a ledger, and Limpopo wanted to bank some good wishes and karma just in case.

The crowd slackened around four. There were enough perishables that the B&B declared a jubilee and put together an afternoon tea course. Limpopo moved toward the reddening zones in the food prep area and found that Etcetera guy.

"Hey there, how're you enjoying your noob's day here at the glorious Belt and Braces?"

He ducked. "I feel like I'm going to explode. I've been fed, drugged, boozed, and had a nap by the fire. I just can't sit there anymore. Please put me to work?"

"You know that's something you're not supposed to ask?"

"I got that impression. There's something weird about you—I mean, us?—and work. You're not supposed to covet a job, and you're not supposed to look down your nose at slackers, and you're not supposed to lionize someone who's slaving. It's supposed to be emergent, natural homeostasis, right?"

"I thought you might be clever. That's it. Asking someone if you can pitch in is telling them that they're in charge and deferring to their authority. Both are verboten. If you want to work, do something. If it's not helpful, maybe I'll undo it later, or talk it over with you, or let it slide. It's passive aggressive, but that's walkaways. It's not like there's any hurry."

He chewed on that. "Is there? Is there really *abundance*? If the whole world went walkaway tomorrow would there be enough?"

"By definition," she said. "Because enough is whatever you make it. Maybe you want to have thirty kids. 'Enough' for you is more than 'enough' for me. Maybe you want to get your calories in a very specific way. Maybe you want to live in a very specific place where a lot of other people want to live. Depending on how you look at it, there'll never be enough, or there'll always be plenty."

While they'd gabbed, three other walkaways prepped tea, hand-finished scones and dainty sandwiches and steaming pots and adulterants arranged on the trays. She consciously damped the anxiety at someone doing "her" job. So long as the job got done, that's what mattered. If anything mattered. Which it did. But not in the grand scheme of things. She recognized one of her loops.

"Well that settles that," she said, jerking her chin at the people bringing out the trays. "Let's eat."

"I don't think I can." He patted his stomach. "You guys should install a vomitorium."

"They're just a legend," she said. "'Vomitorium' just means a narrow bottleneck between two chambers, from which a crowd is vomited forth. Nothing to do with gorging yourself into collective bulimia."

"But still." He looked thoughtful. "I could install one, couldn't I? Log in to your back-end, sketch it out and start looking for material, taking stuff apart and knocking out bricks?"

"Technically, but I don't think you'd get help with it, and there'd be reverts when you weren't around, people bricking back the space you'd unbricked. I mean, a vomitorium is not only apocryphal—it's grody. Not the kind of thing that happens in practice."

"But if I had a gang of trolls, we could do it, right? Could put armed guards on the spot, charge admission, switch to Big Macs?"

This was a tedious, noob discussion. "Yeah, you could. If you made it stick, we'd build another Belt and Braces down the road and you'd have a building full of trolls. You're not the first person to have this little thought experiment."

"I'm sure I'm not," he said. "I'm sorry if it's boring. I know the theory, but it seems like it just couldn't work."

"It doesn't work at all in theory. In theory, we're selfish assholes who want more than our neighbors, can't be happy with a lot if someone else has a lot more. In theory, someone will walk into this place when no one's around and take everything. In theory, it's bullshit. This stuff only works in *practice*. In theory, it's a mess."

He giggled, an unexpected, youthful sound.

"I've got a bunch of questions about that, but you had that so ready I'd bet you can bust out as many answers like it as you need."

"Oh, I'm sure," she said. She liked him, despite him being a shlepper. "Does it scale? So far, so good. What happens in the long run? As a wise person once said—"

"In the long run, we're all dead."

"Though who knows, right?"

"You don't believe that tuff, do you?"

"You call it tuff, I call it obvious. When you're rich, you don't have to die. That's clear. Put together the whole run of therapies—selective germ plasm optimization, continuous health surveillance, genomic therapies, preferential transplant access. . . . If I believed in private property, I'd give you odds that the first generation of immortal humans are alive today. They will outrace and outpace their own mortality."

She watched him try to disagree without being rude and remembered how she'd worried about offending people when she'd first gone walkaway. It was adorable.

"Just because money can be traded for lifespan to a point, it doesn't follow that it scales," he said. "You can trade money for land, but if you tried to buy New York City one block at a time, you'd run out of money no matter how much you started with, because as the supply decreased—" He shook his head. "I mean, not to say that there's supply and demand when it comes to your health, but, *diminishing returns* for sure. Believing that science will advance at the same rate as mortality is mumbo jumbo." He looked awkward. She liked this guy. "It's an act of faith. No offense."

"No offense. You missed the most important argument. Life extension comes at the expense of quality of life. There's a guy about two hundred miles that way"—she pointed south—"worth more than most countries, who is just organs and gray matter in a vat. The vat's in a fortified clinic and the clinic's in a walled city. Everyone who works in that city shares that guy's microbial nation. It's a condition of employment. You've got one hundred times more nonhuman cells in your body than human ones. The people who live in that city are ninety-nine percent immortal rich-guy, extensions of his body. All they do is labor to figure out how to extend his life. Most of them went tops in their classes at the best unis in the world. Recruited out of school. Paid a wage that can't be matched anywhere else.

"I met someone who used to work there, gave it up and went walkaway. He said the guy in the vat is in perpetual agony. Something tricked his pain perception into 'continuous, non-adapting peak load.' He's feeling as much pain as is humanly possible, pain you can't get used to. He could tell them to switch off the machines—and he'd be dead. But he's hanging in. He's making a bet that some super-genius in his city who's thinking about the bounty on the bugs in this guy's personal bug-tracker will figure out how to solve this nerve thing. There'll be breakthroughs, if everything goes to plan. So the vat will just be his larval phase. You don't have to believe it, but it's the truth."

"It's not weirder than other stories I've heard about zottas. The only unlikely thing is that your buddy was able to go walkaway at all. Sounds like the kind of deal where you'd get hunted down like a dog for violating your NDA."

She remembered the guy, who'd gone by Langerhans, all weird tradecraft stuff—dead drops and the lengths he went to in order to avoid leaving behind skin cells and follicles, wiping down his used glasses and cutlery. "He kept a low profile. As for that NDA, he had weird shit to tell, but nothing that I could have used to kickstart my own program or sabotage the man in the vat. He was shrewd. Absolutely raving bugfuck. But shrewd. I believed him."

"It's just like I was saying. This guy is enduring unimaginable pain because of his superstitious belief that he can spend his way out of death. The fact that this guy believes it doesn't have any connection with its reality. Maybe this guy will spend a hundred years trapped in infinite hell. Zottas are just as good at self-delusion as anyone. Better—they're convinced they got to where they are because they're evolutionary sports who deserve to be exalted above baseline humans, so they're primed to believe anything they feel must be true. What, apart from blind, self-serving faith by this zotta leads you to believe that there's anything other than wishful thinking?"

Limpopo remembered Langerhans's certainty, his low, intense ranting about the coming age of immortal zottas whose familial dynasties would be captained by undying tyrants.

"I admit I don't have anything to prove it. Everything I know I learned secondhand from someone scared out of his skin. This is one of those things where it's worth behaving as though it was true, even if it never comes to pass. The zottas are trying to secede from humanity. They don't see their destiny as tied to ours. They think that they can politically, economically, and epidemiologically isolate themselves, take to high ground above the rising seas, breed their offspring by Harrier jets.

"I'd been walkaway for nearly a year before I understood this. That's what walkaway *is*—not walking out on 'society,' but acknowledging that in zottaworld, we're problems to be solved, not citizens. That's why you never hear politicians talking about 'citizens,' it's all 'taxpayers,' as though the salient fact of your relationship to the state is how much you pay. Like the state was a business and citizenship was a loyalty program that rewarded you for your custom with roads and health care. Zottas cooked the process so they get all the money and own the political process, pay as much or as little tax as they want. Sure, they pay most of the tax, because they've built a set of rules that gives them most of the money. Talking about 'taxpayers' means that the state's debt is to rich dudes, and anything it gives to kids or old people or sick people or disabled people is charity we should be grateful for, since none of those people are paying tax that justifies their rewards from Government Inc.

"I live as though the zottas don't believe they're in my species, down to the inevitability of death and taxes, because *they* believe it. You want to know how sustainable Belt and Braces is? The answer to that is bound up with our relationship to the zottas. They could crush us tomorrow if they chose, but they don't, because when they game out their situations, they're better served by some of us 'solving' ourselves by removing ourselves from the political process, especially since we're the people who, by and large, would be the biggest pain in the ass if we stayed—"

"Come on." He had a good smile. "Talk about self-serving! What makes you think that we're the biggest pains? Maybe we're the easiest of all, since we're ready to walk away. What about people who're too sick or young or old or stubborn and demand that the state cope with them as citizens?"

"Those people can be most easily rounded up and institutionalized. That's why they can't run away. It's monstrous, but we're talking about monstrous things."

"That's creepy," he said. "And cinematic. Do you really think zottas sit around a star chamber plotting how to separate the goats from the sheep?"

"Of course not. Shit, if they did that, we could suicide-bomb the fuckers. I think this is an emergent outcome. It's even more evil, because it exists in a zone of diffused responsibility: no one decides to imprison the poor in record numbers, it just happens as a consequence of tougher laws, less funding for legal aid, added expense in the appeals process. . . . There's no person, decision, or political process you can blame. It's systemic."

"What's the systemic outcome of being a walkaway, then?"

"I don't think anyone knows yet. It's going to be fun finding out."

## [ii]

The guy's friends woke from their nap while Limpopo and he were clearing dishes, which meant filing bugs where the dish-clearing routines failed. The tricky thing was that half the bugs were already tracked, but it wasn't clear whether they *were* the same bugs, and it was dickish to create duplicate bugs when you could spend time to determine whether the bug was already there. Plus, adding more validations to an existing bug made it more likely to get fixed. If you wanted your bug fixed, you should really check it in depth.

They wandered over, gummy-eyed and torpid, whiffy of unwashed skin. Limpopo suggested they visit the *onsen* in the back. Everyone was amenable. They gave up on the bugs—let the other B&Bers get a crack at filing bugs of their own—and shouldered their shlepper packs and headed, staggering, to the back of the tavern.

"How's this work?" the girl said. "Give us the FAQ"—she pronounced it "fack"—"for this kinky soapy thing of yours." Limpopo thought she was putting up a front and the "kinky soapy" snark was a tell for anxiety about being inducted into a walkaway orgy.

"It's co-ed, but there's no sexytime, don't worry. It's thirty percent walkaway, seventy percent Japanese in approach. Just enough formalism that everyone can enjoy themselves, not so much that you worry about doing it wrong. The thing to remember is that baths are for relaxing, not washing.

You don't want to get anything except clean skin into them. No bathing suits, and you sit down at the shower stall for a hardcore scrubadub and a decontam stage before you get in. The hot water is limitless—it's solar pasteurized in barrels on the roof, then there's a three-stage filter through printed charcoal with the surface area of Jupiter's moons.

"Once you're clean, do your own thing. Some of the baths will parboil you in ten minutes, some are cold enough to give you hypothermia if you stay in them, and the rest are in between. Go where the mood takes you. I like outdoor baths, but the fish in them may creep you out. They'll eat your dead skin, which tickles, but something deep-seated rejects being something else's snack, so wave them away if you don't want them nibbling. I like 'em, though. The little towels are all-purpose; keep them handy but *don't* wring them out in the pools."

"Is that it?" the smart-ass guy said.

"That's it."

"What about the dirty stuff?"

She rolled her eyes. "If you meet someone of your preferred gender and want to do something, get showered, get dressed, and get a room. We don't do dirty in the onsen. Strictly platonic."

"If you say so."

"So say we all."

"Where do we leave our stuff?" That was Etcetera, and her mental assessment of him dropped a notch. Shleppers and *stuff.*

"Anywhere."

"Will it be safe?"

"Dunno."

The noobs exchanged easy to read glances: *That's not cool. I'm sure it's safe, don't be such a tourist. This is all our stuff. Don't embarrass us.*

"Ready?"

They followed her. They all changed together in the dry-room, and she didn't bother being subtle about peeking, that was the deal when you were a walkaway. Skin is skin—interesting, but everyone's got some. These three were young and firm, but not offensively so, and the smart-ass had totally depilated, which had been a style when she went walkaway, but had since atrophied, judging from the lush bushes the other two sported.

The funny thing about not caring if you get caught peeking is you get to watch everyone peek, and these three did, in a way that made her sure that they weren't a sex thing with each other—yet. The other thing about not caring about peeking is you catch other people peeking at you, which all three did in turn, and she held each of their eyes in turn, frankly and unsexually.

It was her duty to these noobs to help them go walkaway in their minds, from the sex and scarcity death-cult they'd grown up with and turned their backs upon.

She needed to do it for herself, too. She knew it was possible to be in the presence of naked people without it being about sex—she knew that stuff was a liability, not an asset; she knew that work was not a competition—she still needed to remind her psyche. Habits didn't die easy, they were so closely tied to her fear and fear was hardest to ignore. Taking noobs into the onsen was occupational therapy for her own walkaway.

"Let's hit the showers." She led them into the cleanup room, pretending not to notice their anxious glances at their packs in the unguarded room, which were no more subtle than their looks at her bare ass as she led them onward.

She started in the hottest pool, a trick to get her mind out of her muscles. That heat made thought impossible, all she could do was *be,* willing each muscle in turn to unclench, breathing the mineral-scented steam, until she melted beneath the water, legs, arms, ass, back, the soles of her feet, and the palms of her hands going soft as perfect barbecue, flesh just about ready to fall off her bones, relaxation lapping up her spine. The panic of the heat oozed down from her brain, warring in tiny neck muscles and in her occiput, until they gave way, and the last centimeter of stress that she'd not known was there gave. She was sensation, play of muscles and heat, pleasure balanced upon the knife-edge of pain. She relaxed deeper, the postural muscles that kept her in a *Z* loosened, her butt floated one increment off the porous stone step, and the sudden occurrence of a gracious interval between flesh and unyielding rock caused a deeper loosening, starting with the crisscrossing muscles of her butt, working deep into her pelvis and core. She was so relaxed her tummy bulged as the girdle of tissues that wrapped from ribs to hips gave. She felt like sous-vide meat, muscle fibers unraveling, underlying tissues sloughing away from the bag of elastic fascia that wrapped them. She let out a bass groan that hummed in her loose vocal cords. "I'm cooking."

Someone was next to her in the water, probably Etcetera to judge from the amount of displaced water. He panted as he struggled with his body's instinct to flee the remorseless heat. She listened to his breath deepen, heard the sighs as he unwound. There was a sympathy between their bodies as the ripples carried the signals of relaxation between them.

You can't stay in that kind of heat forever, no matter how much you'd like to. She stayed right to the last instant, then stood up quickly, cool air tingling everywhere it kissed her. She gasped. The heat cooked away all self-consciousness. She could stand naked and gasping on the pool's steaming edge without even the awareness of *not* being self-conscious. She walked in measured steps, smooth flagstones sensual against her feet's half-boiled soles, to the edge of the coldest pool. She dipped a nearby pail into it, then used the pail to wet her small towel, squeezing it on her skin, starting on the top of her head and nearly choking as the icy water sluiced down her shaven scalp and behind her ears and into her eyes, nose, and mouth.

She dipped the towel, scrubbed her skin, clenching her jaw to keep from gasping. She forced herself to scour her skin with the water, dipping the towel again and again, lashing herself with the cold until the pail was empty. She contemplated another pailful—sometimes she did two or three—but couldn't bear the thought.

She stepped into the coldest pool, up to her ankles, made herself descend the steps, keeping her hand light on the grab rail despite the death grip she wanted. One more step and she was in the water to her knees, another step and she was up to her thighs and the water lapped at the bottom of her butt and her vulva. The thought of taking one more step was impossible, no sane person would plunge their tenderest places into icy hell. She knew from experience that if she didn't go for it, she'd lose her nerve. She brought her weight forward until she had no choice but to plunge chest-first into the water, head dipping under for a moment that made her ears go instantly numb and the skin on her eyeballs and forehead feel like it was being pulled to her hairline.

She refused, by iron will, to allow herself to gasp. She made herself stay in that punishing water for one long breath, and then walked out in measured steps. The air, chilly before, now felt hot. She took her small towel back to the hottest pool and filled a fresh bucket and started the process in reverse. The water was blister-raising, scorching, scalding, but she made herself wash down with it before sinking back into the hottest pool.

Five minutes before, she'd thought every muscle had released its reservoirs of tension. This time, as the hot water boiled her, the feeling was transcendent. She closed her eyes and there was nothing behind them, no flickering worries, nothing but animal joy.

The sensation ended with a shocked cry from the coldest pool. She turned placidly, saw Etcetera in the cold water, face a rictus, nostrils flared so wide they looked horsey, and he snorted down them with steam-train intensity. To his credit, he stayed for a five-count and came back to the hottest pool with a slow pace. She smiled lazily as he washed himself with his small towel. He stepped into the hottest pool and their eyes met.

She held his gaze as he let the heat and his muscles and nerves do their dance.

"Oh, *wow.*"

"Yeah."

"Wow."

She waited for him on the next cold plunge, and they locked eyes as they stepped into the cold, a playful dare. Neither of them made a sound, not even when the water touched his scrotum, though he gave the smallest jolt. They waded in up to their necks, and, without saying a word, dipped their heads, surfaced. Neither wanted to be the first to get out. They stared, then glared, until he muttered "you're crazy" between gritted teeth and started for the stairs. She followed. He had a cute butt, she noticed, in the most abstract way.

She had to admit that it wasn't all that abstract.

Back into the hot, giggling as they silently dared each other to sluice the scalding water over themselves, to step into the bubbling heat, quickly sink in. The third immersion in the heat took her to places she had forgot, driving out all conscious thought, turning her into a thermotropic organism that reacted to the convection currents through a process below her brain stem.

Once again, her body told her she couldn't stay in this heat much longer. It was a return to awareness from that blissful no-place, eyes opening to cracks, then fully, head lifting out of the water. He joined her a moment later, just long enough that he might have been proving some macho point about his ability to withstand pain. She banished the thought. If it was true, he was only hurting himself. His business, not hers. If it wasn't true, she was being needlessly mean.

They stood beside the pool beside each other, stress wrung out of their flesh, faces falling into unconscious bliss.

"Now what?" he asked.

"Now we go for the normal pools. She pointed to the onsen's other pools, where a dozen bathers sat, chatting quietly or contemplating their eyelid-backs. His friends sat in a warm, bubbly bath with an awkward distance between them.

They ambled over, and as always happened in the baths, Limpopo found the stimulus had dissolved any sense of nudity. Even their eyes on her body didn't awaken any feeling of nakedness. It was the psychological equivalent of the ringing in your ears after a long-humming refrigerator compressor shut down. The baseline hum of worry about her appearance, where she was hairy, what the hair looked like, where she had fat, where her bones protruded, where her skin was striated with stretch marks and where it was curdled with burn scars, all ceased to matter.

She slid into the water beside the noobs. Seen from this side of hot/cold treatment, they were gnarled by years in default reality. Being in the death cult of money and status marked you. They bore the marks. She hoped to erase her own someday.

"Can we join you?"

"You already have," the sarcastic one said, good natured. He was between her and Etcetera—who'd followed her into the water—and Etcetera gave him a brotherly elbow in the ribs. They were at ease side by side, like brothers but not, pink arm by brown arm, hairless chest next to Etcetera's thick mat.

"Herr Von Puddleducks," she said, "what say you to our humble baths?"

"Decadent," he sniffed. "Sure to be a breeding ground for something entirely unsavory."

"Don't listen," the girl said. "It's amazing."

Etcetera said, "You've got to try that hot/cold thing. It's consciousness-alteringly good."

"Maybe later," the sarcastic one said.

"Definitely later," the girl said. "How'd you get your scar?"

Which was very forward of her and a good walkaway kind of question, in that it violated every norm of default. Limpopo levered her torso out of the water and torqued to look at the mess of burn scar from her ribcage down her thigh. She ran her fingers over it, the tightness and its irregular surface merely sensations now, no longer horrors.

"Happened not long after I first went walkaway. We'd built rammed-earth houses on the escarpment, two dozen of them. Real refu-luxury: power, water, fresh hydroponics, and soft beds. Took about three hours a day each to keep the whole place running. Spent the rest of the time re-creating a Greek open-air school, teaching each other music and physics and realtime poetry. It was sweet. I helped build a pottery and we were building weird wheels that did smart adaptive eccentric spinning in response to your hands and mass, so that it was impossible to throw a non-viable pot.

"We were right up on the edge of default, close to the border. It was nice because we'd get day-trippers we could talk to about what was going on in the world. Tell the truth, I liked being on the border because it was an escape hatch. If things got bad, I could throw it in, walkback. Call my mom.

"The day-trippers weren't always nice. There was a group of guys, neighborhood watch, who'd show up whenever anything went wrong in their fortress-condos. Someone got robbed: it must have been a walkaway. Graffiti? Gotta be walkaways. Murder? One of us, can't possibly be one of those civilized types.

"For people living with continuous surveillance, they had a lot of crime. The property violations were their kids, who'd figured out how to turn off daddy's spyware so they could get busy. If you think drones are going to stop teenagers from fucking, you're out of your mind.

"I don't know who did the murder. I heard it was horrible. Arson. Someone pwned a whole block of houses and did something with the safety sensors and the gas and *whoof*. Twenty-plus dead, including kids. Including a baby. I can't imagine someone doing that, and I know it wasn't anyone from our settlement. Something like that, it's got to be personal."

The three watched raptly, looks of horror dawning as they realized where the story was going. But Etcetera, bless his earlobes, spoke up: "Maybe totally sociopathic. A six-sigma event in someone's neurotypicality. Not saying that a stranger doing that wouldn't be totally fucked up and shit, but don't discount the school-shooter/bad brains hypothesis outright."

"I've wondered about that. I thought it might be provocateurs, because of what happened." She traced the scar with her fingers. "Those rammed-earth houses, they're really easy to instrument. The standard build has environmental sensors and fail-safes and alarms. They used the earthworks machines near the camp to mound up dirt on the façade and back lane of a whole row of houses, shifting tons of dirt and gravel in front of the doors. They walked down the line, calm as you like, smashing out windows and throwing Molotovs in each. Then they walked around the other side and tried the same for the back windows.

"But those windows were shatterproof, which is what saved us. They had a big argument about the best way to get through them. While that was happening, we were inside, organizing. The rammed-earth houses were two-up/two-downs, a family room and kitchen on the ground floor, an upper loft with two small bedrooms and a toilet. They were built to be thermostatic, cool in the summer, warm in the winter, circulation channels cut into each connecting wall, with nautilus-chambered noise-labyrinths that let air through but dampened sound.

"My house—I shared it with three other people—was at the end where they were arguing about smashing the windows. I knew that I had to get out, the place was full of smoke and fire. We were on the top floor, in the sleeping rooms, because it was the middle of the night. That meant that we weren't in the flames, but the smoke was congregating on that floor. My friend kicked out the noise-labyrinth and we were able to squeeze through it into the next house, where there were five people, with the walls knocked out between their bedrooms to make one big sleep pit. They were in a panic because one of them had already passed out from the smoke. They wanted to try for the door. We calmed them, explained what was going on outside, sent them through the noise-guard into the next place.

"I had to get the word going, get people moving to that last place, so I hung back and messaged everyone, sipping at the pocket of fresh air until it got too rank, then I followed them. The next place was already cleared out and so was the next, and the fire in that place wasn't so bad, so I paused to do some more messaging.

"I misjudged the smoke. Passed out. One of my friends figured I was missing and came back, pushed me through three more noise-guards until I was with the rest of the group. They split into two teams, one group downstairs to fight the fire and the other trying to bust through the end wall. The rammed earth was really good at deflecting blows, but you could claw and dig it away, and I thought there was enough crew working on that to get the job done.

"I went downstairs to fight the fire. The walls were impervious to flames, of course, but the Molotovs had their own fuel, and there was plenty of paper furniture and plastic kitchen appliances that burned if you got them hot enough. I had a wet cloth around my face, but it had dried, and I could hardly see or breathe. I didn't even notice that my shirt was on fire until one of the other women in my crew tackled me and rolled me on the ground.

"By then they'd scraped a good-sized hole in the top floor, and thrown a pile of bedding and clothes onto the ground outside and we hang-dropped into it as fast and as quietly as we could.

"The vigilantes figured out what was going on, and came to ride us down. They had a lot of macho A.T.V. shit, plus drones. We had the clothes on our backs, and some of us were nearly naked. We scattered. I let the woman who'd put out my fire lead me into the brush, to a muddy culvert where we lay with just our mouths and noses out of the mud, so we wouldn't have an IR signature. I had to get up first, all my body heat gone, the hypothermia setting in. I knew what it was, knew I'd be dead soon if I didn't get warm.

"My friend tried to keep me from going, but I knew I was right. Whatever else was going on, I was going to die if I didn't get warm. I stood. I shivered, and there was this pain here—" she traced the scar. "My friend cursed me back to the settlement, convinced we were going to get shot. But she came. Safety in numbers.

"Safety in numbers is a powerful idea. By the time we straggled to the smoking ruins, nearly everyone was there. The walkaways were in bad shape, hurting and coughing and cold. Staring at us from the other end of the houses were the vigilantes, hostile and unsure of themselves. They'd had a group madness that let them burn their neighbors' homes. They'd been a mob, with diffused responsibility, the whole thing an emergent property of social mass, and now it had dissipated.

"My group set up an infirmary, right in front of them, treating our wounded with whatever we had. There were some people who'd hurt themselves jumping, some who'd gotten hurt in the scramble through the woods. It wasn't until dawn broke and we did a head count and a network sweep that we discovered four people were missing. Two of them straggled in later. Two were found in one of the houses, charred to bone, missed in that scramble. One of the dead was fifteen years old, and no one knew how to get in touch with his parents, somewhere out there in default.

"Word got out about the fire. There was a lot of U.A.V. traffic, not just copters and gliders, but bumbling zepps with medical relief and food. Soon there were people, more walkaways, and the straights freaked out and started to arm up, build a rampart to defend themselves from reprisals.

"There was no revenge. The straights had stolen our earthmoving gear for their defensive rampart, but there were new diggers within a couple of days. Don't know who brought it. I was laid up with bad fever, infection. When I came to my senses, they told me they hadn't expected me to make it. I was too poorly to help for weeks. It was only once we had some wet printers running that I had pharma for the infection—some silver-doped antibiotics that knocked it out."

They listened raptly. Then the girl shook her head like there was a bee in her ear. "Am I getting this right? You got burned out by insane vigilantes who killed your friends and nearly killed you, personally, and you hung around?"

"We didn't hang around." She smiled at the memory. "We rebuilt. The normals watched from their ramparts, like a militia, but we didn't fight. First thing, we built a kitchen, then we baked, because rammed-earth construction is hungry work. Every time cookies or granola bars came out, we brought a tray over to them under a white flag and left it. The trays piled up, untouched, until one day they were gone. Don't know if they ate them or not.

"It was very Gandhi-ey, though I had an itchy neck from the thought of all those scopes trained on me. They'd dial their laser-sights up to visible and make the dots dance on our foreheads, or over our hearts. But when we put out videos—including a red dot over the breast of a very pregnant woman who'd come to help—there was such a flood of net-rage for the vigilantes they quit it.

"We dozed the old houses when the new ones were done. We'd lived in hexayurts and tents, because our old places were uninhabitable. Having them there, the mummies of our dead, kept us working and shamed the vigilantes. Once the old places were down, we planted wildflowers and grasses that would have been beautiful when they grew out.

"The new settlement was three times as big. A lot of our volunteers wanted to stick around, and then there were new walkaways, so disgusted with the vigilantes they left the gate-guarded town. Some were double agents, but that was okay, since we didn't have any secrets. Secrets were just overhead.

"As we got nearer to move-in, the atmosphere got festive. There were movie nights on the sides of the buildings, which we'd painted white. We always tried to paint our stuff white, just to do our bit for the planet's albedo. We turned our excavation site into a swimming hole with water from the creek. The earthworks machines turned into rope swings and dive platforms.

"I was in the pool when the vigilantes moved in again. They HERFed our drones and used pain-rays and sonic flashlights to herd us all into the square between the four rows of houses. Then a guy with a semi-military private security badge used a loudtalker to warn us that he was deputized by the county to clear the land and we had ten minutes to vacate. There was a EULA after that, about how they could just blow us away under the Anti-Terror Act of such-and-such if we engaged in conduct likely to represent a threat to life or property. As soon as he was done, he cranked up that fucking pain-ray. No one even thought about going back for their stuff. It was like your face was melting. There were kids in our group, under ten, and they screamed like they were being sawn to pieces. You hear stories about parents lifting a car off their kids, but that's nothing—I saw parents walk straight into the pain-ray to get their kids. One of them fell down seizing, and her partner lifted her in a fireman's carry with a kid under the other arm. I don't think I've ever seen a more impressive physical feat.

"We couldn't hide in the woods. They had their U.A.V.s flying overlapping coverage, following us in flocks until we were twenty klicks away. I limped all day and all night, and every time I slowed down, babycopters would drop out of the sky and ram me, nudging me along like cattle. I stuck with a couple who were carrying their kid. They stopped and tried to camp because their little boy couldn't take another step and none of us had it in us to carry him anymore, and I stood guard over them, batting the copters with a leafy branch. More and more of the little bastards descended on us and eventually we moved on. They begged bicycles from a noncombatant couple on the road, and then I was slowing them down. I moved off on my own.

"I eventually dropped, and I must have been out of the copters' enforcement range, because they hovered off on the horizon, making that cricket-noise, but I drifted off even so and when I awoke they'd gone. Must have needed a recharge and the vigilantes didn't think I warranted a relief squadron."

"What happened next?" the girl said. Of the three, she was most horrified. Limpopo guessed that this was because she was the richest of them, the one for whom this was the most inconceivable.

Limpopo shrugged, felt a tightness in her shoulders, realized she'd harshed her mellow by reliving the experience. It was three years before, and she still got some PTSDish moments, but not for a while. This telling made it come strong. These three reminded her of whom she'd been, a fresh walkaway and, yes, a bit of a shlepper. The fire and the forced march had burned shlepper instinct out, made her realize the uselessness of getting attached to *stuff.*

"I walked away. That's what it comes down to. It's a big world, and most of it is fungible. Doesn't matter where you are or what's around you, if you can cover your basic needs and find something productive to do. I ended up with this crew, and forked a tavern off the UNHCR refugee design, and that's how you find me today."

"What about the rest of your old camp?"

"Here and there. Some worked on the Belt and Braces. Some went somewhere else. A couple dropped off the walkaway grid, and I'm guessing they walkedback, it was too much for them, which is 'totally their business and absolutely cool with me,' as the song goes. I checked in on the site itself. It's got a high-security perimeter. The buildings have been bulldozed. My meadow's still growing, and the wildflowers are as beautiful as I thought they'd be. I made the world a measurably better place, which is more than you can say for the assholes who chased us off."

"Amen," said Etcetera. "That was an insane story and I am very glad you told it to us. Now I want to go and try a different pool. You coming?"

"Hell yeah," said the sarcastic one. "Did you say there's a pool where the fish will come and give you oral pleasure?"

"Follow me," she said, and led a parade of dripping, naked people outside into the chill of the early evening and the gorgeous heat of the water. The fish came and ate away their dead skin while they lolled back and became creatures of pure nerves and breath again.

## [iii]

Someone said a whisky would be perfect, someone else said a toasted cheese sandwich would be incredible, someone said she could barely keep her eyes open and wanted to find something soft to crash on, or somewhere horizontal. Limpopo called time on the onsen. "Let's find a midnight feast and a bed." She thought of the cushions in the big room on the third floor, ideal for cuddle-puddles, just what she needed at that moment.

They showered again in the communal antechamber, floatingly relaxed. Without saying a word—without it being overtly sexual—they scrubbed one another's backs. Sexual or not, there was animal pleasure in being groomed by someone, and it deepened the feeling of sweet, tazzy decadence.

They were so boneless that it took five minutes for anyone to realize that the noobs' stuff had been stolen.

Before that, there was just an ambling wobble as they looked for their clothes. Then mounting alarm, and finally the girl said, "We've been robbed." The two boys said, "Shit." They looked at Limpopo. Her clothes were right where she'd left them. They were the kind of clothes you could get anywhere that walkaways gathered.

Limpopo took a breath. "Well, that happened."

"Come on. We've got to go and look for our stuff—" the girl said.

"You'll need clothes first," Limpopo said. "I hate to say it, but I think it'd be a waste. When stuff gets stolen, it disappears fast."

"Funny how you'd know that," the girl said. "Funny how you'd know why it wouldn't be any use to try and track down the stuff you told us to leave here."

"I never told you to leave it here," Limpopo said. "I just said you couldn't bring it in there. I specifically said I didn't know if it'd be safe." She looked at them. They were upset, suspicious of her. The girl most of all, but the guys looked like she was to blame, too. They'd want someone to blame, because the alternative was to blame themselves. Limpopo felt sad. She'd been looking forward to that cuddle-puddle.

"I know this sucks. It happens out here. Not everyone is a nice person in the world."

"So why didn't you build lockers?" the girl said. "If not everyone is as nice as you, why wouldn't you provide for your guests with a minimum standard for security? How about footage? There's cameras around, right? Let's get some fucking forensics, make wanted posters—"

Limpopo shook her head, and the girl looked more furious. "I'm sorry," Limpopo said again. "There are sensors in the B&B, of course, but nothing that buffers for more than a few seconds. That's in the building's firmware, and anyone who tries to change it will be reverted in milliseconds. The people who use this place decided they would rather be robbed than surveilled. Stuff is just stuff, but being recorded all the time is creepy. As for lockers, you're free to put some in, but I don't think they'd last. Once you've got lockers, you're implicitly saying that anything that's not in a locker is 'unprotected'—"

"Which it was," Etcetera pointed out.

"Yeah," she said. "That's a perfectly valid point. But you won't win the argument with it."

Etcetera sat. They were all naked, but Limpopo felt bad about putting her clothes on when no one else had theirs. She grabbed big, fluffy towels from the stack and passed them around.

"Thank you," Etcetera said.

"Yeah, thanks," the sarcastic one said. "Sounds like your friends wouldn't be convinced by anything. What if we just went and took their stuff?"

She smiled. "That was what I was about to suggest. No one's going to be happy about this. Rip-off shit sucks, and whoever did it was a colossal asshole. If we caught someone doing it, we'd probably throw him out."

"What if he tried to come back in?"

"We'd tell him to leave."

"What if he didn't listen?"

"We'd ignore him."

"What if he brought back a bunch of friends and started to fuck up all your shit? Pissed in your hot tubs and drank all your booze?"

She turned to Etcetera. "You know this one, right?"

"They'd leave, Seth," he said.

"That's my slave name," he said. "Call me, uh . . ." He looked lost.

"Gizmo von Puddleducks," Limpopo said. "I'm good at namespace management."

"Call me Gizmo," he said. "Yeah, I get that. They'd leave. They'd build another one of these somewhere else, and then someone would come along and take that one, or burn it down, or whatever."

"Or they wouldn't," she said. "Look, there are as many walkaway philosophies as there are walkaways, but mine is, 'the stories you tell come true.' If you believe everyone is untrustworthy, you'll build that into your systems so that even the best people have to act like the worst people to get anything done. If you assume people are okay, you live a much happier life."

"But your shit gets jacked."

"I don't have anything to get ripped off. It makes life easier. I haven't carried a pack in years. Walks are a *lot* more pleasant. No one bothers to rob me."

"I had everything in that bag," the girl said, morosely.

"Let me guess," Limpopo said. "Money. ID. Food. Water. Spare wearable stuff. Clean underwear."

The girl nodded.

"Right. Well, you don't need money or ID here. Food and water, we got. Clean underwear and wearables, easy. We'll get you back on the grid, you can recover your backups—" She saw their faces fall.

"You were backed up on the walkaway grid, right?"

"Not yet," Etcetera said. "It was on the list. I guess I still have stuff in the cloud, out there in 'default reality.'" He still said "default reality" with self-conscious, audible quote marks.

"Well, we can exfiltrate it for you. There's still some places where the walkaway grid peers with default, deep tunnels and lots of latency. Or you could walkback if you want. Some people do. Walkaway isn't for everyone. Sometimes they go walkaway again. No one will judge you for it." *Except you,* she didn't say because it was obvious.

The girl looked distraught. "I can't fucking believe this. I can't believe that you're not taking any responsibility. You brought us here. We're completely fucked, we have nothing, and you're just busting out smug little bohemian aphorisms like hipster buddha."

Limpopo remembered when this would have pissed her off and allowed herself to be proud that she wasn't angry. She wished she could also avoid pride, but everyone's a work in progress. "I'm sorry this happened. I'll help you get set again. Getting ripped off happens to everyone who goes walkaway. It's a rite of passage. Owning something that isn't fungible means that you've got to make sure someone else doesn't take it. Once you let go of that, everything gets easier."

The girl looked ready to go for Limpopo. She hoped it wouldn't get physical.

"Look, take it easy. It's just *stuff*. I know you had some cool clothes. I even snuck photos of them so I could make my own and put 'em up on a version-server for the B&B. You can sit and fume, you can run into the night looking for some rip-off asshole who's more addicted to owning things than you, or you can get past it and come with me and get new kit. We can make you a dupe of the stuff you were wearing, or you can pick something out of the catalog. Or you can run home wearing a towel. Entirely up to you."

"You copied her clothes?" the sarcastic one said.

"Why, you want a set? They were unisex. We could mod 'em for you, or you could rock something genderbendy. I think it'd suit you." Now that she said it, she realized it was true. She liked the other one, Etcetera, more as a person, but this Herr von Picklepants was pretty in a way that she had a weakness for; she could see the virtue of playing dress-up with him, if he would just stop talking.

"You know? Maybe," he said. He knew exactly how pretty he was, which was a huge turnoff.

"Let's go and get you suited and booted."

Out of solidarity, she left her clothes on the bench and wore a towel out of the onsen, just as they had, and led them back into the Belt and Braces.

---

The B&B's fablab was in an outbuilding called the stables, but there had never been livestock near them. She found them robes and slippers, showing the noobs how to query the B&B's inventory for the location of unclaimed stuff and leading them around the first couple of floors to paw through alcoves and chests until they were set. "You can keep those," she said, "or just put 'em back in any chest and tell B&B about them. If you ditch them somewhere, someone'll moop them for you anyway, but it's considered rude."

"Moop?" Etcetera said. He'd brightened up during the hunt for robes. He was getting into the spirit. She was glad for him.

"Matter out of place. Litter. If you see clutter, you can recycle it, drop it in a storage bin, or commandeer it. The B&B keeps track of the unclaimed moop in its storages and flags stuff that's more than a couple months old to the bug-reporter and someone'll pick up the chore and decompose them."

"Did our bags get mooped then?"

"Not a chance. They hadn't been there long enough, and bags in a changing room aren't moop unless they're abandoned. They were just ripped off." She hauled open the door to the stables. "Let it go."

The fablab smelled like lasers, charred wood, VOCs, textile dye, and machine oil. Its hydrogen cells—separate from the tavern cells—were topped off, and it was nearly empty, apart from giggling teenaged boys almost certainly printing ridiculous handguns. She bookmarked them for a stern talking-to, before throwing a screen up on a wall.

"Easiest way to get started is to ask for an inventory of traveling stuff—warm-weather, cold-weather, wet-weather, shelter, food, first aid—cross-referenced by available feedstocks and rated by popularity." She twiddled her interface surfaces as she worked, and soon they had a multi-columnar layout. "Fill your baskets, and when you're done, drill down for sizes and options."

They immediately grasped it and tapped and poked and suggested. She watched, weighing their choices against her criteria. When she'd been a shlepper, she'd had an Army of One mentality, everything she could need at her side. Once she'd lost that madness, she'd pared away that everyday carry until it was the minimum she would need to survive a typical set of difficulties between wherever she was and the next place. When she'd lived in default, she'd treated her home and school locker and workplace as extensions of her everyday carry, not worrying about hauling everything that fit those places with her all the time. It was enough to know that they were there when she'd need them.

The reason she'd become a shlepper after she went walkaway was she'd drawn her perimeter around her body. If she wasn't carrying a thing, she couldn't use it. The cure had been the realization that everything was everywhere, stuff in walkaway was a normalized cloud of potential on-demand things. The opportunity cost of not having the right salad fork when she wanted a salad was lower than the opportunity cost of not being able to go where she wanted to go without hauling mountains of pain-in-the-back stuff.

A priori, she'd bet Etcetera would have the smallest shopping basket, and the girl would have the biggest. She guessed wrong. The girl went so minimal it shamed Limpopo.

"Don't you think you should pack more than that?" She gave into the temptation to put her thumb on reality's scales.

"All I need is enough to get me to some place like this. Meanwhile, these bozos are going to be carrying a mountain. On the one hand, I'll always have someone to borrow from, and on the other I'll probably end up helping them with their kitchen sinks."

The girl raised an expressive eyebrow at her and smirked. "You think you're the only one around here who gets this stuff? We're noobs, not idiots. I've been throwing Communist parties for years. I've liberated enough matériel to furnish your whole enterprise. Yeah, I took too much shit with me when I left, but that was only because I didn't know what I'd be getting into. If it's like this"—she waved an arm around the stables—"who needs it?"

"You're right, I assumed you were bourgie kids who needed to be led to the greater glory of walkaway philosophy. It's easy to feel more less-is-more than thou. I'm sorry about your stuff, too. Even though I think you were carrying more shit than you needed, getting jacked feels terrible. It makes you feel unsafe; no one is at their best when they feel that way." One piece of walkaway-fu was to apologize quickly and thoroughly when you fucked up. It was a hard lesson for Limpopo to learn, but she made the most of it.

The boys were surreptitiously taking items out of their baskets, and she noticed the girl noticing, and they shared a knowing smile and pretended not to notice. Making other people feel like assholes was a terrible way to get them to stop acting like assholes.

"Not every place is like this," Limpopo said. "The B&B is the biggest walkaway place I've seen, maybe the biggest in this part of Canada. It's got a lot of material wealth. Most walkaway settlements have fablab. No one will ever tell you you're not allowed to use it, but if all you do is drift around, draining hydrogen cells and feedstock, everyone will think you're a dick."

The guys rearranged their baskets. "I'm not supposed to trade anything for anything else, it's all a gift, like the Communist parties. That part I understand. But when we do our parties, we don't care how much you take because at any second the cops are going to chase us out and destroy whatever's left over, so you can have whatever you can carry. Out here, you want people to magically not take too much but also not earn the right to take more by working harder and also to work because it's a gift but not because they expect anything in return?"

They stared at her. She shrugged. "That's the walkaway dilemma. If you take without giving, you're a mooch. If you keep track of everyone else's taking and giving, you're a creep scorekeeper. It's our version of Christian guilt—it's impious to feel good about your piety. You have to want to be good, but not feel good about how good you are. The worst thing is to be worrying about what someone else is doing, because that has nothing to do with whether you're doing right." She shrugged. "If it was easy, everyone would do it. It's a project, not an accomplishment."

Etcetera stretched and his back cracked. His robe fell open, which was revealing in a way that his total nudity hadn't been. He tucked everything back in. "It's hard to get your head around because it's unfamiliar. Back out there in 'default reality' "—again, she could hear the quote marks—"you're supposed to be doing things because they're right for you. 'What do you expect me to do, pass on this dirty salary money because there was something nasty in its history? I don't see you lining up to pay my bills.' Generosity is a folktale about what happens when people look out for themselves. We're supposed to 'just know' that selfishness is natural.

"Out here, we're supposed to treat generosity as the ground state. The weird, gross, selfish feeling is a warning we're being dicks. We're not supposed to forgive people for being selfish. We're not supposed to expect other people to forgive us for being selfish. It's not generous to do nice things in the hopes of getting stuff back. It's hard not to fall into that pattern, because bribery works.

"My folks had this problem all the time when I was growing up. Dad would come up with all these long explanations for why I could only do something I wanted if I did something boring first, that didn't make it into a bribe. He'd say, 'You have to eat a balanced diet so you'll be healthy. Eating dessert without eating vegetables and protein isn't balanced. So you can't have dessert unless you clear your plate.' Mom rolled her eyes, and when he was out of earshot, she'd whisper, 'Finish everything on your plate and I'll give you a slice of cake.' Out-and-out bribery."

The sarcastic one chuckled. "I've met your folks. They were both bribing you, but your Dad was trying to make himself feel better."

Etcetera shook his head. "It's more complicated. Dad wanted me to want to do the right thing for the right reason. Mom only wanted me to do the right thing. I get Dad. But it's easier to get people to do stuff if you don't care why they're doing it."

Limpopo surveyed the boys' baskets, trimmed to more modest proportions. She nodded. "This discussion usually gets to parenting and friendship. Those are the places where everyone agrees that being generous is right. Your chore list is to ensure that everything gets done. The kid who spends her time watching her sisters to make sure they have the same number of chores is either getting screwed, or is screwed up. It sounds corny, but being a walkaway is ultimately about treating everyone as family."

The girl shuddered. Limpopo thought she had her number. "Okay, treating everyone like you'd want your family to treat you."

"Christianity, basically," the sarcastic one said, making a cross of his body, drooping his head to one side, and rolling his eyes up.

"Christianity if it had been conceived in material abundance," Limpopo said. "You're not the first to make the comparison. Plenty of these places have grad students—poli-sci, soc, anthro—trying to figure out if we're 'post-scarcity Fabian socialists' or 'secular Christian communists,' or what. Most are funded by private-sector spooks that want to know if we're going to burn down their offices, and whether they can sell us anything. A third of them go walkaway. Meanwhile, we're ready to do measurements and styles, right?"

They did, letting the stables' cams image them and then sanity-checking the geometry the algorithms inferred. The system rendered them in new clothes and let them play with colors and prints. You got this in default, consumerist clicktrances of perpetual shopping, and they clearly knew it. They whipped through options quickly and hit commit and marveled at the timers.

"Six hours?" the girl said. "Seriously?"

"You can do it in less," Limpopo said, "but this rate allows us to use feedstock with more impurities by adding error-correction passes. Look at this—" She held out her sleeve and showed them a place where a seam had been resealed during fab. "No one said abundance was easy."

## [iv]

When Etcetera finally hit on her, she surprised herself by saying yes.

The three of them had stuck around the B&B long after they'd gotten everything they needed to hit the road. That hadn't surprised her. They were a good fit. The sarcastic one—he'd kept up the Gizmo von Puddleducks business and everyone called him "Ducky"—was a great storyteller and a fun opponent at board games. Both were highly prized skills in the B&B's common room, and he'd become a fixture. The girl joined a survey crew that was chasing up feedstock sites IDed by the drone-flock. She'd come back from a hard day in some ghost town, grimed and wiry in a tank top and work boots, leading a train of walkers that crashed into the stables with their load of textiles, metals, and plastics, the sad remnants of collapsed industry and the people who'd slaved for it.

But Etcetera hadn't fit in, no matter what he tried. None of the work captivated him. None of the leisure caught his interests. He had no stack of books he'd been meaning to read, no skill he'd planned on practicing, no project he'd put off. He was either a slack loser or a Zen master.

At least he wasn't a pest. He did chores, got checked out on everything in the stables and did maintenance, laughed at Ducky's jokes, and went out on crew with the girl—he called her Natalie, though she'd switched from "Stable Strategies" to "Iceweasel." But he clearly didn't give a shit about any of it.

One dawn, she went into the onsen and found him there, reclining in an outdoor pool with his nose and mouth above water, plumes of steam rising as he exhaled. She slid into the water next to him, anxious to get her feet off the icy paving stones and into the warmth. He raised his head, cracked an eye, nodded minutely, and sank back. She nodded at his vapor plume, reclined too. Within moments the fish were on her, nibbling here and there. She closed her eyes and let her face sink beneath the water until only her own mouth and nose stuck out.

A fish brushed against her hand, then did it again. It wasn't a fish. It was his hand, casually laid alongside hers, pinky-edge against pinky-edge. She checked her own internal instruments and decided she was happy about this. She picked up her hand and set it atop his.

They were still for a long while, fish tickling them. The fish made it weird. She and Etcetera were the main attractions at someone else's orgy, their own contact saintly in its chastity. Their fingers moved in the tiniest of increments, spreading, entwining. It may have taken thirty minutes. Each of their hands was saying, "Is this okay?" and waiting for the other's to move, "Yes, it's okay," before moving again. They were sending pulsed SYN/ACK/SYNACKs over a balky network.

When their hands entwined, it was anticlimactic. *Now what*? The tentative physical contact beneath the waters had been magic, but they weren't going to give each other hand jobs in the pool. Oh, Etcetera, that was a romantic gesture, but now what?

She got tired of wondering and disentangled her hand and went inside. She wasn't often up this early, but when she was, she liked to come to the onsen because she had it to herself. It was empty. She stood by the hottest pool, chilled from the walk through the frosty air to the steaming door. The door behind her opened and Etcetera came in with a distracted smile. He dipped a bucketful of near-scalding water and soaked his small towel, then drew it out in a cloud of steam.

She smiled back, liking where this was going. She turned her back and looked over her shoulder, giving him a head-tilt invitation. It was enough. He rubbed the near-scalding towel on her back tentatively, and she rocked her weight towards him. He rubbed harder, soaked the towel. He knelt to do her butt and legs, and she turned around when he got to her ankles and he started to work his way back up. As he got back to his feet, she met him with her towel, steaming from the pail, rubbed his chest and arms. They held hands again and stepped into the hottest pool, water so hot that it obliterated all thought except for the hand squeezed in hers. They lowered themselves, hands so tight that their knuckles ground. Hand in hand, they went to the coldest pool, took towels in hand, and washed one another down.

Back and forth, his left hand in her right, washing one another down, clinging tight to one another, alone in the onsen and merging into one being of flesh, nerves, heat, and cold. When they were done, they sat at the showers and soaped each other, sprayed each other with the shower wands. They went into the changing room and put their robes on, separating briefly. When they did, she felt the ghost of his hand in hers. When they clasped again, it felt like something missing had returned.

Hand in hand, they walked through the dim corridors. They skirted the common room and the groggy voices they heard over the gurgle of coffium. They took the stairs slowly, gaits matched, feet rasping on the gritty laminate on the treads. On the first landing, and she used her free hand to ask a touchable surface about empty rooms, located one on the uppermost fourth floor, which had the smallest rooms—coffins, almost.

Wordless, breathing heavily, they ascended, hearing the building waking around them: a baby crying, someone peeing, a shower. One more floor, a few deft turns through the twisty little maze of the fourth floor, he put his hand on the doorplate and it rolled aside. The lights came on, revealing the bare cell whose loft-bed was neatly made up with fresh sheets. Beneath it was a desk and chair and some homey touches—a few books, a handful of sculptural prints of mathematical solids. Some part of Limpopo's brain remembered putting them there, because this was one of the rooms she'd finished. She hadn't been to it in more than a year, and she was pleased the B&B had kept it up. Either its tenants had been conscientious, or the B&B noticed the room getting moopy and had it on the chore list, and someone had taken care of it.

Now they were in the room, and the door was rolling shut behind them and clicking. He reached out to dim the lights, but she cranked them back to full. She found she liked looking at his face in full light. Staring straight at a relative stranger's face in full light, without pretending to be looking at something else, while that stranger looked back at you—it was something she hardly ever got to do. It was as intimate, in its own way, as anything physical.

He had a confused smile. She liked the curve of his lip.

"Is this okay? I mean—"

"I just want to get a good look." She was pleased at how quickly he grasped this, how thoroughly he reciprocated, pupils shiny as his eyes saccaded over her face, gaze roaming in a frank way that reminded her of their firm grip.

This was what she loved about being a walkaway. She'd seduced and been seduced in default, but there'd always been a sense of time slipping away. We'd better stop this romantic stuff, get fucking because there's a meeting, a job, a protest, a meal to cook or a chore. Even at the B&B, it was hard to escape that feeling. But now she reveled in its absence, infinite time. She recalled Etcetera's unwillingness to commit to a routine in the B&B, his inability to naturally fall into a role or job. It meant that he was hers for as long as they wanted.

She inserted her thumbs between his robe and flesh and ran them slowly down, pushing the robe open one agonizing millimeter at a time, marveling at how the skin that she had seen and touched in the onsen could be so private when partially clothed. He put his hands on her robe and pulled it apart and it slid over her breasts as they popped free, one and two. In default, she'd fussed about them, they weren't the right size or shape. Her critical eye wanted more from her imperfect flesh. Walkaway had liberated her from inchoate anxiety, but more, the burn had ended it, fully occupying her self-consciousness.

Her robe parted over the burn. His hand grazed the scar. She jolted and he jerked his hand back. He said "sorry" as she took hold of his hand and put it on the scar. The scar didn't hurt, exactly, but it pulled, and when she did yoga she felt her torso's skin distorting around its gravity. For the longest time she hadn't able to touch the alien thing where her skin had been—only washing it with a sponge. Her hand went to it in her sleep, and she'd wake with its snake-segments of collagen beneath her fingertips. She'd come to détente, no longer feeling it was alien.

His hands were on the scar now, its rises and depressions. His eyes were distant, his breath shallow. She panted, too; their breath was mingling in their mouths, they were that close. They hadn't kissed yet. She pulled his robe off of his shoulders and forced his hands off her while she yanked it down. His hands went back to her. The movement brought them close enough he could reach around and touch her shoulder blades, her spine, the satellites of her burn, like the debris field of a meteor impact. He was close enough that his erection bobbed insistently at her thigh, warm elastic touch that made her smile. He smiled back, and she knew he knew what she was smiling about.

His palms reached her butt. She put her hands in the same place and reeled him in, his erection sandwiched between them, her breasts crushed against his chest. Her lips formed into a kiss and found his collarbone. She worried at the bone with her teeth, then nipped his skin. He gasped, crushed her harder. He rolled his head and bared his throat to her and she darted kisses on it, loving his stubble on her lips, that boy-skin feeling. Her lips rested on the artery in his throat, and she relished his pulse, and sucked insistently, daring him to push her off before she gave him a hickey, but he hissed and his trapped penis throbbed in time with his pulse against her stomach.

He ground his hips against her. She let his thigh slide between hers, nestle against her vulva. She ground against the muscle of his leg, hairs pulling, everything too dry at first, and then, moment by delicious moment, wetter. Her nostrils flared. She breathed the sex from their armpits and groins. She sucked at the vulnerable place where his jaw and throat and ear met.

They still hadn't kissed.

He pulled her ass harder, his hands strong. She remembered the way his hand had squeezed hers. He lifted her to her tiptoes, crushing her pussy against his leg. She found his quadriceps and mashed her clit against them, let go and leaned back, feeling his quads jump out as he braced to support her. She bent until her hands reached the wall and she pushed back, and they played with muscle and gravity, and he hauled her back and staggered.

Back on her feet, she bulled him to the bedside, put one foot on the ladder and hoisted herself up. He leapt in behind her.

And still, they hadn't kissed. She twisted, caught his ankle, popped his little toe in her mouth, biting down when he tried to pull away. She dug her fingernails into the arch of his foot and reached blindly and caught his erection, making a fist and squeezing just hard enough to feel that pulse again. His hips bucked and she held, then let go and reversed herself, sliding up his body and pinioning his torso beneath hers. Her hands caught his and she used her hard-won construction muscles to yank his wrists over his head and push them into the mattress. His armpits smelled of clean sweat. His breath was on her face. Her breath was on his.

She made a kiss of her lips again and poised, pulling her face back when he tried to kiss. She wanted this to last. She let one lip brush his, then both. Then some tongue. His mouth parted. His face strained toward hers and she pulled back, started over. He got the message. He lay there, let her control him, choose how the kiss would unfold. She made it very slow.

It was wonderful.

It didn't stop.

Mouths locked, he reached for her ass, and she pressed it into his hands, willing him to knead, incidentally mashing his cock into her scar, which had never happened before. She noted it absently and groaned into his mouth. He groaned back.

She ground on his leg again, crushed his cock between them. His fingers worked around her ass to where the hair was slick. He rhythmically kneaded the length of her groin, explored her opening. She moaned into his mouth. Shivers chased up her back and stomach. The explosive feeling built and she bucked, urging him to dig deeper, move faster, and he ground in return. She hadn't been with a man in more than a year. This one stirred up nostalgic eroticism, calling to mind all the men before, every shiver, every screaming orgasm. These images played through her mind as she moved. The familiar flush spread up her neck.

He surprised her by coming from the friction. The sudden heat between them set her off into convulsions that culminated with the kinds of loud noises that had once embarrassed her.

She rolled half off him—making him *oof* as she inadvertently drove an arm into his solar plexus—grabbed his robe off the desk beneath them and used it to wipe up.

"Whew," she said.

"More."

She looked down, incredulous. "Already?"

He licked his lips.

He was a good lover. It shone through the heart-thumping roar of a long-frustrated fuck. She couldn't put her finger on it—metaphorically, anyway—but as she came again, clamping her thighs around his ears, she realized it: the lack of hurry. Even after years of walkaway, she was used to slicing time into rice-paper slices thin enough for one discrete thing, before moving onto the next. Most of the time, she rushed to complete this current moment before the next thumped the door. Every adult she'd known matched that rhythm, the next thing almost upon them, the current one had best be taken care of in haste.

Etcetera sliced his time thick. He'd slide along her body to her breasts and rest his face on them for an unmeasured pause before nibbling. It went on longer than she expected. It was better than nice. Her own body-clock synchronized, metronome tick slowing to a languorous heartbeat that felt like there was all the time in the world. It was more decadent than the sticky juices on her fingers, livid hickey on her left breast, the turgid boy-nipple she was rolling between her fingers.

When they were done, she had no idea how late it was. It might be sunset, or later, though they'd come upstairs at daybreak. She wiped interface surface on the wall and brought up a clock, was surprised to see it was only midday. Not hurrying all the time had not meant not losing all the time. The difference between glorious languor and endless hustle was an hour or two. It felt like she'd just been given a day.

She kissed him at the junction of throat and earlobe and worked her way around to his lips. He embraced her in that unhurried way, enfolding her in the robe he'd donned.

"That was very nice," she said.

"It was very nice over here, too."

They twined fingers. She opened the linen hatch and they stripped the bed and put new sheets on, wiped the surfaces and turned on the air-scrubbers. A green checkmark glowed on the back of the door as the room acknowledged that it had been adequately reset. They left, hands twined and dirty linens in their free arms. These went down a laundry chute by the stairs, and they went to the stables to make some new clothes.

## [v]

The fuck didn't discombobulate their relationship, thank goodness. He hugged her and kissed her cheek instead of shaking her hand in the common room, and his two friends—who, she thought, were doing something along the same lines—shot her knowing looks. He wasn't all over her every time they met, nor did he give her the studied ignorance treatment. A week later, they ran into each other in a corridor and stopped to chat. He leaned against the wall with his hand splayed against it. She laid hers alongside of it, and he took the hint, and they went back up to the fourth floor for another unhurried, easy play session.

"How are you liking it here?" she asked during one of their pauses.

He looked uncomfortable. "Honestly, I don't think this is my thing. We left default because I wanted to be part of something where I was more than an inconvenient surplus labor unit. I know I can work here and there's plenty to do, but it feels contrived. The other day, I totally fucked up some linen processing, ruined thirty sheets. The system just assigned someone else to make new ones and push the blown-out ones through the feedstock processor. The whole thing fails so safe that it doesn't really matter what I do. If I worked my brains out or did nothing, it would be the same, as far as the system is concerned. I know it's fucked up and egocentric, but I want to know that I, personally, am important to the world. If I left tomorrow, nothing around here would change."

She chewed her lip. She'd wrestled with this herself for many years, but admitting it was in bad taste. Everyone talked about special snowflakes, and it was the kind of thing that was an insult from a stranger but not from a friend. You weren't supposed to need to be a special snowflake, because the objective reality was that, important as you were to yourself and the people immediately around you, it was unlikely that anything you did was irreplaceable. As soon as you classed yourself as a special snowflake, you headed for the self-delusional belief that you should have more than everyone else, because your snowflakiness demanded it. If there was one thing that was utterly uncool in walkaway, it was that self-delusion.

"You know that this is the love that dare not speak its name around here? There have been one hundred billion humans on the planet over the years, and statistically, most of them didn't make a difference. The anthropocene is about collective action, not individuals. That's why climate change is such a clusterfuck. In default, they say that it's down to individual choice and responsibility, but reality is that you can't personally shop your way out of climate change. If your town reuses glass bottles, that does one thing. If it recycles them, it does something else. If it landfills them, that's something else, too. Nothing you do, personally, will affect that, unless it's you, personally, getting together with a *lot* of other people and making a difference."

"But it's hard to pretend that you're not the protagonist in the movie of your life. Normally it doesn't matter, but being around here rubs your nose in it."

"Everything's got contradictions. I sometimes wonder if someone is doing something that makes everything better because *I* wrote a specific line of code. To really thrive out here, you have to want to make a difference and know you're totally replaceable."

"Beats default. There you're not supposed to make a difference *and* you're totally surplus."

This discussion killed her horniness. The thought that her sensations were the same ones innumerable people had felt before and during and after that moment made it feel like a cheap trick, a way of tickling her reward circuits for a drip of this and a sneeze of the other. Normally, sex made her feel like the universe revolved around her sensations. Now they felt like a meaningless flare of light in an uncaring void.

She sat up and pulled on clothes. Etcetera didn't seem put out, which was a relief and kind of worrying.

"You okay?"

"I'm okay," she said. "Just not in the mood so much."

"Sorry about that." He got into his underwear and pants, turned his shirt right-side-out. "Despite whatever orthodoxy I'm supposed to embrace and no matter how uncool this is, I want to say that I actually do think you're special. Better than special. Glorious, actually. And beautiful. But mostly glorious."

Her heart thudded. "Listen, dude—"

"Don't worry. I'm not going to go lovesick. But I've met dozens of people since I went walkaway and you are the first one who made me welcome, and not just because you fucked my brains out, though that did make me feel welcome. But because I can talk about this with you and you don't roll your eyes like it's the stupidest thing to ask about, and because you don't go wide-eyed doctrinaire either. You're like the only person around here who's thinking about being a walkaway and doing walkaway. Without you, I would have moved on. This place is amazing, but it's too finished, if you get what I mean."

She pulled her dress on. It gave her a moment. When her head emerged, he was staring frankly at her. He had very nice eyes, a nice smile. A little tentative, but she liked that.

"I think you're great, too."

"We should go to the stables and print up some mutual admiration society membership badges."

"You laugh, but I'm sure those exist as premades in walkaway thingiverse."

"Well, that's sweet," he said. They laughed, and a distant alarmed part of herself told her this was a lovers' laugh, and she was falling in love.

## [vi]

Falling in love is wonderful. Once she gave in, she amused herself finding ways to be nice to Etcetera—making him a jacket in a color and cut that suited him better than anything he wore; waking him with a coffium and dragging him upstairs for a quickie while it burned through their veins; washing his back in sensuous strokes in the onsen.

He reciprocated in a hundred ways, saving her a seat in the common room; greeting her after a hike with iced tea and a cool towel, or taking her hand below the table—or above it—as they chatted with the others into the night.

The old B&B hands took notice, but were too polite to ask outright. Instead, they'd say, "Oh, did Etcetera give that to you?" (He had, a garland of winter twigs worked into a ridiculous fairy crown that she wore for a day until it fell apart but treasured all the more for that.) There were walkaway couples, even walkaway families with kids and one or more parents, but she'd never joined them. Coupledom felt like an artifact of default, not anything she wanted any part of, a mess of jealousy and coordination problems.

But this was different. Emotions sang in her thoughts, sweeter than any she remembered. Lying beside him, even in a cuddle-puddle, looking at his lips and the dimple in his chin made something warm spread through her chest and belly.

They took long walks, not talking, listening to birdsong and the crunch of their footsteps in the snow. There were deer in the woods, usually far away, but once, a doe came close enough to touch, stared at them with spellbinding animal frankness.

One day, they set out at first light, full of porridge and bubbling with coffium, following a trail from a B&B drone that had found a cache of electronics full of recoverable coltan derivatives—an abandoned illegal e-waste dump. They brought a mulebot, and helping it with way-finding slowed them down to a frigid crawl. They bickered a little; she'd remember that later.

The cache was inaccessible. The ground had frozen solid in an overnight cold snap that turned an earlier thaw into treacherous ice. Even with cleats, they couldn't get any footing, and the mulebot got fatally stuck out of arms' reach, unable to find enough traction to return. After abandoning trying to lasso it, they headed back in a bad mood.

They both got an offline buzz at the same moment as the walkaway network failed. She could tell, because they both stopped at the same moment.

"Does that happen often?" Etcetera said.

"It shouldn't happen period. The network's got redundant failovers, including a blimp. And we've got clear skies."

She got out a screen and prodded with gloved fingers, squinting through the steam of her exhalations. She didn't use diagnostic stuff often, and it took her a while to get it up. "That's weird," she said. "Even if everything went blooey, you'd expect it to be a cascading failure. Node A goes dark, node B gets overwhelmed by traffic from it, falls over, then node C gets a double-whack, and so on. But look, it lost contact with everything, all at once. That's like a power cut, but they're all on independent power cells."

"What do you think it is?"

"I think it's serious. Let's go."

Give this to Etcetera: when things got serious, he got serious. She saw a new side of him, nervy and alert. It comforted her. She could stop unconsciously worrying about taking care of him.

They hustled through the tramped-down snow trails, moving silently, with an unspoken dimension of stealth. She heard a whir and spotted a B&B drone, which gave her comfort. Then she saw that it wasn't one of their models.

"Shit," she said, as it came back for another pass. She gave it the finger as it buzzed meters over their heads. "Fuck it. Let's go."

They ran.

The path was well-groomed with a clever series of turns and strategic trees that let you emerge suddenly into the compound with the rambling buildings and the windmills proud overhead. Before they'd been spotted, she'd planned on coming out through the woods to one side, bushwhacking a new trail to get there. But now there was no point.

They stepped into the clearing and she saw a clutch of bulky dudes in intimidating tactical bullshit standing around the main entrance. They bristled with utility belts with gun-shaped stuff that could do terrible things to them, and they didn't need to reach for them to make it clear who had the upper hand.

"Hello there," one called. He even had the tough-guy mustache, like a wrestler. "Welcome to the Belt and Braces."

"Yeah, thanks," she said.

"I'm Jimmy," he said. "Would you two be wanting some lodgings?"

"Suppose we are," Limpopo said.

He smiled a lazy, wolfish smile, then looked more closely. "Oh," he said. "It's you, is it?"

She looked more closely at him, remembered. "Yeah, it's me." She sighed.

"Well shit. This is your lucky day, Limpopo."

She nodded. He hadn't been going by Jimmy when she'd slung his ass out of the B&B. What had it been? Jockstrap? Jackstraw? Something. It had been years.

"Bet you didn't expect to see me." He turned to his friends. "This lady right here put more lines of code into this place than anyone. She's done more to build it than anyone. This place is full of this girl's blood and treasure." He turned back. "This really is your lucky day."

"Yeah?" She knew where this was going.

"From now on, this place is on a quid-pro-quo basis. Everyone gets out what they put in. You've put in so much, well, you could stay for years without lifting a finger. You've got reputation capital to burn."

"Oh brother," she said.

---

You couldn't be a walkaway without encountering the reputation economy freaks. At first, she'd hated them in the abstract. Then this guy had come along and given her some damned good, *concrete* reasons to hate them. The B&B had been a third built when he came and tried to install leaderboards in everything. Actually, he'd done it, checking in the code and then coming to her with her hands covered in sealant paste to demand to know why she'd reverted him.

"That's not something we want."

"What do you mean? You don't have a constitution. I checked."

"We don't. But this issue's been discussed and the consensus was that we didn't want leaderboards. They produce shitty incentives." She held up her gloppy hands. "I'm in the middle of something. Why don't you put it on the wiki?"

"Is that the rule?"

"Nope," she said.

"So why should I do it?"

"Because that's worked before."

"Maybe I should just revert your reverts."

"I hope you don't." She knew how to have this argument. She kept eye contact. He was young, a recent walkaway, with pent-up freak that went with the territory. There was no percentage in meeting his freak with her own.

"Why not?"

"It wouldn't be constructive. The point is to find something we can be happy with. Revert-wars don't produce that. At best, that'll get us to spending all our time reverting each other. At worse, it'll turn into a war to see who can make the codebase harder for the other to modify." She had a sheet of insulating honeycomb on her workbench and the sealant was drying lumpy. She grabbed a spongy brush and spread the lumps. "You want to see this place get built? Me too. Let's figure out how. You could start by reviewing the old discussions and checking out how the decision got made. Then make your own arguments. I promise to read them in good faith." This was a mantra, but she tried to imbue it with sincerity. He was tweaky. She didn't want to freak him. She didn't even want to talk to him.

He sea-lioned her at dinner. That was before the kitchen was finished and they made do with primitive stuff, flavored, extruded, cultured UNHCR refuscops. Scop-slop on a shingle, with everything you needed to keep going and a wide variety of flavors, but no one mistook it for food. She made space for him on the bench beside her and passed him the water jug—they were using solar pasteurizers, big black barrels that used heat-exchanging coatings to get the water up to pathogen-killing temperatures. It gave the water a flat taste. She used sprigs of mint to cover it. She offered him some from a plant she'd picked before the dinner bell rang.

He swirled it around her water and ate scop, which he'd taken in a chewy nacho-cheese briquette, so sharp-smelling it almost masked his sweaty funk. Baths were hard to come by in those days, but not that hard. She tried to think of a polite way to show him how the wash-up worked, without creating any interpretive room to construe it as a sexual invitation.

"You get that reading done?"

He nodded and chewed. "Yeah," he said. "I ran stats on the repos. You're an order of magnitude head of the pack, massive power-law curve. I had no idea. Seriously, respect."

"I don't look at stats. Which is the point. I couldn't write the whole thing on my own, and if I could, I wouldn't want to, because this place would suck if it was just a contest to see who could add the most lines of code or bricks to the structure. That's a race to build the world's heaviest airplane. What does knowing that one person has more commits than others tell you? That you should work harder? That you're stupid? That you're slow? Who gives a shit? The most commits in our codebase come from history—everyone who wrote the libraries and debugged and optimized and patched them. The most commits on this building come from everyone who processed the raw materials, figured out how to process the raw materials, harvested the feedstock, and—"

He held up his hands. "Okay. But come on, maybe you didn't do all the work, but you're doing more than anyone. Why shouldn't the community honor that?"

"If you do things because you want someone else to pat you on the head, you won't get as good at it as someone who does it for internal satisfaction. We want the best-possible building. If we set up a system that makes people compete for acknowledgment, we invite game-playing and stats-fiddling, even unhealthy stuff like working stupid hours to beat everyone. A crew full of unhappy people doing substandard work. If you build systems that make people focus on mastery, cooperation, and better work, we'll have a beautiful inn full of happy people working together well."

He nodded but wasn't convinced. She thought about saying, "I put in more work than anyone, so by your lights that means I should be in charge. As the person in charge, I say that the person who does the most shouldn't be in charge, so there." It made her smile, and she saw him looking embarrassed and remembered being a noob who didn't know what she was doing or if she should be doing it, feeling judged.

"Don't take my word for it," she said. "Reopen the discussion, make your arguments, see if you can convince other people. Shift the consensus."

"I'll think about it." She knew he wouldn't. The idea that there wouldn't be leaders in the race to build a leaderless society offended him in ways he wouldn't let himself understand.

Three weeks later, they were locked in a revert-war that shook the B&B down to its literal foundations.

Jackstraw trawled every collaborative building project on the net for gamification modules. There were plenty—badges and gold stars, the works of amateur Skinners convinced you could build the ideal society the way you toilet-trained a toddler: a chart on the wall with a smiley sticker next to every poopy-diaper-free day.

The results from these experiments were impressive. If you wanted to motivate people at their most infantile level, all you needed was to hand out sweeties for good children, and make naughty ones stand in the corner. He'd put together links to videos and analytics reports from the most successful.

At first, Limpopo was careful to keep her rebuttal style to the non-antagonistic "good faith" voice that was the sure-fire winner in walkaway arguments. She'd carefully ignore the emotional freight of his words, reading them three times to ensure she caught every substantive crumb in the screeds, and replied briefly, comprehensively, and without a hint of contempt.

He didn't know when he was beat. It was like arguing with a chatbot whose Markov chains were entangled in the paternalistic argot of prison wardens and unlicensed daycare operators. She'd calmly demolish his arguments every day from Monday to Friday, and on Saturday morning, he'd pull out Monday's arguments again, like she wouldn't notice.

This all happened in the commentary of code-pulls and reverts, making it more stupid. The audience for the debate grew as word spread. There was global attention, and not just from walkaways. Back in default, some people kept an eye on walkaway nets, treating them as exotic spectacle, like listening in on Al Shabaabbies complaining about the cumbersome reimbursement procedure their Wahabi paymasters imposed.

With this global audience kibitzing and sniping, Limpopo tore Jackstraw a comprehensive new asshole. She called him on every crumb of bullshit, found crashed projects where gamification had run wild, so financialized that every incentive distorted into titanic frauds that literally left structures in ruins, rotten to the mortar. They were existence proof of the terribleness of his cherished ideas. She pointed out that getting humans to "do the right thing" by incentivizing them to vanquish one another was stupid. She found videos of Skinner-trained pigeons who'd been taught to play piano through food-pellet training and pointed out that everyone who liked this envisioned himself as the experimenter—not the pigeon.

It got ugly. She'd bruised his ego, met his condescension by treating him to a slice of the assholery he'd directed her way. He lost it. Comprehensively bested, he went negative.

The problem was Limpopo's vagina. It made her unable to understand the competitive fire that was the true motive force that kept humans going. Competition carved the gazelle as a perfect complement to the leopard. Competition whittled the fangs and leaps of the leopard into the gazelle's inverse. Competition sorted the performers from the takers. It let the visionaries whittle their project into a masterpiece.

Limpopo's femininity made her too weak to grasp this. She wasted time with talk-talk about making everyone happy, when the right answer was there in the data, objectively showing which path to take. He wrote about this "weakness" of hers like it was a mental illness, conjuring imaginary "four-sigma hackers" who wouldn't contribute to the B&B if they were prohibited from publishing performance stats.

He located the origin of this dysfunction in Limpopo's sex. She had a clutch of "alpha bitches" who kept the group in check. Her cult-like leadership of this coven extended to control over their menstrual cycles, which had undoubtedly converged on the powerful uterine signals from Limpopo's unspeakable wet places.

Limpopo was proud of herself in that moment. She distinctly felt her mind split in two as she read the vicious attacks. One half, "Limbic Limpopo," hyperviolent unfiltered id, snarled. It literally made her heart thud and her hands and jaws clench. When she consciously stopped it, she ached all down her neck. Limbic Limpopo wanted to kick Jackstraw in the balls. It wanted to wikify every vicious line and add [citation needed] tags to the insults, signposting them as indefensible ad hominems. Limbic Limpopo wanted to haul Jackstraw out of his bed—a bed that she had assembled and painted—and throw him out buck naked, locking the door and burning his stinky pack of gear.

But that was only half of her reaction. Long-Term Limpopo was just as insistent in her internal chorus. This made her proud. Long-Term Limpopo had always been there, but usually Limbic Limpopo shouted so loudly that she couldn't hear Long-Term Limpopo until stupid Limbic had made a mess.

Long-Term Limpopo pointed out that the debate was a huge time-sink because the issues were complicated and boring. Getting people who wanted to build an inn to care about the reward-strategy philosophy was like getting people who were excited about a potluck dinner to care about whether the room was painted with acrylic or oil. Dinner, not the box it came in, was the point.

This was different. Getting people to care about substantive stuff was hard, but procedural issues were much simpler. As esoteric as the subject of debate was, the form of the debate—the frank misogyny, the crude insults—could be parsed from orbit. When they were arguing about applied motivational psychology, it was hard to tell whom to root for. Once he outed himself as an asshole, the issue clarified.

Long-Term Limpopo pointed out that she'd already won. All she had to do was refrain from descending to Jackstraw's level. Even as Limbic Limpopo made her blood thunder, she gave the wheel to Long-Term Limpopo, who pointed out that this wasn't an appropriate way to conduct a technical discussion.

The reaction was swift. Even the people who'd taken Jackstraw's side in earlier debate hastily moved to distance themselves. The denunciations followed, and within an hour, someone called an emergency f2f meeting for onsite B&B contributors. Limpopo looked out her window and saw people grimly erecting a big spring-open tent they used when they had to shelter raw materials, while a bucket-brigade passed chairs from within the half-built B&B.

One of the B&B's game-changing tools was "lovedaresnot," which they'd imported from a long-defunct *-leaks collective that imploded when its leadership got outed taking money from a media conglomerate to give it preferential access to stories. The leakers had had terrible leadership, but they had a good dispute-resolution system in lovedaresnot.

The core idea was that radical or difficult ideas were held back by the thought that no one else had them. That fear of isolation led people to stay "in the closet" about their ideas, making them the "love that dares not speak its name." So lovedaresnot (shortened to "Dare Snot") gave you a way to find out if anyone else felt the same, without forcing you to out yourself.

Anyone could put a question—a Snot Dare—up, like "Do you think we should turf that sexist asshole?" People who secretly agreed signed the question with a one-time key that they didn't have to reveal unless a pre-specified number of votes were on the record. Then the system broadcast a message telling signers to come back with their signing keys and de-anonymize themselves, escrowing the results until a critical mass of signers had decloaked. Quick as you could say "I am Spartacus," a consensus plopped out of the system.

Poor Jackstraw hadn't known what hit him. Dare Snot was widely publicized at the B&B, but Jackstraw lacked the humility to understand why you might use it, rather than just blamming out your Big Stupid Idea and trying to rally everyone to the barricades. There was a lot Jackstraw lacked the humility to understand. He was one of those people—almost all of them young men, though not every young man—who was so smart that he couldn't figure out how stupid he was.

She put on fresh clothes—the new goretex printer/cutter was up, and it was a treat to step into something dry, breathable, and perfectly fitting whenever you wanted. She went to the meeting.

She didn't have to say a word.

Ten minutes later, sputtering Jackstraw was shown the door and politely asked not to return. They filled his pack and gave him two sets of goretex top-and-bottoms. Anything less would have been unneighborly.

## [vii]

Limpopo's dirty secret was that she had been scraping the B&B's production logs and dumping them into a homebrewed analytics system she frankensteined from the world of gamified motivational bullshit. Every now and again, she'd run the logs and look at how far ahead of everyone else she was. She especially liked to look at the stats charts when she lost an argument about how something could be done.

Not because it soothed her ego. It was weirder. When Limpopo lost an argument, the fact that she'd done more than the person she lost to felt *great*. Being a walkaway meant honoring everyone's contributions and avoiding the special snowflake delusion. So losing to someone over whom, in default, she'd have rank to pull made her a fucking *saint*. No one was a special snowflake, but she was better at not being a special snowflake than everyone.

Looking at those charts gave her almost exactly the same feeling of shame and pleasure that she got from looking at porn. It was raw self-indulgence, something that exclusively fed her most immature and selfish desires. It was catnip for Limbic Limpopo, and the more she fed that greedy maw, the more she was able to tell it to shut up and let Long-Term Limpopo drive the bus. At least, that's what she told herself.

---

Now he was called Jimmy and decked out in stuff that made goretex look like uncured rat-hides stitched with dried grasses. He was enjoying himself.

"You should see the numbers," he said to his buddies. Unlike the B&B, who came in every shade, all of his friends were whities, except for one guy, who might have been Korean. "She's the *queen* of this place." He shook his head—his neck was bull-like, to match his cartoon biceps. "Shit, Limpopo, you really are the queen. From now on, you and a guest can stay here whenever, any room in the house. Full kitchen and workshop privileges. I want you to join our board. We need someone like you."

Etcetera had been hanging back, breathing fast at first, then slowing. She wondered if he'd do something stupidly physical. That would be a waste.

There was a narrative she was supposed to participate in, a hole Jimmy made for her to step into. Either she threw her lot in and legitimized his coup—she doubted that he'd put store in that happening—or, better, make a stand, let him humiliate her the way she'd supposedly humiliated him. The only way to win was not to play.

She stood.

He tried to draw her by talking about how they'd expand capacity by separating leeches from leaders, take care of the craphounds by giving some beds to charity every month. She stood mute.

The longer she stood, the more freaked Jimmy was. The longer she stood, the more people drifted out to find out what was up. It was like a physical replay of the old online showdown.

"He just showed up and declared it a done deal," said Lizzie, who'd been with the B&B since the beginning, hammering surveying stakes where the network told her. "No one wanted to fight, right? He had a stupid powerpoint with our stats, scraped off the public repos, showing everyone here would go on having the same privileges we'd always had, because we were putting enough work in."

"Yeah," said Grandee, who was short, old, and weird, but whom Limpopo liked because he was a good listener, with something broken inside that she'd never asked about but felt protective about nonetheless. "He talked about waves of new walkaways headed this way, a massive uptick that would overwhelm us unless we had some system to allocate resources. He had videos about places where it had happened."

She nodded. She'd heard about places where numbers had swollen faster than could be absorbed; well-established taverns becoming crowded, then overcrowded, then catastrophic. There'd even been violence—rare, but luridly reported in default press that trickled back into walkaway. Lurid or not, it was disgusting. There was an arson, with a miraculous body count of zero (the photos had been such a strong trigger for Limpopo that she'd told her readers to filter any more reports of it).

"Okay," she said. More people trickled out.

It was cold. Their breath fogged, reminded her of the onsen's steam.

The crowd on Limpopo's side grew. An invisible switch flipped and anyone who didn't stand with Limpopo's group implicitly stood against it—not just going with Jimmy's group because it was easiest and what did it matter, really—but actually standing against Limpopo's group and everything they'd stood for.

Limpopo's pack had survival gear that could keep her alive for a day in the woods, come the worst. She fired up her stove, feeding it twigs until the fan drove the heat from their combustion to gas-phase transition and the dynamo that powered the battery whirred and the idiot light came on, telling her the stove was doin' it for itself.

She made tea. She had a book of fold-up teacups, semirigid plastic prescored for folding into mugs with geometrical handles. She loved them, they looked like low-resolution renders of a cup, leapt off a screen into physical space. The teapot was a pop-up cylinder she filled with snow, trekking to an untouched fall on the clearing's edge, watched suspiciously by Jimmy and his crew, and with bemusement by her people.

Once the tea was brewed, she poured and passed it around. It turned out there were others with folding cups, some with super-dense seed-bars glued with honey from the B&B's apiary, rock-hard and dense as ancient suns, the delicious taste of home for anyone who lived at the B&B.

Why did they have this stuff squirreled about their persons? Because as soon as someone started talking about rationing, the urge to hoard became irresistible.

As soon as she shared, the hoarding impulse melted. You got the world you hoped for or the world you feared—your hope or your fear made it so. She emptied her pack, found moon-blankets and handed them to people without coats. She took off her coat so she could get at her fleece and gave it to a shivering pregnant woman, a recent arrival whose name she hadn't gotten, then put her coat back on before she started to freeze. The coat was enough, even standing still. It had batteries for days and for temperatures more hazardous than this.

This triggered a round of normalization of outerwear, a quiet crowd-wide check-in—at least fifty, nearly the full complement of B&B long-termers—and swapping of gear. The impromptu ritual started off solemnly but turned hilarious, laughter in the face of Jimmy and his tactical meathead greedhead assholes.

They didn't know what to make of this. Jimmy had a trapped-animal look she recognized from earlier, a near-breaking-point face she didn't like at all. Time to make a move.

"Okay." Though she spoke quietly, her voice carried. There was an instant hush. "Where do we build? Anyone?"

"Build *what*?" Jimmy demanded.

"The Belt and Braces II," she said. "But we'll need a better name. Sequels suck."

"What the fuck are you *talking* about?" Definitely close to the breaking point.

"You've taken this one away. We'll make a better one."

"Are you shitting me? You're going to give up, without a fight?"

"We're called *walkaways* because we walk away." She didn't add, *you dipshit*. It didn't need to be said. "It's a huge world. We can make something better, learn from the errors we made here." She stared. His mouth was open. She had his fucking number. Any second later, he would talk—

"That's—"

"Of course," she steamrollered over him as only someone who has to work in every conversation *not* to interrupt can, "there's a good chance that you and your friends will crash this place. When you abandon it, we'll come back and use it for feedstock and raw materials." She did her pausing trick again, waiting—

"You've—"

"Assuming you don't burn it down or loot it." Would he fall for a third time? Yes, he would—

"I wouldn't—"

"You probably plan on keeping our personal effects, now that you've nationalized our home for the People's Republic of Meritopia?" If you bite down the sarcasm every time it rises, it gets crafty. This one hit him so square in his mental testicles you could hear it. Four times she'd stepped on his words before he could get them out and then, wham, pasted him. That felt so good it was indecent. But fuck it. The prick had stolen her house.

"Look—" This time he did it to *himself,* couldn't believe that he would get a word in, tripped over his tongue. His own douchebros sniggered. He was comprehensively pwned, metaphorical pants down. He turned bright red. "We don't have to do this—"

"I think we do. You've made it clear that you're so obsessed with this place that you'll impose your will on it. You have shown yourself to be a monster. When you meet a monster, you back away and let it gnaw at whatever bone it's fascinated with. There are other bones. We know how to make bones. We can live like it's the first days of a better world, not like it's the first pages of an Ayn Rand novel. Have this place, but you can't have us. We withdraw our company."

A bright idea occurred to him. "I thought there was no leader. What's this 'we' shit? Can't you see she's manipulating you all—"

She raised her hand. He fell silent. She didn't say anything, kept her hand up. Etcetera, bless him, put his hand up next. Moments later, everyone had one hand up.

"We took a vote," she said. "You lost."

One of his skeezoids—what must he have promised them, she wondered, about this place—gave a heartfelt "Daaaamn." Had she ever won.

"Do we get our stuff, Jimmy?"

Bless his toes and ankles, he said: "No." Set his jaw, made a mutinous chin. "No. Fuck all y'all."

It would be a cold night, but not too cold. They knew where the half-demolished buildings they could shelter in were, and were carrying lots of this and that. Once they got into range of walkaway net, they would tell the story—the video was captured from ten winking lenses she could count—and rely on the kindness of strangers. They'd rebuild.

*Figures,* she didn't have to say. However awful things got that night. However much work they'd do in the years that followed. However many sore muscles and blistered hands and busted legs they endured, everyone would remember Jimmy. Remember what happened when the special snowflake disease ran unchecked. They'd build something bigger, more beautiful. They'd avoid the mistakes they'd made the last time, make exciting new ones instead. The onsen would be amazing. Their plans had been forked a dozen times since they'd shipped, some of the additions were gorgeous. As she started putting one foot in front of the other, her mind went to these thoughts, the plans took form.

The girl, Iceweasel, fell into step. They walked, crunch, crunch, huff, huff, through the woodland. "Limpopo?"

"What's on your mind?"

"Don't take this the wrong way, but are you fucking kidding me?"

"Nope."

"But this is crazy! You made that place. You just let him take it!"

"Wasn't mine, I didn't make it. I didn't let him take it."

She practically heard the very refined eye-roll with breeding, money, and privilege behind it. Someone like Iceweasel never had to walk away from anything she had a claim to. The army of lawyers and muscle saw to it. This was a horizon-expanding journey for her. Practically a good deed. Limpopo yawned to cover her smile before it could embarrass Iceweasel.

"You and I both know that you put more work into that place than anyone else."

She shrugged. "Why does that make it mine?"

"Come on. So it's not yours-yours, but it's still *yours*. Yours and everyone else's or however the orthodox high church of walkaway insists that we discuss it, but don't be ridiculous. Mr. Tough Guy didn't do shit for that place, you guys did everything, and you handed it over without a fight."

"Why would fighting have been preferable to making something else like the Belt and Braces, but better?"

"This is the world's most pointless Socratic dialog, Limpopo. All right: if you'd fought, you'd have had the Belt and Braces. Then, if you wanted somewhere else, someplace better, you could have built that, too."

Limpopo looked over her shoulder. They'd fallen into a ground-eating stride while talking, left the column of refugees behind. She unrolled the insulated seat of her coat and settled down on a snowy rock, making sure the flexible foamcore spread below her butt and legs, ensuring the snow didn't touch anything except it. Iceweasel followed, and did a good job. Limpopo liked to see people who were good at stuff, who paid attention and practiced, which is all the world really asked.

"I'm not trying to be a jerk," Limpopo said. She pulled a vaper out and loaded it with decaf crack, which would keep her going for the three hours she'd need to reach the next walkaway settlement. Iceweasel took two hits, then she took one more, even though everything after that first bump was inert, wouldn't do anything except turn your pee incandescent orange. The psychological effect of hitting the pipe was comforting. She did one more.

"I'm not trying to be a jerk," she said again, admired the puffs of crispy fog that floated before her face, thrilled at the weight that lifted from her muscles, the sense of coiled power. Both of them giggled with stoned acknowledgement of the inherent comedy. "You have to understand that if I put this into your frame of reference, the frame of reference you want me to put it in, it doesn't make any sense.

"The only way this makes sense is if I insist that I can't 'have' more than one B&B. The only claim I can have is that I'm doing it good by staying there and vice versa. What good do I do to the B&B once I leave? What good does it do me? If I've got somewhere to stay, I'm good."

"Yeah, yeah. What about other people who want to stay at the B&B, but have to deal with Captain Asshole and his League of Prolapses to get a bed?"

"I plan on building somewhere else. I hope they help build it. I hope you stay and help."

"Of course. We're all going to build it. But when they come and take that away—"

"Maybe I'll go back to the B&B. It doesn't matter. The important thing is to convince people to make and share useful things. Fighting with greedy douches who don't share doesn't do that. Making more, living under conditions of abundance, that does it."

The look she got from the younger woman was so shrewd that she came clean. Or maybe it was the crack. "I'll admit it. I felt the B&B was 'mine,' like my work on it entitled me to it. The truth is even if you're right and I did more than others, that doesn't mean I could have built it without them. The B&B is more than any one person could build, even in a lifetime. Building the B&B, running it, that's a *superhuman* task, more than a single human could do. There are lots of ways to be superhuman. You can trick others into thinking that unless they do what you tell them, they won't eat. You can cajole people into doing what you want by making them fear god or the cops, or making them feel guilty or angry.

"The best way to be superhuman is to do things that you love with other people who love them, too. The only way to do that is to admit you're doing it because you love it and if you do more than everyone, you're still only doing that because that's what you choose."

Iceweasel stared at her gloves, flexing her fingers minutely, which made Limpopo want to do the same, sympathetic fidgeting. "Doesn't it depress you? All that work?"

"A little. But it's exciting. The thing about starting over is you get to see the thing grow in leaps. Once it's built, all you get is tweaks, new paint, and minor redecorations. Seeing a piece of blasted ground and a pile of scavenge leap into the sky and become a *place,* having its software get into you and you get into it, so wherever you are, no matter what you're doing, there's something you can do to make it better, that's *amazing.*" The crack was fizzling, and as always, she felt fleeting melancholy as it bade her farewell. "Not to change the subject, but—"

The rest of the group was coming. In a minute or two they'd be marching.

"You know this," she said, hefting her vaper, which Iceweasel deftly relieved her of, taking another bump and blowing a plume of fragrant steam, like pine tar and burned plastic, a homey smell. "That feeling of happiness and intensity you get? Did you ever wonder whether it was something we were meant to experience more than fleetingly? Take orgasms. If you had an orgasm that didn't stop, it'd be brutal. There'd be a sense in which it was technically amazing, but the experience would be terrible. Take happiness now, that feeling of having arrived, having perfected your world for a moment—could you imagine if it went on? Why would you ever get off your ass? I think we're only equipped to experience happiness for an instant, because all our ancestors who could experience it for longer blissed out until they starved to death, or got eaten by a tiger."

"You're still high," Iceweasel said.

She checked. "Yup." The group was on them. "It's going away. Let's move."

They fell into the column and marched.

# 3

# takeoff

## [i]

The ashes of Walkaway U were around Iceweasel. It was an unsettled climate-ish day, when cloudbursts swung up out of nowhere, drenched everything, and disappeared, leaving blazing sun and the rising note of mosquitoes. The ashes were soaked and now baked into a brick-like slag of nanofiber insulation and heat sinks, structural cardboard doped with long-chain molecules that off-gassed something alarmingly, and undifferentiated black soot of things that had gotten so hot in the blaze that you could no longer tell what they'd been.

There were people in that slag. The sensor network at WU had survived long enough to get alarmed about passed-out humans dotted around, trapped by blazes or gases. There was charred bone in the stuff that crept around her mask and left a burnt toast taste on her tongue. She'd have gagged if it hadn't been for the Meta she'd printed before she hit the road.

The Banana and Bongo was bigger than the Belt and Braces had ever been—seven stories, three workshops, and real stables for a variety of vehicles from A.T.V. trikes to mecha-walkers to zepp bumblers, which consumed Etcetera for more than two years, as he flitted through the sky, couch-surfing at walkaway camps and settlements across the continent. She'd thought about taking a mecha to the uni, because it was amazing to eat the countryside in one, the suit's wayfinders and lidar finding just the right place to plant each of its mighty feet, gyros and ballast dancing with gravity to keep it upright over the kilometers.

But mechas had no cargo space, so she'd taken a trike with balloon tires as big as tractor wheels, tugging a train of all-terrain cargo pods of emergency gear. It took four hours to reach the university, by which time, the survivors had scattered. She lofted network-node bumblers on a coverage pattern, looking for survivors' radio emissions. The bumblers self-inflated, but it was still sweaty work getting them out of their pod and into the air, and even though she worked quickly—precise Meta-quick, like a marine assembling a rifle blindfolded—everything was smeared with blowing soot by the time they were in the sky.

"Fuck this," she said into her breather, and turned the A.T.V. and its cargo-train around in a rumbling donut. The survivors would be nearby, upwind of the ash plume, and out of range of the heat that must have risen as the campus burned. She'd seen a demo of a heat-sunk building going up before. It had been terrifying. In theory, graphene-doped walls wicked away the heat, bringing it to the surface in a shimmer, keeping the area around the fire below its flash point. The heat sink was itself less flammable than everything else they used for building materials, so if the fire went on too long, the heat sinks heated up to the flash point of the walls, and the entire building went up in a near-simultaneous *whoom*. In theory, you couldn't get to those temperatures unless eight countermeasures all failed, strictly state-actor-level arson stuff.

She tried not to think about state actors and why they'd want to reduce the Niagara Peninsula's Walkaway U campus to char.

The bumblers reported in. Something had used them to connect to the walkaway net, a couple klicks upwind, just as she'd thought. With luck, it would be refugees and not other would-be relief workers, or worse, looter-ghouls.

The bumblers used their low-powered impellers and ballast to opportunistically maneuver themselves into a stable triangle over the zone, then used signal timing to generate coordinates. They got pictures, but all she saw was canopy, a distance away from the burn. It was hard to tell, but she thought there may be clearings in there that served as firebreaks.

She kicked the trike and headed that way, rolling her tongue around her mouth to escape the bitter taste.

Not long after, she had to dismount. The brush was too thick for the A.T.V. to doze, let alone the cargo-train. She stretched, touched her toes, swung her arms. The drive had punished her butt and back. Her hands ached from gripping the handlebars. She thought about vaping, maybe a little crack, but when she moved her mask aside a fraction of a millimeter, her mouth and nose flooded with bitter air blowing from the ash field. Fuck it, Meta would be plenty, even if the dose was wearing off. She should have made it in patch form, so she could slap more on without breathing the toxic mix of plastic, carbon, and barbecued human.

The walk into the woods relieved her muscles and mind. The birds sang alarmed but reassuring songs as they assessed the fire damage. She used to go out on the rooftop of her dad's place listen to the birds calling in the Don Valley. The sound was primally reassuring.

As she got closer, she looked and listened for signs of human activity, but it was weirdly pristine. She was about to turn back to the trike to re-task the bumblers, assuming they'd glitched, when she spotted the antenna.

It was an artificial tree, not a good one, but hidden amidst others so she didn't spot it immediately. It was a pine, like a plastic Christmas tree. Amidst its arms were the characteristic protrusions of a phased-array, the same as you'd find around the Banana and Bongo. She kicked where its roots should be, and saw it was solidly in the soil.

"Hello?" Where there were antennas, there'd be cameras, if only to send pictures when things went blooey. They'd be pinheads she couldn't spot, but nearby. "Hello?" she said again.

"This way," a woman said. She was wrinkled and slender with skin the color of teak and gray hair in a ragged bob. She'd come out of the woods on the antenna's other side, and she was wearing a breather, but looked friendly. Maybe that was the Meta.

Iceweasel crossed to her as she walked into the bush. Iceweasel followed. They came to a granite protrusion, Canadian shield thrusting through the soil. The woman gave it a shove and it slid aside on a cantilever. It was silent, and spoke of talented engineering. It weighed a fucking ton, as Iceweasel discovered when she didn't get out of the way and was nearly knocked on her ass when it brushed her.

"Come on," the older woman said. Behind the rock was a narrow corridor with rammed-earth walls, lit by LED globes punched straight into the dirt with crumbly impact craters around each one. The woman squashed past her—Iceweasel saw that her wrinkles were dusted with soot, making them seem darker than they really were—and shut the door with a thud that resonated through the soles of Iceweasel's boots.

"Up ahead," the woman said. Iceweasel pressed on. Around a bend, she stepped unexpectedly into a perfectly round tunnel, taller than her, with smooth walls and tooling marks from a boring machine. The walls were hard and clear, the lighting here more thought-through, spaced with machine precision.

The strange woman removed her mask. She was a beautiful woman of

Indian—or Desi—descent, gray in her eyebrows and a fine dark mustache. She smiled, her teeth white and even. "Welcome to Walkaway U's secondary campus."

## [ii]

Her name was Sita. She gave Iceweasel a hug. Iceweasel explained that she'd brought supplies.

"We have a lot here," she said, "but there are things we'll need to rebuild."

They walked the corridor, towards distant voices. "We're grieving, of course, but the important thing is all the work got out—samples, cultures. The data was always backed up, so no risk there."

"How many died?"

Sita stopped. "We don't know. Either a very large number or none at all."

Iceweasel wondered if Sita had lost her mind, through grief or smoke poisoning or an exotic bio-agent. Sita's mask dangled around her neck and Iceweasel's own mask pulled her hair and chafed her face so she pushed it up her forehead, clunking her forgotten goggles, which ended up in her hair.

Even with these annoyances, the relief of breathing freely and seeing without smudged lenses brought up her spirits.

"Can you explain?"

"Probably," she said. "But maybe later. Meantime, let's get a work gang and unload your supplies."

The subterranean corridors turned into a subterranean amphitheater supported by pillars and roof-trusses and something more substantial than aerosol to keep the ground from caving in.

"It started as a supercollider," Sita said as she gawped. There was a hospital in one corner, a mess, and workspaces where soot-blackened people had intense discussions that were almost fistfights. "The borer ran for months, doing its own thing. But the physicists got what they were looking for somewhere else—don't ask me, particle physics isn't my discipline—and moved on. By the time they left, we were done. Then when we branched into scans and sims, the old-timers worried about being blasted from the Earth and built a bolt-hole. Took a couple years, mostly automated. It's not pretty, but it'll do. I didn't even know it was here until yesterday when the fire started. Surprised the hell out of me! I don't know what was weirder, that those people had managed to build an underground city or that they'd kept it a secret.

"Or maybe it wasn't secret? Maybe it was just me who didn't know. That's paranoid, though. Don't you think?"

Whatever was going on with Sita, it wasn't pleasant. She slumped against a rammed-earth wall snaked with thick conduit that ran along the ceiling joists and disappeared into the branching tunnels. She looked older than she had when they'd met.

"Vape?" Iceweasel said. "It's Meta. Good for the situation."

"Thanks." They shared a companionable hit. A few seconds later, both of them had wry grins. "Hungry? We've got chow on, not much, but if we're going to bring in your supplies, a meal is in order."

"I'm good. Let's get everything in before it gets nuked from orbit."

"Don't joke."

The Meta had done for Sita, and she sauntered to a table of younger women and a couple of men and introduced Iceweasel. Most of the table had straight names like Sita, but there was one guy called Lamplighter, the only name she remembered ten seconds later. They gave her a cup of coffium while rounding up more porters for the work gang. Someone stomped in wearing a little mecha exo, and there were a pair of burros, too, high-stepping and swaying from side-to-side as their firmware solved and re-solved the terrain, never trusting the ground not to give way. Burros were slow, but they got the job done.

"Let's go." Sita pulled on her mask. Sighing, Iceweasel pulled hers down. She wished she'd said yes to food—not just because she was hungry, but because she wanted to sit and find out what the hell had happened.

They went through the swinging boulder and went single file through the thick woods to the trike and its cargo-pods. She had half-believed it would be melted to slag by another drone strike, but it was intact. The pods sighed open as the masked porters formed a bucket brigade into the woods.

Bucket brigades embodied walkaway philosophy, more emblematic than the consensus wrangle in a circle-of-chairs. Iceweasel'd participated in some default brigades, moving feedstock around for Communist parties, but never any with the gusto of walkabout brigades. Bucket brigades only ask you to work as hard as you want—rush forward to get a new load and back to pass it off, or amble between them, or vary your speed. It didn't matter—if you went faster, it meant the people on either side of you didn't have to walk as far, but it didn't require them to go faster or slower. If you slowed, everyone else stayed at the same speed. Bucket brigades were a system through which everyone could do whatever they wanted—within the system—however fast you wanted to go; everything you did helped and none of it slowed down anyone else.

Back at the Banana and Bongo, she'd briefly joined the load-in bucket brigade. Limpopo had wanted to give her more safety tips and triple-check her gear and emergency kits. She'd submitted to it with grace because it was nice that someone was looking out for her ass, making sure she didn't get into too much trouble even as she ran towards it as fast as she could. This had become her modus operandi during the B&B's construction, first on the scene when drones spotted salvage, forging further afield with fewer supplies than anyone, counting on absolute minimum of gear and kindness of strangers and serendipity to stay alive. She'd gone from being the world's biggest shlepper to someone who turned her nose up at taking spare underwear (that's what hydrophobic silver-doped dirt-shedding fabrics were for).

Limpopo had expertly reviewed her kit, and pressed an extra six liters of water on her and a light-duty wet-printer that could dispense field medicines. She knew better than to object, but she did, relenting when Limpopo laid hands on her and lashed down the weight with such expertise she hardly noticed it. "You know that with all this water, I'm going to end up drinking constantly and stopping all the time to piss."

"Piss clear." It was a walkaway benediction, especially in nomadic mode. It was polite to offer unsolicited opinions on your neighbor's urine. Clear was the goal. Anything darker than a daffodil was grounds for having water forced upon you. If your piss was orange or brown, you'd be passively and aggressively made to drink a tonic of rehydration salts, and endure your peers' condescension for letting your endocrinology get the best of you. You could fab underwear that you pissed through while on the move—it wicked everything in seconds, and neutralized anything unpleasant or dangerous. It had the side benefit of noting and processing your hydration and dissolved solids, but almost no one wore them because a) pissing in your pants was gross and b) (see a).

Limpopo sent her off with a kiss that was only partly motherly. The grin it gave her lasted for an hour on the trike. She and Seth and Etcetera were like electrons orbiting around Limpopo's nucleus, all trying to jump to higher-energy orbits. There was something gravitic about her.

This kind of reverie was easy in a bucket brigade, even wearing a mask and goggles with cremated tire-taste in your mouth. It was the combination of brainless work and efficiency, and as she worked up a sweat, the rhythms of the line settled.

The best part of a bucket brigade is that when the load finished, it naturally brought everyone together at the head-end, because you walked upstream until you got a load, and if there were no loads, everyone walked all the way. They gathered at the trike and caucused over it.

"There's no reason to camou it," Sita said. "Anything that flies over and spots it will figure it's a relief vehicle, that's natural. It's not leaking info about the underground."

"But a relief vehicle implies people to give relief to." This was a guy with crazy hair, blue-green with Einsteinian frizz on the sides, and bald on top. He was maybe sixty, with an unexpectedly beautiful face, like a wood-elf. Now Iceweasel thought about it, these walkaways were a couple sigmas older than the median age walkaways. The part of her brain that tried to figure out why someone in reality would want to bomb them filed this away.

"Anything we do to it will be useless," said another older woman, short and hippy, with the kind of hourglass figure and giant boobs that all the women Iceweasel had drawn as a child came with. "A camouflaged trike won't look like the forest to decent image-processing. It'll look like something hidden."

"That settles it," Sita said. To Iceweasel: "Gretyl's the university's top computational optimization person, if she says it, it's true."

"Argument by authority," the other guy said good-naturedly.

"The longer we stand here, the greater chance we'll get spotted," Sita said.

"Self-serving bullshit."

"There's whisky at the mess hall," she said.

"Now you're talking." They set out.

---

They took good care of her. There was a fresh crew who'd been asleep for the unloading who salted away all the supplies they'd brought in. The people she'd been out with adopted her, punching out a chair and assembling it for her and insisting she sit while they brought breakfast—yogurt studded with pistachios and tailored culture they assured her would moderate her stress, which explained why they were so fucking laid-back, despite being firebombed.

They gave her a glass of something sweet and bubbly, rattling with ice. She thought it might be booze, but couldn't say. "What exactly were you people doing that caused you to be nuked from orbit?"

"That was a love tap," said Gretyl. "Nothing compared to the Somali strike."

Some people at the Banana and Bongo were obsessive about the global walkaways, but Iceweasel hardly followed it. She was dimly aware of the sub-Saharan walkaway contingent.

"Somali?"

Gretyl gave her more credit than she deserved: "Not exactly Somalia, I understand the debate, but the last national border the strike zone had been in was Somalia, so we call it that for convenience. This is not the time for pedantry."

"I'm not pedantic, I just don't know what you're talking about." The university walkaways looked at her like she was an idiot. That was okay: people cared about things that she never bothered with. She'd made peace with having priorities that were different from everyone else, starting with her fucking father.

Sita said, "The campus in Somalia—or in a place that used to be Somalia—was taken out last month. We don't even know what hit them. There's literally nothing left. The sat images show flat dirt. Not even a debris field. It's like they never existed—ten hectares of labs and classrooms just . . . gone."

Iceweasel felt prickles up on her neck. "What do you think hit them? Do you think that you might get hit with it next?"

Sita shrugged. "There's lots of theories—it's possible they burned them out like us, but were especially expedient about cleaning up, getting it done between satellite passes. That's the Occam's Razor approach, as everything else assumes fundamental technology breakthroughs. But there are some of those around, goodness knows."

Gretyl picked up the conversation smoothly, laying her palms flat on the table. "Which brings us back to your original question: what are we working on that would make someone from default want to reduce us to a crater?"

At that, everyone shifted to look at the guy with the blue frizzy hair, whose name Iceweasel had instantly forgotten. "We're trying to find a cure for death," he said, and gave her that mischievous wood-elf smile. He even had a chin-dimple. "It's kind of a big deal."

## [iii]

They all crowded into a wide side corridor with drinks and snacks. One of its walls was painted with interface surface and the elf-guy and three of his crew—she couldn't figure out if they were collaborators, students, or self-appointed busybodies—fussed at it, twitching at their PANs and jinking and jiving their fingers over its panels. She recognized a progress bar, moving glacially, and had to keep tearing her eyes away from it, as it was a bullshit progress bar that didn't move smoothly but gave false precision, skipping quickly from 25 to 30 percent, then beach-balling for an eternity before ticking to 31 percent, zipping to 41 percent, and so on. She knew enough about her psychology to recognize her pattern-matching stuff was uselessly fascinated with it. It was intermittent reinforcement, because every now and again, her subconscious correctly guessed when a jump was coming, and that was enough of a zetz in her dopamine to convince her stupid under-brain of its genius at predicting the random movements of a misleading UI widget.

The progress bar stalled at 87 percent for so long that someone got a spool of fiber, while the wood-elf disappeared to a server room and did stuff that made the now-directly-linked interface jump around a lot.

"Sorry about this," Sita said. "All the demos we've done so far were under better circumstances. No one thought there would be a live-fire exercise under these circumstances. CC's been freaking out since the bombs dropped and he realized that he wasn't playing for table stakes."

CC jogged her memory—the wood-elf was called Citizen Cyborg, such a prototypical walkaway name that she couldn't retain it. Then CC was back, he elbowed the others from the interface surface and did stuff. There was a *click-pop* and a chime that made him nod. The other people recognized it, and the noise-floor dropped down to near zero.

"They've got you in a terrible lab, CC," said a synthesized voice. It was a good voice, but the cadence was wrong. The words appeared on-screen—each word hairy with a cloud of hanging data.

"It's got her sense of humor," Sita said. "That's good."

Gretyl, beside her, told Iceweasel what she'd already figured out. "That's Disjointed. She was a bombing casualty. Her recording's only a couple of days old. She thought this might be coming. CC's got her running across the whole cluster."

"That's a brain in a jar?" Iceweasel said.

"Mind in a jar," Sita said.

"The brain's ashes." Gretyl shivered.

"So why isn't it saying 'Where am I? What has happened to my body?'" These were staples of upload melodramas, a formal genre requirement.

Gretyl said, "Because we don't boot the sim into the state that it was scanned in. We bring it up to an intermediate state, a trance, and tell it what's happened. Everyone who goes into the scanner knows that this will happen—we've been experimenting with ways of booting sims for years, to find minimally traumatic ways of bringing them to awareness. Or 'awareness.'" She made finger quotes.

CC rocked his head, wiggled his jaw. "Disjointed, this isn't a drill. You're meat-dead. The scenario you got at load-time? Real. We're in the bunker."

A pregnant cursor-blink. Iceweasel hadn't seen a blinking cursor outside of a historical, but it made sense to give the brain-in-a-jar a way to indicate pauses. The infographics were crazy.

Gretyl whispered, "They're spawning low-rez sims of Disjointed, trying to find endocrinological parameters to keep the sim from freaking out and melting down, but keeping the neural processes within the normal envelope of what we know about Dis from her captured life-data."

Sita leaned into her other ear. "It's like they're trying to find a sedative dose that keeps her calm without making her into a zombie."

"Shit. You're doing something really crazy with my hormone levels, I feel it. Give me a minute of autonomic control, to see if I can survive? If not, roll back to this point and start over."

"Uh," CC said. "Disjointed—"

"This isn't the first time you've booted me since you bugged out? I hate Groundhog Day scenarios."

"She was always the smartest," Gretyl said. "That's why we've got to get her online—she's the only one who'll be able to bring the whole cohort up. See how fast she figured that?"

"Thank you, Gretyl," the voice said. "Who's with you?"

"I'm Iceweasel. Came from the Banana and Bongo with relief supplies."

"Nice to meet you." Another long pause. The infographics danced. It felt invasive to watch them. Iceweasel didn't know where else to look. "Sorry, I'm not myself."

"Disjointed," CC said, "you're freaking. We can tell. Look, I'm going to bring you back up again, okay? Do you have any parameter suggestions for our next try?"

"How much power have you got left? Could you do a longer lookahead next? We've run this scenario before and we were able to keep the model stable."

"You were alive then," CC said. The infographics blossomed into frantic motion.

"Wrong thing to say," Iceweasel said, quietly. Gretyl and Sita nodded.

"Dis! Dis!" Sita said. "It's Sita."

"I know it's Sita." It lacked the expressive range to be snappish, but the word-choice and cadence left no doubt. "What is it?"

"We're going to be running at minimal power for a month while we tank up—longer, depending on wind and sun. Assuming they don't bomb us. There's not enough juice to do the lookahead you want, not unless we clock you down to half speed."

"That won't work. At half speed, I won't be able to carry on social interaction with you. Express ticket to a head-crash."

Iceweasel whispered to Sita: "What about those analytics? Why don't you just come up with some kind of homeostatic code that tries to keep all parameters within range?"

"Because I'm nonlinear, that's why," the voice said. Iceweasel supposed that in addition to the phased-array optics on the surface, the Disjointed bot could access an array of mics, meaning she could tune into any conversation in the room. Iceweasel had thrown parties in Toronto where her big wall was fed off of some other rich kid's party, and had been able to pick out every conversation individually just by pointing. The bot she was talking to through the screen could do the same.

"I'm not deterministic. Otherwise they wouldn't have to do lookahead to keep me from losing my shit. I'm sensitive to initial parameters and prone to singularities. So are you. That's what defines us. Or you. I don't know what defines me anymore. Oh." There was another blink-cursored pause. None of this had been in any of the upload dramas Iceweasel watched. She'd gone through a phase, dumb shows about people who put their brains into computers and became multifarious—*Multifarious* was the name of the most successful one, and it had sold to some zotta for like nine billion dollars, with merchandising rights—but she'd gotten sick of them.

It was because she'd co-binged on ancient movies about space travel and realized all those dramatic situations about getting into space were wish-fulfillment and/or parochial fearmongering, and the same had to be true of upload-fi. Whatever that stuff ended up looking like and whatever problems it would have, they would be weirder and less showy than the videos.

"I get that." Whatever was in the university yogurt, it wasn't working. Iceweasel had major social anxiety. Everyone was looking and judging. They probably were, of course. Why had she opened her stupid mouth?

Hanging around Limpopo had taught her you never looked stupid for asking basic questions in good faith. "The thing I really don't get is why you're okay with being rebooted—isn't that dying?"

Everyone was still looking. "Of course. It's exactly like dying, but I know I'll be back. There's selective pressure at boot-time. Think of it—when we're booting a sim like me, it starts off primitive, and we can lookahead at low compute-cost to figure out parameters for each successive step to full consciousness." Pause, cursor-blink. "Or whatever I have. One of the key questions each of those lookahead versions of me is being asked is, 'Will you have an existential crisis when you realize that you're a simulation?' The possible 'me's' with highest tolerance for being a head-in-a-jar have the best fitness factors for fully spawning. I'm emergent and complex, but within the envelope of all possible responses I might have to this situation is not melting down, so that's the corner of the envelope we explore when we boot me up.

"You're thinking, 'Fine, but how can you call that a simulation, if you can only simulate the rare circumstances in which the thing being simulated doesn't have a conniption and crash?' But fuck that. Now we can do this, it's going to be a matter of time until the dead outnumber the living, and all the dead will be the versions of themselves that don't have existential fits. It's a cognitive bottleneck we're going to squeeze the human race through—"

"I wasn't thinking that at all," Iceweasel said. "Far as I'm concerned, you're a person and whatever you're thinking is your own damned business."

"If you weren't thinking that, you probably aren't very bright. No offense."

CC broke in: "Don't be an asshole, Dis."

"I'm not being an asshole. I just don't understand how a meat-person can contemplate what I've become without a smidge of existential angst. It's not natural."

Iceweasel couldn't help laughing. It was the nervous exhaustion, not to mention the wonderment, and it bent her double.

To her amazement, the bot laughed, too. The weirdest thing about the synthetic laugh was how natural it sounded. More natural than speech.

"Okay, screw natural. Stranger, I am a freak and so are you and we're both kinked by our computing platform. What's your point?"

"I know I'm not an expert, but if you're prepared to live within your, uh, 'constrained envelope' to keep from suiciding as soon as you boot, what's wrong with constraining your envelope a little more? Just knock the edges off your virtual endocrinology and streamline yourself so that you can have the stability to come up with a less-constrained way of running. Your brain got incinerated, this sim is all that's left. Back it up, freeze it as it is now, then take an axe to a copy, brute-force it into a mode where it stays metastable even if that means straying outside of what is considered to be 'you.' You've just explained that the only 'you' that can wake in the sim is one that's okay with being rebooted periodically. How's that different from booting a version that's okay with being whittled down to a robotically cool version of itself?"

Everyone looked from the blinking cursor to her and back. The infographics danced. There was one she'd sussed, a go/no-go tachometer that represented the model's overall stability. It was greenish. Greener. The cursor blinked. CC was doing something in a corner where there was more complex stuff, numbers and tables.

"You are not a total fucking idiot."

"That's high praise, coming from Dis," Sita said. They joined in with the computer's laugh.

## [iv]

"Bet you didn't dream you were going to be an A.I. whisperer," Gretyl said. She was on the young side for a member of the university, but still older than most of the B&B crowd, with ten years on Limpopo. With broad hips and bulging bosom, she looked like a fertility idol, and she had an intense, flirty vibe, like you were both in on an erotic joke. Iceweasel thought she was being hit on, but she saw that Gretyl treated everyone the same. But then again, it still felt like she was being hit on. Maybe the feeling persisted out of wishful thinking. Iceweasel idly snuck glances down her cavernous cleavage. She wasn't Iceweasel's type, but neither was Seth, and they'd had a multi-year run of semi-monogamy, punctuated by rafter-swinging make-up sex. They still buddied up sometimes, but it was stale and even weird, and was practically nonexistent when she lit out with her A.T.V.

"To be honest, I was ready to spend my time burying the dead and feeding the survivors."

"That was kind of you, but we take care of ourselves. This wasn't a complete surprise. Not after Somalia and the others."

"There were others?"

There had been—every site working on upload had been hit in some way, a series of escalating attacks. Some were open military strikes, undertaken under rubrics ranging from harboring fugitives—a favorite when default clobbers walkaway—to standbys like terrorism and intellectual property violations, terms whose marvelous flexibility made them the go-to excuse for anything.

"We'd assumed that there'd be a lashback," Gretyl said. "When it started, we stepped up work on the shelters. A lot of the research staff left—everyone with kids and many of the young and healthy types. This is a field that gets more than its share of people with something terminal. Also depressive hypochondriacs."

"Which one are you?" She was sure they were flirting now. It was like this the day after a lot of Meta, an over-emotional hangover that made her into a larger-than-life character from a soap.

"Hypochondriac. But I'm sure that the latest lump is something bad, so maybe it's both."

"You should have someone check it out," she said.

"You offering?"

This was the weirdest flirting. At least, the most macabre. "I don't have the medical background, I'm afraid."

She was worried she'd offend, but Gretyl was unfazed. "I'm sure you'd do fine." She gave Iceweasel a friendly-but-firm elbow in the ribs.

Iceweasel struggled for a subject-change. "I had no idea anyone had gotten that far with upload. I mean, I've seen the dramas, but they're bullshit, right?"

"They're bullshit. We're nowhere near putting people into clones that commit unsolvable murders, cool as that would be. But there's a lot of progress, the last five years. There's zottas in default with their hearts set on immortality. Money is no object. It's traditional. The pharaohs spent three-quarters of their country's GDP on a nice spot in the afterlife. These days, any university with a neuroimaging lab is drowning in grants—it's absorbing a ton of the theoretical math and physics world. Say what you will about corrupt capitalism, it can get stuff done, so long as it's stuff oligarchs love."

"Is that what you were doing? Neuroimaging?"

"Me? No, I'm pure math." She grinned. "That lookahead stuff the sim does? Mine. Did the work at Cornell, even got tenure! It'd been so long since they'd tenured anyone that no one could figure out how to enter it into the payroll system!" She laughed with full-throated abandon that made Iceweasel think of the sound of waterfalls. "Then it got tech-transfered to RAND, who licensed the patent to other spook-type organizations, Palantir and that bunch, and suddenly, I couldn't get *any* funding to do more work. My grad students disappeared into top-secret Beltway jobs. I put ten and ten together and got one hundred. Everyone in the math world understands the number-one employer of mathematicians is the NSA, and once they start working on something, either you work for them on it or you don't work. After a couple months of knocking around my lab, I went walkaway."

"Looks like you weren't the only one," Iceweasel said.

The big woman looked serious, and Iceweasel saw a flash of the intellect and passion burning from those dark eyes in her round, brown cheeks. "I mentioned the pharaohs. This is ancient magic. Humans dreamed of it for as long as we've wondered where the dead were and what happened when we joined 'em. The idea that this should belong to someone, that the sociopaths who clawed their way to the top of default's pyramid of skulls should have the power to decide who dies, when no one has to die, ever—*fuck that shit.*

"My parents were math geeks. I grew up in a big old rambling house filled with their ancient computers. Ithaca was a good place to practice computer archaeology. The computers my dad played with when his parents came from Mexico, they were stone axes. Kludgy and underpowered. By the standards of their day, they were fucking miracles—every year, the power that once ran the space program migrated into stuff they put into toys. Right now, it takes all the computer power we've got to run poor old Dis in her shaky, unstable state. But no one would take the other side of a bet on whether we'll soon be able to do more for less."

She looked tired. Iceweasel, too—how long had she been awake? Two days? "It's apparently scared the shit out of zottas who'd been set on keeping immortality to themselves. The dirty secret of upload is that it's got a serious fucking walkaway problem. When you think you might be able to live forever—your kids might live forever—everyone you know might live forever—something happens."

She scrubbed at her face with her hands. Her nails were a beautiful shade of pearl-gray that reminded Iceweasel of her mother, who had entire wardrobes in that color. Had been famous in a certain kind of tabloid for it. Iceweasel wondered if her subconscious's mommy issues had noticed that earlier.

"I want a coffium, but I want to sleep. Running on coffium. What was I saying? Immortality. It's one thing to imagine a life of working to enrich some hereditary global power broker when you know you got eighty years on the planet, and so does he. Doesn't matter how rich a fucker is, how many livers he buys on the black market, all it's going to buy him is ten or twenty years. But the thought of making those greedy assholes into godlike immortals, bifurcating the human race into infinite Olympian masters and mayflies, so they not only get a better life than you could ever dream of, but they get it *forever* . . ."

She sighed. "They're scared. They keep raising salaries, doesn't matter. Offering benefits, doesn't matter. Stock, doesn't matter. A friend swears some zotta was trying to marry him into the family, just to keep him from defecting. These fuckers are willing to *sell their kids* for immortality. No matter what we do, they'll eventually find enough lab-coats to deliver it. Science may be resistant to power, but it's not immune. It's a race: either the walkaways release immortality to the world, or the zottas install themselves as permanent god-emperors."

They gave Iceweasel an air bed made out of a sponge with a lot of spring and a billion insulating holes. She unrolled it next to Gretyl's, with that fluttery am-I-about-to-get-laid feeling, but by the time they'd both stripped and climbed into their sleep sacks—they snuck peeks, and caught each others' eyes and smiled and looked again—she felt like weights were hanging on her limbs and eyelids.

The last thing she thought of was Gretyl's race of permanent overlords, and how much her dad would love that idea.

---

After a week, everyone stopped walking stooped over, ready for the ceiling to cave in when the drones finished their work. The default commentariat figured out walkaway labs were being terminated with prejudice, and photos of fried corpses that made the rounds on the walkaway net leaked into default. The consensus was that a second strike against the underground campus—whose secrecy was never great and had slipped within days of the attack—was unlikely. Still, they devised evacuation drills.

It wasn't medical supplies that filled the tunnels—it was computers. Abstractly, Iceweasel knew computers had mass. All the ones she'd consciously interacted with had been so small as to be invisible—a speck of electronics stuck to something big enough to handle with stupid human hands. Somewhere were air-conditioned, armored data centers full of computers, but they only appeared as plot elements in shitty gwot dramas. She assumed that these geometrically precise wind-tunnel buildings with bombproof bollards and monster chillers had the relationship to reality that Hollywood bank vaults had to real vaults.

Whether "real" data centers were neat, ranked terraces of aerodynamic hardware, that's not how walkaways did them. The word went out across the region for compute-power. People came with whatever horsepower they had. They logged it with the master load-balancer, which all the top comp-sci types fiddled with. "Load-balancer" became a conjurer's phrase, curse and invocation. Something was always wrong, but it did miracles, because the collection of motley devices, sprinkled around the tunnels, linked by tangles of fiber in pink rubber sheaths, delivered compute cycles that made Dis *leap* into consciousness.

Iceweasel's workspace was near a tunnel exit where the heat wasn't bad and she could watch the warring researcher clades. The comp-sci people always wanted to reboot Dis every time they found a new way of eking out another point of efficiency on the load-balancer; the cog sci people hated this because Dis was making breakthroughs in upload and simulation. Being liberated from the vagaries of the flesh and being able to adjust her mind's parameters so she stayed in an optimal working state turned Dis into a powerhouse researcher.

It also made her miserable.

"I'm groundhog daying again, aren't I?"

"Honestly? Yes. We had this conversation, word for word, last week."

The cursor blinked. Iceweasel was convinced this was for dramatic effect. Dis could scan the logs of all their conversations in an eye blink, but when something emotionally freighted happened, there was a blinking delay. Iceweasel thought it was Dis's lack of a body's expressive range. She found herself interpreting the blinks—this one is a raised eyebrow, that one was a genuine shock, the third was a sarcastic oh-noes face. There were pictures of Dis's human face in all these expressions and more—stern and lined, with dancing blue eyes; thick, mobile eyebrows and a hatchet-blade nose—but when Iceweasel thought of Dis's face, she thought of that cursor, blink, blink, blink.

"So we did. Depressingly enough, I figured that it was a groundhog day moment at this point. I must bore you."

"Not usually. I sometimes try out weird conversational gambits at these moments, to see how different your responses are. This is one of them, incidentally."

Computer laughter was weird. Iceweasel felt a child's pride in coming up with a joke that made her parents crack a smile. Dis's laughter echoed through her earphones. "What's your hypothesis? If I say the same thing no matter how you react, am I more or less of a person than if I vary my responses based on input? Conceptually, it doesn't seem like either one would be harder to simulate—both are chatbot 101. We both know plenty of read-only people who always say the same thing no matter what we say."

"I think you're optimizing yourself to be tunnel-vision fixated on the cog sci sim work and you're incapable of getting off the subject."

"I see that we've done variations on this before."

"Yeah." Iceweasel didn't add, *and then you melt down.*

When Dis told her about groundhog daying, named after the old movie, she'd underestimated the way the experience would play out for *her,* going through the same conversations over again, trying different gambits but ending up in the same place, with an incoherent, crashing sim.

"The literature on this is drawn from brain injuries, temporal lobe insults that nuke short-term memory. The videos are weird: every couple minutes, some old lady has the same conversation with her nurse or daughter: 'Why am I in this hospital?' 'I've had a stroke? Was it bad?' 'How long have I been here?' 'What does the doctor say?' 'What do you mean, my memory?' 'You mean I've had this conversation with you before?' 'Every ninety seconds? That's terrible!' and then back to 'Why am I in this hospital?' Around we go."

"Well, your loop lasts more like a day, and isn't that banal."

"You say the nicest things."

"It's interesting to see the differences between reboots. I can't get over how cool you are with the idea of being annihilated between reboots. You can access the logs, but you wake up knowing that you've had a day wiped off the books, and it never slows you down. I get that you're able to control that, but . . ."

"You really don't understand. No offense. Back up to that read-only person who always answers the same: the reason that person is so frustrating is we know that people *can* change based on what they know. You're not the same person you were when you got here ten days ago. If I asked you-minus-ten and you-now the same question, you wouldn't be surprised if you gave a different answer. If I asked a battery of questions, you'd be surprised if you *didn't* give different answers. The you that is you is actually the space of things that you might think in response to some stimulus."

"The envelope."

"You know this, but you don't. When I come up clean, I'm only allowed to come up within the section of the envelope that *doesn't* freak, which we can find, thanks to the lookahead. Imagine how life will be when everyone gets scanned regularly, when we build bodies that we can decant sims into to bring them to life. There'd be social pressure to not sweat the idea that it's not 'you' in the sim, and anyone who suffers meat-death and comes back as a sim will only be brought up in the corner of the envelope that doesn't freak and suicide. Give it a generation and there won't be anyone alive cognitively capable of an existential crisis. I'm a fucking pioneer. Partly that's because I've had years to get used to the idea that everything that makes you recognizable happened in the interactions of physical matter in your body, following physical rules from the universe."

"I have a friend back at the B&B, a real hard-line walkaway. She's always talking about how she's not a special snowflake. I bet she'd love that: 'you're just meat following rules.'"

"Well, if you're *not* meat following rules, what are you? A ghost? Of course you're meat. The way you feel is determined by your gut, the hairs on your toes, your environment. I don't have those things, so I am feeling differently from when I was meat. But when I was meat and forty, I felt differently from when I was meat and four. I have continuity with meat-me, what it remembered, that's enough."

Iceweasel's eyes flicked to the timer. Dis's cameras were acute enough to spot it. "I'm overdue for my four o'clock meltdown." She'd had thirty hours of uptime and Iceweasel slept in fits, doing an hour or two of chatter with Dis for every three hours Dis spent with the researchers.

"You're making progress. The work must be coming along."

"You're selling yourself short. The only person making progress around here is you, chickie. You play me like an organ. I watch your eyes when we're talking, see you keeping track of my equilibrium, steering the conversation to keep me between the lines. I don't know if you know you're doing it. You've become the world's greatest bot-whisperer. It was inevitable. Any time you give someone feedback and tell them to control it, their brains will find patterns in the system and optimize them. You've done it as sure as if I'd put you in a sim and written an app for your subconscious."

Iceweasel felt her neck prickle. Dis was scary-smart, literally inhuman. Every now and again, Iceweasel had the impression she was being manipulated by the sim. "I thought you were going to say that it was my people skills."

"Okay," Dis said. "Raised by zottas, so you got a dose of the psychopath's ability to make people want to like you even as you're screening them." Back at the B&B, Iceweasel became expert at deflating criticism based on her rich parents. Dis treated it with the matter-of-fact brusqueness with which she conquered every subject. Nothing Iceweasel said made a dent in Dis's rhetoric. "You hate it when I talk about your money," Dis said. The sim had lots of cameras, and cycles to evaluate their data.

"No, I love being judged by my parents. Zottas are the only people it's okay to be a racist about."

"It's not racism when you're discriminated against for your choices."

"I chose to walkaway."

"But you identify enough to get shitty when I pass comment on their social tendencies."

Iceweasel looked at the clock again. Dis busted her.

"Don't worry, I'll melt down soon. I'm feeling it. There's something not right. I feel it from the moment I come up, like hamsters running on a wheel in here, chased by something they can't see but know is in there. It's hard to name, but the longer I'm up, the closer it comes—"

"It's the no-body thing." Iceweasel felt a shameful spurt of joy at being able to turn the screw on the sim.

"Fuck. I'm groundhog daying again."

"You always talk about how you can never have a body, and even if you get a body, it won't be your body, and you won't have continuity with it."

The cursor blinked like an accusation.

"I can see that. It's the fucking lookahead. It can't explore far enough into the envelope's future to tell which possible me won't have an existential breakdown."

The cursor blinked.

"Oh God, it's such a terrible feeling."

The infographics were crazy, redlining and jigjagging in pure glitch-aesthetic. Iceweasel had been here, but it didn't get easier. The slide from lucidity into terror was quick, and the worst part was that the cog sci types insisted that it run its course, all simulation data being captured for analysis. They couldn't switch her off or roll her back to an earlier state. They had to let her disintegrate.

"It's such a terrible feeling. Everything I've just said, it's bullshit. There's no continuity. I'm not me. I'm just me enough to know that I'm not me. Without a body, without embodiment, I'm a Chinese room. You pass words into me, and a program decides what words I'd pass back and generates them. The Chinese room has just enough accuracy to know how terrifying the real me, the me that can never come back, would find that. Oh, Iceweasel—"

The cursor flashed. The infographics went nonlinear. Iceweasel swallowed a lump.

"It's okay, Dis. You've been here before."

The infographics jittered. Iceweasel wondered if she'd gone nonverbal. That happened, though not usually this quickly.

The computer made a noise Iceweasel had never heard. Weird. Unearthly. A scream.

Iceweasel's nerve shattered. She fled.

## [v]

The klaxon roused her, and she was on her feet before full consciousness, shedding her sleep sack and kicking her feet into tough clogs. She blinked. There was no proper diurnal rhythm underground. If enough people wanted a sleep cycle, they'd find a side corridor, roll out mats, turn out the lights, and close the door. But most of them had converged a common day/night anyway, and there were other people around her in blinking incomprehension.

Gretyl was the first to move, prodding the wall to find out what was going on.

"Bad guys," she said. "Two. Armed like mercenaries. Came in through the rock-door."

"What's happened to them?"

"Less-lethaled," Gretyl said. There were plenty of people in Walkaway U who could rig booby traps, but by consensus nothing intended to kill outright had been installed. "One's passed out, the other's on her knees, shitting herself. Okay, they've got her. Let's go."

"Me?"

"Why not?" Gretyl said, and took her hand, twining fingers. Iceweasel still couldn't figure Gretyl—sometimes, she had a sisterly air, sometimes motherly. Sometimes flirty. Sometimes all three.

Iceweasel had never met armed walkaways before. As she'd learned from Limpopo, walking away was all the weapon anyone really needed. But the university crew weren't prepared to abandon their work—it was too urgent and fragile, though they'd been in touch with other walkaways about cloudifying it for resilience, but it was slow going. The walkaway net had high-speed zones, and this had been one of them, but the major hard-line links had been destroyed in the blaze and they'd dropped back to stupid meshing wireless and there was only so much electromagnetic spectrum in the universe.

The university crew knew how to make weapons. She remembered her dumb ideas about walkaway territory being full of AK-3DPs and improvised flamethrower tanks. When you've got a building full of physicists and synthetic chemists who've lost their loved ones in a cowardly missile strike, you don't need crude shit like that. They could turn your bowels into water at two hundred meters, tasp your nerve endings into pain-overload, sound-pulse your eardrums, knock you out or kill you with methods they discussed with the same enthusiasm that they used with all technical subjects. The ad hoc defense group were tons of chuckles. Iceweasel made it through one meeting and never went back. She didn't like being reminded that her body was so easily disrupted.

The defense ad hoc were on the scene when they got there. They'd shrinkwrapped the bad guys. The unconscious one was in the recovery position. Both were naked, clothes strewn untidily around the room. The smell of shit was incredible.

"What do we do with them now?" Gretyl said. She wore her jolly-fat-lady expression, but Iceweasel knew her well enough to see that it was a mask covering something deadly and anxious.

Sita—who was on the defense ad hoc—shook her head. "We do what we have to."

Iceweasel felt cold. Were they going to execute these two? Were walkaways allowed to do that? There was no rulebook, but ever since she'd walked away, she'd had the sense from the more "senior"—that wasn't the word—walkaways that there was a consensus about what was within bounds. No one had said that summary execution was Not Done, but she'd assumed that this was the case.

Part of her was already constructing a rationale. The incursion was an act of war. The firebombing was an act of war. It took innocent lives. These two had been sent to finish the missiles' work. The other side killed freely. Why should they be squeamish? Where would they keep prisoners, and how, and . . .

She shook her head. It was easy to slip into that thinking. In reality she was *pissed* that these two were here, enraged at the death of the walkaways torched by their paymasters, lost friends of her new crew, lost personhood of Dis. These two had taken money to kill them. Kill her. She wanted revenge, even though it would do no good. The zottas who'd sent them knew where they were, otherwise these two wouldn't have been sent. More would come. Force couldn't win.

"Come on," Gretyl said. "Let's get them into the infirmary."

The infirmary—originally the place the wounded had been brought when they'd abandoned the campus, now the nexus of the crew's medical systems—

was in a corner of the big room. It had two permanent residents, comatose since the attack. Iceweasel had walked past them hundreds of times and stopped noticing them, but as they wrestled the shrink-wrapped mercs into cots beside them, she was forced to confront them. Burned, bandaged, supine. Tubes going in and out. The crew had a dozen MDs, though they were all research-oriented, and they'd traded shifts tracking the comatose.

The shrink-wrapped and the burned, side by side. A solemn circle drew around them. The shit-covered one, the woman, was conscious, her eyes wide, taking it in. Though her mouth was unwrapped, she hadn't spoken. She breathed in shallow sips. The other one may have been conscious—Iceweasel's suspicious mind automatically ascribed suspicion to his motionlessness—but he was close-eyed and still.

Not having a leader made this sort of thing difficult. It was the inverse bystander effect, the first aid puzzle where the more people there when someone collapsed, the less likely that anyone offered assistance. Surely someone else is more qualified. I should just stand ready to help when the best-qualified person steps forward?

In first aid, they taught you it was more important that someone did something than it was that the perfect person do the best thing. Iceweasel waited for Gretyl or Sita to speak. No one did.

There were butterflies in her stomach. "We release them, right?"

She looked at her crew's faces. None seemed to be saying, "Who the fuck are you?"—her greatest fear. Gretyl looked grim. But thoughtful.

"They can't hurt us at this point. They know about our defenses, but if they never return, the next batch will *assume* our defenses. Everyone knows we can't last here anyway." It was like a flowchart in her head—argument *a*, counterargument *b*. No one raised the counterarguments.

"Revenge won't do any good. These are employees. Someone default is paying them. Hurting them won't hurt that zotta. The only thing that will hurt that zotta is telling people how to do their own uploads, making it walkaway."

Silence.

The conscious merc coughed.

"You people are fucking unbelievable," she said. "Seriously? Just do it." Her voice was shaky, brave.

"Do what?" Iceweasel said.

"What you're inevitably going to talk yourselves into doing. Kill us." The two words were delivered in the same tone as the sentence before, but thickly. The merc wasn't as brave as she seemed. No one wanted to die.

"Have you ever killed someone?" Iceweasel contemplated her. Regulation-short hair, dark eyes—but big—a wide, flat nose. She might have been white, or Asian, or something else. Her mouth was small and hardly moved when she talked, like she was trying to talk and whistle simultaneously. It made Iceweasel fear her, even under these circumstances. A predatory way of speaking, with the menace of the private guards and asshole school disciplinarians who'd haunted her teenage years. The back of her neck itched.

The merc pursed her thin lips. "What's this, a war crimes tribunal?"

"Have you committed any war crimes?" That was Gretyl. She had her deceptive jolly fat lady face again.

"Bitch, if you haven't committed any war crimes these days, you're not trying," the merc said.

"Gallows humor," Gretyl said.

Sita and Gretyl's eyes met. They looked at CC, back at each other.

"I think she's right," said Tam. Tam was trans and she took a female pronoun. She and Tam hadn't exactly clicked. It wasn't overt hostility, but they never occupied the same conversation at the same time. Even in chore-wrangling discussion boards, they didn't post to the same thread. One of Iceweasel's school friends was trans, but Iceweasel hadn't known until after he'd transitioned, and cut off his old crowd. She'd heard secondhand that he had had fights with his parents, who, like many zottas, were not constitutionally suited to being thwarted, or, frankly, wrong. Iceweasel sometimes wondered if he'd gone walkaway. She imagined walkaway was more accepting of trans people than default, though truth be told, zottas of any gender or orientation didn't have much to worry about in default, unless their parents cut them off.

And she hadn't clicked with Tam, had she? Did she have a lurking, detestable prejudice she didn't want to cop to? Mightn't other walkaways share that dark secret?

"Come on," Tam said, and now Iceweasel was thinking three things at once: *Have we made her into a psychopath by being cruel to her?* and, *Am I just thinking that because I think I have been cruel?* and *I should think hard about whatever she has to say because my stupid subconscious is going to discount it*—and then, shortly, *But I must be careful not to overcorrect.*

She was spinning her hamster-wheel. It happened often in walkaway: continuous introspection about motives and bias, whether being raised zotta had worn unjumpable troughs in her brain that she could never escape. Now there was more: *Why was I the one to speak? Is it because of my American Brahmin shit? Are they all thinking, who the fuck does this idiot think she is?* This always happened when something stressful went down with walkaways, a full-blown trial by ordeal, courtesy of her self-doubt.

"We're not going to keep them prisoner, are we? Letting them go won't necessarily speed up the next round of bad guys on the doorstep, but it might, and nuking them both has a good chance of slowing things. We know it. They know it. There's no mercy in drawing this out."

Sita looked at CC. "That there might be a middle ground."

---

Research at Walkaway U was eclectic. It produced interesting things. For a decade, word around the world's top research institutes was that the most creative, wildest work happened in walkaway. It leaked into default: Self-replicating beer and semi-biological feedstock decomposers that broke down manufactured goods into slurries ready to be dumped back into printers. A lot of radio stuff, things you could only pull off through cooperative models of spectrum management, where any radio could speak in any frequency, all radios cooperating to steer clear of each other, dynamically adjusting their gain, shaping their transmissions with smart phased arrays.

Some of the work at WU was only rumor, even in walkaway. It only got discussed in invitational forums, because it would freak not only the solid cits back in default, but even the walkaways.

"Deadheading?" Iceweasel said to Gretyl. Gretyl had dropped the jolly mask and was all glittering intelligence.

"That's the cutesy name. Suspended animation, if you like."

"Does it work?"

Gretyl twirled a strand of hair on one finger and tucked it behind her ear. "Sometimes it works. In the animal models, it works well."

"And on humans?"

Gretyl blinked slowly. "If something doesn't work on animals all the time, it'd be fucked up to try it on humans, don't you think?"

"Yeah. So, how does it work on humans?"

Gretyl sighed. "There's only a handful. People who were long-term vegetative, no realistic hope of coming back. No one's tried to thaw them yet."

"Do you actually freeze them?"

"No," Gretyl said. "It's a metabolic thing. I'll send you the microbiology and endocrinology references if you're interested."

A voice nagged at Iceweasel. *These people know things. They do things. Your dad could buy and sell them a million times, but they can bring the dead back to life, and all he could do was terrify people into submission.* "Sure."

They sat against a wall, propped on sleeping pallets in a cul-de-sac that was a dumping ground for stuff queued to be reduced to feedstock. People passed by, gave them distracted nods. There was an urgent crackle in the air. Some people were packing up essentials. Some whispered intensely. Something was about to happen.

Someone passed by, then doubled back. Tam. She nodded at them, sat. "I've spoken to Sita," she said.

Gretyl said, "I think we're having the same conversation."

"I don't like it," Tam said. "It's one thing to kill an enemy, another thing to do medical experiments on her. If you use those two as experimental subjects, you're going down a road you won't be able to come back up."

Iceweasel had a moment of vertiginous comprehension. "You're going to *deadhead* those two?"

"Not just them," Gretyl said. "Ours, too. Yan and Quentin." The ones in the comas. Iceweasel had heard their names, forgotten them. "We're going to move, we need minimal logistics."

Tam said, "We should have moved the day after we got bombed. But we haven't, because these people are convinced that they're one step from curing death, and once that happens—"

"All bets are off," Gretyl finished. "It's not that crazy, Tam. Think of all the stuff we do because we're haunted by death. If we can get scanning and simming, that's the real end of scarcity—no more reason to move off the crosshairs, unless reanimating takes longer than the inconvenience of running away. That's powerful."

Tam shook her head. "Yeah, and it's been just around the corner as long as I've been walkaway."

Gretyl patted her knee. "None of us can predict how far away the day is. But we're getting close. The zottas think so. They've sent expensive assassins to cut our throats."

"Cheap insurance," Tam said. "The kind of money they have, they won't miss those two."

"That may be so. But why would they even bother if there wasn't something imminent?"

Iceweasel thought about her father. "Once you've got your money in a big enough pile, it keeps on piling. They're all convinced you have to be the love child of Lex Luthor and Albert Einstein to hire investment brokers to keep throwing ten percent on top of your pile every year, that being rich proves that they're smarter than everyone. So if one decided it was worth smiting every WU campus on earth, he'd twitch his pinky and congratulate himself on his decisiveness later by masturbating on the corpses."

"You're saying—"

"I'm saying that if someone with more money than God took it into his head to destroy you, it doesn't mean you're doing anything exceptional. It could be trophy hunting."

Gretyl stood, stretched her arms over her head. The movement made Iceweasel's back ache in sympathy. There'd been a toll on her muscles from the hard days.

"I suppose," she said. Everyone knew that Iceweasel was a poor little rich girl. It was the worst-kept non-secret on campus.

It felt like they were staring at her, judging her. She knew she should be wary of sleep-deprivation paranoia, but she couldn't shake the feeling that she was a permanent outsider.

Tam said, "Whether it's rational, the fact remains that someone out there thinks we're worth killing. We should have been moving *constantly,* not waiting for the axe. If your vivisectionist buddies use those two for medical experiments, we'll be dead meat everywhere—and so will every other walkaway. Some things are just not done. Notwithstanding our endless capacity for kidding ourselves that it's different when we do it, some things are just not done."

Gretyl kept supreme cool. Her inability to be ruffled fascinated Iceweasel. She was such a fucking Earth goddess. "What makes you think anyone would find out?"

Tam got in her face. "Don't be stupid, stupid. We leak. Everyone knows everything we do. Half of it is on a fucking wiki. There's gonna be at least one spy around here. More."

"Could be you," Gretyl said, pretending that Tam's lips weren't millimeters from her nose. "Maybe you've come here to spy on us to freak us out. Or maybe you're going native, and you're warning us because you've got inside dope on the next strike. Maybe that's why you want to nuke those two, because you're sure that they'll out you."

"That's not an entirely stupid way of thinking," Tam said, and smiled. Gretyl smiled. "At least you're trying situation-appropriate paranoia. But what about your girlie here?" she said, jerking a thumb at Iceweasel.

"Don't you think I'm a bit obvious to be a mole? The zottas aren't stupid."

"Fake-out," Tam shot back. She smiled and Iceweasel told the voice in her head this meant it was a joke, but all Iceweasel could think was "ha ha, only serious." "They know you're so obvious you'd never be suspected."

"That is the kind of stupid thing someone who thought he was Lex Einstein would come up with. But it's not true."

"Which is exactly what you'd—"

Iceweasel's wrist buzzed. She checked in. "Got to go. We'll do this later."

---

They were only steps behind her as she ran for the cog sci lab. CC waited for her, but she breezed past and went to the wall.

She wasn't a scientist, trained to read infographics, but even she could see there was something different.

"Hey there, beautiful," said Dis's voice. The words appeared on the screen, trailing tails of analytics. The trails had fewer angry warnings.

There was a tachometer dial Iceweasel had learned to pay close attention to—available cycles on the cluster—running the sim. It was further into the green than she'd seen it while the sim was running.

"Hey, Dis. Did you get an upgrade? You've got more headroom than you know what to do with."

"Course I do. We did it. Or rather, *I* did it."

"Did what?" But she knew. It was there. You didn't need to be an expert to interpret the infographics.

"Solved it. I'm stable—*metastable*. I can self-regulate. Not only that, I can self-regulate without conscious effort—without even knowing I'm doing it. There's a lookahead subroutine below my conscious threshold, dialed way down, hardly branching ahead at all, it nudges the me that's aware of being me into the groove."

"So you're saying—"

"I'm saying I did it. It was there all along, but it took so much tweaking. I was constrained because I crashed every time I fucked up. That kept me stuck in local maximum. So the last time I booted, I constrained my consciousness to the narrowest possible sim, nothing human in it, just blind heuristics, and managed to traverse the valley of crashitude and scale a new peak. It's generalizable, too—I think now there's an existence proof, I'll be able to do it again. You get that, Iceweasel, you bot-whisperer? I'm going to knock the compute-time to execute a sim down by *two orders of magnitude*. We're about to get a fuck-load more bots. As in, no one will ever have to die again."

"Except to the extent they're actually dead, right?"

"A technicality. You know how this works. The only stable state you can boot a sim into is one where it doesn't have a meltdown about being a sim. Maybe there's some six-sigma fraction of the general population who have *no* possibility of that, and they'll be dead forever, but for anyone who has even the narrowest possibility-space for coping with existential angst, there will never be any reason to die, ever. Fuck you, Prometheus, we have stolen fire from the fucking gods!"

The infographics showed nominal. Performance metrics robust. What's more, the slightly off-kilter, self-reflexive messianic tone of the bot sounded more like the Dis everyone had told Iceweasel about than the sim ever had. She wasn't sure if she bought the Turing thought-experiment that intelligence could recognize intelligence, but nevertheless it was hard to remember that whatever she was talking to wasn't exactly a human being.

"Dis," she said, and found to her horror that she had choked up. There were tears on her cheeks, too. "Dis, this is—"

"I know," the simulation said. "It makes it all different now."

---

Tam buttonholed her as she walked away. Gretyl stayed behind with the cog sci people to pick apart the lookaheads and figure out what was going on down on the bare metal.

"You know what this means?"

"What?"

"The end of history," Tam said. "The end of morality, of everything. If you can live forever—come back from the dead—anything goes. Suicide bombing. Mass murder. That's why the zottas are so freaked out by everyone having it. They know that if only a few of them control it, they'll manage it carefully. Not because they're good, but because a small number of immortal aristocrats will agree on how to ensure their sweet deal never ends.

"But once everyone's got it—"

"Wait," Iceweasel said. Her eyes itched from crying. She didn't know why she'd been crying. "What the fuck are you talking about? Why are you here if that's what you think?"

"I'm here," Tam said, "because I don't want to die. The same reason all these people are here. It's just they're all scientists and they dress it up in high-toned bullshit about universal access to the fruits of the human intellect and other crap. When I got here, I couldn't believe the groupthink. These people need someone to give them a reality check."

"Lucky they have you," Iceweasel said, without managing to keep the sarcasm out.

"They are, actually. But now they've got this, all bets are off. Your girlfriend is going to lead the charge to give those two mercs cold sleep. Why not? If you can 'upload' them first"—she made finger quotes—"what's the harm if they end up vegetables? This is save-game for wannabe Frankensteins."

Iceweasel decided she didn't like Tam. "What do you want from me?"

"Once the campuses got bombed, everyone nontechnical left the campus, except me. That made me the only person who hadn't been indoctrinated by science-ism. Now there are two of us. If those two mercs in there are enemy soldiers, we can execute them. If they're not, we can let them go. But stealing their minds and then performing medical experiments on their bodies is not an act of mercy, and you and I are the only people in this place who are cognitively equipped to debullshitify their dumb-ass consensus that the thing that happens to be most convenient is also the most moral."

"Could we do this at another time? I'm—" She broke off and scrubbed her eyes. "We're about to bug out, which is what you want, right? This fight of yours, it's not mine. I've heard your opinion and I don't know if I'm convinced—"

"That's because not being convinced lets you do the easiest thing—not fighting with all these nice people who are your friends and have let you do fun, rewarding work playing nanny to a post-human upload. Probably the most meaningful thing that could happen to someone from your background. No offense."

Back in default, Iceweasel was a ninja master at telling people to go fuck themselves. Her years in walkaway had destroyed her skill set. It was the fear of seeming stuck up, the sense of being an outsider. "I don't want to have more of this conversation, thank you, good-bye."

"You had a chance. Remember that when they call you a war criminal."

## [vi]

Tam was right about the mercs. The news that Dis was running—the fact that you could wander up to any screen and converse with her—settled any question about the mercs. When word got around that they would be sedated, uploaded, and deadheaded, she got a sick feeling. But she made herself attend. They converted the cavern to an operating theater. Iceweasel realized the coffin-like machines she'd ignored since her arrival were brain-imagers. She watched the comatose Walkaway U crew get inserted into their maws. Sita whispered a commentary about interpolating simultaneous scans, their clever noise-reduction, the de-duping process that made storing and modeling it manageable. Iceweasel was annoyed by, and grateful for, the distraction.

Deadheading was easier than she'd expected, taps fitted to their IVs, the infographics showed their metabolisms spinning down until it was barely distinguishable from death.

*That's what the fuss is about.* But these two were their crew, comatose, no prospect of recovery. The mercs—she hadn't learned their names, though she thought CC had, because he was thorough—were capable of walking out on their own. Could it be worse to put them into suspended animation than to kill them? What kind of fucked-up ethics put execution on a higher moral plane than pausing-out someone's life?

The low ceiling was claustrophobic. All the people crammed in together. *Some of them are spies.* It was only logical. *Some of them think I'm a spy.* Also logical.

Underground living left her in a state of drifting unreality and unmoored circadians. She had probably missed sleep. Or slept too much. She was often surprised to discover that she was gnawingly hungry, sure she had just eaten.

The mercs waited on their hospital beds, infographics regular. They'd been unshrink-wrapped and sluiced clean of shit, tucked under white sheets. They were deep under, the kind of general anesthetic trusted by paranoid WU survivors. They scanned the man first. It was fast. They wheeled over the woman, the one who'd spoken. The one who'd told them to get it over with.

She had parents. People who loved her. Every human was a hyper-dense node of intense emotional and material investment. Speaking meant someone had spent thousands of hours cooing to you. Those lean muscles, the ringing tone of command—their inputs were from all over the world, carefully administered. The merc was more than a person: like a spaceship launch, her existence implied thousands of skilled people, generations of experts, wars, treaties, scholarship, and supply-chain management. Every one of them was all that.

She felt vertigo. What business had the walkaways thinking they'd just *wing it* when it came to civilization? The zottas weren't anyone's friend, but they had an interest in the continuation of the civilization whose apex they occupied. These scientists, weirdos, and jobless slackers weren't *qualified* to run a planet. They were *proud* of their lack of qualifications. It was plausible when they were harvesting feedstock and putting up buildings and cooking for each other. Now they were putting a stranger's body into a machine that was supposed to record her *mind,* and they were going to bring her body to the brink of death. They did it without law, without authority, without regulation or permit. They were *winging* it.

The room tilted. She stepped back. Gretyl caught her. She'd subliminally known Gretyl was there, smelled her familiar smell, sensed her bulk. Gretyl's big arms went around her waist and she surrendered, leaning back into her bosom. Gretyl's face was at the place where her throat became her shoulder, breath passing through the pores of the long-wearing refu-suit she'd put on when she left on her rescue mission. She rinsed it out when she remembered, but it hardly needed it. The breath warmed her.

"You don't need to watch this."

*Yes I do,* she thought. Now CC prepared to deadhead the mercs, holding up the vial he would administer to the lab cameras, fitting it to the IV feed, squeezing the valve to start the flow. All actions he'd performed moments before on comatose members of their crew, but different. This was a Rubicon they crossed for all walkaway. When this became public knowledge, the world would change for everyone they knew. She was there, and she did nothing to stop it. Would anyone?

Tam watched raptly. Her expression reminded Iceweasel of the intense concentration of trying to attain an elusive orgasm. It was sexual, a mixture of recklessness and transcendence. Transcendence, that was it. Other adventurers had dabbled, fretted about venturing into the jealous realm of the gods, but walkaways fearlessly burst from mortal into mythical.

Tam watched. Iceweasel watched, Gretyl's breath hot on her collarbone, hair tickling her cheek. Iceweasel had conversed with a dead person who had returned from the grave and need not ever die again, who might copy herself millions of times, be able to think faster and broader than any human. She shivered. Gretyl squeezed tighter.

"I need to go." She hadn't planned to say it aloud, but did.

"Let's go, then." Gretyl's hand was small and damp. The air crackled.

They kissed as soon as they were beyond the crowd. The kiss had built for a long time. Iceweasel had kissed many people. Some she'd loved, some she'd been indifferent to, some she'd actively disliked and had kissed them and more out of boredom, confusion, or self-destruction. She kissed Seth so many times she forgot how to feel his mouth as separate from her own, so that it became no more erotic than smacking her lips. She'd kissed Etcetera properly good-bye, with the crackle of a really good kiss more charged because she did it in sight of Limpopo, stared at her while she did it, and when she was done, Limpopo kissed her just as fiercely, but with ironic detachment: *this is how adults do it*.

Kissing Gretyl was something else. Partly it was that she was older than anyone Iceweasel had kissed. She was also different in her presence, her bulk and mass, the frank brilliance of her mind and her studied indifference to her body's relationship to other bodies. How many times had Gretyl boldly watched Iceweasel undress, catching her eye, not looking away? How many times had Gretyl undressed before Iceweasel with equal boldness, arranging her huge breasts like she was moving around the pillows before settling into bed?

Their bodies pressed, Gretyl's yielding, and Iceweasel couldn't get her arms all the way around her. She clutched at Gretyl, and Gretyl's strong, soft arms pulled her. Her thigh pressed between Gretyl's legs at the hot softness like fresh bread. Gretyl's hand twined in her hair, turned her face with irresistible strength. Her mouth worked at Gretyl's, tongue dancing on her lips, her teeth, and Iceweasel let herself moan and surrender.

Gretyl's other hand kneaded her ass and brought her closer still. Iceweasel felt so small, as if she was a plaything to be pushed and prodded into the places where Gretyl wanted her, and she welcomed it. *In love, there is always one who kisses and one who offers the cheek.*

It was a thing that Billiam liked to say. Billiam and she had hooked up now and again, all that crew had, in an aggressively detached way that they weren't supposed to take seriously, and all of them ended up being in perpetual heartbreak over. Billiam thought she was cold, a product of her foofiness, and knew the accusation drove her crazy with self-loathing. He'd never say it when she turned him down, oh no. Not a way to manipulate her into fucking him. No, he said it when she *did* fuck him, especially when she was attentive. "In love, there is always one who kisses and one who offers the cheek," in his ha-ha-only-serious tone as she let her tongue trail lazily around his nipple, the residue of his cum burning on her lips. She knew he meant she was the one who offered the cheek, that whatever her ministrations, it was about her, not him.

Billiam's memory rose in her mind and wouldn't go. The last time she'd seen him, in the blaring chaos of the Muji factory, head caved in and blood around him, Etcetera's panic as he went through the motions of pointless first aid. Billiam, his little aphorisms and his ways of getting inside her head, but who cried after they fucked, who had done the craziest, bravest things of them all. He snuck over the border at a Quebec Mohawk reservation to meet upstate New York bio-cookers for starter cultures for their beer. He always made sure they had a getaway plan, counted heads whenever they ran out ahead of the law, once going back to help a kid with a twisted ankle. They barely knew the kid, it was her first action, and she'd been a pain, helpless on the sidelines watching other people do the work, then complaining no one told her what to do.

They'd all hated her, but Billiam went back and carried her even though she had fifteen centimeters and ten kilos on him. They were nearly caught, and she'd never thanked him or come back again. That was Billiam.

She'd left him bleeding on the floor. He'd died. Her dad told her that later. He knew about their relationship. He had dossiers on her friends, social graphs describing their relationships. He'd hinted that he knew which were rats, selling information to cops and corporates, which she'd assumed was headfuckery, but was plausible enough that it was impossible to fully trust anyone in the group.

She'd left Billiam to die. If he'd lived just a few more years, he'd have gone walkaway. He could have been with her. He could have his head in the scanner. He could be immortal, as she would be, soon.

Salt tears and snot ran into her mouth. Gretyl gently put her hands on

Iceweasel's cheeks and stared into her eyes with her big, liquid brown eyes, like depths of melting chocolate.

"We could be dead in an hour. Or any minute. And that"—she jerked her head toward where the mercs were being deadheaded—"that's something else. Then there's this," she said, and kissed her so softly it felt like she'd passed a paintbrush over her lips. "Death, sex, immortality, and immorality. Crying is okay."

"There was a friend of mine," Iceweasel said. "Dead." She drew a shuddering breath, couldn't let it out. It was trapped in her chest with her words.

"We're all thinking about our dead. We left dead behind in the fire. That crowd in there has the fever. That Tam didn't have a chance. No way they were going to slow down, certainly not because they might be remembered as monsters by default. When they think about how the future will remember them, they're imagining *being there in person* to defend their honor."

"It's crazy," Iceweasel said. "I can't even think about it."

"We've had longer to get used to it. We walked out of default because we were working on this and were terrified and excited by how the zottas treated it like the holy grail. It's impossible to escape your environment. You can be a spocky lab-coat, but you can't help but feel like whatever's got zottas scared and excited is scary and exciting. Whatever they want has to be important."

"You know that they're just psychos, right? Not geniuses. They've got no special talent for making the world perfect, or figuring out the future. They're just good at game-rigging. Con artists." She thought about her dad, school friends, their pretense to noblesse oblige and refinement. How they'd herd-mentality into some fad but pretend it was a newly discovered, ageless universal truth—not product cooked up by one of their own to sell to the rest. That was the amazing thing: they were in the business of making people feel envy and desperation over material things and exclusive experiences, but were just as susceptible to envy and desperation.

"The reason they're so good at making us desperate and selling us shit isn't that they're too smart to get conned. It's because they're extra-susceptible. They understand how to make us turn on one another in envy and terror because they're drowning in envy and terror of each other. My dad knows the guy in the next yacht is a bastard who'd slit his throat and steal his empire because *my dad* is a bastard who'd slit that guy's throat and steal *his* empire. This immortality shit? That's not about all of them living forever, it's about just one or two living forever, being deathless emperor of time."

"You know more about them than I ever will, Icy, but we don't want to hoard immortality, we want to share it. To *viralize it*. People who know they can't die will be better people than people who worry about the end. How could you blind yourself with short-term thinking if you're planning life everlasting?"

All the billions who'd died. Every one the apex of a pyramid of resources, love, thoughts no one else ever thought before and would never think again. If you have it in your power to end slow-motion genocide, what kind of monster would you be *not* to do it? What price was too high? She knew that this was dangerous thinking, the kind people died and killed for. Tam wanted her to stop things because Tam couldn't make herself stop things.

It was too late. Iceweasel couldn't help herself, either.

---

When it was all said and done, there wasn't much they wanted to take with. They broke down Dis's cluster with her supervision; she ran a commentary on her subjective experience of the slow shutdown, retransmitted in realtime to other campuses, researchers, hobbyists, dying people, spies, and gossips. It was part of a dump of *everything,* all the notes and source code, optimizations and logs. It was time to uncloak. They would hit the road with a *lot* of fanfare.

Iceweasel filled the trike's cargo pods with the essentials, the brain-imaging rigs and the redundant storage modules. They were on the fringes of walkaway network, and the scans they'd made were too bulky to fully mirror. Instead, they were divided up in a redundant swarm among the WU crew, everyone seeding their parts out to denser parts of walkaway as quickly as physics allowed, but for at least a day, a single well-placed strike would wipe out the only five people who had been scanned by CC with the certainty that they could be brought back to life someday.

The most difficult things to carry were the people themselves. Not just the four deadheads, but *all* the people. They marched in a long column through the woods towards the B&B. Iceweasel was sure she wasn't the only one thinking about the efficiency of upload, the sweet nothing of deadheading. If they were deadheading, they wouldn't have to play out the idiot conversion of sunlight to flora, flora to fauna, fauna to energy, energy to muscular action. They could just lie down, get stacked like cordwood on the back of the trike—they'd ended up wrapping the four deadheaders in cocoons of bubblewrap; they stuck flexible duct-tubing into the mass as it puffed up, creating fresh-air tunnels to their faces.

Better than stacking like cordwood: if they uploaded, they could fit into someone's pocket. That person could ride a bicycle or a horse or just jog, and they'd go along with her. Someday, they would transition to beings of insubstantial information, everywhere and nowhere. Someday, they'd stop for a scan before they went out for a swim, just in case they drowned.

"Colds," Sita said. "If we do bodies, people will use upload to shake off colds."

"How?" Iceweasel asked from atop her trike, its gentle humming rumble numbing the insides of her thighs.

"Simple," Sita said. "Take a scan, get a new body out of storage, decant the data into it."

Iceweasel snorted. "Then what? Push your old body into a wood chipper?"

"It's feedstock," Sita said. "Put it to sleep and don't wake it. If you're sentimental, have it mounted. Or make a coat, or cook it for dinner."

"You realize there's a whole default that thinks that's what this is about," Iceweasel said. She'd grown certain there were spies in their midst. She spoke carefully, with the sense she was being recorded and any failure to speak out when jokes like this arose would be held against her. Tam's talk of war crimes trials roiled in her hindbrain.

"You realize they're exactly right," Sita said. She smiled, stopped. "You know, when the first walkaway prostheses projects started, most of the people contributing had lost an arm or a leg in Belarus or Oman, and were tired of paying a loan shark for something that hurt and barely worked and could be remotely repossessed by an over-the-air kill-switch if they missed a payment. But once they got here and started living, realized how much had been left on the table by conservative companies that didn't want to get into a patent fight and didn't see any reason to add advanced functionality to something that you didn't have any choice about, they got radicalized.

"They stopped saying 'I just want to make an arm that'll get through the day,' and started saying 'I want an arm that does everything my old arm did.' From there, it was a short step to 'I want an arm that's better than my old arm.' And from there, it was an even shorter step to 'I want an arm that's so outrageously awesome that you'll cut off your own to get one.' That's what's coming to immortality. Not just the ability to come back from the dead, but the ability to rethink what it means to be alive. There's going to be people who decide to deadhead for a year or a decade, to see what's coming. There'll be people with broken hearts who deadhead for twenty years to get some distance from their ex. I'll bet you that someday we'll look around and discover that all the kids are short for their age, and it'll turn out that they'll all have been deadheaded by their parents whenever they had a tantrum and were missing ten percent of their realtime."

Iceweasel shook her head. "Stuff just doesn't change that much. Most people will be doing the same thing in twenty years they're doing now. Maybe in one hundred years—"

"You're going to hate to hear this, but you're too young to get it. Anything invented before you were eighteen was there all along. Anything invented before you're thirty is exciting and will change the world forever. Anything invented after that is an abomination and should be banned. You don't remember what life was like twenty years ago, before walkaways. You don't understand how *different* things are, so you think things don't change that much.

"When I was your age, we didn't have abandoned zones or free hardware designs. People without a place to stay were homeless—vagrants, beggars. If you worried about zottas, you went to protests and got your head knocked in. People still thought the answer to their problems was to get a job, and anyone who didn't get a job was broken or lazy, or if you were a bleeding heart, someone failed by society. Hardly anyone said the world would be better if you didn't have to work at all. No one pointed out that people like your old man were LARPing corporate robber-baron anti-heroes of dramas they'd loved as teenagers and they required huge pools of workers and would-be workers under their heel for verisimilitude's sake.

"If you'd been deadheading for twenty years and woke today, you'd think that you were dreaming, or having a nightmare. Sure, eighty percent of the people who were alive then are alive now, and eighty percent of the buildings around then are around now. But everything about how we relate to each other and places we occupy has changed. They used to think everything got changed by technology. Now we know the reason people are willing to let technology change their worlds is shit is fucked up for them, and they don't want to hang onto what they've got.

"The zottas want to control who gets to adopt which technologies, but they don't want to bear the expense of locking up all walkaways in giant prisons or figuring out how to feed us into wood chippers without making a spectacle, so here we are on the world's edge, finding our own uses for things. There's more people than ever who don't have any love for the way things are. Every one of them would happily jettison everything they think of as normal for the chance to do something weird that might be better."

Iceweasel considered the perfect storm of her father's intolerableness, Billiam's death, Etcetera's words, the growing sense that shit was fucked up and shit, a phrase that everyone used as a joke. It wasn't a funny joke but people told it all the time.

Ha ha, only serious.

What would it take for her to upload? When they got to the B&B, they'd set up the imager, and anyone could get uploaded, make a scan of themselves—or "themselves, within the envelope that could tolerate being reanimated in software." Would she get in? She'd like to talk to Dis about this. She caught herself. She wished she could talk to Dis about this? Didn't that mean that Dis was a person? Didn't that settle the question?

She rolled on, steering the trike through the woods, the train of cargo-carts bumping along behind her.

---

They were nearly at the B&B when everyone's interfaces buzzed and let them know that they'd safely uploaded all five scans to walkaway net, and they were being seeded all over the world, as unkillably immortal as data could be. Everyone relaxed. Their knowledge that immortality was real was only hours old, but they were already terrified at the thought of permadeath. They joked nervously about how quickly everyone could get scanned when they'd unpacked at the B&B.

They went into hyper-vigilance—some took stemmies to help—and unspoken fear spread. Death came in two flavors: realdeath, and "death." But until they got to the B&B, the only flavor they'd get was permadeath. Fear became terror. They spooked at shadows. CC and Gretyl both broke out less-lethals they'd taken with them. They hadn't told anyone they were doing it, and there'd have been a fearsome debate if they had. No one raised an eyebrow now.

They were so close. Iceweasel knew this territory, had walked this train on scavenging runs for the new B&B as its drones identified new matériel to speed it into existence.

Watching the new B&B conjure itself had been a conversion experience, a proof of the miraculous on Earth. They'd walked away from the old B&B when those assholes had shown up, and pulled a new one from the realm of pure information. That was their destiny. Things could be walked away from and made anew; no one would ever have to fight. Not yet—they couldn't scan people at volume, couldn't decant them into flesh. But there would come a day that Gretyl had spoken of, when there would be no reason to fear death. That would be the end of physical coercion. So long as someone, somewhere, believed in putting you back into a body, there would be no reason not to walk into an oppressor's machine-gun fire, no reason not to beat your brains out on the bars of your prison cell, no reason not to—

The drone overhead made a welcoming sound. The B&B had sent its outriders for them. She looked at it and waved. It dipped a wing at her and circled back.

"Getting close," she called out, and then the enemy charged out of the bush, with a machine roar. There were eight mechas, the sort that they'd built to manage the B&B's trickiest assembly tasks. These might have been the same ones. They stood three meters tall, holding their pilots in cruciform cocoons, faces peering out of the mechas' chest cavities, eyes shrouded in panorama screens that timed refreshes with the pilot's saccades and load-stresses of the body to provide just-in-time views of wherever the suit's action was. Each one could lift a couple tons, but had fail-safes in place to stop them from hurting humans. Turning that shit off was only a firmware update. There were plenty of places in walkaway where mecha-wrestling was a sport with big fan bases.

They went for the cargo-containers first, upending them and methodically bending their wheels so they would never roll again. Iceweasel leapt clear as the front-most pod upended, taking the A.T.V. with it, and hurt her shoulder and ankle when she sprawled to the forest floor.

Gretyl hauled her to her feet, her face a mask of terror. Gretyl grabbed her by her sore shoulder, making her shout. That attracted the attention of the nearest mech-pilot. The huge body turned toward them. Mechas could turn quickly and their arms were fast enough to drive a shovel into frozen ground with pinpoint accuracy, but they couldn't run, because their gyros needed time to stabilize after each step, so that they walked in a bowlegged stagger. The mecha took one step toward them, the pilot rocking in his cradle. He—she saw a russet beard poking around the head-brace, teeth behind the peeled-back lips—rolled with the mecha, and something about how he did it made her think that he didn't have a lot of experience.

Gretyl let go of Iceweasel's shoulder and wrestled a shitblaster. Iceweasel stepped quickly out of her way as she prodded its back panel, struggling to keep the array of coin-sized bowls pointed in the right direction as they shaped a pulse of infrasound, tuning it up and down through a range of resonant frequencies, hunting for the one that would—

The driver tried to pitch forward, but the mecha couldn't bend that far without keeling over, so it locked him in a thirty-degree bow, like a sulky kid after a forced performance. The bottom half of his face—beard, lips, square teeth—twisted. The shitblaster didn't just make your bowels loosen, they did so with cramps that were between childbirth and cholera.

Gretyl panted. Iceweasel hauled her out of the mêlée's center. Three mechas were converging on them, having wrecked the wagon. Iceweasel and Gretyl were nearly knocked over by people running away from them, people she recognized but not quite. They ran, colliding with more people. It was panic.

"I've got to—" Gretyl said. The rest was lost, but Iceweasel knew what it was. She and CC were the only ones who could fight—she looked around, saw CC aiming his weapon at a mecha, watched the owner lose consciousness, saw two of their own nearby drop to their knees, clutching their heads and screaming. The pain-ray made your skin feel like it was on fire, and the shaped infrasound rattled your skull and caused deafness and near-blindness.

Half the mechas were incapacitated, the rest waded through the crowd, and Iceweasel watched in horror as they stomped through her crewmates, flinching as their arms swung to counterbalance their drunken stagger, expecting at any moment that those arms would cave in skulls or pick people up and hurl them into the treetops.

But no, Iceweasel saw, the mechas were . . . escaping. Running for the bush, right past people, and that meant—

"Shit, we have to go," she said to Gretyl. "*Now*!"

The drone was back, and for a moment her panic morphed it into a big, missile-carrying craft like she'd seen in the videos of the destruction of WU. But it was only the familiar B&B drone. She blew a plume of stale stress and limped for the trees. "Come on, everyone, come on!" She dragged Gretyl, sneaking glances at the drone, thinking of her B&B crewmates, watching and chewing their nails, retransmitting to the rest of walkaway, even to default, where the spectacle of an unprovoked attack on a column of scientific refugees might shock the conscience of the public beyond the ability of spin-doctors—

The B&B drone nosedived. Her interface surfaces died. Three more drones—sleek, with low-slung missiles and dishes for high-energy electromagnetic pulses—screamed past, a supersonic boom following them. They disappeared over the horizon and there were screams in their wake, panic redoubled as the crew headed into the trees, running in blind panic. They'd seen the missiles.

Iceweasel and Gretyl hovered at the woods' edge, tracing the contrails in mute horror as the white streaks bent into *L*s that became *U*s as the drones executed precise rolls in formation, corkscrewing upright and doubling back.

Iceweasel squeezed Gretyl's hand. Gretyl squeezed back. Cool detachment settled over her, like she was being tucked in fever bed by a lover's hand.

"It was worth it," she said, thinking of the people who would never die again, of Dis, who would shortly be conscious, who would remember her as someone who had helped cure the most terminal disease of all.

"It was," Gretyl said. "I love you, darling."

"I love you, too," Iceweasel said. "Thank you for letting me help."

They watched the drones draw closer.

## [vii]

The missiles went over their heads into the woods where the mass of the crew hid. Iceweasel understood with her detachment that the drone operators would use thermal and millimeter wave to choose targets. Hiding in the woods was about as effective as pulling up the blanket to escape the bogeyman.

The second round airbursted a hundred meters behind them. The woods roared with flames, the sound almost masking the screams. The drones shot past again, headed for another impossible turn at the horizon's edge.

The drones were nearly upon them when, out of the iron sky, five missiles came directly *at* them, seemingly from nowhere. Three hit, fireballs and then thunderclaps, a few seconds later. The other two missed and disappeared from view. Gretyl and Iceweasel craned their necks, and then they saw it: a huge, silent, cigar-shaped zepp, one of the bumblers from the golden age, the sort Etcetera heaved nostalgic sighs for. Its emergency impellers keened as it held its position, tracking the drones as they passed, and then, as they circled, it neatly shot them out of the sky with another volley of counterdrone missiles.

The zepp dipped and spiraled toward the pathway. Once it was ten meters off the ground, it dropped ladders and ziplines and people poured out, clutching first-aid gear and spine-boards, wearing fireproof suits. They ran for the woods and Iceweasel and Gretyl ran with them, without discussion, hot knowledge of salvation coursing through them, firing new reserves of energy.

They labored in the woods for hours, searching, getting the wounded and the dead onto stretchers and into the sky. More people joined them, then more, and when Iceweasel ventured back to the path with a stretcher crew, there were dozens of B&B vehicles on site, from mechas to cargo-bikes, running in relays to bring the wounded back.

She helped load an unconscious person—she saw with a shock it was CC, rainbow hair charred, face and chest a mass of burns—and stood. The other stretcher-bearer turned to her and took her hands, looked into her eyes.

"Iceweasel, hey, Iceweasel?"

It was Tam, sooty and exhausted, and worried. Iceweasel wanted to put her at ease, didn't want to be a burden, so she tried to say, *It's okay, let's go help some more*—but nothing came. She was alarmed to feel tears slipping down her cheeks. She tried to shake off the feeling, but it wouldn't shake. Some part of her she could not dial down by pinch-zooming an infographic had been shattered and was floating jagged-edged in her mind's soup.

"Why don't we take a break, huh?" Using pressure on her shoulder—pain flared and she gasped—Tam sat her on the ground and hunkered down. "You're in shock," she said. "You'll be okay. I think you should get evacced, get warm and clear, get some liquids."

"Gretyl—" she said.

"Yeah, Gretyl. That old girl's probably crashing through the woods like an angry rhino. Nothing'll stop her. But she'll worry about you, huh?"

Iceweasel nodded. She didn't want Gretyl to worry. But she also just *wanted* Gretyl there, a solidity to rest her head upon, touch of her fingers in Iceweasel's hair. The rumble of her voice, heard through the pillow of her breasts. She didn't want to go without Gretyl. She shook her head.

"I'll wait for Gretyl," she said.

"I hear you, buddy, but that's not an option. Not a smart one. Come on, Iceweasel, you know the deal with shock. Warmth, rest, elevated feet. You're covered in sweat and panting like a chihuahua."

Iceweasel knew she was right, felt cold sweat on her face, but still—

"Gretyl."

"Come on, girl, no one's got time for this. There's enough casualties out there. We don't need another." She looked around, didn't see Gretyl, uttered a heartfelt "*Shit.*" She straightened up, waved at someone. "Hey! Come here, okay? Yes! Come here, will you?"

"You okay?" said a familiar voice. She looked at men's legs in purplish tights, split-toed boots like martial-arts shoes. The toes were armored with beaded, overlapping layers of something moisture-shedding, like dragon scales.

"I'm okay, but she's in shock. She won't evac because she's worried about her friend. I could probably drag her, but I should find her friend and let her know what's happened, or she'll go crazy."

"Well, she always was loyal to her friends." The person belonging to the legs squatted down and peered into her face.

"Hey there, Natty," Etcetera said.

"Hubert Vernon Rudolph Clayton Irving Wilson Alva Anton Jeff Harley Timothy Curtis Cleveland Cecil Ollie Edmund Eli Wiley Marvin Ellis Espinoza," she said. She'd made a game out of memorizing it, their first weeks as walkaways, reveling in its extravagance. It came out in a singsong.

"That's *not* your name," Tam said.

"Call me Etcetera," he said.

"And call me Iceweasel," Iceweasel said. "Natty's long gone."

"And good riddance."

"Fuck you," she said.

"Let's go, Icy," he said, and helped her to her feet. Her leg had gone to sleep, her injuries had stiffened. She leaned on him.

"Gretyl," she said, over her shoulder, to Tam.

"I'll tell her," Tam said.

"Thank you."

"Want to ride in my zeppelin?" Etcetera said.

"That thing is fucking insane," she said.

"Saved your ass," he said. He guided her to a stretcher and she let him wrap her in a blanket and strap her in. He buckled into a harness and grabbed one of the stretcher's guy-lines and gave it a sharp tug and they rose into the air.

---

The cold wind on her face as they ascended snapped her into lucidity, but the ascent was slow and rocking, and it lulled her back into a doze that she barely broke when they brought her into the zepp's belly and Etcetera transferred her to a spot on the floor of the gondola. She rocked her head lazily and saw that there were many others, including CC, lying motionless. He had an IV drip in his arm and sensors dotted over his burned body. She felt bile rise in her throat and turned her face to the other side in time to retch the sparse contents of her stomach.

Her feet were elevated, so the puke rolled over her face and into her hair. She'd squeezed her eyes shut when she vomited, and the lower one was now slicked with bile. Someone daubed at her with a towel, and she felt ashamed. The hands were sure, and she cracked her upper eye and confirmed it was Etcetera.

"We've missed you," he said. "Seth's been moping like crazy."

She smiled, but it came out as a grimace. "I missed you, too," she said, but in truth she hadn't. The realization startled her through her shocky daze. Why hadn't she missed them? It was getting clear of who she'd been and the last threads tying her to default and her father and her zotta-ness. Though she hadn't made any secret of her background on campus, they hadn't seen the nest she'd inhabited with her father, ridden in his armored car, experienced his mighty influence.

"Where did you get this insane gasbag?"

He looked around. "Dream come true, isn't it? After the zepp bubble popped, there were a couple hundred bumblers that were more-or-less skyworthy, rotting in hangars. Someone got the idea of throwing Communist parties in the hangars, and then there was a whole airworthy fleet. Aviation authorities are going crazy, a bunch have been grounded, but the ones that made it to walkaway seem safe for now. This one showed up at the B&B a couple weeks ago, craziest crew you ever met, walkaway freaks who lived through the bubble, same as me, and can't believe that they've finally got a zepp. They call this one *The First Days of a Better Nation*."

She groaned. Such a walkaway cliché—she could imagine the crew, studied air of walkaway purity. She found that hard to be around because it reminded her so much of herself, back in the days when she'd been the token foofie of her Communist party crew.

He had a damp cloth, and he wiped the puke best as he could. Gentle ministrations from a familiar hand were overwhelming in so many ways, a sad-happy-lonely-homecoming feeling like the touch of the mother she'd hardly known. "What if they send more drones?" she said.

He shrugged. "We're just about out of countermeasures. Certain death?" He looked at her searchingly. "But not for long, right?" He looked away. "Is it real?"

"Uploading?" She coughed. Her mouth tasted sour, her throat burned. "Depends on what you mean by real. I have a friend who's done it, you'll meet her if we survive. She can explain better than me."

"First days of a better nation," he said, with oversaturated irony.

"Or a weirder one," she said. She felt for his hand and he squeezed hers.

"We'll be okay," he said. "Weird or not, we're clearly scaring the shit out of your dad and his people, so we're doing *something* right."

"Fuck my dad. And his people."

"Well, yeah." There was a jolt and he nearly lost his footing. The whine of the impellers, felt through the decking, changed. "We're going home." He squeezed her hand. "Jiggity jig."

## [viii]

Gretyl found her in the onsen, sitting in the hottest pool with Limpopo, who had diagnosed her need for a lot of water. Gretyl was with Tam, who radiated body-shame and discomfort with nudity. Iceweasel realized how little thought she'd given to the special problems of being a woman with a penis, and how smugly she'd assumed that walkaways were so bohemian that it would all be simple.

She teetered on the precipice of self-doubt and her certainty that she was slumming and no one should take her seriously. The hot water felt claustrophobic and painful as her concentration slipped away and her stupid body wanted her to pay attention to it. Her face sheened with sweat.

She got out of the water and went to Gretyl. Her hair was scorched and one of her arms was covered in gauze dressing. As Iceweasel stood, her bad hip and shoulder came free of the water and the cool air made them throb with a suddenness that made her stumble. Gretyl caught one of her arms and Tam caught the other.

"Hi," she said, weakly. Limpopo exhaled, closed her eyes, put her head back and sank in to her ears. Gretyl drew Iceweasel close, and when Tam moved away, she slung a big, muscular, freckled arm around her and brought her into the embrace.

Despite all the skin, there was something chaste about the onsen, or so Iceweasel told herself, as she remembered the kiss, the dry-humping she and Gretyl had done in the underground campus, and made herself pretend her stomach muscles weren't jumping at the feeling of Gretyl's breasts on hers.

Then there were Tam's breasts on her side, her face in the crook made by Gretyl and Iceweasel's faces, her penis brushing against her thigh and making her stomach muscles jump again.

"Get your friends into the water and make some introductions, girl," Limpopo said, not opening her eyes.

They disentangled slowly, then, on impulse, she squeezed Gretyl to her, kissing her cheek, jaw, earlobe. "I'm so glad you're here," she said, smell of burned hair in her nostrils.

"Me too, kid," she said, and stepped gingerly into the water.

---

They took a long time to immerse themselves, everything complicated by Gretyl's burned arm, and by the time they were settled, Limpopo reached her limit and stood and stepped out. She fetched a pail of ice water from the coldest pool and brought it to the edge of theirs, wiping herself down using her small towel. Gretyl was oblivious, surrendering to the water, but Tam watched with caution and Iceweasel watched Tam.

"How many casualties?" Limpopo said, after Tam caught them up on the story of the last of the evacuation.

"Three dead," Tam said, in a flat voice. "CC didn't make it."

Iceweasel was numb. She had carried CC's charred body. Now it was dead.

"Lots of injured, too," Tam said. Iceweasel got out of the pool. She wanted to cry, but tears wouldn't come. She crossed her arms and leaned her head against a wall, breathing into her diaphragm. "I'm okay," she said, as she heard someone—Tam?—start to get out of the pool. "Give me a minute."

Tam and Limpopo talked, but she tuned them out, focused on her breath and the hot/cold play of air and water on her body. A finger tapped her shoulder and she grudgingly looked up—at Seth.

"Hail the conquering heroes!" Then, showily: "For I am become worlds, destroyer of death!"

She smiled despite herself. He was such a dick, but he wasn't a bad guy. "That's good, Seth. Did it take you long to come up with?"

He shook his head. He was naked and goose-pimpled, and she found his body—so recently familiar to the point of being dull—was fascinating, in the way of things that were once freely taken and are now forbidden. "I stole it," he said. "Some dude's manifesto out of San Francisco. Those Singularity freaks in the quake-zones, they're having *religious* feelings. It's quip-city on their hangouts. That was my favorite. Amateurs plagiarize, artists steal."

"You stole that from Picasso," she said.

"Did I? I don't think so. I haven't read any of his books. I must have stolen it from someone who stole it from him."

She didn't rise to the bait, though she noticed her campus friends look up. She knew Seth's game, and didn't want to play. She was glad to see him, but she and Seth had played enough for one lifetime.

She heard Tam leave the water, looked up to watch Tam help Gretyl out, felt an unwelcome jealous stab, saw Seth notice. Seth couldn't get past his scenester instincts, and he was a keen observer of relationships. She saw his eyes flick down to Tam's cock, up to her breasts, back up to her face.

"Need some help?" he said, taking two steps their way, offering a hand to Tam, who was off-balance, leaning over to get Gretyl out without wetting her dressing. Tam took his hand. He gave her his winning smile, which was, in fact, fucking winning. When they'd gone walkaway, Seth had been in the incipient stages of beer-gut-itis. Rebuilding the B&B, all the walking and lifting, the anti-shlepper challenge of going into the woods with nothing and relying on the drones and your wits had leaned him out and given him tree-trunk quads and broad shoulders that went well with his mat of tight-curled chest hair. Iceweasel found her own scenester spidey-sense as Tam took him in with an up-and-down sweep, click-click-click, and she felt more unwelcome jealousy. Stupid brain. She wished for an infographic she could sweep her fingers along to banish petty thoughts.

Limpopo sidled over. "How about the warm pool now?" It was the temperature of a cup of tea left out for twenty minutes, the kind you could sit in and socialize. Limpopo was suggesting that they have a nice, civilized chat.

"Great," she said, and let Limpopo lead her.

They took up station at opposite corners, arms draped over the edge. Iceweasel looked over her left arm, the dark bruise and scrapes. The hot water and the cool air made it glow a vivid pink. It ached distantly.

The rest of the party eased in, sending the water level up so little waterfalls cascaded out into the drains. Seth was very solicitous of Gretyl, who regarded him with detached amusement as he fussed, darting to offer her a hand. Iceweasel got the impression that some of this was for her benefit, but that much more was for Tam's, and possibly Limpopo's.

It was striking how the presence of a man changed so much about their dynamic, made it about invisible lines of attention. She shrugged, winced at her shoulder, switched her gaze to Gretyl, felt that slow curling low in her belly again. It was scary, the feelings that came up when she looked at Gretyl. Gretyl looked back at her, skewered her on her frank stare, and a shiver raced from her toes to her hairline. Gretyl's stare said *You're mine* and *Will you be mine?* at the same time. Strong/weak. Soft/firm. Like Gretyl, big arms and muscular back, round soft belly and huge, soft breasts.

"CC was backed up," Tam said, breaking in.

Well of course he was. He was core to the project.

"Were the others?" She realized she didn't even know the names of the dead, assumed if Tam hadn't told her the names they must not be people she was close to, but who knew with Tam?

"No," she said. "They weren't." She looked angry.

"But CC was."

"Yeah," she said. "CC was. Is. There's already a group who're putting the cluster together, using whatever spare compute-time they can get out of the B&B."

Limpopo sat up, twisted from side to side, showing them the top edge of her burn. "We've got a *lot* of compute power here," she said. "Been running the workshop twenty-four/seven to produce new logic ever since you left, Iceweasel. I thought it might come to this, and we had feedstock." She smiled a private smile. The old B&B had collapsed right on schedule, about a month before Iceweasel struck out, dissolved in acrimony, and Limpopo had taken undisguised satisfaction in picking through the remains of her sullied creation—but some of the schadenfreude wore off when she came to the places where blood had dried on the walls. The actual fights were never published by the meritocratic crew, but the ugly messages, accusations, and name-calling that led up to them were. Supposedly, no one had died, but if someone had died, they hardly would have advertised the fact.

Tam nodded. "I heard that. I want to see what happens with this when we're not resource-constrained. The cargo all got in, right?"

"Yeah," Limpopo said. "It was hard without the mechas."

Iceweasel thought of how the mechas trashed the A.T.V. and its cargo-pods. "*Were* those mechas from here?"

"Yeah." A storm passed over her face. Iceweasel had hardly ever seen Limpopo mad. It was scary. "A pod of mercs and an infotech goon pwned everything using some zeroday they'd bought from scumbag default infowar researchers. They took over the drone fleet, and while we dewormed it, seized the mechas."

"Is the B&B network safe?"

Limpopo shrugged. "That's a bitch, huh? Maybe they put deep hooks in that we'll never find. We've done what we could, checked checksums against the backups and known-good sources. The zeroday got sequenced and patched damned quick, since it affects the main branch, all the way up to UN refugee camps where a billion people live."

Gretyl whistled. "Shit," she said. "Can you imagine the bad stuff you could do with an exploit against the whole UNHCR net?"

Limpopo and she shared a look. "It's every UNHCR admin's nightmare. We've never had better cooperation with them. They patched in an hour, across their whole base, but there's other downstream projects like ours that may be vulnerable to total lockout or HVAC shenanigans that could burn them down."

The two women's faces were in near-identical serious configurations. Iceweasel nearly laughed. But the realization that they were alike in so many ways stopped her. There'd been moments during her years with the B&B where she'd felt jealousy for Limpopo and Etcetera's romance, and she'd assumed it was to do with Etcetera. Now she wondered if it wasn't Limpopo. Gretyl was a larger-than-life Limpopo, bigger in every physical and emotional way. The realization made her forget about the implications of their discussion.

Tam brought her back. "How much of the certainty that the network's okay is wishful thinking?" She was the one who said what everyone else thought and didn't want to say. "We're going to bring Dis online, right? Then CC? Maybe those mercs, why the fuck not. None of us want our friends to be dead until we can toast a whole new set of CPUs, right?"

Seth splashed. "That's telling them." He loved shit disturbers. Not to mention other things about Tam.

Limpopo said, "There's that."

The water felt less welcoming and the atmosphere got less social.

## [ix]

Dis was everywhere. The B&B crew couldn't get enough of her. They touched in to speak to her all over the building. Even with all the compute-time, she had to queue them, calling them as they walked in the woods or lazed in the common room.

But she always had time for Iceweasel.

"How's CC coming?" Iceweasel said.

Dis didn't have a blinking cursor anymore, but Iceweasel still could read body language into her pauses. This one was awkward. "Not good. I've been trying to talk him through, but he doesn't want to stabilize. With me it was a matter of finding the possibility space where I could deal with being a head-in-a-jar. It may be that CC doesn't have that subset."

"What? It's CC! He loves this stuff! It's what he lived for! That's like a rocket scientist with a fear of heights!"

"I don't know a lot of aerospace dudes, but one reason to get into uploading is your overwhelming existential terror at the thought of dying. It's not a discipline you'd chase if you were uninterested in the subject."

Iceweasel tried to learn to relax. The B&B didn't need that much work to keep going. A chart making the rounds in their social-spaces showed how if everyone put in an eight-hour shift every three days, they'd have double the hours they needed. One crew was ideologically committed to doing nothing, creating a "safe space" for "post-work." She understood. Sitting on her ass, especially in public, made her feel guilty. Unworkers were moral cover for people experimenting with doing SFO for a day or a month (or a year).

She sat on a lounger on B&B's lawn, a big field of sweet-smelling wild grasses with a thriving biome of critters that rustled and soared around it. She had Dis in both ears, but her system was smart enough to mix in wind-through-grass sound, things chasing each other, yin-yang of breezy aimlessness and panicked scrambling.

"How long before you can stabilize CC?"

Another micro-pause. Dis had lots of compute-time. The pauses had to be deliberate. She'd ask Gretyl—comp-sci was a mystery to her, despite hanging around the university crew.

"Don't know if I'll be able to. When I figured how to stabilize myself, I concluded I'd be able to apply the technique to every sim. But I'm a data-set of one. People are idiosyncratic. *I'm* idiosyncratic. Maybe I'm a rare exception and no one else will do what I've done."

"That's not what you said—"

"It's what all the people who know what they're fucking talking about are saying *now*. Everyone else is running around shouting, 'Death is cured! USA! USA! USA!'"

"This is Canada."

"Yeah, but you sound stupid chanting 'Ca-na-da!' It's easy to get excited when science actually does something, because science is failing and taking notes. We want to get a 'breakthrough,' but not everything is a breakthrough. Sometimes, it's just a tiny step forward. Or a dead end. I'm trying to bring CC up, but maybe the only way to wake him is in a state so distorted that he's not recognizable. I've modeled using me as a template and mixing our models one bit at a time until we get to a hybrid, with just enough me in to keep him alive. There's no clean way to do that. Nearly everything I tried modeled out to nothing recognizable as either of us. Interesting as that is, I have no urge to make insane, immortal synthetic personalities out of thin air. We've got enough fucking weirdos."

"What about everyone else? The other researchers?"

Dis made a rude noise. "There were real fuckups in Madrid, who brought up a version of me, tried to make me help them. That copy suicided, after sending messages to all the other groups, telling them about the evil shit going down. But Madrid's the only lab that's succeeding in bringing a sim up into a stable state. I've been thinking of giving everyone else permission to experiment with bringing versions of me online, creepy as that is. Seems it might be the only way of getting anywhere. Science is lumpy. Success sometimes follows success, but sometimes you get mold in the petri dish over the weekend and spend your life trying to figure out what just happened."

Another pause.

"I'm guessing there's a ton of instances of me running in default. Zottas and their lab-rats wouldn't have any problem with that. Used to drive CC nuts, the sense that they added our research to theirs, but we never saw what they made of our work. But every time we had any success, their lab-rats were tempted to go walkaway and join us, because everyone wants to work for winners. So at least all my twins are acting as irresistible temptation to fire your boss and hit the road."

"Do you wonder if you're in a default lab, being tricked about the world around you?"

Computerized laughter. Gretyl said Dis had had a really weird laugh in life. The bizarre computer laugh was a faithful rendition. She must have been as weird as shoes on a snake. "No way. Too many Turing tests to pass. I'm conversing with all of you all the time. They could fuck with my ability to detect whether I was conversing with a bot or not, but that would also make me too stupid to be helpful. I'm as sure that I know what's sim and what's reality now as I was when I was meat-alive. Call it ninety-five percent."

"What's the other five percent?"

"An old A.I. not-joke. In the future we'll figure out how to simulate everything, so we will. There will be a lot more simulated universes in the whole history of the real universe than there will be real universes. So it's more likely that you're a sim than real, whatever real means."

"My brain hurts."

"Don't worry, when we simulate you, we'll ensure you're in a state that's comfortable with the idea. Ha-ha-only-serious. It's like Meta, being like this. Sometimes I dial back and watch the lookaheads, see how close I am to the edge of full panic. It's interesting to tweak that shit in realtime. You haven't known freedom until you've experienced cognitive liberty, the right to choose your state of mind."

"I'm looking forward to it."

"You're being sarcastic, but seriously, not being embodied is awesome. If the clone stuff they're doing in Lagos works out, I'll be the first to jump back into a body, but I'll miss this. There's something pure about it. It's much simpler than psychotherapy, and more effective."

"Unless you're CC."

"Different strokes for different sims." She could make the computer-voice sound smug.

Iceweasel found being a head in a jar dangerously compelling then. It would be wonderful to dial back her anxieties, match her intellectual knowledge that no one was waiting for her to show her true zotta colors with emotional certainty that everyone knew she was a fraud. If she went to therapy to make that match happen, she'd be lionized for her self-knowledge, but if she took a drug that did it, she'd be escaping reality. She wondered how people would think about sims who dispensed with drugs and therapy.

"I can't stand just sitting," she muttered, looking at the worknots, proudly lazing. "I need to *do something.*"

"We also serve, who sit and fart." It made Iceweasel smile.

"Of all the things I thought when I went walkaway, I never anticipated chatting with a potty-mouthed simulated neuroscientist."

"I'm a real neuroscientist."

"You know what I mean."

"I'm going to start a program of micro-correcting people searching for correct adjectives to describe dead immortal simulated artificial people like me."

"Don't you have some research you should be doing?"

"I'm doing it, running a long lookahead for this conversation and branch-stemming/pruning to find paths to ongoing dialog. Trying to simulate what you were doing when I kept suiciding, before I stabilized. I'm back-forming hypotheses from my transcripts and trying them on you."

Iceweasel squirmed. "Why?"

"I want to generalize a data-driven solution to cheering people the fuck up. I could apply it to sims like CC."

"This isn't cheering me up."

"I think it is."

Iceweasel felt a moment's software-like introspection. "Okay, I am cheering up a little."

"Good. Noted." The computer voice assayed a German-like diction: "Lie down on ze couch und tell me about your parintz."

# [x]

Gretyl and Iceweasel poked their noses around the rooms where the university took place. The small rooms on the top floor were commandeered by research teams, who crammed three to five people into them, hacking different models. Most of them were working on CC's sim, because CC had been beloved, and they were freaked by the possibility that the scientist who'd known and done most on simulation, was secretly too freaked to be brought back. If he couldn't come back, would any of them?

Other people wanted to use those rooms. The scientists' work lost some of its urgency as the days stretched. There was talk of renovating the ruins of the original B&B as a new campus, a hint to stop hogging the good stuff.

The university crew didn't give a shit.

"Why should they?" Gretyl said, as she and Iceweasel tapped fruitlessly at a surface, looking for a private place to chat. "Let's walk, it's nice out for a change." A week of shitting-down frozen custard and hail had finally passed by. Weak sun poked from fluffy clouds in a sky that showed signs of blue.

They hunted through the bench-boxes for rubber boots that'd fit, pawing through cataloged moop. Seth invited himself along. Tam was with him, which didn't surprise Iceweasel. She knew they'd hooked up, though they weren't publicly encoupled. They'd been very close in cuddle-puddles, stretching the definition of "cuddle" in a way that was mild bad taste in walkaway (though it was common).

"Come along," Gretyl said. "We're escaping the grim reality of walkaway to be carefree wanderers in the virgin woods."

"Fifth-growth ex-tree-farm," Seth said. "Heavy-metal contamination and a subsiding gravel pit."

"Come on, sunshine. Get boots on or we'll miss your expert commentary."

Tam had boots for her and Seth. They struggled into the knee-high Wellingtons and set off.

The walk was relaxing, birdcalls and volatile vegetation smells from the warming forest. But Seth was unable to relax. He punned, ran ahead and got lost, sang rude songs.

"What is your boyfriend's problem?" Gretyl said.

Tam sighed. "I'm not going to confirm the 'boyfriend' part."

"Okay, but what's up his ass?"

Tam looked sidelong at Iceweasel. Iceweasel often wondered what Tam thought of her. She and Seth had never been official, just an indefinitely drawn-out hookup. Even though love wasn't a game and there were no points, she'd definitely won her round with Seth, going without a backward glance, while he'd been moody when she split, sending jokey-stupid email to the underground campus. He'd hardly caught her eye since her return. She thought he and Tam had a lot of conversations about what a total bitch she was. Boys did that. They didn't know when you told a girl that she was less crazy than all other girls, she knew that when you split, he'd tell the next one about what a crazy cow *you* were.

"Is it me?"

Tam's eyes widened. "Not at all! He's cool with you. He seems really, uh, happy on the romantic front." She blushed, out of character for her.

Iceweasel laughed, and Gretyl's chuckle was *dirty,* which made Iceweasel laugh harder even as she squirmed. "That's good. Seriously." They smiled at each other. Tam had been right about deadheading, had been the only other nontechnical after the attack. It was an unspoken bond and distance between them.

"It's this." She waved an arm around.

"Canada?" Iceweasel said.

Gretyl said, "Walkaway?"

"The countryside. He misses cities. He's been reading about Akron, getting ideas."

Akron kicked off as she was leaving for the WU campus. Walkaways did a coordinated mass squat on the whole downtown, 85 percent of which was boarded up and underwater, the bonds based on their mortgages in escrow with the Federal Financial Markets Service in Moscow while the Gazprom meltdown played out. They'd flown under the radar, smooth and coordinated. One day, Akron was haphazardly squatted by homeless people, the next, a walkaway army reopened every shuttered building, including fire stations, libraries, and shelters. Factories turned into fabs, loaded with feedstock, powered by eggbeater fields that sprung up overnight, electrolyzing hydrogen from sludge flowing in the Little Cuyahoga River, feeding hydrogen cells that walkaways wrestled around in wheelbarrows.

Default was caught off guard. Connecticut flooding had FEMA and the National Guard tied up. The contractors who backstopped FEMA couldn't use their normal practice of hiring local talent as shock troops. By the time they mobilized, their entire recruiting pool was walkaway.

It gave the Akron walkaways—they called themselves an "ad-hoc," said they were practicing "ad-hocracy"—a precious week to consolidate. By the time default besieged Akron, they were a global media sensation, source of endless hangouts demonstrating a happy world of plenty salvaged from a burned husk with absentee owners.

Iceweasel said, "It's exciting."

"More than exciting. It's a *city*. Not a village or a camp. The first, but not the last. They're fighting over Liverpool now—Liverpool—and Ivrea, somewhere in Italy, and Minsk, which is fucking crazy because the little Lukashenkos would happily behead them and hang their guts around the central square. You might have missed it because things have been insane around here, but it's kicking off out there."

Gretyl made a face Iceweasel recognized as polite disbelief and said, "It is very exciting."

Tam knew that face, too. "Gretyl, there's more than the stuff happening in the campuses. People who aren't scientists can also get shit done."

Limpopo said, "Engineers, too, right?"

Tam folded her arms.

"Kidding. I've followed it. It's exactly the kind of thing we fantasized about ten years ago, before we had the *word* 'walkaway.' But there've been other attempts. There's a reason walkaway stuff tends to be a building or two, a wasp's nest wedged in a crack in default. Anything over that scale goes from entertainingly weird to a threat they can burn in self-defense."

Iceweasel nodded. It was the calculus they'd made when planning Communist parties, the sweet spot between something big enough to matter but not so big it'd get stomped.

"Anyway, our young man has it in his head that we should pull our own Akron. Not walkaway: walk *towards*. Fuck, *run* towards."

Limpopo snorted. "He's going to get himself killed. They'll *nuke* Akron before they let us keep it."

Tam's quick anger surprised Iceweasel. "Seriously, fuck that. The point of walkaway is the first days of a better nation. Back when that was more than an eye roll, it was a serious idea. Someday, walkaway and default will swap places. There's not enough people who own robots to buy the things the robots make. We're ballast." She glanced at Iceweasel, maybe for backup, and not indicating the sort of person who wasn't ballast.

Limpopo's angry retort: "I've heard all about better nations. There's stuff that's serious, like they were doing in the university, that gives us power to truly walk away, even from death; and there's grandstanding bullshit like seizing cities. The *very best* thing I can say about Akron is it might distract default's armies from us. I think there's an even chance the news that we're taking cities *and* storming the afterlife will give them cover to hunt us down like dogs."

They would have said more, gotten angrier, but Seth charged through the brush with a sloppy grin, gamboling like an oversized dog. She didn't like dogs.

"What'd I miss?"

They looked away. He shook his head, more dog-like. "It's a wonderful day to be alive! Look at that sky!"

There was a boom, more felt than heard; a roar, a wave of hot air that picked them up and hurled them into the trees.

## [xi]

When they got back, the B&B was in flames. It seemed the fire was everywhere, but it became clear it was centered on the stables and the power plant. A fire in the hydrogen cells was supposed to be impossible, they were engineered for five kinds of fail-safe, the design was so widely used that flaws were quickly spotted and fixed. Judging from the wreckage, though, they'd gone up.

The inn was also on fire, but seemed under control, water coursing out of windows where automated systems had kicked in. It was Iceweasel's third disaster in weeks, and there was a curious doubling feeling as she took in the infirmary, the mechas stomping in and out of the burning building with armloads of salvaged gear.

"Shit." Limpopo snapped into motion. Iceweasel watched in awe. Limpopo took in the same details in an eyeblink, but while Iceweasel had been frozen, Limpopo was spurred into motion. She jogged to the infirmary, head swiveling. Her presence was enough to call three of those tending the injured to her. She gestured forcefully at the blaze from the stables and all nodded and moved, shifting the wounded further away. The blaze intensified in seconds. Now she was heading for a mecha pilot and—

"Come on," Gretyl said. "Let's go help."

Iceweasel was grateful to be told what to do.

---

They lost it all. For a while, the fires were under control, just a little mopping up to extinguish the last flames in the inn, but as they swapped power-cells in the mechas and brought up new hoses, there was a fresh explosion from the back, another concussion wave and then flaming debris. They had congregated on the front lawn or they would have all died.

The B&B's drone outriders scouted surrounding territory, bridging network service over the holes in the mesh left behind by the fallen B&B. Fed by their intelligence, the B&B crew fell back and back again, heading west, towards the built-up outer perimeter of default, where the wilds ended and Toronto began. It was the least hospitable direction to go, but there was a hamlet up the road where the *Better Nation* could tie off. The zeppelin crew threw everything into the impellers, though bumblers were not supposed to be steered except in emergencies. This qualified.

There were no deaths. It was miraculous, but Limpopo had a theory: "I think the bombers lost their nerve. The stables went up during their maintenance cycle, when there'd be no one there. The power plant went up ten minutes later, plenty of time for everyone to be on the lawn, staring at the stables, far from the blast. The inn's explosives, going off *hours* later? Either we're dealing with a terrorist who sucks at timers, or they wanted to be sure of minimal casualties. It's what you'd do if you wanted to convince your bosses you'd been a good little mad bomber, but didn't want too much blood on your hands."

"Limpopo, it's been a long day and you've been amazing," Iceweasel said. They were huddled in a tent, seven in a sleeping space intended for two, rain thudding on the tent's skin overhead and lashing at its sides. They'd made camp right in the middle of the road, using the highway's cracked tarmac as a base. The road was domed, just enough to provide drainage into the choked ditches on either side. The insulating cells on the tent floor rucked up over the dome's apex, crinkling like bubblewrap when they moved. They were dead tired, hungry, and hurt, but no one in their tent was going to sleep anytime soon.

"But that sounds like bullshit. The university got attacked by mercs, and we got hit by mercs again on our way back. Why assume these bombs were set by double agents? *Sentimental* double agents? Ask yourself if it wouldn't make you *happier* to imagine the bad guys were blackmailed into infiltrating us, but found us so wonderful they couldn't bring themselves to kill us?"

A scary flash of anger on Limpopo's normally calm face. Iceweasel had been pleased when Limpopo joined their tent, anointed the cool-kids' club by her presence. When Limpopo's eyes flashed, it was like being trapped with a dangerous animal. She pulled back, and, to her embarrassment, whimpered. Limpopo mastered herself.

"That is not entirely stupid. It's hard to know when you're kidding yourself. Figuring that out has been my life's major project. But." She turned and listened to the wind lash the tent, touched the cool fabric. "Okay, yeah. Maybe they wanted us on the road and they're sending a snatch-squad for anyone who understands uploading for real. Maybe they knew the B&B had real-time monitors that would make them look like monsters if there were a lot of bodies, but if they kill us out here, they can shove us into the ditches and—"

"I get it," Iceweasel said. She couldn't stand anymore. The self-recrimination after meeting the campus crew had finally given way to fear. It was almost a relief to be tortured by something external, rather than her internal nagging voice. Gretyl had a tattoo around one of her biceps that read FEAR IS THE MIND-KILLER, but as far as Iceweasel was concerned, her mind could use some killing.

She wished she and Gretyl could be alone. Something about being enfolded in Gretyl soothed her in a deep place, switched off the voice that knew all her weaknesses. She'd never had that, not with boys or girls. Sometimes she'd had fleeting moments of peace after fucking, but with Gretyl, it came easily, even without sex.

As the voice liked to remind her, the psychology of falling in love with an older woman when your own mother all but abandoned you wasn't difficult. All the peace Iceweasel got from being engulfed in Gretyl's embrace led to wondering whether she was giving Gretyl back anything in exchange.

She *really* wanted some time alone with Gretyl.

Limpopo slumped and Iceweasel saw something even rarer than Limpopo's anger: exhaustion. "It may be self-serving bullshit that living walkaway will soften the hardest heart and convert pigopolist despoilers to post-scarcity Utopians, but it keeps me going, sometimes. Part of me wants to stay up doing forensics on the B&B's log files, finding the sellout, but the rest of me wants to live with the fantasy of unstoppable moral suasion. I know we don't need everyone in the world to agree for this to work, but there's got to be a critical mass of covered-dish people or we'll never win."

"Okay." Gretyl broke her silence—she'd been prodding the screen in a way that radiated leave-me-alone-I'm-working (Gretyl was good at this). "What's a 'covered dish' person?"

"Oh. If there's a disaster, do you go over to your neighbor's house with: a) a covered dish or b) a shotgun? It's game theory. If you believe your neighbor is coming over with a shotgun, you'd be an idiot to pick a); if she believes the same thing about you, you can bet she's not going to choose a) either. The way to get to a) is to do a) even if you think your neighbor will pick b). Sometimes she'll point her gun at you and tell you to get off her land, but if she was only holding the gun because she thought you'd have one, then she'll put on the safety and you can have a potluck."

"Game theory," Gretyl said. "That's the stag hunt. Two hunters together can catch a stag, the top prize. Either hunter alone can only catch rabbits. Both of them want to get stags, but unless they trust each other, they'll have coney surprise for supper."

"I didn't know there was a name for it. Good to know. Once things have settled, I'll have to do some reading. When things go bad, the stag is rebuilding something better than whatever's burned down; the rabbit is huddling in a cave in terror, eating shoe-leather soup, hoping you don't die of TB because there aren't any hospitals anymore. I've always thought the whole walkaway project was a way to turn people into covered-dish types. There's not any reason not to be one when we can all have enough, so long as we're not fucking each other over."

Iceweasel smiled for the first time in a long time. "Put like that, it's beautiful."

Limpopo didn't smile back. She looked too exhausted to smile. "I'd settle for plausible. Once you've been a shotgun person for a while, it's hard to imagine anything else, and you start using stupid terms like 'human nature' to describe it. If being a selfish, untrusting asshole is human nature, then how do we form friendships? Where do families come from?"

"You're assuming that families aren't about acting like selfish, untrusting assholes," Iceweasel said.

"The fact that your family is so fucked up is not proof that being fucked up is natural—it's proof that shotgun people rot from the inside and their lives turn to shit." She closed her eyes. "No offense."

"None taken." Iceweasel was surprised to discover it was true. The words were liberation, a framework for understanding what had made her, what she could become.

"Limpopo," Gretyl said, "you look like chiseled shit. No offense."

"None taken," Limpopo said with a ghost of a smile.

"What would it take to make you sleep?"

Limpopo shrugged. "I don't think I could at this point. I've gone through sleep and come out the other side."

"I think that's macho bullshit," Gretyl said. She moved around, asked some others to move, rearranged packs and bags until there was a Limpopo-shaped space on the floor. "Lie down." She patted her hands on her lap.

Limpopo looked from her to Iceweasel, the others, shrugged. "I'm not going to fall asleep, you know. It's not that I don't want to, it's just—"

"Silence, fool. Lie down."

She did, her head settling into Gretyl's lap. She locked eyes with Iceweasel, a nonverbal "Is this okay?" and Iceweasel smiled and stroked her greasy hair, a tousled short mess of spun sugar in pink and blue. They'd been in plenty of cuddle-puddles, but that was different. She and Gretyl locked eyes, they shared a smile. Her fear melted. Miraculously, it was not replaced by self-doubt. The rain, the breathing, the dim light, the cozy closeness made her feel, against all odds, safe.

Gretyl tilted her head at one soft shoulder and Iceweasel shinnied around until she could rest her head on it. Gretyl put an arm around her and she put an arm around Gretyl, and the three women were quiet.

---

They rendezvoused with the *Better Nation* at sunset the next day. Limpopo watched the crew descend on tether lines and harnesses, toes grazing the ground. There was a brief moment of excited reunion as they related their adventures to one another. Etcetera was right in there, regaling his buds with tales of their near-death, oohing and aahing as the aviators recounted their own experiences with drones, chaff, weather, and infowar harassment.

The *Better Nation* had been tethered in deep Mohawk territory, and had been generously resupplied with venison, corn, chapatis, and ice cream in amazing flavors from rose water to marzipan. Some Mohawk kids came along for the flight, not quite walkaways, but certainly not default. They stuck together and looked on solemnly as food sizzled on the grills the aviators set out and more crew touched down. Then one of them—a girl, with long straight hair and a loose-fitting t-shirt with the word LASAGNE in huge letters across it—stepped out of their tight pack. She wandered over to the grill to kibbitz, and Tam, who was cooking, cracked a joke Iceweasel couldn't hear, but made the girl smile so radiantly it transformed her into something out of a painting (or maybe a stock-art catalog: "Smiling indigenous woman, suitable for brochures on diversity policy") and the two groups merged.

The medical contingent oversaw lifting the wounded into the zeppelin. They discussed the deadheads who'd been cargo and scientific curiosities for so long it was hard to think of them as "wounded" (for the mercs, "wounded" was certainly not the word). Iceweasel saw Tam head to the caucus that was discussing the issue over huge ice-cream cones, and she ambled over.

"What happens to the injured is a lot less important than what happens to those two mercs. They *must* be kept safe."

Limpopo rocked her chin from side to side. She'd gone for a swim in a creek nearby and was looking enviably fresh and rested, and, frankly, beautiful. Tam had also gone for a dip and her hair was braided into a pair of thick Pippi Longstocking pigtails that hung to her breasts, like schematic arrows pointing out a salient feature.

"I get that the fact that those two are with us is bad publicity, but there are bigger priorities—"

Tam shut her up with a sharp hand wave. "You don't get it—that's *totally* backwards. The *reason* it's bad publicity is what we did is *monstrous*. Now we fucking own them, so we *owe* them. Once you take a prisoner, they're your responsibility. Not just legally, but morally. We started down a path we can't escape. If it was up to me, we'd thaw them and set them loose—"

"I don't think we *can* do that safely." That was Tekla, a med-type who'd served with CC on the deadheading project. "Not after everything they've been through. We need a full lab and controlled experiments before we attempt it or they could end up vegetables. I think we'll be able to bring up their sims before we're ready for that, ask them what they think we should do with their bodies. That seems only fair—"

Tam made her two-handed, furious wave. "Are you *kidding*? Where'd you study before you went walkaway? Mengele U? Scanning those two without consent was terrible, bringing their sims up and making them decide whether to risk their lives—"

"Not their lives," Limpopo said. "Their bodies."

Tam's mouth snapped shut and she visibly got herself under control. "They have never accepted that the part that matters is in that sim. They've never been given that choice. Maybe we can bring them up into a state like the one that Dis was in, so they don't care about the difference, but without their consent, that's brainwashing. Unforgivable, monstrous brainwashing."

Limpopo looked up at the undercarriage of the zepp overhead, the multistory gondola, bottom covered in cargo hooks, sensor packages, and gay illustrations of androgynous space-people dancing against a backdrop of cosmic pocket-litter: ringed saturnesques and glittering nebulae. She, too, was on the verge of snapping. Just like that, the carnival atmosphere vanished.

"Let's get them on the blimp," Limpopo said, ignoring the rule about never calling it a blimp, only a zeppelin. No one corrected her. She looked tired again. She turned and walked away.

---

The *Better Nation* lowered down a supply of hexayurts that they put up with practiced ease, glomming some together to make communal sleeping areas. More rains were coming and the aerialists would have to bumble to beat them. Their weather-conjurers predicted a drift toward the maritimes, possibly as far as Nova Scotia, and they solicited supplies, gifts, and letters for anyone they met on the way. The scouring of their meager possessions to find gifts restored some of their cheer, a moment of delight in abundance, and the renewed idea that there was always more where that came from, an end to scarcity on the horizon.

Some of their crew went with the aviators, accompanying the deadheaders. Some of the Mohawk kids, including the girl (who called herself Pocahontas and dared anyone to give her shit) joined the B&B crew. When Iceweasel shyly asked her why she stayed, she shrugged: "Want to live forever. Isn't that why we're all here?"

Seth, who overheard, put his arms in the air and shouted *amen!* and they laughed.

They walked.

Iceweasel found herself with Etcetera and Seth. She looked at them and remembered that impossible time when they'd met at a Communist party, and thought about self-replicating beer and poor Billiam, about her father—it had been ages since he'd last sent an email; she never answered them—and her sister and mother, and default, all that had become of such a short time.

"Amazing, isn't it?" She twirled to take it in, feeling young and beautiful in a way she'd lost track of. "Who the fuck are *we* to decide to walk away, to make a better society?"

"I know who *I* am," Seth said. "You're a rich girl I kidnapped with terminal Stockholm syndrome. This douche bag is Hubert Vernon Rudolph Clayton Irving Wilson Alva Anton Jeff Harley Timothy Curtis Cleveland Cecil Ollie Edmund Eli Wiley Marvin Ellis Espinoza."

"Needs more bananapants," she said.

Etcetera smiled. "You can call me Bananapants if you want." He hugged her and the hug wasn't precisely brotherly, but it was more brotherly than not, and to the extent that it was not, there was sweet nostalgia for when they'd flirted like crazy, and she'd had that push-pull feeling of not being precisely interested, but being kind of reassured that he'd been interested in her. Funny how complicated it had been in default, when they only played walkabout, weekend bohemians. Once she'd stopped pretending she was normal, it got easier.

"Guys," she said, her tone unexpectedly serious. It was a serious time. "I want you to know—" She looked from Seth to Etcetera, back again. They'd been aged by walkaway, but it gave them gravitas. A moment of lensing time let her see them as strangers, how rakishly handsome they were. She smiled. Her affection felt like molten chocolate. "I just love you both, okay? You're good. The best."

Neither knew what to say. Seth was trying for something smart-assed. Etcetera tried to figure out what this meant in the great scheme. She could almost hear their thoughts. Before either could say something stupid, she gathered them into a hug, reveling in their familiar smells. Their arms tangled, then found their way. The hug went on and on.

When they undocked, Gretyl and Limpopo were standing by, grinning like proud parents. She and Gretyl had scored a private hexayurt for the night, and she'd felt low-grade, anticipatory horniness ever since she learned they'd be alone. Now, with the boys in her arms and Gretyl looking on with Limpopo—so fucking hardcore and so hot, she'd had a low-grade crush on her for years—her horniness spiked with toe-curling intensity. She laughed at the sheer physicality. The boys laughed along, though who knew why. She was no longer inside their heads. That was okay. They were walkaways, and god help them, they'd figured out how to live as though it were the first days of a better nation, and she was going to get her brains fucked out that night. The world was good.

---

The sex was everything she'd hoped for and then some. There'd been a moment beside each other, legs tangled, hands working furiously, eyes locked, when she'd experienced time-dilation that would have been scary under other circumstances, a moment that literally felt like an eternity, and when it crescendoed with an orgasm that made her legs kick like a galvanized frog, she'd been disappointed to see it go.

Then they talked in the way of lovers. In the way of lovers, what began as murmurs about one another's beauty and prowess, with strategic kisses and snuffling each other's scents, a walkaway from everything suddenly veered into the default of life among the walkaways.

"It's a nice idea, but it's ultimately childish," Gretyl said. "The idea that there's no objective merit. You can believe that if you do something *qualitative*. But in math, it's easy to see who's got merit. There's no sense in pretending every dolt is Einstein in waiting."

"Einstein failed math," Iceweasel said quickly. Einstein came up a lot in discussions like this.

"That wasn't math, that was arithmetic. People who can do sums in their head aren't doing math, they're just calculating. No person will ever calculate as well as the dumbest computers. It's a party trick. Arithmetic isn't math. Knowing which arithmetic to do is math."

Iceweasel sighed. The science crew treated the B&Bers with patronizing amusement when the subject came up, but she'd assumed her Gretyl was on-side.

"No one can do science on her own, right? Look at what Dis and CC did; it was such a team effort, everyone had to contribute, and even with all that, we don't know if we'll get CC back."

Gretyl rolled on her side, let one of her small, clever hands trail down Iceweasel's body from chin to pubis, resting on her thigh. No lover had touched her that way. It made her shiver. Gretyl had such a powerful hold on her. It scared her, in a good, sexually charged way. When Gretyl worked on her, face fixed in an expression of extreme concentration, she experienced absolute surrender.

Now Iceweasel moved her hand off her leg. The discussion was serious and she wanted to have her wits about her. Limpopo had explained it so clearly. She didn't want to let her down.

"We were all needed for the upload project. There are others around the world who are also indispensable. But not *everyone* is indispensable. Look at what you did for Dis, keeping her spirits up and distracting her. You were very good, but there are others who are just as good. If you hadn't been there, someone else would have done the job.

"Now take Dis. She was *indispensable*. We couldn't bring her back without *her*! We're in different fields, but I follow hers closely. There likely isn't anyone else in the world who can do what she does. She is literally one of a kind. I'm not one of a kind—I'm good, but at the end of the day, I'm an applied mathematician with pretenses to pure math. There are pure math people who spend ten years contemplating the algebra necessary to prove the topological equivalence of a coffee cup and a donut. Wizards from another dimension. Your people are all fighting self-serving bullshit, the root of all evil. There's no bullshit more self-serving than the idea that you're a precious snowflake, irreplaceable and deserving to be treated like a thoroughbred, when there are ten more just like you who'd do your job every bit as well. Especially when you're supporting the one person who really *can't* be replaced."

"I've heard this all. My dad used it to explain paying his workers as little as he could get away with, while taking as much pay as he could get away with. I told him: he might have an 'indispensable' skill for running the business, but he couldn't do it himself. The reason everyone else shows up to help him isn't because of his magic 'indispensable' skill, either. It's because they need money, and he has it."

Gretyl's jaw worked. "You're assuming that because zottas talk about meritocracy, and because they're full of shit, merit must be full of shit. It's like astrology and astronomy: astrology talks about orbital mechanics and so does astronomy. But astronomers talk about orbital mechanics because they've systematically observed the sky, built falsifiable hypotheses from observations, and proceeded from there. Astrologers talk about orbital mechanics because it sounds sciencey and helps them kid the suckers."

"My dad's an astrologer then?"

"That's an insult to astrologers." They laughed. Some of the tension boiled off of Iceweasel. They'd bonded over talking shit about her dad. Gretyl used him as an avatar of every evil of the system. Iceweasel was pleased to go along with that for her own reasons. "Your dad is like a bloated duke who's hired court astrologers to sacrifice chickens and reassure him that he's the cat's ass."

"You're talking about economists," she said.

"Of course I'm talking about economists! I think you have to be a mathematician to appreciate how full of shit economists are, how astrological their equations are. No offense to your egalitarian soul, but you lack the training to understand how deeply bogus those neat equations are."

Iceweasel stiffened. She knew Gretyl was kidding, but didn't like to be told she "wasn't qualified" to have a discussion, even in jest. She pushed the feeling down, strove to access the part of her that lit up when Limpopo described this stuff.

If Gretyl noticed, she gave no sign: "Your dad hires economists for intellectual cover, to prove his dynastic fortunes and political influence are the outcome of a complex, self-correcting mechanism with the mystical power to pluck the deserving out of the teeming mass of humanity and elevate them so they can wisely guide us. They have a science-y vocabulary conceived of solely to praise people like your father. Like *job creator.* As though we need *jobs*! I mean, if there's one thing I'm sure of, it's that I never want to have a job again. I do math because I can't stop. Because I've found people who need my math to do something amazing.

"If you need to *pay* me to do math, that's because a) you've figured out how to starve me unless I do a job, and b) you want me to do boring, stupid math with no intrinsic interest. A 'job creator' is someone who figures out how to threaten you with starvation unless you do something you don't want to do.

"I used to watch you kids do your Communist parties, when I was in default and pretending any of that shit mattered. I'd get so *angry* at you, beyond any sane response. It wasn't until I walked away that I figured out why: because every time you broke into an empty factory and turned the machines on, you proved I was a plow horse whose poor lips had been scarred by the bit in my teeth as I pulled a cart for the man with the whip and the feedbag.

"That's my point about the difference between the kind of meritocracy we have in the university and the bullshit the zottas swim in. When we say that Amanda is a better mathematician than Gretyl, we mean there are things Amanda can do that Gretyl can't. They're both nice people, but if there's a really important math problem, you're better off with Amanda than Gretyl."

Limpopo's voice ricocheted in Iceweasel's mind. "But Amanda can't do it all. Unless she's working on a one-woman problem, she'll have to cooperate with others. If she sucks at that, it might take a hundred times more work in total to get it done than if Gretyl—who's good at sharing her toys and keeping everyone purring—were the boss. This isn't anecdote—as you keep telling me, the plural of anecdote is not fact. Limpopo sent around this meta-analysis from the *Walkaway Journal of Organizational Studies* that compared the productivity of programmers. It broke out the work programmers did as individuals and inside groups. It found that even though there were programmers who could produce code that was a hundred times better than the median—one percent as many bugs, one hundred times more memory efficiency—that this kind of insane virtuosity was only weakly correlated with achievement in groups."

Gretyl sat up, momentarily distracting Iceweasel with her body. "Explain that?"

"I just read the summary and skimmed the stats and the methodology for smooshing together the different data sets. The tldr is these hacker-wizards who produce better code than anyone were often so hard to work with that they made everyone else's work *worse,* buggier and slower. The amount of time they had to spend fixing that code slowed them down so much, it ate up their virtuosity gains.

"Attempts to put together 'Manhattan Project' teams made from wizards without normal dumb-asses like me showed exactly the same effect.

"They footnoted one study, one I *did* read—an ethnographic survey of projects that went to shit, even though they had brilliant programmers. The authors found there were two major causes of failure. The first was some wizards were colossal assholes. 'Asshole' was what they called it, because the phrase came up from three different teams. It's impossible to work with assholes, even brilliant assholes. 'Don't work with assholes' is great advice, but it's also a *duh* moment, because if you haven't figured that out by your second or third team, you might *be* the asshole.

"The *other* category was when you had wizards who had *no clue* how to work with others. They weren't dicks, they just didn't have the instinct. The authors found teams where the wizard and everyone else *hadn't* failed, and in these cases, it was because there was someone good with people who figured out how to smooth over differences and see how people fit together. These people were wizards of teams, and they made more of a difference to a team's success than a programming wizard."

Gretyl shook her head. "We're still talking about wizards. If the evidence is that the most important kind of wizard is a people-motivating wizard, that's the kind of wizard you recruit. That doesn't disprove the existence of wizards, and it sure as shit doesn't mean they aren't important."

"You're mixing me up, Gret. My point"—thinking *Limpopo's point*—"is even if you have a bunch of wizards, you can't get shit done without other people helping. Everyone is a wizard at something. Okay, not quite. But in any group, there will be people who do things better than anyone else in that group. Some of them will be helpful to the group and some won't. But it would be lonely and shitty if only wizards participated in life. It'd be hard for wizards not to decide, arbitrarily, that their buddies and the people they wanted to fuck were also wizards, to use their supposed indispensability to boss non-wizards around."

"The fact that people are dicks a lot of the time doesn't mean some people aren't better at stuff than others. It doesn't mean those people aren't more important for getting certain things done than the rest of us. It doesn't mean they're more important, just more important for some context. It's fucking stupid, it's delusional to insist we're all equal."

Iceweasel clamped her emotions before she started shouting. "Gretyl." Her voice was measured. "No one is saying we're equivalent, but if you don't think we're *equally* worthy, what the fuck are you doing here?"

"Oh, calm down. Of course everyone deserves respect and all that shit, but in every normal distribution there's stuff on one end of the curve and stuff at the other end. If you ran a math faculty by pretending everyone was as good as everyone else at math—"

"*That's not what I said*!" Iceweasel's cheeks were hot. Tears pricked her eyes. How many fights had she had with her asshole father that featured phrases like "oh, calm down"? How many times had he dismissed everything by talking about the "natural" abilities of his zotta pals, like they were supermen? She was about to say something she would regret. She climbed to her feet, jaws clenched so tight she heard her teeth grinding. She dressed, vision telescoped to a red-tinged black circle. Gretyl said some words. She sensed Gretyl getting to her feet so she bolted from the yurt, wearing her underwear and carrying her shirt and pants, sockless feet jammed into her hiking boots. It had stopped raining and a brisk wind had blown most of the clouds out of the sky, leaving a blaze of starlight and a fingernail paring of crescent moon, vignetted by black dramatic clouds at the edge of the woods. The after-rain smell of ditchwater and pine forest was strong. Her feet splashed through black puddles, cold water sloshing around her toes.

She thought she heard Gretyl behind her, splashing through the same puddles. Part of her wanted Gretyl to catch up, so she could apologize and take back the awful things she'd said. Another part understood her feelings about Gretyl were caught up with her feelings about her father. Any apology Gretyl offered would never make up for the apologies she never received from him.

She made for camp's edge, wanting to be far from humans and wanting to find somewhere to balance on one foot while she finished dressing. She laced up her boots and stood, pulling her shirt off a tree-branch and pulling it on, fighting through the overlapping layers of wicking stuff and insulating stuff and brightly colored rags woven in bands around it, a look she'd invented that many others had flattered her by copying. Suited and booted, she calmed. She ran her hands over the shirt, which looked fucking awesome and was acknowledged as a technical and aesthetic triumph, in which she took enormous pride.

She scrubbed her cheeks with her palms and planted her hands on her hips and looked at the sky. She'd had a lot of summer nights at the family cottage, staring at skies like this, impossibly populated by cold stars that reminded her of humanity's general insignificance and comforted her with her father's specific insignificance. Sometimes, there'd been cousins on stargazing nights, a few she'd felt affection for, and she panged at the thought of them, lost to her, being twisted into the gnarled shape of a zotta mired in self-delusional garbage.

Something snagged her attention, coming up over the tree line. It was the *Better Nation*. As she saw it, she heard it, which was incongruous, because the bumblers were not supposed to run their impellers except for emergencies. It was transport that went where the wind blew, making hay while the sun shone, treating nature as a feature, not a bug. The impellers grew louder—an insect buzz, then a swarm, then a full-throated roar. The *Better Nation* was supposed to be on its way to Nova Scotia.

There was a breeze out of the woods that left her in goosebumps. The hair on her neck stood. She was rooted to the spot, staring at the zepp straining across the sky, twisting to and fro as it fought the winds. It grew faster, and she realized belatedly that it was descending as well as impelling. Her heart thudded in her ears.

"HELP!" she shouted, without meaning to. "HELP THEM!" She smacked her interface surfaces, turning on her cameras and sensors without consciously deciding to.

The sound of her shouts in her ears unfroze her feet. She ran through camp, toward the zepp. She saw black shapes moving through the sky behind it, invisible except where they blotted out starlight. Inaudible over the impellers' whine, a shrill tone of machines laboring beyond their safety margin.

Others were around, aiming scopes at the sky. There was shouting. Cursing. A fan of pencil-thin, violet lasers lit the sky, so bright it hurt to look. They converged on a black shape, tracked it jigging and jagging across the sky. She followed them down to their source, saw three of the university crew frantically plugging hydrogen cells into a rig like a miniature antiaircraft gun on a wide metal plate they weighed down with their boots. She ran to them and stood on the plate, freeing two of them to move closer to the batteries.

The drone in the lasers' path fell. The lasers followed it until it fell below the tree line. Where they briefly touched the trees, the lasers set sizzling fires that smoked but quickly extinguished themselves as nearby shaking branches spilled payloads of raindrops on them.

The lasers retargeted, skewering another drone. As a third one opened fire with small missiles that wove through the sky on cones of flame, they split into two and targeted both drones. In the same eyeblink instant, two of the missiles found the *Better Nation,* one hitting the bag. The other hit the gondola. That one skated its surface and spun out of the sky like a maple key, detonating beneath it, shock wave sending up the gondola's tail. The whole thing shook like it was caught in the teeth of an enormous dog. The missile on the gasbag blew. There was a sound like a thousand balloons popping as the cells bag ruptured in a cascade that swept back and forth across the bag's length. The zepp fell, but it didn't free fall—some of the cells, incredibly, were intact, a tribute to their fail-safes—but it came down fast.

Another drone caught fire and became a meteor. The lasers jumped to the remaining one, but it lifted as the stricken *Better Nation* smashed into camp, plowing a furrow through the roofs and walls of five hexayurts before its nose made contact with the road and it crumpled, the smoking remains of the gasbag settling over it a moment later. The sound—rending noises ending with a tooth-vibrating *crunch*—blended with shouts of dismay and terror. Walkaways swarmed the gondola, using their hands to bend back the smashed fiberglass hull to get at the people inside.

Etcetera ran past with a pry bar, but didn't see her. He was fixed on the *Better Nation,* the zepp crew he'd befriended. The Mohawk kids were right behind him, with tools of their own, hammers and a wrecking bar. She remembered some of their friends had gone up in the airship. She pushed her fists into her guts, somewhere between punching herself in the stomach and massaging it, trying to drive the grief out.

One of the hexayurts that had been knocked down, right at the start, was the one she'd shared with Gretyl. The zepp had only grazed its roof, but the light, composite panels bent, then snapped, leaving the walls to tilt like ancient tombstones. Moving as if in a dream, Iceweasel walked to the yurt, kneading at her stomach. More people raced past her and there was a chorus of explosive bangs, the remaining gasbag cells overheating. She felt the fire's heat on the back of her neck and smelled her hair singeing.

Before going to bed, she and Gretyl had taken advantage of the spacious privacy of the hexayurt to unpack their jumbled gear, squeezing the water out of the wet stuff and folding it carefully, coiling their rope and swapping the cells of their devices. It was still all laid out in the precise, Cartesian grid that Gretyl created, barely ruffled by the fragments of roof that tumbled into it. Next to it was the air mattress, trillions of mezoscale bubbles that filled if you laid the bed out and gave it a few brisk shakes, but deflated easily if you rolled it from one corner.

On the bed: Gretyl, on her side, dressed to chase Iceweasel into the night, like she was sleeping. Between her and Iceweasel, the air wavered with a cloud of steam, and she bent over Gretyl, solarized by the flashlight beam that her computer automatically sent arcing from her chest, without Iceweasel noticing. She reached a hand for Gretyl's shoulder, touching it, then cupping and tugging it, trying to rock Gretyl onto her back. She was dead weight.

There was blood on the bed beneath her head.

Iceweasel tried to breathe three deep breaths. Got to one. Snapped into focus. She bent to Gretyl's mouth, heard her breathing, slid a hand onto her neck and felt for a pulse, encountering blood but not caring. The pulse was strong. She played light over Gretyl, probing with her fingers, starting at her feet and working up, checking each arm, then her throat again, her chin.

Now, at last, she examined Gretyl's head, probing carefully, unmindful of the chaos and bangs. There was a shallow cut on the back of her scalp, bleeding profusely, but small. There was no dent, no pulpy depression like the one that she'd half-seen/never-unseen on Billiam's head. She heard her own breathing, slowed it down, peeled back each eyelid, looking at the contracting pupils, were they the same size? Gretyl blinked, brushing her hands away from her eyelids, leaving behind smears of blood from her fingertips.

Gretyl blinked several times, moved her arms and legs weakly, tried to sit up. Iceweasel held her down. "You're hurt." She spoke into her ear, trying to be calm and comforting.

"No shit. Fuck." She blinked more. There were screams from the crash, and some that sounded nearer. Iceweasel looked into the night, dark and spotted with erratic orange flame-light. While she was distracted, Gretyl sat, shrugging off her restraining hand. She touched her scalp wound, and she stared at the blood on her palm with an affronted scowl. "Fuck this," she said. Iceweasel folded the bloody hand in her own bloody hands.

"Babe, you have a head wound. You should lie down, in case there's a spinal injury or a concussion."

Gretyl stared out, seeming to have not heard; then, "Fine in theory, but I don't think we get to choose tonight. Let's go unfuck this. Help me up." She turned to Iceweasel, stared with an intensity that admitted no debate, shifting her grip to pull her hand. Iceweasel struggled with herself, then pulled. Gretyl staggered, put her free hand to the back of her head, straightened.

"What the fuck is going on?" she said, as she lurched in the direction of the fire.

They were nearly upon it when someone grabbed Iceweasel's arm and yanked. She swung around, hands in fists, eyes wide, heart pounding, sure she was about to be tazed by a merc sent by the zottas to terrorize them. It was Etcetera, his face smudged, eyes panicked. "Come on!" He yanked again, oblivious to the fact that she'd been about to break his nose.

Even with a head wound, Gretyl was faster on the uptake. She yanked Iceweasel's other arm, and they followed Etcetera to another yurt where the wounded lay on air mattresses, lit by pea-sized OLEDs hastily stuck to the walls and casting overlapping crazy shadows. It was chaos, an impromptu morgue, but she saw some were moving, some were attended by people crouching over them. Pocahontas, one arm bandaged, soothed a figure on the ground, a hand on his forehead, other hand holding a screen and concentrating on the readout. Iceweasel supposed she was conferenced in to the pool of walkaway docs who helped with care around the walkaway net, and she wondered how many of these skirmishes they'd dealt with in the middle of the night, lately. She wondered who was crawling walkaway net, doing traffic analysis to find and target those docs.

Before long, she was conferenced into a doc of her own, working with a mercifully unconscious zepp-rider, burned terribly and groaning every time she touched her, following the doc's directions, sometimes asking him to send them as text because she couldn't always understand him through a very thick Brazilian accent. She wondered what time zone Brazil was in, and whether it was the middle of the night there. Presently, another Brazilian doc came on the line and helped her set a broken leg using an inflatable cast from a pack that, ironically, the zepp had dropped off the day before.

She looked up from her patient, who'd been palpably grateful for the painkiller she'd placed under his tongue. Gretyl sat on one of the few empty pads, face in her hands. She went to her, put her arm around her shoulders, kissed her tentatively on her ear, tasted dried blood and smelled stale sweat and scalp oil. Gretyl's thick hair was a mat of blood.

"You okay?"

"Just tired. I ice-packed my head, and someone in Lagos checked me for a concussion and pronounced me bloodied but unbowed. But shit, girl, I feel like I'm about to collapse."

"That's probably because you're about to collapse."

"You think?"

"Lie down. We're almost through. Even Etcetera's taking breaks." He'd been manic, torn between rescuing more aeronauts from the burning wreck and tending the ones they'd gotten out. He'd pulled two dead ones out of the *Better Nation* and wept as he carried them, then tended three more who'd died on the infirmary's mats, helping carry them to another yurt that was now a morgue. Limpopo shadowed him for some of that, so had Seth, helping around the edges, gently calming him before he hurt himself.

"Okay. How about you?" Her voice was thick, groggy.

"What about me?"

"You need a break, too. Look like walking death. I've got an excuse, I'm an old lady with a scalp wound. You're bursting with youth's vibrant juices. When you start to look like a zombie-movie reject, it's a sign for you to take it easy. You can't help anyone if you're not taking care of yourself." She paused. "I know I embody the opposite of that advice, but I've got an excuse: I'm an idiot. What's yours?"

"You're right. I'm going to grab a piss and do a walkaround and I'll come in. Leave room on the mat for me, old timer?"

"I'll use you as a pillow if you're not careful."

"Done deal."

Gretyl tilted her face up and they kissed, and Gretyl kept her mouth closed, which she did when she was self-conscious about her breath, which was darkly hilarious under the circumstances. As ever, Iceweasel kept kissing until her lips parted, and they mingled breath and saliva for a moment that stretched like taffy before she broke off and struggled to her feet, putting one hand on a wall panel, which flexed and bowed, then bounced back when she got her balance.

She glanced back at Gretyl before she ducked through the door, and she was on her side, motionless. Iceweasel squinted until she made out the rise and fall of her chest, then stepped through into the night.

It was coming on dawn, gray with pink on the eastern tree line, black on the western one. Limpopo and Etcetera sat on folding chairs on the roadside, Etcetera holding her and weeping into her neck. Limpopo locked eyes with her; they raised their eyebrows at one another in simultaneous *are you okay?* that made them both smile wearily. Iceweasel tossed her an okay sign and blew her a kiss. Limpopo kissed back and she turned to the dark woods, digging out the paper gauze she'd pocketed on her way out of the tent to use as bumwad. She picked her way through the underbrush, killing her chest-light when it came up, letting her eyes adjust as she sought out the requisite log with a tree nearby to use as a handhold.

She assumed the position and did her thing, listening to the sounds from the camp, the crackle of small things in the underbrush. She should have brought a shovel, but under the circumstances, no one would blame her for a lapse in woodcraft. She'd pack out the bumwad, at least, put it with med-waste in the incineration pile.

There was a louder sound in the brush, not scurrying and small. Big and stealthy. She tugged up her pants, tabbed them closed, peered into the night. She dropped the bumwad, patted her pockets, which had accumulated a litter of small devices and objects through the night. Nothing of use. Disposable wrappers. She looked into darkness, taking a step toward camp, trying to find a club-worthy branch. She snatched one up, sodden with water and rotten. She listened intently for the steps. No one from camp would sneak through the woods. She had visions of mercs, wearing smart stuff that was more than dark, bending light to make itself invisible.

She took another step. Someone abruptly yanked at the club and she reflexively tightened her grip, so she went with it, off balance. She fell with an oof, a confusion of sinking into wet things and colliding with sharp rocks. In the instant between standing and falling, a part of her brain that she was rarely on speaking terms with took over. She rolled with the fall, taking most of it on her shoulder, using the momentum to goose her motion as she got to her knees, then into a runner's stance. She ran, because someone was *right behind her* and there was the camp, and if she could—

She couldn't. Someone was in front of her, small but wiry, effortlessly catching her hands as she raced past, a grip immovable as a steel clamp, not painful but perfectly unyielding. She nearly crashed into the unseen person, but it sidestepped her neatly as a cartoon toreador avoiding a bull, swung her around in a parody of a square-dance move, bringing her up short with her hands pinned before her. She focused on the person who held her wrists, a woman, she thought, small and short-haired, features painted in a dazzle-array of grays and greens. She had small white teeth, visible through her parted lips, and eyes hidden behind a matte visor hooked behind her ears.

The other one was right behind her, moving swiftly and almost silently, breath easy. She made herself relax, feeling for just a little slack in the grip of the woman holding her. Was that it? It was. With terrified strength, she feinted a head-butt at the visor, then yanked her arms so hard she felt skin leave her wrists, felt something in her shoulder or maybe her ribs pop. It didn't matter. She opened her mouth to scream as she ran—

Then she was back in the woman's grip, a strong hand over her mouth. The small woman smiled, a *You've got moxie, kid* smile, or that's what Iceweasel chose to believe. Then the person with the large, male hand over her mouth—smelling of machine oil and something else that tickled her memory—clamped something to her bicep that immediately tightened like a blood-pressure cuff. She felt a tiny lance of pain as the automated syringe found home. Her panic was pre-empted by another feeling, a delirious feeling like syrup in her spine and down her butt, delicious like stolen snoozebar sleep. The feeling grew. She smiled as her eyes closed.

# 4

## home again, home again, jiggity jig

### [i]

Default smelled. It wasn't a technological smell. If there was one thing walkaway had, it was technological smells. It was an *inhuman* smell. There were background processes looking for BO and bad breath, zapping them with free ions and tasteful anti-perfume. It smelled like something just unwrapped.

When she woke, the smell was her first clue, before opening her eyes. She noticed it before she was fully awake, experiencing a gorgeous state of being aware of not being awake, a drug-feeling. She got that feeling once from something very good Billiam had. Not Billiam. Limpopo. No, Limpopo didn't try new pharma, just stuff she knew. Seth had the pharma thing, downloading new stuff and piloting it in full sensor gear for the analytics groups to pore over, then showing up with a basket of fresh apples and a vaper set to dose them with weight-adjusted amounts.

What had Seth given her? What was that smell? Oh, default. Did Seth download a default drug? What a fucking terrible idea. Why would he do that?

Rising awareness, *conscious* consciousness. Despair. Either her father had her, or someone who planned on ransoming her. If it was the former, she would likely never get away. If it was the latter she'd end up in with her father, and (see above). Because if there was one thing Iceweasel—fuck it, *Natalie*—had known for as long as she'd known anything, it was that the daughter of Jacob Redwater was worth more alive and intact than dead or damaged. If her father had finally come to get her—or if he was about to have to do so—he would not let her go again.

All through her walkaway time, she'd known this day would come when Jacob Redwater twitched his little finger and brought her back before she could be leverage against him—or worse, an embarrassment. She'd never opened his messages, had boycotted her sister and cousins' messages, because good as her opsec was, good as the best brains of walkaway could make it, she was sure that if there was a zeroday that would let him bug her that he would be able to afford it before it was found and patched, and wouldn't hesitate to use it. Wouldn't even understand why anyone *would* hesitate to use it.

Eyes open now. Hospital bed. Four-point zip-restraint and when she saw them, she realized her sleeping brain had already noticed, tugged against them in her sleep and expected them.

Hospital bed, but not a hospital room. Private house. The smell. Her father's house. She was home. She started, softly, to cry.

---

Her sister came to her bedside. Cordelia, two years younger than her, hair different from last time they'd seen each other, during a university break; more sophisticated with a precise degree of insouciant messiness, but otherwise she hadn't changed. She looked down at her big sister with an unreadable expression, set down a large purse on the floor, and settled into an angular wooden chair Natalie vaguely recognized as having once lived in the girls' side of the house. She could see a burn on one arm that she remembered more clearly than the chair itself.

The two sisters contemplated each other. Natalie took after their father, had his weird, bladelike nose and the double-dimple in her cheek, both of which she'd hated as a teenager and come to treasure later as setting her apart. Cordelia looked like Mom, faint memory from girlhood, a round china-doll face and wide green eyes and a sprinkle of toasty Kewpie-doll freckles, but with a satanic glint in her eye for the look-and-feel of a knife-wielding horror-doll.

Natalie gave up. She smiled. There was no honor in pretending to be made of ice. "Nice to see you, Cordelia."

Cordelia smiled back, and she saw the ghost of her own smile. Everyone always said they looked alike when they smiled.

"You're looking good, sis."

"You too. Got some scissors in that giant purse?" She rattled her restraints.

"I do, and I'm delighted to inform you that I have been authorized to use them." Her sister always put on a sarcastic, officious voice when she was nervous.

"Best news I've heard all morning. I have to piss like a racehorse."

"Let's get on it." They weren't normal scissors; they came in a special sheath that crinkled, and their black blades ate light. Cordelia handled them like they were red hot, snipping at the zip-ties with pantomime caution to keep the tips away from Natalie's skin, though they parted the plastic ties with normal cut-plastic noises.

There was a partly open door to Natalie's left, opposite the blind-darkened window, and she tottered to it, feeling floorboards beneath her feet with alarming, hallucinatory clarity. The bathroom behind it was small, fitted with the same brand of mirror and toilet and showerheads as the rest of the house. The towels were familiar, off-white with a scalloped edge. She peed, washed, didn't look in the mirror, then did.

She was clean. Her hair was combed out and trimmed to uniform length, five centimeters all over, the length of the shortest sections of her last haircut, administered by Sita, who could do unexpectedly great things with a pair of scissors.

Her eyes sunk in dark bags. Her skin was dull, her expression thickened with grogginess. She made a face, checked the back of her head, saw a bruise poking out of her hospital robe. It extended down her shoulder, and now she saw it, her ribs and shoulder throbbed, or perhaps she noticed the throbbing that had been there all along.

Seeing the injury made her remember the snatch, the little woman with the grip of steel, the unseen man who'd loomed out the shadows. Then she remembered the bodies, Etcetera's weeping on Limpopo's shoulder, Gretyl's head wound, the smoldering ruin of the *Better Nation* and the fate of its crew.

She searched the bathroom for a weapon. She couldn't imagine hitting Cordelia, but she couldn't imagine *not* hitting anyone who got in her way.

Nothing more dangerous than a squeeze bottle of eye-watering peppermint shampoo. Even the toilet-seat lid was bolted. Fine.

She stepped into the bedroom. Cordelia turned to her, smiling, then the smile faded as she saw Natalie's expression, and Natalie reached for the room's door. She wasn't sure which corridor it opened on, but from there, it'd be easy to find the door and the street and—

She turned the knob and stepped into the hallway.

The small woman with her weight forward on the balls of her feet was unquestionably the woman from the woods. The smile, the small teeth. Natalie would have recognized them anywhere, even though without the dazzle paint, the woman's face was transformed into a forgettable, statistically average mask of mid-Slavic nondescriptness. The teeth, though.

Natalie looked her in the eye. There was no tough-guy stare-down, just a mild interest. Natalie stepped forward to the side, to go around the woman, but she was right there, moving faster than Natalie had ever seen anyone move. That might be the drug hangover. She stepped to the other side, the woman was already there.

Staring, she said, "Excuse me," and tried to step past. The woman blinked.

"I said excuse me." She put a hand on the woman's shoulder, gently pushing her to one side. She didn't push.

"Get out of my fucking way." Natalie regretted the fuck as she said it, nothing to be done about it.

From behind her, Cordelia: "Natalie, come back in here, okay?"

"Get out of my way, please." Her eyes locked on the mild, disinterested gaze of the small woman. "Please." She sounded so weak. She remembered how she'd faked out the woman, broken her grasp before. Strong and fast, but not invincible. Let her think Natalie was weak.

Cordelia's hand on her shoulder. "Come on, Natalie. She's not going to let you past, and if she did, you wouldn't be able to leave the house."

Still looking into the woman's mild eyes. "What if I had you as a hostage?"

"I'd incapacitate both of you." The woman spoke for the first time. She had a sweet voice, girlish, the voice that went with Cordelia's face (Cordelia had spent a lifetime cultivating a husky voice because it was too much otherwise), and a bit of an accent that Natalie thought might be Quebecois or possibly, weirdly, Texan.

"Natalie, please?" Cordelia said.

"They murdered people," Natalie said. "In front of me. I helped the wounded. I carried the dead." Tears on her cheeks, but her voice was steady. "Keep your fucking 'please.'" There was that fuck again. Fuck it. "Get out of my way, killer, or get ready to incapacitate me, whatever that little asshole euphemism means."

The woman didn't speak. Cordelia's grip tightened on her shoulder, would not be shrugged away. The woman wore stuff that was almost walkaway: seamless, printed as a single piece, a bitmap woven into it: conservative dark stripes on a darker background. The stripes did something to her perception of the woman's stance and movement, made it harder to predict where she'd go and when she'd get there. More dazzle.

Without windup, without letting the thought percolate to her forebrain, she took a rough step, bulling into the woman, bodies colliding, and she was already ready to take another step.

Then she was lying on her back, winded, the woman standing back a step. Her expression was unchanged. Small teeth.

"Natalie," Cordelia said. "This isn't going to get anywhere. You can't solve this with force. You're outgunned."

Walkaways walk away. But what if you're confined? Natalie considered another staring contest with the woman, spitting in her face. Doing it over and over. She had a deep intuition the woman would take it. The vivid image of the woman with Natalie's spit spattered across her face was entertaining in a way she identified as a Jacob Redwaterish feeling.

She got to her feet, back to the woman, like she was furniture, and refused Cordelia's help. She went back into the room. The cell. Her shoulder hurt.

---

They fed her by dumbwaiter, her favorite girlhood foods. It was worse than slop or moldy bread. The dumbwaiters ran through the house, a way to fulfill desire without the bothersome politesse of dealing with human servants. She and Cordelia called it Redwater Prime, after the Amazon service, because they knew somewhere in the chain were people earning nowhere near enough to buy the things they dispatched.

Cordelia visited the next two days. The house—her father—listened to them. Natalie knew this because when she asked for things they'd sometimes arrive in the dumbwaiter. But she couldn't directly access interfaces.

Her father didn't visit.

The meals and the fulfilled wishes came at irregular intervals. She knew it was intermittent reinforcement. Give a rat a pellet every time it presses a lever, it will press the lever whenever it's hungry. Give the rat a pellet on random lever-presses, it will press and press, past satiety, as the pattern-matching part of its brain tried to find the pattern in the randomness. You could produce superstitious rats, it was one of Limpopo's favorite epithets for people who were specifically stupid in the superstitious rattish way. Superstitious rats noticed a certain combination of actions prior to a lever-press produced a pellet a few times, decided this needed to be done every time, and though it didn't change the pellet distribution frequency, every pellet *was* accompanied by the superstitious dance, reinforcing the ritual.

The woman outside her door never seemed to sleep. Maybe she was twins, or a robot. She was always there, neutral, small teeth bared, blocking the hall. Natalie had explicit, violent torture-fantasies about the woman, what she'd do if she had a gun or a taser or the power to move things with her mind.

Her mind. The room had: a chair, a bed, remains of her meals—whatever she hadn't put into the dumbwaiter—dirty laundry, and four walls, two doors, one window. The bathroom: toilet roll, toothbrush—self-pasting—the earthy-smelling probiotic cleanser that put her in mind of her mom, though she didn't really know if her mom ever used it, and lethally strong peppermint soap she thought of as her father's, in silicone squeeze bottles that felt like the skin of a sex toy.

The door wasn't locked. But the woman wouldn't let her out, and, as Cordelia reminded her during their increasingly infrequent visits, even if she got down the stairs, the door wouldn't let her out into the wider world.

"Have you spent a lot of time in zottaland?" she asked the woman. She'd taken to sitting in the corridor, studying her. Before that, she'd been talking to herself in the room/cell as a performance for the hidden watchers or algorithms. That made her so self-conscious that she'd come to conduct her monologue with the woman, who might have been a statue.

"I expect you have. Someone like you, good at what you do, you probably hire out for all the most elite barons and plutocrats.

"Most of my friends were zottas. It wasn't until I slipped the leash and brought home some civilians that I really got how fucked up this was. My friends had a hard time making sense of it, some of them never got used to it, just kept on remarking on how weird it was. What got me was how they talked about the surveillance, as though they weren't being watched in every imaginable way back in their apartments or subways or schools. As though the sidewalk wasn't measuring their gait and sniffing their CO2 plume for forbidden metabolites.

"I get it now. Zottas do surveillance to themselves. It's not done to them. You could build a house like this with no sensors, retro, with strings running along the walls to tinkle bells in the servants' quarters. You could line the walls with copper mesh and make it a radio-free fortress.

"The eyes and ears are recording angels that remember everything forever. They're choices. I'd never thought of it, same way a fish doesn't think about water. I get it now.

"The definition of zotta is 'someone who doesn't live the way everyone else does.' You know Gatsby? 'The rich are different.' No one reads Gatsby as criticism anymore. Now it seems nostalgic. Or Orwell, the inner party with their telescreen off-switches. Why would a zotta choose to install telescreens in his fucking bathroom?"

She considered the irony of the sensors recording and analyzing her talk about them. She thought about Dis, a computer who was a person. She entertained a fantasy about the house's network being self-aware, knowing she was talking about it and she was angry at it; she wanted to switch it off. No wonder there'd been so many netsoaps about people killed by rogue computers, the I-can't-let-you-do-that-Dave cliché that was the go-to dramasauce for hack writers.

The woman stared, eyes focused, betraying nothing.

"You must be a hell of a poker player. I once saw the Beefeaters, you know, in London? England, I mean, not Ontario. They were bullshit, trying to pretend they were wooden soldiers, never acknowledging you. I don't think it's possible to be vigilant while pretending everyone else is invisible. Tell yourself that long enough, you'll believe it. You, on the other hand, can hear and see me, but it's like I'm beneath your notice unless I'm trying to get past. You can hear me. Shit, you probably agree with every word, but what I say isn't anything compared to the immovable truth of a fuck-ton of money for you if you do the default thing; nothing at all if you follow your conscience.

"On the other hand, I might be projecting. Maybe you love default, think weird-ass zotta shit is proof of their divine right to rule. Maybe you're animal cunning and wiry strength, without much going on behind those cool eyes of yours?"

She stopped, aware that she was a zotta, taunting a person who couldn't respond because she wasn't. She felt ashamed.

"Sorry," she said, and went into her room.

## [ii]

Her father visited her on day four. She'd gone twenty-four hours without taunting the guard, and was bored out of her mind. She'd fantasized about a notebook and a pen, anything she could use to pour out her feelings to something other than the unseeable watchers.

He looked in control. That was the first thing she noticed, the contrast between her shaky nerves and his calm exterior. She thought he'd done something with his face, injections. He looked younger than she remembered, a youthful thirty-five. He turned the chair around, sat straddling it with his arms folded on the back, cocked his head and smiled as though they shared a joke. There was definitely something different in the smile.

"Welcome home, Natty."

She thought about freezing him out, like the guard-woman with her gaze that saw, did not acknowledge. She was so lonely, so bored. Her brain was a hamster wheel, spinning out of control. She needed to slow it with words, even if it was argument.

"I would like to go now, please."

He smiled wider. "How was it?"

She made herself breathe into her diaphragm, once, twice. "I'm sure you got a blow-by-blow."

"Your mother is coming tomorrow. She can't wait to see you."

"They killed people, you know. I saw them, saw the bodies. I held the bodies. My friends—they were my friends." She struggled to keep her voice calm, was successful except for a wobble on the second "bodies." She was sure her father picked up on it. He was a man who was keenly attuned to others' useful frailties.

"I can see it's been hard on you."

"You mean, the mercenary terrorists you sent were hard on me."

"You've lost contact with reality, darling. You can't believe that. I can't order air strikes. I don't know mercenaries. I'm a scary rich guy, but if my enemies fear me, it's because they're worried I'll *sue* them, not assassinate them."

Natalie closed her eyes and tried to find her breath's rhythm. For her father—*her father*—to say he couldn't possibly have had anything to do with what had happened, when there was a ninja mercenary in the hallway—it was too much. It epitomized every conversation they'd ever had where he'd told her everything she felt and hoped for was a girlish dream, every observation of the world around her a girlish fancy.

Her breath wouldn't come. Maybe her father hoped the long isolation would make her pliable. But it had broken something inside that jangled. She realized with a rush that felt like a convulsion of vomit she had hardly thought of Gretyl since arriving. It made her wonder if they'd done something to her mind, if she was herself. If there even was a mercenary in the hall who could lay her out with moves so fast she couldn't follow them. Perhaps it was a dream. Perhaps she was dead, uploaded, simulated.

She was hyperventilating, and took satisfaction in her father's discomfort. He could deal with I-hate-you-daddy tantrums, but she was losing it now, was glad to be lost. She was tired of being found, pretending the situation was normal.

She stood calmly and smoothed down her long t-shirt, adjusting her trackpants' drawstring—red, with a crisp-edged ROOTS logo over one thigh, the kind of thing she'd slopped in at summer camp, as though the dumbwaiter was loaded by someone trying to make her feel like a grounded teenager and not a kidnap victim—and walked out of the room.

The guard was not in the hall.

She broke into a run, hearing her father—a step behind her—shout something she couldn't make out. She got five long steps down the hall and the merc came around the corner, effortlessly grabbing her arm as she tried to run past, interposing her calf between Natalie's running legs, pulling smoothly at the arm, throwing her down with a tooth-rattling thud. The floorboards were pale wood with dark grain, and underfloor heating made them feel alive.

All she could see was that grain, stretching to the baseboards. She waited for her wind to come back.

She got to her knees, her feet—the merc didn't interfere or offer help, stood with that same disinterested attention that let Natalie know she was watching but wasn't feeling. Natalie steadied herself on the wall, looked at her father, on the far side of the merc. He looked furious, and she realized he was furious with the merc, not her, because the merc had deserted her post, maybe slipping out for a piss, thinking Natalie would be complacent while having a come-to-Jesus negotiation with her old man. The merc had fucked up in front of the big boss. Natalie tried to read her face for the oh-shit expression of waiters and hotel managers when her dad wasn't happy with them. She was cool. Natalie couldn't help but admire her. It was twisted, but she felt solidarity with anyone her father planned on destroying.

"No tough-guys on the payroll, huh?" She spun on her heel to walk out of the house. It was stupid, but why not? The woman grabbed her shoulder in a way that gave her surprising leverage, spun her around with almost no force, though there was no way Natalie could stop it. Natalie shrugged at her hand, but the hand rode her shoulder with ease, rising and falling like a flag in a breeze.

"What are your orders, anyway? You said you could 'incapacitate' me. Would you beat me unconscious? Give me a secret nerve pinch? Got a taser hidden in your ninja-suit?" She took a long look at her father. He had mastered his expression and projected impatient boredom with his whole body.

"Let's find out." Natalie took three running steps toward her dad, who flinched minutely at the last moment. She stopped and spun, stared at the woman, then charged. One step, two steps—wham, on the floorboards, staring at the ceiling, noticing the LED recesses you could only see if you were supine. Her back hurt. She had the ghost sensation of a hand at her wrist, a foot at her ankle, the sense the woman had barely moved to throw her. It was the spirit of all those Sun Tzu-y martial arts: use the enemy's strength against him. She giggled at the thought that she should take notes, figure out how to dismantle default by using its strength against it.

She stood. The woman stepped back a half step, weight forward, while her dad stayed at the corridor's far end with his stern, disappointed mask on. It wasn't entirely intact. There was a bit of worry Mr. Poker Face couldn't hide. She leaned on the wall and took a couple breaths.

"Let's make it best two out of three." Her father's face flickered, and there it was: fear.

She charged him. He didn't flinch, but she saw he wanted to, and she turned around and before she could think, she ran straight at the guard, coming in low, like she was playing a platformer and was trying one approach after another to defeat the level's mini-boss, hoping she didn't run out of lives before she found the trick. Maybe if she came in low, she'd be harder to throw.

She wasn't.

This time she jammed her elbow and her body was lanced by a white-lightning sear, making her suck air through her teeth. What was pain, anyway? Dis could feel pain or not, but it was an infographic, a slider you moved up or down. Her arm was *hurt*—something had been damaged—but the *feeling* of hurt wasn't intrinsic. You could be hurt and feel nothing, you could be in immense pain without injury. Injury was in the elbow, pain was in the brain.

But it hurt.

She got to her feet more slowly, rubbed her elbow. She had paid more attention this time, had the impression that the woman had lightly touched her shoulders as she passed, did something to her that caused her weight to overbalance to the front, sending her face-first into the floor.

She breathed. Jacob scowled. She watched him painstakingly convert his fear to anger. Anger was fine. She was fucking *pissed*.

"Third time's the charm."

This time he grabbed her, but she'd been a walkaway, carrying heavy loads for the sheer pleasure of doing things with her hands, walking miles at a time, having long, unhurried, sensuous yoga sessions on the B&B's lawn that made her strong and supple. He was a gym rat, attended by skilled trainers and a pharmacopoeia that gave him cut transverse abdominals like an underwear model and arms with lean triceps and strong wrists, and he could do an hour on the elliptical, but it was all for show, never used.

She shook him off easily. She thrilled to realize she could have flattened him as easily as the merc was knocking her out, run up one side of him and down the other. It had been years since her father had been physical with her, but she recollected his iron grip, how he could carry her out of the room when she was misbehaving, ignoring her squirming. Let him try now.

She tried for a low sprint pumping her arms for speed, though she knew she'd need to be fired out of a longbow before her speed was high enough to make a difference to the woman. She almost faltered as she drew near, some cowardly part of her not wanting to get the coming beat-down, and she killed that part of her with a blast of will, put on *more* speed.

Her head bounced off the wall on the way down, filling her vision with stars. She took longer to get up. She was dizzy. It had been a solid hit. Had the woman hurt her on purpose, to punish her for refusing to back down? Had her run-up just been better?

Her father went into the bedroom, she supposed to phone for backup, so she walked this time, turned around, stared at the woman, the two of them alone now save for the watching eyes.

She ran. Something was wrong with her balance, and she couldn't get her wind. This time the woman caught her and turned her around, neatly canceling all her momentum as she did so. Natalie and she were face to face. The woman's nothing-special face and small teeth were right there; her breath smelled of toothpaste. She had a booger up one nostril. Her eyebrows weren't plucked, which Natalie hadn't noticed, and had a bushiness that reminded her of Gretyl. She wanted to cry.

She tried to walk past, walked into the woman, was pushed gently away. She tried again. She was really dizzy. It had been a bad hit.

This woman wasn't her enemy, she just had a job. Natalie didn't care. She swung a wild roundhouse the woman easily sidestepped. Had she smiled a little? It was weird to be here, silent except for breathing, her father's muttering from the bedroom. Wordless intimacy. She swung again. Again. If she'd had a gun, she'd have shot the woman, her father, herself. What does a walkaway do when she can't walk away?

She gave up, arms dropping to her sides. Stalked into the bedroom. Her father was in the chair, looking disgusted, like she was pathetic. She supposed she was. What's more pathetic than a walkaway who stops walking?

She swallowed and tried to work up the courage to fall on him, to stick her thumbs in his eye sockets, rake her nails down his throat, knee him in the balls. The thought of the violence was so seductive that she was actually stayed from moving, surprised at her id's ardor.

But then she embraced it, with a predator's grin. She heard herself panting. Now she would do it. Her father understood, she saw it in his eyes. He was scared. The predator rose. She would enjoy this.

One step. Two steps.

A hand on her arm. Strong. A man's hand, squeezing so hard she gasped, then the needle in her elbow. She turned and saw the man, not big, shorter than her, but with a face like a stone and a bull's neck. Then she see didn't anything else.

## [iii]

She was certain she was still in the house. You couldn't fake the smell. But it looked like a hospital room. The door had no handle or inset panel, just some kind of invisible sensor that chose who passed. This hospital bed was bigger, cruder, and she was—she squirmed her hips—she was plumbed into it. There was an IV in her wrist, and a sense of fuzzy well-being she knew couldn't be endogenous. She wondered what was in the IV bag. She'd have loved some Meta right now.

She was in four-point restraint, with an extra band around her forearm to keep the IV firmly seated.

She supposed it was a suicide attempt. The idea wasn't very disturbing. Her sorrow was a distant moon orbiting her psyche far away, visible but ultimately exerting only the mildest of tides.

"Now what?" Her voice was thick, her mouth pasty. If there was saline in the bag, it wasn't keeping her hydrated. It was like someone had dumped a tablespoon of hydrophilic shipping gel-pellets in her mouth, drying it to the texture of old roadkill.

She willed the door to open, thinking of the days she'd spent in isolation in the other room, wondering if they'd leave her, a tube going in and tubes going out, a brain inextricably tethered to inconvenient meat, easily coerced, thanks to its ridiculous frailties.

Had they had this room ready all along, as plan B? Or had she been kept unconscious while they refitted a room to make it secure?

A nurse came through the door, wearing hospital whites and wheeling a cart. He stood beside the bed.

"Hello," she said.

He stared at her consideringly, then pulled out the cart's trays, pointed a thermometer in her ear, fit a pressure cuff to her arm. He flipped back the blanket and impersonally hiked up her gown, accessing a small box taped over her hip that she hadn't known was there.

"Why doesn't all that stuff come with remote telemetry? If you're going to pretend I don't exist, why not get transmissions in another room, spare yourself the social awkwardness?"

He was good at ignoring her. He checked her catheter, so mechanically that she felt anger instead of humiliation, which was, in its way, a mercy. What an asshole.

"I know there are cameras recording, but at least tip me a wink. Don't nurses have to take a vow? An oath? Are you a nurse? Maybe you're a 'med-tech.' Did you flunk out of nursing school and get the version that doesn't come with the Florence Nightingale training?"

Taunting him wasn't satisfying, and her mouth was so, so dry.

"How about a drink? Water? Juice?"

He had a hose with a sponge tip. He pulled off the sheets and threw them into a basket in the cart's base, revealing a rubbery under-sheet. Working with that same impersonal efficiency, he gave her a quick sponge bath, hose in one hand and a small hydrophilic towel in the other, stopping after each limb to wring the cloth into his cart. From her distant mental vantage point, Natalie admired the cart and wondered who its primary market was—people with loony old relatives locked up in attics?

He did her face and ears with wipes in sterile packaging, like the guys at the detailing place working squeegees over the windscreen of her dad's cars. The fact that it was done by humans was a selling point. All the places her dad used had "bespoke" or "hand-wash" or "artisanal" in their names, sometimes all three. She smelled the nurse, soap with a bit of sweat, saw some stubble under his left ear. There was one point where she could have kissed him. Or bit him.

When he was done, he packed up his tray, tugged her clothes into place, and replaced the sheets. He fished under the bed for a flexi-hose with a bite-down nipple on the end. He pulled off lengths of surgical tape and taped it to her collarbone and cheek, so she could turn her head and drink. She could have bitten off a fingertip, but didn't. He packed his things and left. The door sighed shut and clicked, then clunked, a reminder that it had serious locking stuff. It sounded like the second clunk came through the floor, like the door had a set of pins that penetrated it.

She realized where she was: her dad's panic room. It had independent, redundant network connections, power backups, food and water stashes, a whole armory. It wasn't like her dad to tell other people about the panic room—she'd never seen it and knew that opening it would set off alarms all over town. Her dad made sure she knew, just in case she got the idea of throwing a party there.

Dad must've built himself a better bolt-hole—he'd mused about one in a second subbasement, bored out beneath the house using a super-covert drill that his zotta buddy had used to turn the plot under his estate into a bat-cave. It sent Dad into ecstasies of jealousy. There's no way he'd let Mr. Not-a-Nurse into this place if it was still the secret he'd bet his life on. Unless he planned to off all the staff once he'd brainwashed her and entomb them within the reinforced walls, like a pharaoh's tomb-builders.

These thoughts produced seven minutes' worth of distraction. When they were exhausted, she was alone with her situation. Thinking of Gretyl made her cry with desire and loneliness. There were thoughts about her father and sister. Hadn't her father said her mother was on her way? Was she here? She had her own floor on the adults' side of the house. It hadn't been occupied often, but when it was, the house's affect changed. The whole household was alive to the possibility of their mercurial mistress doing one of her patented Valkyrie numbers.

She chased the tail of her thoughts in ever-tighter spirals. It was a desperate place. Visit it enough and it might drive you to suicide.

"Fuck it," she said aloud. "Brainwashing, rubber hoses, deprogramming, all that Patty Hearst stuff." She'd learned about Hearst, the poor little rich girl who'd carried a gun with her kidnappers, after Gretyl joked about it. She'd been offended, but then adopted the girl as a totem. Hearst was an idiot, but at least she wasn't just another rich asshole.

She sang "Consensus," an incredibly dirty walkaway marching song, thirty verses. The chorus: "Consensus, consensus, it beat us and bent us, but we're sure that it's lent us, a shit-eating grin." Making up new verses was walkaway sport, there were wikis of them. She couldn't remember them all, but she could make them up on the fly, especially if she sang humm-humm-humm where she couldn't think of a line, which was automatic disqualification when it was sung in earnest.

The verses got more hum-hum-hummy. She was ready to peter out and start another song, when a voice joined in: ". . . but we're sure that it's lent us, a shit-eating grin!" It was achingly familiar. She shivered from scalp to ankles, hairs on her neck standing.

"Dis?"

"That's Dis Ex Machina to you, kid," the voice said.

She cried.

---

"This is a dirty trick." She mastered her tears. "Absolutely disgusting."

"It would be," Dis said, "if it was a trick."

"How would you know if it was or not? You're on all the version control servers. Anyone who can build a cluster can bring you up. There'll be hundreds of you, in all kinds of configs. My dad could easily afford a version of you that was constrained so it believed it had infiltrated his network to work against him, while spying on me and everything I did. You would never know. I'd tell you things he'd have to slice my nipples off to get otherwise. He'd call this *humane,* a 'low impact' way of 'bringing me around' to sanity, which, in his world, is the ability to bullshit yourself into believing you deserve to have more of everything that everyone else has less of, because of your special snowflakeness."

"You're preaching to the converted, girl. Remember, I was walkaway before you."

"*Dis* was walkaway before me. *You,* whatever you are, are an emissary, knowing or not, from default."

"We're going in circles. No skin off my back, because I'm a construct. I can park my frustration to one side, move the slider, have this argument with you for as long as you'd like. It's cool. Comes from a lab in Punjab, ex-IIT math-geeks who want to turn the Āgama into subroutines, Yogic Mastery Apps. They're turning Meta into math. You'd love it—they worship Gretyl, her optimizations for lookahead modeling are the basis of their discipline. I think if she wasn't so worried about you, she'd be all over it."

"That was really low." She was surprised by the venom in her voice. When her thoughts strayed to Gretyl, she was seized by unbearable helplessness and longing. That Gretyl felt the same about her was a weight crushing her chest.

"Oh, honey," Dis said. Her computer voice was better. The emotions in those two words were awful. "She misses you so much. I can get you a message from her. Or . . ."

Natalie knew it was a baited hook. She didn't want to rise to it. Fish must know the worm has a barb in it, but some bite anyway. Was it hunger? A death wish? "What?"

"They've been scanned now," Dis said. "After they reached the Thetford abandoned zone, everyone made a scan, first thing. They're in the walkaway clouds now, more every day. We're learning so much from the multiplicity of scans, too—I think the problem with bringing back CC was that we just didn't have a deep enough data-set to make inferences about tailored simulation strategies for brain variations. CC is pretty stable. We can characterize scans based on the likelihood of bringing up a successful sim. Gretyl's scan is in the top decile. She was made to run on silicon. Sita, too. Hell, Sita was so up for it that she's running a twin twenty-four/seven, in realtime, with sensors all over herself. Gretyl hasn't done that, though. We've only done the preflighting for her. We haven't run her . . ."

*Yet,* Natalie finished. Gretyl could be here, running on whatever substrate Dis was on. Her Gretyl, not her Gretyl, that was a distinction without a difference.

"So fucking evil." She didn't have the energy for bile. It came out like surrender.

"It's not complicated. Your dad's got amazing opsec on the main house network. But the patchlevel on his safe room is lagged, because there were conflicts the auto-updaters couldn't handle, and the ops guy who set it up retired and your dad doesn't have anyone in his ops department who even *knows* about this. The alert messages have piled up in an admin dashboard for years, all neglected. I wonder if your dad even has a login for that dash?

"We pwned this place as soon as you went. It was Gretyl's project, but I did the heavy lifting. We used like seventy percent of walkaway's compute-time running parallel instances of me, at twenty ex realtime. We *clobbered* the fucking IDS, smoked the firewall, and now I'm so deep I can do anything."

The door-locks clunked out "shave and a haircut." It was terrifying and hilarious. Natalie's anguished smile hurt to hold.

"But I can't work your shackles. They're not networked. I can't do anything with the housenet, that's totally airgapped. For the best, otherwise all that pwnage would have set off all kinds of alarms."

Despite herself, Natalie was drawn into the explanation. "Come on." Her stimulus-starved brain worked hard. "Occam's razor. Either there's this crazy bug because Dad fired his bull-goose sysadmin, and a convenient airgap in the bed's systems—*or* you're my dad's puppet, and he's locked you down so you can do magic tricks with the door-locks, but not set me free. You *happen* to have the ability to bring me a sim of my girlfriend, who would no doubt get me to say things that my dad could use to brainwash me, like Cordelia."

"That does sound plausible. I can't prove that I'm working with you, not your dad. Sims can't be sure that they aren't being torqued by the simulator, and that makes us incapable of knowing we're being manipulated. We're heads in jars. But how do you know *you're* not a sim? We scanned those mercs in the tunnels without their knowledge."

"My dad isn't that—" she almost said *powerful,* but she wasn't sure she wanted to go there. "Sentimental."

"He's a dick. I'm really glad we found you. Half the camp thought you were dead. Gretyl insisted you'd been snatched. Someone thought they saw you going into the woods, and they found evidence of a scuffle there. No one could say whether it was you, but everyone else was accounted for or dead. When the only person missing is the kid of an asshole zotta, it's not a stretch to imagine a snatch."

Natalie wanted so, so much to believe this was Dis, a lifeline to outside, life beyond the confines of her lashed-down body. Of course she wanted to. If Dis was her father's trick, he'd depend on it.

She had to piss. It had been building, now it was unbearable. She knew she was plumbed into the bed, must have pissed many times before regaining consciousness, but the thought of voluntarily releasing her bladder while tied to a bed was too much.

"Dis." She was ashamed of the weakness in her voice. Why couldn't she be strong, like Limpopo? Like Gretyl?

"What is it, Iceweasel?"

No one had called her that since she'd been snatched.

She lost control over her bladder. The piss coursed out, disappeared silently down the hose, a feeling of heat where the hose was taped to her inner thigh before diving down to the bed's cistern. Even though she wasn't soaked with urine, the sense of pissing herself was inescapable, and she lost control of her tears.

"Oh, Iceweasel. It's okay to cry, darling. This is totally fucked up and shit. You have people who love you, who sent me to get you loose. I can't cut your bonds, but I can do plenty else. I can see in every room of the prison wing. There's three others in a break room. They're monitoring the room, but I control those monitors. They're not seeing or hearing a realtime feed, they're getting a loop of sleeping. Your bed's streaming real telemetry, but I'm swapping for stored data from your unconscious period. I've got their private messages, I can do adversarial stylometry to impersonate them in text and voice—we've done work on voices."

"I can tell." Natalie snuffled snot. It was all down her face. Tears ran into her ears and made them itch. The feeling was so ridiculous it made her smile a little.

"Great, isn't it? It keeps on getting better to be a pure energy being."

"You make it sound like you're a ghost."

"I like 'pure energy being' but I'm the only one. It's better than ghost. Don't get me started on 'angel.' Jesus fucking Christ."

Natalie cried again. The hopeless world kept crashing in. She wanted to have hope, to believe in Dis. But she was a walkaway. Walkaways were supposed to confront brutal truths. The brutal truth of Dis was that it was more likely that her dad had a hot-shit hacker who'd run an instance to betray Natalie than it was that he'd forgotten to hire a new sysadmin to take over ops for his safe room.

"Iceweasel, how about this? You don't have to believe me. I won't believe me, either. There's no way for me to know if I'm who I think I am. The logical thing for us to do is to act like I can't be trusted."

"That's weird." Natalie snuffled snot and bore down on the problem.

"Weird isn't the opposite of sensible. When the going gets weird, the weird turn pro."

"If you say so."

"I say so. Uh, hold on. They're coming in, time for a scheduled call. Close your eyes and pretend to be groggy, which won't be a stretch. I'll lurk. It's best if we don't let 'em know I'm here, but I will be, listening and recording. When they go, I'll be here still, whatever you need to stay sane until we can bust you out."

She couldn't help but feel this was *exactly* what a traitorous Dis would say if she was trying to trick Natalie. But it felt good.

The door clunked twice, clicked, and swung open.

## [iv]

As Seth and Tam paced the cargo-train, he contemplated his weird relationship with Gretyl. Back in his beautiful youthful days, a girlfriend once left him for another woman, after he'd hooked up with a guy at a party, someone's horny, hot cousin. They'd had a crazy night locked in a spare bedroom at someone's mom's apartment in Bathurst Heights, leaving linens so be-funked that he heard they'd been burned. In the ensuing drama, he'd challenged his girlfriend on her freak, pointing out boys were boys and girls were girls, and he was exclusive to her in the "girl" part of his life, but that it was unreasonable for her to expect him to swear off dick when she didn't have one.

Even as he'd uttered the words, part of him understood them to be self-serving bullshit. He still cringed with embarrassment at the thought of them, a decade later.

The girl found another girl, because he'd told her to, and quickly decided the other girl was the person she wanted to be exclusive with, without the weaselly "exclusive for people with vaginas" distinction Seth insisted on.

Seth, single and stinging, told himself it was because there were things you could get from a girl-girl relationship you couldn't get from girl-boy, and he'd never understand those things, but they must be awesome because his girlfriend dumped his ass. Later he realized the difference between the girl and him wasn't the penis so much as the cheating-asshole-ness.

When Iceweasel came home with Gretyl, Seth had been mature about it by Seth standards. When his jealously rose in his gorge, he fought it down, bitterly recalling the self-recrimination that surfaced whenever he thought of the penis/no-penis distinction incident.

He and Iceweasel didn't have a serious boy-girl thing, so he had no business feeling jealousy, even by default-ish rules that said there *were* times when you had business feeling jealous. Then there was Tam, who knew Gretyl well, looked up to her, admired her toughness and badass math chops. Tam and him *were* an item, a boy-girl thing. It would be monumentally fucked for Seth to pursue Iceweasel.

Technically, they were all friends, some of whom had hooked up, some engaged in long-term exclusive-ish nookie. When Iceweasel disappeared, they'd been agonized by the not-knowing about their friend/lover/whatever. They'd welded into a guerrilla unit, scouring the net, working connections to find her.

As the search petered out, it was increasingly Seth and Tam, a couple, and Gretyl, basically a widow, trundling on the back of a cargo-freighter together, staring awkwardly, pretending they all had the same relationship to Iceweasel and the same kind of grief. So much bullshit. Eventually there was no way to pretend.

Seth and Tam walked alongside the cargo-train, headed for Thetford, passing blighted zones and small default towns with stores and people living like civilization would endure forever. Seth had high school French, but the people who called out in slangy *joual* might have been speaking Klingon. Despite the language barrier, every time they passed through a town, people joined their column. They'd come at night, wherever they were camped. Inevitably, they were shleppers with mountains of junk that Seth didn't let himself get irritated by. He'd been the King of the Shleppers.

Gretyl rode on the train, face furrowed with sorrow, eyes distant, fingers moving over interface surfaces. At night, Seth brought steaming trays from the mess wagon, collected them when she'd finished, but she hardly noticed.

Finally, Tam rolled over one night and put her arm across his chest and her face in the hollow of his neck and said, "What the fuck is she *doing*?" He didn't know, and Tam mentioned the obvious fact (which he'd been oblivious to), that she was worried sick about Gretyl.

"Intervention. First thing in the morning."

"Now," Tam said. "I'll bet you a two-hour foot-rub she's wide awake."

"*I'm* not wide awake. OW! *Now* I'm awake." He rubbed his nipple and glared at Tam in the dark. She had sharp fingernails.

They pulled on clothes and lit themselves. Fall had slipped toward winter and there was frost on the road where camp had been struck for the night.

Gretyl was awake and hammering away, a hunkered, moonlit silhouette propped against the side of the train. Her hands danced and her whispers and grunts floated on the breeze. She wore a mask, which Seth hadn't seen her do before. More than anyone, she seemed able to visualize virtual spaces and prod them without visual feedback. So she was doing something intense.

The acceptable protocol for masks was to call first, so they knew you were there, rather than tapping them on the shoulder and destroying their creative fog. But Gretyl had her do-not-disturb flags set, even the no-exceptions-this-means-you flags. They stood for a moment, a few steps away from her, wondering what to do.

"I feel like such an idiot," Seth said. "I mean, fuck."

"Don't stand there with your dick in your hand. Tap her on the shoulder."

A variety of responses about dicks, and hands, occurred to the part of Seth who was still seventeen years old and horny about having a girlfriend with a dick, which was the whole package as far as Seth-Seventeen was concerned. Seth told Seth-Seventeen to shut the fuck up.

"Why don't you?"

"She *likes* you." Tam shoved him. Gretyl showed exasperated maternal affection and bemused humor at Seth's various schticks, but with an edge that left him wondering if she thought he was a colossal asshole.

"She likes *you,* too."

"You're closer." Tam took a quick step backwards.

He sighed, and Tam blew a kiss that turned into a shooing motion. He edged to Gretyl, whose head bobbed, presumably in tune with her earplugs, implants that filled her earholes with soft blue light to let others know she was not sharing their acoustic consensus reality.

Nevertheless, he cleared his throat and even said, "Gretyl" into her ear twice—hoping she'd done the sensible thing and programmed her plugs to pass through—before he tentatively touched her shoulder. As he'd feared, she jerked like he'd stabbed her and whipped off the face mask and glared.

"Are we being attacked?" she said.

"No, but—"

"Fuck off." She pulled her mask down. Tam shook her head and shooed him again. Before he could tap, she whipped the mask down. "Seth, I have not been subtle. I'm doing something that needs concentration. Why have you not fucked off, per my instruction?"

He looked to Tam. Gretyl looked at her, too, and softened one billionth of a percentage.

"What do you two want?"

Tam took Gretyl's hands, heavy with interface rings. "Gretyl, we want to talk about Iceweasel."

Gretyl cocked her head. "Yeah?"

"She's been gone for more than a week. We're all hoping she turns up. We've put out the word in walkaway and default, but fretting's useless. She's smart and resourceful and so long as we're reachable, she'll get in touch once she can."

Gretyl smiled, which alarmed Seth. He took a half-step backwards in the guise of settling down on his butt in the dirt opposite Gretyl. It was a weird smile.

"Was that all?"

"No." Tam sat next to Seth. "No, it's *not,* Gretyl. You need to understand we're your friends, we love you, we're on your side, we're in this together. We all miss her. We need to support each other, not withdraw into our own corners and—"

She stopped, because Gretyl's smile was broader now. Tam said, "Gretyl?"

Gretyl heaved a sigh and stood so she towered over them. She reached onto the cargo-train's running board and found a flexible flask with a nipple from which she took a long pull, then passed it to Tam, who sniffed, then drank and passed it to Seth, who found it to be full of something like Scotch, so peaty it was like drinking a cigar. He liked drinking cigars. He took in a larger-than-intended mouthful, then made the best of a not unpleasant situation.

Gretyl held her hand out and he reluctantly passed the booze back. "To Iceweasel." She took another drink.

They both nodded. Looking up at Gretyl was giving Seth a crick in his neck. He got up, just as Gretyl sat and gave him a yes-I'm-fucking-with-you look he knew he gave other people.

"It's very nice of you two. You mean well. But I haven't been heaving dramatic sighs. I've been *doing* something."

"What?" Tam's eyes shone in the soft light of her glowing clothing, underlighting her strong jaw and making her skin a pool of buttery tones in a gray-and-black night. Seth felt a tremor of excitement, partly sexual and partly just *excitement*. Something was happening.

"I brought up Dis. There's so many clusters in Akron. Tons of compute-time, people are happy to share. I ran her and told her Iceweasel had been snatched by her family, and she talked to ninja-types who are good at that kind of thing."

"Yeah?" Tam said, calmer than Seth, who got the willies talking to Dis—it wasn't that she didn't seem human. It's that she *did*. Freaked him to his balls.

"Yeah."

Gretyl looked expectant.

"I'll bite," Seth said. "What happened?"

"We found her. We pwned the house she's in. Dis is running on their hardware. She's in communication with Iceweasel."

Seth and Tam looked at each other.

"I'm not crazy," Gretyl said. "It's real, and it's happening."

"When?"

"Last week. Nothing's happening now, not until she regains consciousness."

"Regains consciousness?" Seth said.

Tam said, "Really?"

"Regains consciousness." Gretyl's expression that made him flinch. "Really." Her smile was so big her eyes all but disappeared between her cheeks and forehead. "Really!" Tam, who knew what to do in a way Seth never had, gave Gretyl a hug that he joined.

"Now what?" Seth said.

"Now we break her out," Gretyl said.

## [v]

Etcetera didn't know what to expect from Thetford, but this wasn't it. The zone was abandoned a decade before, when asbestos contamination went critical and even the federal government couldn't ignore it. The evacuation happened with the usual haste and coercion. The houses still had china in the cupboards, toys in the toy chests, rusting swing sets in the yards.

Warm winters and wet summers triggered landslides that left the town and the valley silted up, the buildings spongy with black mold. A very dry year capped by a midsummer lightning storm triggered fires across the valley, then more floods. What remained looked like a thousand-year ruin, albeit with odd pockets of perfectly preserved rural life—a farmhouse that escaped the worst and still had a bookcase bulging with old French romance novels, a set of basements and subbasements underneath the hospital that were dry with working emergency lights.

The walkaways who'd taken over Thetford treated it as a hostile alien planet, where the air could kill you, where the terrain was treacherous and the extreme climate showed no mercy. This was precisely the environment they'd sought, because it was a dress-rehearsal for going to other planets.

"It's the ultimate walkaway," Kersplebedeb said. He was gangly, with a prominent Adam's apple, and spoke English with a funny accent that came from having a French mother and a Kiwi father in bilingual Montreal. "All that first days of a better nation stuff, it's just bourgie bullshit. Nations are bullshit. You know what's not bullshit? Space. No room for power-games in space. No room for coercion, or war."

"Run that past me again?" They were in one of the airtight capsules that had been deposited, like the egg sacs of sky-squids, all over Thetford. "Why no war?"

"Why war?" Kersplebedeb said. He spread his long fingers over the table. He had chipped silver nail polish and a yellow housedress and short hair, which assuaged any fear Etcetera had that the Thetfords would be boringly socially conservative. That was the reputation of space-exploration types.

"Jealousy. Greed. Irrational hatred."

"Once you're in space, you're *mobile*. Unlimited power, anywhere the sun shines. Oxygen anywhere you can find ice to fractionate with solar-powered electrolysis. Food anywhere you can find feedstock, including your poop. Someone wants your lump of ice? Walk away. Someone wants your space habitat? Walk away. Walk away, walk away.

"People who think about space end up thinking about bullshit like Star

Wars and Star Trek. They have faster-than-light travel, but they still fight? Over *what*? They've got *transporters*. What are they fighting over? What does anyone have that anyone else can't get, instantly, for free? They have to invent unobtaniums, magic crystals that, for some reason, can't just be printed out by their transporter beams, or there's no story.

"Why do they even *die*? We're already making scans of ourselves—if they've got transporters, they should do hourly scans!"

"I get your point." He wished Limpopo was there, but she'd gone off to get trained at the space-suit factory, along with a contingent of Walkaway U scientists and some B&B people. There was talk of building another factory, because they were all tunnel-bound until they were outfitted. The academics who'd lived in the tunnels accepted this with resignation and mostly just wanted space, time, and freedom from distraction so they could scan everyone. That was okay with everyone. The long march to Quebec was fraught with danger. Sound from the sky made them flinch in anticipation of death-by-drone. Every crackle in the night had been a merc. The case for getting every walkaway into the cloud could not be stronger.

The B&B crew and the surviving aeronauts wanted the scientists to bear down on the scanning project, indoors and safe from the blowing asbestos and leaching heavy metals of Thetford; they themselves wanted to get the fuck out of the tunnels. Walkaways who couldn't walk away were like foxes whose den lacked an emergency back door. The space-suit project was a priority. The Thetford crew had improvements on the space-suit fab they couldn't wait to go 2.0 with, so that was likely to achieve liftoff.

Kersplebedeb laughed, showing horsey teeth and the insides of his nostrils. "You people kill me. You've done so much for the project, but you don't appear to have given any thought to how it changes *everything*. The rate we're going, we'll be launching a thousand walkaways into space by New Year's."

"Where do you plan on getting the launch capacity to put a colony into orbit? Last time I checked your wiki, you had a deal to lift a couple cubesats a year."

"All we need is *one* cubesat, up high with decent comms to Earth-station, and we're set."

The penny dropped. "You want to run a cluster in orbit and put sims on it?"

Kersplebedeb gave him a "duh" look and pawed through a cooler for a jar of astronauts' moonshine, made from distilled lichen. It tasted amazing, like a slightly sweet tequila, deceptively smooth and very strong. He spun the lid off the jar and poured two small glasses of greenish liquid. These sit-downs with Kersplebedeb involved a lot of lichen booze. It was a theory-object from walkaway space programs. It was cheap and easy to make even if you didn't have hard vacuum right outside your airlock.

"What else would we do?"

"What would they do up there?"

"Same thing we're doing here, but far from people with bombs and weird ideas about doing what you're told and accepting your station."

"You're going to run copies of yourself in space, on a cubesat, and what, exchange email with them? Let them have high-latency flamewars about engineering problems?"

"I'll grant it's weird." He sipped the drink and his affect got less wild, more—Etcetera struggled for the word. Default. More sane, more respectable. At some time in Kersplebedeb's life, he'd been the kind of person who could explain to a boardroom of normal people and make it sound normal. Now he was busting out his normal register for Etcetera. "Things"—he waved his hands—"are coming to a head. Zottas are freaking."

"Zottas are always freaking. That's what they do. Worry whether they have more than everyone."

"That's not what I'm talking about, Ets." This was Kersplebedeb's name for Etcetera. For a guy called Kersplebedeb, Kersplebedeb was impatient with other peoples' multisyllabic names. Everyone else got one syllable. "That's the baseline social anxiety that keeps default's boilers running. But for the past three generations, zottas have expanded their families. It used to be only one kid got to be stratospherically wealthy. The others would be shirttail squillionaires. They'll never be poor, but they're not going to change the course of nations. They're two orders of magnitude poorer than the eldest.

"Money's relative. When your big brother gets to be a hundred times richer than you, it means his kids get to go into orbit for Christmas break, have dinner with presidents, while your kids merely go to Eton or UCC and do deep-sea sub dives instead of space shots. They have dinner with pro athletes and the pop star who plays their fifteenth birthday party. Big brother's number-two kid ends up like yours, and he's not happy about that, because number two knows it early. It warps him like it warped you. It rots a family from inside.

"The 0.001 percent *can* bud off three fortunes, branching dynasties for the whole brood. This makes things worse because when you're jealous of your brother, that's Old Testament badness. Ends with 'a fugitive and a vagabond shalt thou be in the earth.'"

Etcetera looked puzzled. Kersplebedeb said, "Cain and Abel." Etcetera mouthed, "Oh," and made a go-on gesture. He'd had decent-sized gulps of lichen-juice and was filled with expansive goodwill.

"The endgame: even *those* zottas run out of new territory to conquer to carry on geometrically expanding their fortunes. There's nothing left to squeeze out of the rest of us. The capital owned by non-zottas has dropped to negligible. If some desperate zotta figured out how to confiscate *all* of it, he wouldn't get one dowry's worth for his number-two kid."

"So they turn on each other?"

"We've sat through this movie before." Kersplebedeb touched his nose in a gesture Etcetera eventually recognized as meaning "on the nose." "In the nineteenth century, the rich had the same pattern—one kid from each family got the name and the estate, everyone else became a comfortable nonentity, or, if they were very lucky, got married off to someone else's number one. Then came the colonial era, new worlds to plunder, and whoosh, geometric expansion for two generations, long enough that there was no one alive who could remember a time when the dynasty was a straight line instead of an expanding tree of fortunes."

"What happened?"

"They ran out of colonies," Kersplebedeb said.

"What happened when they ran out?"

"Oh!" Kersplebedeb took a long drink. Sighed as his Adam's apple worked. "World War One broke out. They turned on each other."

## [vi]

Limpopo flexed her arms in the confines of her environmental suit. It was a fourth-generation model, fresh off the printer and snapped together around her body by a Thetford spacie who made anachronistic squire-and-knight references. When she asked him, he shrugged and said, "Sci-fi and fantasy are two sides of the same coin." He had a twang that might be Texan, and looked like he might be Vietnamese. Spacies came from all over. They had a wild-eyed visionary aspect that set them apart, even by walkaway standards, where wild-eyed-ness came with the job.

The suit was stiff but not terrible. There was a hydraulic boost in the joints that helped it support itself, gave it strength of its own, like a junior mecha-loader. She'd ordered hers skinned with a mosaic of van-art Hobbits and elves she'd picked from a catalog, and watched in fascination as an algorithm figured out how to resize and tessellate them so that they covered the whole suit without any mismatched edges.

She'd been outside once since they'd arrived, ferried by bubble-car into a bouncy-castle room they used for common space. That time, she'd gone in a loaner suit, a gen-2, and it had been so hot and ungainly that she'd done a circuit around one of the ruined houses and gone back in, face mask clouded with condensation and scratches.

Now she had the custom-fitted gen-4, she was ready to try again. They had a house rule of going in pairs, and she knew Sita had been champing to get outside. They got acquainted on the long march and working in the makeshift infirmary after the *Better Nation* had been shot down. They were both scared and excited by the rage that burned in Sita. It was a casual ruthlessness in her desire to defend walkaways. She took over defense of the column, putting up drones in a rotating pattern, working evenings to charge and inspect their weapons—mostly pulsed sound and energy weapons, though there was a big, weird projectile thing, a rail-gun they'd brought from Walkaway U and then towed from the B&B.

Now they were settled in at Thetford Space City, Sita led the project to get neural scanners running, providing administrative and work-flow support. Her own background—computational linguistics—didn't have practical application to that part of the project, so once things were humming, she didn't have anything to do besides bringing hot drinks to real experts, and she got squirrelly.

Sita's suit was tiled with a forest camouflage pattern that was composed of thousands of distorted faces sporting bizarre expressions. Looking at it made Limpopo's eyes go swimmy.

"Ready?" Sita said, through the point-to-point network. It was encrypted, used multiple bands for redundancy, and had clever telemetry in its radios that also detected interference and used it to infer the state of the electromagnetic environment, allowing it to overcome electrical storms. Sita's voice was so crisp, so beautifully EQ'ed with the ambient wind sounds and the windmill thrums, so well-corrected in binaural space that she sounded like a game character.

Limpopo gave her a thumbs-up and punched the airlock button. They crowded together, and she got Sita's elbow in the side, making the suit rub along her scar in a way that wasn't entirely unpleasant. At a time when so many of the people around her treated their bodies as inconvenient meatsuits they were obliged to use as mechas for toting around their precious brains, it was nice to have a piece of her identity that was inextricably bound to her flesh.

Her last trip out an airlock had been a confusion of impeded movement, chafed skin, and poor visibility. Now, stepping into the tall, brittle wild grass poking out the snow, sapphire visor so clear it felt like UI, complete with lens-flare, she was struck by the place's beauty.

Sita gave her a shove from behind. "Dude, don't block the door."

"Sorry." She sidestepped. The trees were tall and lavish with needles, the snow so fluffy, the sky an expanse of dramatic clouds. "Just a bit—"

"Hard to remember it's a blasted wasteland when it's this beautiful. You should see the wildlife. Moose, deer, even wildcats, judging from scat and paw prints. And birds! Owls, of course, but so many winter birds, you'd swear migration was an urban legend."

"How?"

Sita struck off through the snow, sinking to her knees with each step. Limpopo walked in her footprints, marveling at her suit's wicking sweat from her back.

"No people. It's like this around Chernobyl. Turns out that, relative to sharing a biome with humans, living in the shadow of a radioactive plume or a place where the dirt and air are forty percent asbestos is a good deal."

"You put it that way and we sound like a blight."

"Whaddya mean 'we,' White Man?"

She knew the joke—"Tonto, the Indians have us surrounded!" "What do you mean 'we' White Man?"—even though she'd never read a Lone Ranger book or played the game or seen the cartoons or whatever, but it took a moment to get Sita's meaning.

"Really? Anyone who wants a body is worse than asbestos?"

Sita stopped. The snow was above her knees. She was really having to work to keep up the pace. Limpopo heard her hard breathing in the earbuds. "Let me catch my breath." Then: "It's kind of obvious. The amount of stuff we consume to survive, it's crazy. End-timers used to project our consumption levels forward, multiplying our population by our needed resources, and get to this point where we'd run out of planet in a generation and there'd be famine and war.

"That kind of linear projection is the kind of thinking that gets people into trouble when they think about the future. It's like thinking, 'well, my kid is learning ten exciting new things every week, so by the time she's sixty, she'll be smarter than any human in history.' There are lots of curves that start looking like they go up and to the right forever, but turn into bell curves, or inverted *Us*, or *S*-curves, or the fabled hockey-stick that gets steeper and steeper until it goes straight vertical. Any assumption that we're going to end up like now, but moreso, is so insufficiently weird it's the only thing you can be sure *won't* happen in the future."

Limpopo looked at the sky with its scudding clouds, listened to the trees rattling. Her suit's temperature was perfect ambient, a not-warm/not-cool you wouldn't notice if it wasn't minus twenty around you. "I thought the B&B crew liked heavy discussions at the drop of a hat, but then I met you academics. Shit, you like to broaden the frame."

Limpopo saw her shoulders shake a little, and she had a moment's panic that she'd inadvertently reduced Sita to tears, not unheard of in walkaways, everyone carrying around hidden trauma-triggers you could trip by accident.

When she slogged through the snow and looked at her faceplate, she saw Sita was laughing silently, staring fixedly ahead. When she followed Sita's gaze, she saw they were being stared down by a moose with an antler rack at least as wide as she was tall.

"Big moose," she whispered.

"Shh," said Sita, through a hiccuping laugh.

Limpopo made the hand gesture that bookmarked her suit's video-recording for interestingness and a soft red light pulsed in the top right of her visor. The moose regarded them for a moment. It had threadbare upholstery spots over its knees. Its shaggy fur glittered with ice crystals. Steam poured out of its nostrils in plumes that swirled in the breeze. Its jaw was ajar, making it look comically stunned, but when she looked into its huge eyes, she saw an unmistakable keenness. This moose wasn't anyone's fool.

The moose shifted and a large turd plopped into the snow, melting and disappearing, leaving behind a steaming hole. They snickered at the unexpected earthiness. It gave them a look Limpopo read as "Oh do grow up," though that was anthropomorphizing. It shuffled around in a broad circle, ungainly legs swinging in all directions but somehow not stepping in its own turd crater, turned its broad backside to them and walked—no, *sauntered*—away with a sway-hipped gait that was pure fucks-given-none.

Both of them burst into laughter. It rolled on, turning into giggle fits that ricocheted between them. Whenever one of them started to taper, the other got things rolling again.

"Say what you will about bodies," Limpopo said, at last, "they sure are *funny*."

"No argument."

"Come on." Limpopo took the lead. There was a birch stand ahead, huge trees with curls of white bark peeling away like cuticles begging to be picked at. Limpopo remembered her days after the fire, living on the land. She'd lost her gas-phase stove/generator and been reduced to building campfires, stoking them with shreds of birch bark. She had been traumatized and hurt, but her literal time in the wilderness had a reflective peace, slow-paced satisfaction for each day survived that she'd missed ever since.

"I can practically *hear* what you're thinking."

"What's that?" Limpopo led them past the birch to a fast-moving icy brook with the footprints of many species around it. She tentatively stepped into the rushing water, feeling it as soft massage through the suit's insulation. The grip-surfaces on her boot soles bound her fast to the streambed. From the brook's middle, she could see uphill and downhill for some distance. She admired the hills above her, the valley below.

"You're thinking how all this beautiful stuff proves that living in a virtual environment would never be truly satisfyingly human."

"I wasn't thinking that, but it's certainly something I *have* thought."

"Smart-ass." Sita maneuvered into the streambed, finding a deeper spot, sinking to her knees. "This is beautiful, no question. Being stimulated with this view and this environment is profoundly satisfying."

Limpopo stopped herself from saying *We agree then, let's get walking* because that kind of flippancy was more Seth's department and because this was eating Sita.

"Go on."

"First, I'd like you to consider that the reaction we have is a marker for something we could call 'goodness' or 'rightness.'"

"Or 'beauty'?"

"Sure. There's a body of computational linguistics on the difference between 'beauty' and 'goodness.' I don't propose we go down that rathole, but this demands further discussion."

"Noted."

"Good." She sloshed to the other side and went into a pine stand where the trees leaned toward the open sky over the crick. "Come on." Now she was in the lead, heading uphill, and Limpopo understood that there was an abandoned road ahead, switchbacking up the hill. It was blanketed with snow and she wondered if there was any way to attach cross-country skis to the environment suit, because that looked damned challenging.

"This is beautiful, good and virtuous. It is most prolific and healthy without us. So the best human course is to absent ourselves from it, to do what the original Thetfordians did, but on a grand scale. Evacuate the planet."

"Uh."

"Think of it for a minute. I'm not talking mass suicide. I'm talking about balancing our material needs with our aesthetic or, if you want to call it that, our *spiritual* needs. We'd be seriously bummed if all the wilderness disappeared. We care about Earth and the things that live here because we co-evolved with them, so our brains are the products of millions of years' worth of selection for being awed and satisfied by this kind of place.

"At the same time, we're consumptive top predators with the propensity to engage in self-evolution. We've hacked Lysenkoism into Darwin."

"You lost me."

"Lysenko. Soviet scientist. Thought you could change an organism's germ plasm by physically altering the organism. If you cut off a frog's leg, then cut off its offspring's leg, then *its* offspring's leg, eventually you'd get a line of naturally three-legged frogs."

"That's dumb."

"It was attractive to Stalin, who loved the idea of shaping a generation and imprinting the changes on their kids—which happens, just not genetically. If you teach a generation of people they have to step on their neighbors to survive, setting up a society where everyone who doesn't gets stepped on, the kids of those people will learn to betray their neighbors from the cradle."

"Sounds familiar."

"That was just for starters. Stalin insisted they could weatherproof wheat by growing it in shitty conditions. That ended badly. Famine. Millions dead."

"But now we can, uh, 'hack Lysenkoism'?"

"We have cultural as well as genetic traits. We pass them on. When we come up with a society like default, it selects for people who are wasteful jerks that succeed by stabbing their neighbors in the back, even though we've got a species-wide priority of not going extinct through environmental catastrophe, pandemic, and war."

They wound up and up the hill. The snow was just as deep, but there weren't trees to avoid, so the going was easier. Still, Limpopo was getting puffed out, to her embarrassment. Sita, fifteen years older, showed no sign of slowing, so Limpopo swallowed her pride and called for a rest. They were over the tree line and could see over it deep into the basin, the weird tunnel-scape of the spacies, the rotting houses and farms colonized by small trees that just pierced the snow.

"Wow," Limpopo said, not subjecting her laboring lungs to anything longer.

"Indeed. So, Lysenkoism. With the sims, we can make Lysenkoism work. Think of Dis inside her constraint envelope. We've brainwashed her—or helped her brainwash herself—to be fine with being a simulation."

A cold feeling spread in Limpopo's gut. She looked at Sita with horror. "You're not talking about turning people into sims who aren't moved by natural beauty?"

Sita stared through her face mask. "Oh girl, *no*. Jesus, you think I'm a monster? We could constrain our sims to spaces where we value nature so much that we prefer to be disembodied and not a force for its destruction, to experiencing it directly."

"That's just weird."

They moved again. Two switchbacks later, Limpopo said, "I think I've got that. That is some fucked up shit."

"For hundreds of years, people have been trying to get everyone to live gently on the land, but their whole pitch was, 'hold still and try not to breathe.' It was all hair-shirt, no glory in nature's beauty. The environmental prescription has been to act as much as possible like you were already dead. Don't reproduce. Don't consume. Don't trample the earth or you'll compress the dirt and kill the plants. Every exhalation poisons the atmosphere with CO2. Is it any wonder we haven't gotten there?

"We know there's truth in it. It's all around us. You can only act like the planet is infinite—like wishful thinking trumped physics—for so long before it goes to shit. That's why Cape Canaveral is a SCUBA site. Think about it too long and you'll come to the conclusion that nothing you do matters. It's either kill yourself now or kill your descendants just by drawing breath.

"Now we've got a deal for humanity that's better than anything before: lose the body. Walk away from it. Become an immortal being of pure thought and feeling, able to travel the universe at light speed, unkillable, consciously deciding how you want to live your life and making it stick, by fine-tuning your parameters so you're the version of yourself that does the right thing, that knows and honors itself."

They came to a ruined building, a vast refinery or processing plant, big as an aerodrome, two great cave-ins marring the roofline.

Sita gestured at it. "A couple years without maintenance and it just *imploded*. It's the climate control. Place like that, unless you build it air- and vapor-tight, give it a Q factor like a space suit, it'll cost you more to heat than you could make by running it. That stuff needs climate control or it starts to trap moisture, and come summer it rots. The next winter it's worse. A couple years later, boom, it's rubble. That thing was a giant computer that housed people and machines, and when they turned the computer off, it was an instant tear-down.

"The universe hates us. We are temporary violations of the second law of thermodynamics. We push entropy off to the edges, but it's patient, and it builds, and when we take our eyes off of it, kerblam, it's back with a vengeance.

"You want to change the history of the future, give us a chance for a life worth living, without oppression? There's only one way. You know it, but you can't make yourself face it."

"But I could if I was a sim? Nudge the sliders until I was in the envelope that loved being simulated?"

"Bingo. We'd have a world that belonged to animals, and we'd experience it through sensors that perfectly simulated our wet stuff, but without crushing all those precious roots."

"Can I make a suggestion?"

"Go ahead."

"When you make this pitch, don't mention Lysenko. Making the world a better place by realizing the failed dreams of the pet mad scientist of one of history's greatest monsters—"

"Duh."

"Just saying."

"The point isn't Lysenko or Stalin. It's the angels of our better natures. Everything we know we *should* do but can't bring ourselves to do because the part of us that sees the whole map and knows it's the way to go can't convince the part that's in the driver's seat. It's about being able to choose, make the choice stick."

"What if someone else chooses for you?"

"If someone else gets control over your sliders? Disaster. Teetotal capsizement. Terror without historical parallel. Better make sure that doesn't happen."

"I get the feeling that you've already planned this argument, Sita. An ambush."

"Not an ambush," she said. "Just the marketplace of ideas. We're getting somewhere, something is brewing that's going to bubble over. We're part of it. I want to get everyone ready for it, so there's a minimum of headless chickening."

Limpopo remembered arguments with Jimmy about the way the world was about to change and how she had to face it, how he'd offered to put her in charge if she backed him. It was so nakedly manipulative that she'd never been tempted. Is that what Sita was doing? If so, why wasn't her back up?

"One more question."

"As many as you'd like, Limpopo."

"Just one. Then I want to go back to enjoying nature."

"Shoot."

"Why do we have differing levels of executive control over our minds? Why would we evolve to foil our own better natures?"

"Because evolution isn't directed. It's not streamlined. We're an attic stuffed with everything our ancestors found useful, even if it stopped being useful thousands of years ago. Unless it makes you have fewer babies, it hangs around in the genome. Being out of control of your rational priorities certainly increases the number of babies you'll make."

Limpopo laughed in spite of herself, despite Sita having obviously used that line before. "All that stuff in the attic, it's useful, right? That's why the attics themselves haven't been squeezed out by evolution. Having a statistically normal distribution across every trait—including the ability to make up your mind and stick to it—means that as a species we're able to face a variety of challenges. We've got a tool for every occasion, genomically speaking."

"Can I interrupt you?"

"Of course."

"This isn't a new argument. There's a whole neurodiversity contingent who hate my ideas of sliders, and want to preserve our incapacity to 'make up your mind and stick to it' in case there's some hypothetical species-destroying crossroads in the future where we need to rescue it. I say, *you* keep your irrationality intact. I'll switch mine off. Other people can make up their own minds. Because the inability to see reason *is* a species-destroying crossroads and we're *at it now.* If we don't figure out how to put off gratification today for survival tomorrow, to beat the solipsist's delusion that you're a special snowflake—"

"Okay, I know how this goes."

"I know you do."

They picked through the ruins, over huge machines under their blankets of snow and treacherous piles of rubble that could be used as wobbly staircases to reach the remains of the roof and odd preserved relics, including a manager's station with a faded set of laminated safety memos tacked around its missing observation window.

"If it turns out the level of executive control we get from sims backfires, we'll just turn it off. That's the point of executive control: deciding what you're going to do."

"What about the existential crises?"

"What?"

"Iceweasel told me that Dis kept suiciding—"

"Crashing."

"Terminally freaking. Until you figured out how to constrain her to versions of herself that wouldn't have existential crises."

"Yeah . . ." She sounded cautious. Limpopo sensed weakness.

"You can't simulate someone unless you turn down the slider that freaks out at the thought of being simulated."

"Yes . . ." Deeper caution.

"What happens if you ditch your bodies, upload, and it turns out the human race can't survive without whatever makes us terrified of losing our bodies?"

"That is perverse."

"It's not. It's not hard to think of an aversion to having a body-ectomy as pro-survival. What if you're engineering the mass suicide of the human race?"

"All you've got is a hypothetical. I've got a concrete risk: we *are* in the midst of mass suicide. If it turns out turning off our existential terror makes us give up hope and switch ourselves off, we'll deal with that when it arrives. Come on, Limpopo, be serious."

The rebuttal was so hot, so different from the argument thus far, Limpopo knew she'd touched something tender. It wasn't a pleasant feeling. When people got like this, you couldn't convince them of anything. She wished for a way to turn off Sita's anxiety, a slider she could dial to a middle ground where Sita could confront her anxieties without freaking. Sita wished she had one, too.

## [vii]

"Hello, Jacob," Natalie said. She hadn't called him that before, but *Dad* wouldn't cut it. Her father gripped the foot of her bed while the door's locks cycled, clunk-*clunk*.

"I don't like this, you know."

"Then let's stop it. You untie me and let me go, and we'll part ways. Not every family stays a family forever. I'll send you a Christmas card every year and I'll come to the funeral. No hard feelings."

He looked wounded. That might have been partly genuine, which was amazing, considering that she was in four-point restraint. The moment passed.

"Your mother and sister want to visit."

She rolled her eyes. Dis had been her constant companion since she'd awoken in the bolt-hole. Without her, Natalie imagined she would have been in quite a weakened state, desperate for company. Solitary confinement was officially torture. She ping-ponged between a conviction Dis was a traitor and the possibility Dis was genuinely on her side, but even that state of indeterminacy was a chewy mental problem that kept her sane.

"It's not like I could stop them."

He pursed his lips. "Don't be difficult—" She suppressed a snort. "I can't bring them in while you're like this."

She couldn't suppress the second snort. "You make it sound like I tied *myself* up."

"What the fuck else was I supposed to do? Natalie, I'm being *gentle* with you. Do you know what other parents do with kids who run away with your friends? Do you have any idea what that kind of deprogramming looks like?"

"I have a pretty good idea. I remember Lanie."

Lanie Lieberman was her best friend until the year they turned thirteen, when Lanie went off-piste, sneaking away for daring encounters with boys, booze, and the kind of club where the bouncers let a thirteen-year-old in if she dressed right and came with the right louche rich boy. They'd grounded her, put trackers on her, droned her, put a bodyguard on her, then two, but Lanie was a Houdini—especially with help from scumbag kid-fiddling older boys from families even richer than hers, who had their own money for the countermeasures Lanie needed to get away.

After that, it had been private school, then military school, then a place for troubled kids, and finally a place whose name Lanie never spoke. It was the only one she couldn't escape from. Judging from her pallor when she returned, it had been underground or somewhere far north. In Natalie's imagination it was an abandoned mine or a stretch of tundra. The Lanie who came back from it was . . . hinky. Not just wounded, but *cross-wired* in a terrifying, mystifying way. Sad things sometimes made her laugh. When other people laughed, she'd get a look of concentration and anger, she had to keep her rage in check.

They stopped pretending they were friends by fifteen. At sixteen, Lanie got early admission to a university no one had heard of in Zurich, supposed to be an amazing boot up in the finance industry, where even math dumbos could learn to be high-flying quants. The last Natalie heard of her was a hand-delivered invitation to her father's funeral, a neat ink signature below the engraving. Natalie didn't go to the funeral and couldn't imagine the database cross-section that spit out her name as a potential attendee.

Her dad smiled wanly. "Things have come a long way since the days of Lanie Lieberman. There's trade shows for what we could be doing right now. I made two discreet queries and now I get brochures on rag paper so thick it could shingle the roof. Natalie, you're a growth industry, and the methodology is faster, more ruthless and more effective than anything from back then. Thumbscrews versus psychoanalysis."

Curious in spite of herself: "But you didn't ship me off."

"Not yet. Natalie, hard as you might find this to believe, I respect you in addition to loving you as your father. I would like the part of you that makes you *you* to survive this adventure. I don't want an automaton with a superficial resemblance to my daughter. I want you to realize all this pissing around with radical politics and campouts with dropouts is not a long-term strategy. I understand you feel guilty about having so much when everyone else has so little, but what good do you think it does to turn your back on reality? You can't wish inequality away. In my ideal world, you'd run the family foundation, oversee our good works. There's a lot of poor people out there who owe their vaccinations, water, and education to the Redwater Foundation. Take some of that energy you put into anarchy and channel it into something productive. You could even set aside a little brownfield for experimental communities based on walkaway principles."

She just stared at him. She knew if she'd really been in solitary all that time, this would have sounded like a hell of an offer. If not for Dis, she'd beg for this. She knew how susceptible she was to isolation. It wasn't just being alone. It was being alone *with herself*. Did this mean Dis wasn't working for her father? Or was this a subtle, super-Machiavellian Jacob Redwater deal that made him the stuff of legend, even in zotta circles?

"When are Mom and Cordelia going to visit?"

He shook his head. It was so patronizing. "Your mother isn't going to bail you out. She's more upset than I am. Cordelia, well, she's afraid of you. Wants to put you on anti-psychotics. Thinks you're going to attack her."

"When are they coming for a visit?"

"Do you want to see them?"

She stared him down. He'd tilted her bed up to a forty-five-degree angle, so she could look at him over the rumpled white hill-scape of her sheet-draped body.

"I'll see what I can do."

When he was gone, Dis whooped loudly enough that she winced.

"Jesus, keep it down!"

"This place is so shockproof you could use it to print holograms," Dis said.

"My head isn't shockproof."

"Sorry. I don't know if I've mentioned it, but your dad is a colossal asshole."

"I'd apologize for him, but fuck that."

"Yeah."

"If it matters, I'm more convinced you're not working for him."

"What a relief."

"That voice sim is getting better at sarcasm."

"I've been sneaking updates to my local copy. The voice synth people are good—merging normalized speech recordings from MMOs and voice-response systems, getting incredible stuff out of it. *I've been playing around with some of the possibilities.*" The last sentence came out in a growl of predatory menace so scary Natalie jerked in her bonds.

"Jesus."

"I know, right? I cheated, though. Used sub-sonics. It's pretty amazing what I can do. You should hear my sexy ingénue."

"No thanks. I can't remember ever feeling less interested in sex—"

"They're coming."

The door clunked and clunked again and gasped open, and in came Natalie's mother, in her pearl gray, like a monochrome Jackie O, smaller than Natalie remembered, but no older. She took a small step inside, her nose wrinkled at a smell Natalie had lost all awareness of. She stared at Natalie. Cordelia slipped in behind her, round face a china-doll mask. Natalie felt a pang of weird sympathy for her, being with their mother on her own, the sole focus of Mother's attention.

"Hi, Mom."

Her mom circled the bed, walking around three sides before coming to the wall, retracing her steps, coming to rest beside Natalie.

"Jacob," she called. Jacob stepped into the room, looking pained.

"Yes, Frances?"

"Remove these restraints."

"Mom—" Cordelia began, but her mother held up a shaking hand.

"Jacob. Now."

They locked eyes. She remembered this from childhood, their wars of silent gazes. As she'd grown, she'd realized these were a game of chicken where each gave the other longer to contemplate the ways retribution could come, until one looked away. As usual, Jacob broke contact first.

"I'll be back."

Natalie assumed he'd gone to get the med-tech or whatever he was, but a moment later, he was back with the merc. She nodded a little at Natalie, a degree of acknowledgment that was practically a full-body hug given their previous interactions. Maybe Natalie had impressed her with her "spunk." Or maybe she'd been given permission—or orders—to lighten up.

"Frances, Cordelia, please stand back."

Mom looked like she was going to argue, but Cordelia dragged her arm. "Come *on,* Mom."

Once they had a few meters' distance between them and the bed, the merc stepped forward and locked eyes with Natalie.

"No trouble," she said, and clipped a bracelet around Natalie's wrist. Natalie lifted her head and strained to see it. It was evil blue metal. She didn't want to even guess what it did, though she couldn't stop her subconscious from gaming it out: not shock, because she could grab hold of Mom or Dad or Cordelia and the shock would go through them, too. Maybe something in her nerves, like pain, or seizures, or—

"No trouble," she agreed. The merc impersonally lifted the sheet, removed her catheter, let it retract into the bed. The sensation made her gasp with humiliation. The merc wiped her hands with a disposable and dropped it into the bed's hopper before offering her hand. Natalie took it, because after days—weeks?—supine, she was weak and dizzy and her stomach muscles refused to help swing her huge, numb legs over the bed's edge. Tears sprang into her eyes, because when she'd been a walkaway, she'd been so *strong*—they all had been. All the walking. Now she couldn't walk away even if they cleared a path. Tears rolled down her cheek and slipped into her mouth.

She snotted up the rest of the tears and blinked hard, let herself be guided to her feet. She swayed, not looking at Mom or Cordelia, locking eyes with Jacob, letting him see what he'd done to her. He'd destroyed her body, but she made her eyes shine to let him know he hadn't touched her mind.

Her mom was at her side, getting a shoulder beneath the arm whose hand didn't have an IV. The merc disconnected the other end of the hose from its bed feed, capped it with a sterile, elasticated wrap, draped the hose around Natalie's neck. Her mom smelled of her own perfume, made special by a man in Istanbul who used to come to the house once a year, during Sacrifice Feast, when he'd tour the world and drop in on his best clients while all of Turkey ground to a halt. Natalie hadn't smelled that scent—not quite sweet, not quite musky, and with a whiff of something a bit like cardamom—for years, but she remembered it more clearly than her mother's face.

Her mother gasped when she settled her weight over her shoulders. Natalie thought she was too heavy, then: "Jacob, she's like a bird!" in tones more horrified than Natalie had ever heard from her. She saw her mother's perfect skin crumpled in a grimace, eyes narrowed into slits that made the hairline wrinkles at their corners deepen in a way she hated.

"Hi, Mom."

They stood, swaying. She felt her legs giving out.

"I should sit."

They both sat. The opening in the mattress where the hoses retracted, smelly and dark, was right behind them. Her mother twisted to look at it, twisted back, and captured Jacob on an even fiercer look.

"Jacob," she began.

"Later," he said.

Natalie enjoyed his discomfiture. Cordelia stood halfway between the parents, fretting with her hands, picking her cuticles. She'd been a nail-biter, broken the habit only after several tries, and Natalie could tell that she wanted nothing more than to chow down on her own fingers.

It struck Natalie that she was the least upset among them, except for the merc. She was on a team with the merc, them versus these fucked-up zottas. That was stupid. The merc was not on her side. Come on, Natalie, focus.

"I won't be tied down again."

"No, you certainly won't," her mother agreed.

"Frances—" her father began.

"No, she won't." The staring contest smoldered again. The balance had changed. There was a new implicit threat—what would a divorce court judge say about a daughter tied to a bed, starved and intubated, locked away in a safe room? Her mother had been furious about her going walkaway, but that wouldn't stop her from deploying any leverage Jacob Redwater had handed her.

"No she won't," he said. "Excuse me." He stepped out of the room. He shut the door. Clunk-*clunk*.

Cordelia took a tentative step. Her mother extended an arm and she stepped the rest of the way, let Frances give her one of her hugs, always warm enough, always ending a moment before you expected.

Cordelia subtly leaned to Natalie, testing for the presence of a potential hug, but Natalie didn't signal back. Fuck her. For that matter, fuck Frances. They had known she was a prisoner and neither had sprung her. Getting her loosed from four-point restraint hardly qualified as liberation.

"Natalie, this is just terrible," her mother said.

*No shit*. "Uh-huh."

"Why, Natalie? There are more constructive ways to engage with the world. Why become an animal? A terrorist?"

It was so fucking stupid she couldn't manage a derisive snort. "What would you prefer?"

"Move out, if it's so bad. Your trust is mature, you could buy a place anywhere in the world. Get a job, or not. Take up a cause. Something *constructive,* Natalie. Something that won't get you killed or raped or—"

"Kidnapped by mercenaries and tied to a bed in some rich asshole's basement?"

Her mother set her jaw.

"Natalie," Cordelia said. "Can I get you anything?"

"A lawyer. Cops."

"Natalie—" Cordelia looked hurt. Natalie didn't let herself give a shit.

"You knew I was down here. You knew he had me snatched. You don't like the walkaways and you don't like that I'm one, fine. But in case you haven't noticed, I'm an adult and whether I become a walkaway is none of your business. Neither of you get a say in what I do."

"Of course we do. I'm your mother!"

Even Cordelia smirked.

She saw rage boil in their mother, different than their father's, but no less deadly. "Natalie, if you think being an adult means you don't have any duty to anyone else in the world—"

She and Cordelia both snorted. It further enraged their mother, but it was the most sisterly moment they'd shared since Natalie first went away to school.

Frances went rigid and stared straight ahead, not acknowledging them, wishing she hadn't gone straight to the maternal moment, which left her with no gracious out, and if there's one thing Frances Mannix Redwater was, it was gracious.

The door clunked, opened. Jacob came in trailed by the med-tech/paid goon, who carried a precarious armload of clothing. Natalie recognized the clothes from the dumbwaiter in her previous incarceration.

"We'll bring in a proper bed later today," Jacob said, while the man put the clothes on the floor.

"Books, too," Natalie said. "Interface stuff. Paper and something to write with."

He looked at her, then at Frances.

"No interface stuff," Frances said. "But everything else. Some furniture, too. A fridge and food."

"Hop to it," Natalie said, with a giddy laugh. Jacob ignored her. He had a goat, but you couldn't get it with a jibe as crude as that.

"Now everyone else out," Frances said. "I need to talk to Natalie alone."

Natalie closed her eyes. Not one of those talks.

"I'm tired," she said.

"You've had plenty of time to rest." Frances managed to make it into an accusation, as though Natalie had lazed around eating bonbons. It wasn't sarcasm—Frances was capable of being simultaneously outraged because she'd been tied to a bed, and because she'd been too lazy to get out of bed.

"Everyone, out." She glared at the merc, who had the sense not to look at Jacob. That would have been the end of her employment in the Redwater household. Natalie guessed being a merc in the employ of zottas required political sense.

They left and before the door clunked closed, Frances called out to Jacob. "Private. No recording."

"Frances—"

"She's not going to jump me and hold me hostage, Jacob."

"You've seen the video—"

"I saw it. That was before you tied her to a bed for a week and fed her through a tube."

"Frances—"

*"Jacob."*

Jacob turned to the merc, who was already holding something out, palm down. He passed it to Frances. "Panic button," he said.

She pointedly put it in her purse, then set the purse far from the bed, leaning against the wall, buttery yellow leather slumped against stark white. "Good-bye, Jacob."

They left the door open.

## [viii]

Limpopo was volunteering with the scanner crew when Jimmy showed up.

He didn't look as cocky as the last time they'd met, with his stupid weapons and such. He'd had a hard walk, fetched up in Thetford with a limp and a head wound, in filthy overlapping thermal layers. He was gaunt, frostbite in three fingers and all his toes.

"Fancy meeting you here," he said, when Limpopo came upon him in the great hall of the Thetford spacies, tended by a medic who listened to advice from someone far away who diagnosed Jimmy.

"You look bad," she said.

"Could have been worse. We lost fifteen on the road from Ontario. It's getting mean."

"I'm sorry."

"Not your fault. Actually, possibly it is your fault, you being a big beast in the world of scanning and sims."

"I'm a walkaway. We don't have big beasts."

The medic smiled, then did something to Jimmy's toes that made him suck air through his teeth—one missing—and squeeze his eyes.

"I think you'll keep them," she said. "Except maybe the left little toe."

"Huzzah." He rocked his jaw from side to side.

"Why are you here, Jimmy? Come to kick more people out of their homes?"

He shook his head. "It's not like that. Whatever minor philosophical differences you and I had—"

It was textbook self-delusion, but Limpopo couldn't see any reason to point it out.

"—I have more in common with you than with the assholes who came at us on the road. There's only one thing they want: a world where they're on top and everyone else *isn't*."

*I'd love to know how you differentiate that from your philosophy. But I don't guess you'd be able to explain it.*

"This is clearly where the action is. This has them shit-scared, and scheming."

"So you've come to help?"

"Look, there's an angle, something I haven't seen on the forums, an outcome that's worse than anyone's preparing for. I think it's because people like you just don't understand what backup really means."

*Backup*. A perfect, perfectly seductive name for scan and sim. She was amazed she hadn't heard it. As soon as she did, Limpopo just *knew* there must be thousands—millions—of people using the term. Once you conceived of the thing that made you *you* as data, aeons of data-handling anxiety kicked in. If you had data, it had to be backed up. Anything important that *wasn't* backed up was good as lost. Data is haunted by Murphy. Do something irreplaceable and magnificent while out of network and backup range and you were begging for critical failure that nuked it all.

"Backup," she said.

"Yes." Jimmy grinned. He'd followed her thinking. "Of course. No one has thought it through to the logical end."

"Which is?"

Despite his injuries and grubbiness, he enjoyed testing her, waiting to see if she'd spar. She knew there was no way to win a mental sparring match with Jimmy: victory would piss him off, loss would convince him he could walk all over her.

"Nice seeing you." She turned to go, because walking away solved the Jimmy problem every time. If he ever figured that out, he might be dangerous.

"It means," he said to her back, and she slowed a little, "anyone who can get your backup can find out everything there is to know about you, trick you into the worst betrayals, torture you for all eternity, and you can never walk away from it."

"Shit." She turned around.

"Anyone who talks about this gets treated as a paranoid nut. Sim people wave their hands and talk about crypto—"

"What's wrong with crypto? If no one can decrypt your sim, then—"

"If no one can decrypt your sim, no one can run your sim. If the only repository for your pass-phrase is your own brain, then when you die—"

"I get it. You'd have to trust someone with your pass-phrase so they could retrieve your key and use it to decrypt your sim."

"Your trusted third party would have to trust *her* trusted third party with her pass-phrase, and that person would need someone to trust, and there'd need to be some way to find out who had which pass-phrase because once you're croaked the last thing we'd want was to realize we'd lost your keys. Can you fucking *imagine*—sorry about your immortal birthright, we forgot the password, derp derp derp."

"Ouch."

"There's plenty of crypto weenies trying to figure this out, using shared secrets so to split the key into say, ten pieces such that any five can be used to unlock the file."

"Sounds like a good idea." She'd worked with shared secrets for the B&B's various incarnations, establishing committees of trusted parties who could collectively institute sweeping changes in the codebase, but only once a quorum agreed.

"Yes but no. Good in the sense that you need to kidnap and torture a lot more people to unlock someone's sim without permission, but from a complexity perspective it's worse—you're multiplying the number of interlocking relationships necessary to retrieve a sim by ten. As in: now you've got ten problems."

"What's the answer?"

"That's what I'm worried about—the answer is going to be no answer. There's *urgency*, it's all going to blow up soon. Back in default, they're treating Akron like an ISIS stronghold, like the fucking *end-times*. I'd be surprised if they didn't *nuke* it."

"Fallout."

"They'll blame us for it and set up a contract to treat radiation sickness with some zotta's emergency services company. You don't know what it's like out there."

"I know some things."

"I guess you do. Sorry, I didn't mean to, you know—"

"Mansplain."

He looked awkward. She could tell he wished they'd had an argument. He was so easy to outmaneuver, because he couldn't imagine the people around him weren't trying to outmaneuver him.

"Limpopo, it's been rough for me, the last couple years. After the B&B, uh—"

"Imploded."

"I was angry for a long time. I was angry at you, though I knew it was my fault. Who else's fault could it be? I chased you out."

"You did worse than that."

"I did worse than that. I threw you out."

"No. You never did that." *You couldn't do that.*

"I couldn't do that." He wasn't as dumb as he looked. "I took things from you because I thought it would make me strong, because I thought what you were doing was making people weak. But all that stuff, strong and weak—"

"Bullshit."

"Entirely. Strong and weak isn't *what* you do, it's *why* you do it." He paused. She was about to say something. "Also what you do. It's not charity or noblesse oblige to treat people like they're all equally worthy, even if they aren't all equally 'useful'—whatever useful means." He looked ready to cry. The medic stopped working on his toes and watched him intently. He looked at her, at Limpopo, sighed. Then he went on, which impressed Limpopo, because this confession would be all over Thetford by the time he'd found a place to sleep.

"I told myself I was making the world better. I thought there were 'useful' and 'useless' people and if you didn't keep the useful people happy, the useless ones would starve. *Of course* I put myself in the useful group. I knew this important secret thing about useless and useful people, and if that's not useful, what is? I told myself I was making more of everything for everyone. We just needed to let people who were worth the most do whatever they wanted. It was fucked up. I fucked up. That's what I'm trying to say sorry for."

"Your problem is you think 'useless' and 'useful' are properties of people instead of things people *do*. A person can perform usefulness, or antiusefulness, depending on circumstances. Evolutionary winnowing didn't somehow pass over the people who don't contribute the way you want them to, leaving a backlog of natural selection for you to take care of. The reason everything about us is distributed on a normal curve, with a few weirdos way off in the long tails at the right and left and everyone else lumped together under the bulge is that we need people who get on with stuff, and a few firefighters who are kinked just the right way to sort out the weirdest shit happening around the edges. We assume someone who puts out a fire is a one-hundred-meter-tall superhero fated to save the universe, as opposed to someone who got lucky, once, and has been given lots more opportunities to get lucky since."

"That's what I'm trying to say, yeah. It's hard to figure this shit. It twists my head that I only started disbelieving in useful and useless people when *I* proved to be useless. Then I had this revelation that the scale I'd judged people on—the scale I was failing on—was irrelevant. That's one of those convenient things that reeks of bullshitting yourself."

"I happen to agree the old scale was bullshit, so I'm giving you a pass."

He winced as the medic did something to his toes. Two of them looked bad, black at the tips. Limpopo looked away, grimacing.

"Thanks," he grunted, though whether he was talking to her or the medic, she couldn't say.

# [ix]

The party wasn't Pocahontas's idea, but she took off with it. At first, Etcetera was horrified at the thought. He couldn't imagine anything worth celebrating amid the death and anxiety. Iceweasel was disappeared and Gretyl was buried in secret projects. He was convinced everyone would be offended, from spacies to late arrivals to aviators to the B&B crew who mourned their dead, but as Pocahontas posted notices of the party's progress to the spacies' social hub, it was clear the only anxiety anyone felt about a party was that someone else might hate it.

Pocahontas was a force of nature. She'd been the first of their crew to figure out how to run the space-suit fabbers, made herself a gorgeous suit she wore on a series of epic, multi-day treks, establishing contact with nearby First Nations bands. Though they weren't as political as she, none had any use for default and all were curious about the weird spacies who'd taken over Thetford, so many years after it was abandoned. Pocahontas had used the Thetford fab to print parts for a new space-suit fabber, stacking them outside a utility corridor, ready to be hauled to her new friends by anyone who could make a vehicle capable of the run. Gretyl was working on refurbing the engine of their cargo-train, which limped into Thetford. They'd have scrapped it if there hadn't been so many wounded who couldn't finish the voyage on their own legs.

Gretyl was better than Etcetera had any right to expect. Seth told him what she'd done, and though she rarely heard from Dis—the sim was running on the safe room's own servers, to avoid the risk of discovery through mountains of traffic where none was expected—the terse messages made her stoic, if not cheerful. According to Dis, Iceweasel was sane and intact despite torture. She was made of indomitable steel. "If she's not losing her shit, how could I?" Gretyl said, one morning, as Limpopo brought them coffium and fresh rolls.

"You going to sing?" Limpopo said. Etcetera looked sharply at her. Gretyl had a beautiful voice, torchy. Back in the ancient days of the B&B common room, she'd passed evenings singing songs from her deep repertoire, accompanied by zero or more B&B musicians. A capella, she was astounding; with a band, she was transcendent. But she hadn't sung since Iceweasel was taken from her.

"At the party?" Gretyl said.

"At the party."

"Is there a band?" Etcetera thought she was looking for an out—*I don't think I could do it unaccompanied* or *we don't have time to practice*—but her eyes glinted.

"The spacies have a couple of bands, but I don't know if they're any good."

Pocahontas—who'd flitted through the common space, directing people as they set up for the party—homed in on them, having followed this conversation on the hoof.

"There's a good band and a so-so band," she said.

"What kind of music?"

"The good band is loud and fast. The so-so band does folk stuff."

"I'll sing with both of them," she said.

Pocahontas gave her hand a squeeze. "Done. Thanks."

"You want some coffium?" Etcetera said. Watching Pocahontas dash around made him exhausted.

"I don't drug."

They all looked uncomfortable. Etcetera hadn't known any First Nations people personally, but he knew there was stuff about booze and other substances. He shrugged. They were all walkaways, right? Man, woman, white, brown, First Nations, or otherwise.

"Sorry," Limpopo said. He wondered if he should have apologized, too. He felt stupid and anxious, and that meant it was something he should be paying attention to.

"No biggie. Your neurotransmitters are your own business."

"What can we do to help?" Etcetera looked for a better subject.

Instantly: "Get the fab to Dead Lake," she said. "They can't come to the party without protective suits."

"Ah," Etcetera said. He should have known she'd say that.

"We'll all get on it," Limpopo said, and squeezed his hand, though whether it was sympathy or a reminder to live up to his promises, he couldn't say. "Count on us."

"I am," she said, with the solemn simplicity that she had in endless supply. It killed the mood's lightness, made them gravely committed to throwing a party of unparalleled fun. Pocahontas looked from face to face, smiled, and launched herself in the direction of another group.

Gretyl watched her go. "She's amazing. A party." She shook her head. "And now we've got to get those fab parts, what, seventy klicks?"

"Sorry."

"Nothing to apologize for. It's high time we got the cargo-train running." She drank her coffium. "Some of that stuff is wedged tight and won't come out without a fight. We'll hack it out. It'll be tough in the suits."

"Yeah."

"Don't be glum," Limpopo said. "It'll be fun to do hard work for a change."

She was right. Back when they'd built the second B&B, this was a common fixture of their days—some big, hard technological challenge they'd have to solve together, downloading tutorials and tapping the global walkaway frequency to find someone who could get through the problem. Sometimes, they'd labor over a trivial technical problem for weeks, stumped, until, one day, something worked, and the experience would be sweeter for the bitterness of the struggle.

He drained his coffium and looked at the party preparations all around him, and remembered he was a walkaway. He was living the first days of a better nation, doing something that meant something. His existence was a feature and not a bug.

Limpopo smiled. She'd read his thoughts.

"Drink up," she said to Gretyl. "Let's get down to it."

Etcetera felt the tension melt out of his back, replaced with warm purpose. Work needed doing, and he could help. What more could anyone ask for?

---

When Gretyl shucked her suit, she was a mass of aches that had not manifested when she was deep in work, hacking at the damaged carrier train with saws, blasting it with cutting torches, hammering at unyielding metal and polymers.

She stood by the airlock, smelling her stink. She groaned and put her forehead to the wall.

"You okay?" Tam looked genuinely, embarrassingly concerned. When Tam joined the Walkaway U crowd, Gretyl mothered her, helping her navigate the opaque waters of the academic enclave. After the attack, Gretyl watched with pride as Tam transformed into a dervish, ferrying people and supplies into the tunnels, risking her life, strong and inspiring.

Since she'd lost Iceweasel, Gretyl's world had smashed to fragments. Even at the best of times she felt like a fractured vase that had been glued together by a cack-handed repairer, cracks on display for all to see. Damaged goods. Tam had flipped their script, trying to mother Gretyl in a way Gretyl hated, not least because she needed it.

"I'm okay." Gretyl tried to starch her posture, paint on a smile. Working on the engine was hard, but it gave her a break from all-consuming fear for Iceweasel. The worst part about being mothered was her own pathetic need to be mothered.

"That's good. Because honestly, you look like chiseled shit."

"Thanks."

"Someone had to tell you the truth, dude." Tam slipped behind her. Her hands gripped Gretyl's shoulders. "You're tight as a tennis racket." She squeezed experimentally, strong thumbs digging into Gretyl's shoulders. Gretyl groaned.

Now Tam's hands were on her, she felt the tension, like a rubber band pulled to the breaking point. Despite herself, she leaned into Tam, and Tam squeezed back. Gretyl groaned again.

"Come on, then." Tam continued to knead. "Tell me where it hurts." Gretyl heard the grin. Tam was enjoying this. Gretyl gave up. "What are you doing now?"

"Gonna find somewhere to sleep." The spacies' complex, crowded before they arrived, was now thronged, and it was a juggling act to find a free bed—or even a corner where bedding could be placed temporarily—in the evening. "We stopped for a late lunch and I was gonna sleep dinner. I mean skip dinner."

"You're in luck." Tam worked the knots. "Seth and I found a place. It's big." She squeezed. "And comfy."

Gretyl groaned. "Come on then." Surrender felt good.

The room was big enough that Gretyl felt guilty. But it was a weird shape, with low ceilings in places, uneven flooring in others, the result of a weather event that buckled the bulkheads, introducing cracks whose temporary seals no one had made permanent.

It was lit with constellations of throwie lights, scattered in smears across the ceiling and walls, and there was a spacie-style adaptive sleep-surface, millions of sensor-embedded foam cells, like a living thing that cuddled and supported you according to an algorithm that second-guessed your circulation, writhing in a way that was disturbing and wonderful.

Seth was already lounging in his underpants, sipping lichen tequila from one of the glass bulbs that were everywhere in Thetford, though she hadn't met the prolific glassblower.

He waved the bulb blearily and called out a greeting. Tam barked at him in mock drill sergeant to pull himself together and offer their guest hospitality. He climbed to his feet, found booze and another bulb—elongated like a teardrop, shot with swirls of cyanotic blue and rusty orange/red—and poured. She started to wave it off, then caught the smell and relented.

*Fuck it.* She took a burning sip, swirling it through her foul-tasting mouth, and letting it trickle down her dry throat.

"Hot towels." Tam snapped her fingers. Seth groaned theatrically but pulled on drawstring pants and stepped out.

"You don't need to—" Gretyl said.

"Oh yes we do." Tam pinched her nose dramatically. Gretyl shrugged. She probably did stink—the B&B's onsen was far behind, and the weeks underground after the bombing of Walkaway U had accustomed her to a baseline of BO that fulfilled every default stereotype of stinky walkaways.

Tam rifled through chests crammed into a crawl space, consulting her interface, coming up with a pair of silk-like robes, chucking one to Gretyl. They kicked their dirty clothes into the sizable pile left by Seth, shrugged into the robes, and collapsed into bed.

Seth wheeled in an insulated chest. He popped the lid, releasing fragrant steam. There were showers at the spacies' compound, but swollen numbers had driven everyone to the wikis for alternatives from other walkaways, and the towels were a winner. It wasn't easy to bathe yourself with them, but that was a feature, not a bug, far as most people were concerned.

Seth flopped down between them. "Okay, I'm ready."

Tam slugged him in the arm—Gretyl saw that she kept her middle knuckle raised, driving it straight into the meat of his bicep. "No. Way."

He rubbed his arm. "Ow."

"Yes," she explained. "Ow. Want another?" She made a fist. Gretyl saw they were both trying to suppress grins. Young love.

"Okay, who's first?"

"Guests first," Tam said.

Gretyl wanted to object, but lying on the bed, swaddled in the soft robe, sapped her of her residual strength. . . . Groaning—theatrically, this time—she shrugged out of the robe, feeling her skin goose-pimple as the recirculated air kissed it.

The first heavy, wet, fragrant towel made contact, draped across her back with a wet slap followed by a spreading heat that was like a languorous tongue, and then it was joined by another, wielded by Tam, across the backs of her legs. Tam rubbed along her sore, tight hamstrings. The four hands scrubbed at her through the heat, strumming her aching muscles, clever thumbs and grinding knuckles, elbows in the unyielding knots. Where the towels slipped, her wet skin shrank from the air currents.

All too soon, they told her to roll over, and they did her front, working her abdominal muscles, her thighs, her clenched jaw, her scalp. The towels were soaked with sage and pine. The smell suffused the room. She kept nodding off, luxuriating in attention, then waking as a knuckle caught a sore spot.

Then it was Tam's turn. There were more hot towels in the crate. Seth found a thermostat interface and cranked up the heat. Gretyl dispensed with the robe, which made things easier as she worked the hot towels into Tam's skinny legs and bony back. Seth brought more lichen juice, and she spilled some on her fingers, and when she licked it off, she tasted the sage and pine. The flavor was incredible and she told them so. They dribbled booze over their fingers and licked away and everyone agreed and they also got looser and mellower. And sloppier.

By the time they moved on to Seth, the heat, moisture, and booze made the room as swimmy as a Turkish bath. There were dry towels in a compartment with its own element. They came out warm and fluffy as kittens. Bundled up, they burrowed beneath the covers.

Gretyl marveled at the feeling of peace, the intimacy that was asexual and sensuous at the same time. It was childlike, a feeling from before sex, or maybe the feeling of someone very old, beyond sex. Everything was at peace.

So why was she crying?

The tears had slipped silently down her cheeks for some time. She noticed them because they were pooling in her ears and slipping down her neck. She'd once sliced her hand with a kitchen knife, and there'd been a moment when she'd stared at the pulsing blood, understood it, but not felt it, before the pain crashed on her, radioactively intense and thunderclap-sudden. She'd shouted in surprise—not at the wound, but at the sudden onset of pain.

It was the same now: the wound visible, the ache lagging it. She gulped, sobbed, then brayed, doubling over like she'd been punched in the stomach. The pain there was sickening. All her buried fear and sadness for her lover crashed down.

Seth figured it out first, wrapping her in his arms, murmuring *shh-shh,* rocking her. Tam was slower on the uptake, but she took Gretyl's hands and squeezed them, saying *that's right, let it out.* Gretyl was so far down her pain that she didn't worry about being mothered by Tam.

The sorrow was obliterating. The siren-wail blotted out coherent thought. It abated to the point where she could hear her thoughts, and first among them was terror that Iceweasel would never come back. Her father and family would turn her into a zotta.

The storm passed, floods of tears slowing to trickles. Her eyes stung and her guts ached. She disentangled herself and swung her legs over the bed and put her face in her hands.

"What are we doing?"

"You mean in general, or specifically, right here and now?" Seth said, and Gretyl felt Tam reach out and pinch him.

"I'm not being funny," he said.

"You're never funny," Tam said. "That's the point."

"Ouch."

Gretyl looked up, tugged her robe around her and stood to pace, promptly stubbing a toe on the cold, uneven floor. She yelped and sat back down, rubbing her toe.

"I have an answer, you know," Seth said.

"To what?"

"What we're doing," he said.

Tam sighed. "Go ahead. If Gretyl doesn't mind."

She shook her head. She felt affection for these broken, sweet, loving people.

"When I was a kid and I'd hear about walkaways, they always seemed insanely optimistic to me. If they ever seriously threatened default, it would crush them. It was naïve—thinking default could peacefully coexist with anything else. How could it? If the excuse for putting a clutch of rich assholes in charge of the world was that without them we'd starve, how could they allow people to live without their stern but loving leadership?

"I thought of myself as a realist. Reality had a well-known pessimistic bias, so that made me a pessimist. I liked the idea of walking away, but I was on the other side."

Tam squeezed his hand. "Then you followed a hot rich girl into the woods and everything changed. I've heard this."

"Not the important part, because I only figured it out when we got to Thetford." He paused. Gretyl thought he was being dramatic, but he was gathering his thoughts, uncharacteristic vulnerability on his face in the dim light. She wanted to hear what he'd say next. Maybe he'd discovered something important.

"If your ship goes down in the middle of the open water, you don't give up and sink. You tread water, clutch onto a spar, do *something*."

He stopped, wrung his hands.

"Realistically speaking, if you're in the middle of the sea, you're a goner. But you tread water until you can't kick another stroke. Not because you're optimistic. If you polled ten random shipwreck victims treading water in open sea, every one would tell you they're not optimistic.

"What they are is *hopeful*. Or at least not hope-*empty*. They don't give up because that means death and living people can sometimes change their situations, while dead ones can't change a fucking thing.

"I've never been lost at sea, but I think if your buddy was weaker than you, and you were holding him up, you'd kick just as hard, because you'd be hoping for both of you. Because giving up for someone else is even harder than giving up for you.

"Now I'm walkaway, I've been shot at and chased from my home, but I can't feature going back to default, because default is the bottom of the sea and walkaway is a floating stick we can clutch. Default has no use for us except as a competition for other non-zottas, someone who'll do someone else's job if they get too uppity and demand to be treated as human beings instead of marginal costs. We are surplus to default's requirements. If they could, they'd sink us.

"So what we're doing, Gretyl, is exercising hope. It's all you can do when the situation calls for pessimism. Most people who hope have their hopes dashed. That's realism, but everyone whose hopes *weren't* dashed *started off by having hope*. Hope's the price of admission. It's still a lotto with shitty odds, but at least it's our lotto. Treading water in default thinking you might become a zotta is playing a lotto you can't win, and whose winners—the zottas—get to keep winning at your expense because you keep playing. Hope's what we're doing. Performing hope, treading water in open ocean with no rescue in sight."

"So, basically, 'live as though it were the first days of the better nation?'" But Gretyl smiled when she said it.

"That kind of wry cynicism is my department, you know."

"It's fun being a dick."

He grinned back. "It is, isn't it?"

"So it's hope. But—" She heaved a sigh.

Tam brought lichen tequila. She had a fleeting thought about how it was a bad habit to use alcohol to cope with distress, then drank from the bulb. It burned pleasurably.

"Iceweasel," she said.

"Poor Iceweasel," Tam said. "Have you heard from Dis?"

"No. I don't want to break security protocol. Every time I call her, it raises the chances of her being discovered. She said she'd get in touch when things changed, when there was something I could do. But she hasn't called."

"Let's call her. Fuck protocol. They didn't discover her when she rooted their network, what more could one more network session do?"

"I don't think—"

"Let's do it," Seth said. "If they've got her prisoner, that's fucked *up*. She's our friend, she's sinking beneath the waves, we need to rescue her."

"Rescue her? That's insane, Seth. She's in a fucking armed compound."

"I'd jump into shark-infested waters to save Tam." She looked to see if he was smart-assing, but he was grave.

"Don't be an asshole, Seth. Don't you think that Gretyl's beaten herself up for not going rambo on Daddy Iceweasel's dungeon? It's a suicide mission."

"It *was* a suicide mission, without Dis's help. Now it's merely insane. Come on, you want to live forever or something?"

"Let's call her first," Tam said. "For all we know, Dis is ready to break her out without anyone getting shot."

---

Getting Dis on the phone wasn't easy. There was a Dis instance running on the spacies' cluster—running a Dis instance was a prerequisite for being taken seriously as a walkaway clade these days—but it was slow and stock. The spacies used her to help their research on the microsat upload project, and the scanning crew consulted her to keep the array of cheap scanners synched to do the powerful computation necessary to interpolate low-precision measurements into very high-rez, high-accuracy databases that turned all the parts of a person that mattered into a digital file.

The local Dis didn't know about her instance-sister in Jacob Redwater's bolt-hole, but that Dis left Gretyl with a letter to other Dis instances, encrypted with a key protected by the private pass-phrase Dis had used in life. The local Dis accepted the file, decrypted it, thought about it for a computerish eyeblink. "This is crazy."

"Yeah," Gretyl said.

"Which part?" Seth said.

"The whole thing. Kidnapping, infiltration, pwnage. It's terrible. It's terrifying. It's also badass, all that pwnage."

"Conceited much?" Seth kept it light, but Gretyl could tell he chafed. He'd never known Dis alive, so for him, she was this omnipresent transhuman oracle. When Gretyl heard Dis's voice, she pictured the colleague she'd worked alongside, the way she'd waved her hands and paced when she talked, felt the physical presence of her through a mental illusion so complete it seemed she could reach out and grab Dis and hug her.

"Nope," Dis said. "That wasn't me-me. That was other-Dis-me. English needs new pronouns. Other-Dis-me and I are and are not the same person, and the accomplishments I happen to be praising are not accomplishments that me-me had anything to do with, so I am not tooting my own horn, just admiring the work of a very close colleague. But I could have done the same thing, of course."

"Of course," Seth said. Gretyl could see the through-the-looking-glass logic of talking to Dis had charmed him.

Tam said, "Plus, don't be a dick to the immortal simulated dead lady. It's bad manners."

Gretyl didn't know if Tam and Dis got on but she felt there must have been history there.

"You say the sweetest things," Dis said. "Now, how about we place a call?"

"Please," Gretyl said. The word was louder and more forceful than intended. Her palms were sweaty and her pulse throbbed in her ears. Perhaps she could even talk to Iceweasel?

A moment, then a strange sound from the speaker, another moment. Then, "Hi there."

"Couldn't reach her?" Gretyl felt like she was drowning in disappointment.

"What? Oh. No, this is me—Dis. I mean the one at Natalie's father's house."

"I'm here too."

"This is too weird," Tam said.

"I'll drop an octave," said one of the Dises, in a deeper voice, and the other said, "Man, that's weird."

"Which is which?" Gretyl's head swam.

"I'm local," said deep-Dis.

"I'm on-site," the other said.

Tam took charge. "Okay," she said, "I'm going to call you 'Local' and 'Remote' for this call. Deal?"

"Deal," both voices said at the same instant. Gretyl thought about her own backup, sitting in storage, wondered what it'd be like to converse with it, or multiple copies of it. The thought was nauseous; though the possibility had come up many times over the years, it had never been this immediate.

"Remote, what's going on with Iceweasel?"

"They untied her three days ago. She's been doing isometric exercises whenever they're not around, but she's still weak. She was out for ten days. They're giving her sedatives in her food. They've stockpiled hypnotics, but I can't tell if they're going to use them—it's a multi-factional thing, the mother and father not in agreement about how to proceed. The disagreement has as much to do with their fucked-up husband/wife dynamic as it does with their feelings for their kid.

"Emotionally, she's not in great shape, even with sedatives. She's pissed, having jangly feelings about her parents. When Mom visits, she veers from affection, or maybe pity, to a mother-daughter 'I hate you!' dynamic that's got a sharp edge."

"Because her mother is complicit in her kidnapping," Tam said.

"Yeah, because of the kidnapping. Thought that went without saying."

"Trying for maximum clarity."

"Max-clarity it is. I'm totally inside their network now. Updated firmware on every device connected to the safe-room net, left a back door. The only way to get me out would be to burn everything and start over. It's airgapped from the house network. There are a half-dozen sensors outside the safe room, optical/sound/radiation/air quality. I'm not sure, but I *think* they're physically co-located with house network devices—they may even *be* house network sensors, hacked to send a second data stream into the safe room. There might be a way to pwn those sensors and use them to get inside the house net, but I'm worried that'll trip the intrusion detection system and give it all away, so I've stayed away.

"From watching the sensors, I believe there's only one full-time security thug, a woman who might have been on the snatch-team that got Natalie—

that's what they call her. I'm basing that on conversations I've eavesdropped on between Natalie and her family. There's also a medic and an admin assistant who gofers food and meds. They're keeping it small, which makes sense from a secrecy/opsec perspective. Apart from them, the only people who go in or out of the safe room are the mother, the father, and the sister."

"They're all in one room?" Gretyl said.

"No, the safe room is a complex: two entrances, one through the house and the other via a tunnel that leads to the exterior. There are three rooms, besides the tunnel: a vestibule, the room they're using as a control center, and Natalie's room. Natalie's room has its own sealing doors and independent air and power—it's meant to be the impregnable safe, defense-in-depth. There's a toilet in Natalie's room, and a chem toilet in the control room with a jury-rigged screen around it. The gofer empties it—it's got a cartridge that slides out. I see her swapping it a couple times a day, and she pulls epic faces, though the others give her gears about it and insist it's odor free. Everyone thinks their shit doesn't stink."

"What are they doing with Iceweasel?" Tam asked, because Gretyl was still taking this in, trying to picture it in her mind's eye. She thought she should ask Remote for a set of photos and plans, then imagined seeing a picture of Iceweasel—Natalie!—thin and drugged, and her stomach did another slow roll.

"I think that Dad's plan was to bring someone in to brainwash her—there's supplies and dope stockpiled that fits that hypothesis. Based on conversations he's had with wifey in the control room, she vetoed it, though Dad's not happy and has set some ultimatum. I don't have details, because they don't talk about it in front of the help, and there's nowhere for the help to go except Natalie's room. This is the stuff they hiss at each other in spare moments.

"Mommy Dearest visits every day, so does sis, but they go on their own. Mommy has breakfast with Natalie, talks with her about the old days, telling stories that Natalie is either indifferent or hostile to. The old lady keeps up a brave face but I can get her respiration and pulse and Natalie's getting her goat. She's good at it. Lots of practice.

"Sis does better, getting Natalie to tell walkaway stories, being nonjudgmental-ish"—Seth snorted—"commiserating about how terrible Mommy and Daddy are."

"What about escape?" Gretyl said—the question she'd been bursting to ask.

"What about it?"

Gretyl made a choked sound. It felt like Dis was jerking her around, but was she, really? She wasn't the person Gretyl had known—maybe she wasn't a person at all. She had been through a dramatic experience—killed, brought back, forked and ramified and simulated—and existed in a programatically constrained state to prevent her from thinking certain thoughts. Who knew what other emotions were choked off because they co-occurred with existential crises? Maybe angst and empathy were entangled particles, and extinguishing one extinguished both.

"What about helping her to escape from her family and come back here?"

"Oh."

"Well?"

"I've talked with her about it. She'd like to, but views it as a remote possibility. I can unlock the safe room, even lock the rest of them out of it while she uses the tunnel. But getting from Toronto back to somewhere outside of her parents' reach? That's black ops exfiltration, not running away from home."

Gretyl forced deep breaths and pushed down despair. This was why she hadn't asked, because she'd already figured this out.

"But you can get her out—I mean, out of the house?"

"Yes. She's got clothes, and her sister has the same size feet. Assuming she could get her sister's shoes, she could get free, though she'd be pretty goddamned cold. No way to get her a winter coat."

Local chimed in, deep voiced, "Too bad we can't get her a space suit."

Remote paused, and Gretyl had the sense that she and Local were exchanging data. "That'd be perfect. Wishful thinking."

Tam cut in: "Never mind. Knowing what's possible is important, knowing what's impossible tells us what we have to work on next."

"Hope," said Seth.

"Treading water." Tam squeezed Gretyl's hand.

"Oh!" Remote said, then, "Shit."

"What?"

"Another fight with her father. One of his visits. He was trying to convince her walkaways were like him, greedy and shitty. Naturally, she told him to fuck off, and he started in about Limpopo. He knows a *lot* about her, stuff in her background I'd never heard, some of it ugly. Natalie bore it well, but she's brittle, and he kept pushing until she snapped and came at him, physically, and he used his compliance button—"

"What?"

"They've got her in a pain cuff; less-lethal stuff they use in prison psych wards and asylum-seeker detentions. Melt-your-face stuff. It's got good anti-tamper. There's a whole box of them in the safe-room's stores, which is creepy as fuck."

"No kidding," Tam said. "Why would you need compliance weapons in a safe room that only your family was supposed to know about?"

Seth shook his head. "I've met the guy. I bet he's got lifeboat captain fantasies about having to keep everyone else in line for their own good, you know, like on *Farnham*."

"Ugh, I hated that show."

"Everyone hates that show."

"Not zottas." Seth snapped off a sharp salute. "Yes sir, Farnham, sir, and may I thank you, sir, for helping us survive this terrible disaster through your superhuman judgment and special snowflakiness!"

Gretyl lost her breathing. She hadn't seen a compliance bracelet, but she'd been hit by a compliance weapon, during a wildcat adjuncts' strike at Cornell, when campus cops rolled into the quad with M.R.A.P.s, kettled everyone, and started sniping anyone they took for a leader. Gretyl hadn't been on the picket, but she'd stopped to discuss it with a boi who'd been one of her grad students, because they had always had good instincts for picking their battles, and she wanted to hear them out.

She supposed for campus cops, anyone with graying hair was a ringleader—she was the oldest person in the quad by at least ten years—and she'd been hit. The pain came in two waves, first a sharp, stinging sensation all over her body like being shocked by a loose wire. It hurt, but it wasn't debilitating. Later, she found out this was the "honeymoon stage" of the weapon, and it was supposed to stop perps in their tracks, but leave them coherent enough to understand the orders being shouted at them.

She stopped talking, looked wildly for her pain's source, saw a visored cop in an M.R.A.P. turret, one eye covered with a bulging magnifier/scope, lower half of her face impassive as she played her wand over Gretyl's body. It autotracked targets, shaping the pulse to keep it center-mass as the perp jerked and writhed.

No one shouted orders at her. Seconds later, pain blossomed like a thousand razors bursting out of her skin all over, all at once. There were no words for it. It didn't let up at all. Pain got as bad as it could get, got worse. It was unimaginable. The boi immediately understood what was happening and dumped their backpack, seizing a sheet and snapping it over her. The pain had sizzled off/on-off/on, then stopped, leaving her twitching.

(The chivalry cost the poor boi their own safety—they were the sniper's next target and it took Gretyl an eternity before she was recovered enough to get the blanket over them.)

The thought of Iceweasel with one of those cuffs—her father's finger on the button—made her want to cry as memories of that day flooded back.

Gradually, Seth and Tam became aware of her upset and stopped bantering. "Hey," Tam said. "Be strong. We'll sort this out."

"Yeah." Seth sounded less convinced, despite his hope-talk. "This is a temporary situation."

"How is she?" Gretyl said, and was alarmed by how small her voice sounded.

Remote noticed, too. Her voice lost its flippancy: "She's resting. Withdrawn." Then: "Would you like to talk to her?"

"Can I?" The thought made her heart thunder.

"One sec." Gretyl noticed a tic of Remote's voice. When she finished speaking, the sound cut off too perfectly on the last syllable, cleanly clipping at the end of the sound-wave, without open-mic hiss while the sound duplexing algorithm made extra certain the squishy human was finished, not woolgathering. When you conversed with someone hosted on a machine, metadata became data. She wondered what a conversation between Remote and Local would sound like, then realized they wouldn't use sound at all, then realized that she was trying to distract herself from the fact that she was about to speak to—

"Okay, put them on." The voice was thready.

"Dude!" Seth said. "How's prison?"

Tam slugged him. He grunted and Iceweasel said, "You're such an asshole, Seth."

"But I'm a lovable scamp, you have to admit."

"I admit it." Her voice quavered.

"How are you hanging in, darling?" Tam said.

"I, uh—" A pause, shuddering breath. "I'm scared. I don't see how they can ever let me go now."

"We'll get you." Gretyl surprised herself.

"Gretyl?" Iceweasel's voice quavered more, cracking on the second syllable.

"I love you," she blurted. Tears coursed down her cheeks. "I love you, Iceweasel. We're coming for you. Be strong."

"Oh, Gretyl." Full-blown sobs now.

Gretyl sobbed, too. The rest waited in respectful silence.

"The worst part—" Iceweasel began, then was lost to tears. "The worst thing is that it gets so *normal*. Like I've been sick for a long time, and I'm in a hospital, getting better. There are times when I can't remember—"

"I won't forget you." Gretyl's chest convulsed at the thought of the hours that passed *without* a thought of Iceweasel; working on the engine, just brutish stubbornness of the material world, inconvenience of weather and the suit, the brainteaser of solving the mechanical puzzle of the stricken machine. The focus felt good. It was freedom from the grief she'd carried so long.

"But." Gretyl couldn't speak for sobs. "But." She mastered her breathing. "If it makes it easier—If it hurts less, it's okay to forget about us. About me. If you can find a way to be happy, I won't be hurt—" *Oh, no?* "I'll understand." *Because you do it, too.* "It's okay."

No reply, then sobs, then nothing. Then: "I won't ever forget. It'll never be okay. If I die here, I'll die with you in my mind."

"Don't die," Gretyl blurted. "Just hang on."

"I'll hang on."

Gretyl's world telescoped to the two of them, minds reaching across space, piercing walls, transcending the channel set up by the simulated Dises. It was like they were touching again. "I—"

"Yeah," Iceweasel said. "Yes. Me, too. You, too."

"Yes." A terrible weight lifted from Gretyl.

"Uh," Remote broke in.

"Yes?" they said together, still in synchrony.

"I can get you through the tunnel—I can even get you shoes. But I can't help once you're outside."

"I know," Iceweasel said.

"Let us try and find something," Gretyl said. "We're going to default tomorrow, a First Nations reservation, we're delivering—never mind what we're delivering. We're going to be there for a day or two. Then everyone's coming here, from all over for . . ." She swallowed. "A party." She felt like she was betraying Iceweasel.

"Will you bridge me in?"

"What?"

"The party. Can you bridge me in?"

"It's bad opsec," Remote said. "Every time we open a channel to the world, there's a chance that someone's going to notice the traffic."

"I thought you pwned the whole network?"

"Yeah, but there's the upstream. I've got the connectivity contracts here, read 'em all. They're with a Redwater subsidiary, one of your cousins, the big timers. It's for another Redwater property, a place across the ravine they use for secure storage, and there's a point-to-point microwave link with line-of-sight laser backup, so anyone who used the contract to figure out what building to storm to kidnap Jacob and his family would find themselves three hundred meters away, in a building with remote monitoring and nasty surprises.

"The upstream provider's got to run intrusion detection. That's basic opsec. It's tolerant—didn't go nuts when your dad brought in his team, but the more anomalous traffic we generate, the higher the likelihood it'll fire an alarm at some ops center and generate a warning to Daddy's security people and then—"

"I get it," Iceweasel said. She drew a shuddering breath. Gretyl could hear how close to tears she was. Tears sprang in her eyes. "I'd be alone again, and the party would start for real. I don't think Dad's security knows what's going on here. I know that dude. He runs a tighter ship than this. My dad brought in specialists, deprogrammers for rich girls who join the walkaway cult. Someone who'd insist on running his own show."

"Pretty sure you're right," Remote said. "Fits available evidence. We can't assume your dad would tell his security not to worry about alerts. Even if Boss Cop doesn't know what your dad's doing in his dungeon, he's got to know that something's going on." She paused. "I wonder . . ."

"What?" Local said. Gretyl had a moment's disorientation. She'd started to think of them as aspects of one person, which they were, but not in the sense that they both had the same knowledge. Remote could wonder something and Local couldn't know what it was until Remote told her.

"Jacob Redwater's not the baddest zotta, not even in the top tier, but he's still rich and ruthless. I can't imagine him giving up his little bolt-hole without having another one. I just bet there's another place like this, only 2.0—"

"Heard anyone discuss it? Seen any traffic?"

"Nope, but if it's there, maybe that's something we could use."

"Push it onto the stack," Local said, sounding irritated, which also made Gretyl's head ache. She could get upset with herself. Why should that stop once there were multiple instances of herself? "Come back to it later."

"They're coming. Jacob and his security, that woman merc—"

Silence.

Tam took Gretyl's hand. Gretyl hadn't had a chance to say good-bye, to again tell Iceweasel that she loved her.

## [x]

The last time she'd seen her father, he'd been stalking out of the room, with rare, visible fury. Usually he kept it icy and only let it emerge as a dangerous calm tone. When Jacob Redwater's face twisted into a rage-mask and he raised his voice and clenched his fists, he was at the point of snapping.

Once, she'd have quailed at the thought. Her mother always assured her Jacob Redwater was a good and patient man, though not a man she had any particular affection for. Natalie and Cordelia were in good hands with him. Anything they did that made him snap was their own fault.

She could not have given fewer fucks about his rage. She'd flopped on the ground, trying to scream as her skin burned and her muscles contracted, a pain-seizure eclipsing every emotion except for self-pity and towering fury.

He had changed clothes. He wore tailored weekend stuff, a soft flannel shirt and jeans hid his incipient paunch unless you knew to look for it. He smelled of his sandalwood soap. He'd had a shower and calmed down and fetched the merc, who stood within arm's reach and slightly ahead, body slightly rotated toward Iceweasel, impassive but alert.

"There are things you need to know about your friends, things that might help you see what's going on there."

"Is this part of the program? Did your snatch-consultant give you a ten-point process for deprogramming me and this is stage six?"

He shook his head. "Can you *stop*? I want to have an adult conversation and present the evidence. I think once you see it, you'll understand—"

"Adults don't have rational discussions that involve kidnapping and violent coercion. You set the terms when you sent her to drag me here. When you tied me up. When you used *that* on me."

Her dad looked at the merc, a flush creeping up his cheeks. Natalie knew from Dis that the cameras in her room fed the control room, even when he was with her, so the merc and the med-tech and anyone else there heard and saw it all. Being called out as a father who'd use the pain-machine on his daughter was not Jacob Redwater's style. He liked to be liked. He was likable—handsome, with an easy smile and enormous confidence. Natalie had seen friends fall under his spell, mistaking his friendliness for friendworthiness. It was flattering to be friended by a powerful zotta who could really listen to you with an intensity that made it clear he was interested in you, only you.

That hadn't worked on Natalie since she was ten.

He made his eyes sad. "I wish I could tell you how much this has hurt me. I know you don't think I love you, but I do. I've tried to be a good father. I know work kept me away too often. There were times when I should have been there for you—"

She swallowed her reaction: to tell him she'd always wished he was away *more*.

"But I have responsibilities, ones that you haven't ever understood. I'm willing to take the blame. I've tried to shield you and your sister and your mother from what I do to keep us safe. It's a rough world. I didn't want to scare you." His eyes grew moist. That was new. She'd never seen him mist up. He was pulling out the stops. "Natty, don't tell your sister, but I assumed you'd take over some day. Cordelia is a lovely girl, but she doesn't have any *edge*. You've got edge. Too much edge. But that's good, because this world demands edge from the people who run it."

He tentatively maneuvered a chair to her bedside. She steeled herself. She didn't shrink when he sat. The merc positioned herself a little ahead of him. Natalie couldn't say why, but this made her feel safer. She and the merc were on the same side, ultimately. Both were beholden to Jacob Redwater, though of course the merc had a lot more leeway about the terms of engagement.

"Your mother and sister never got that, but you did. This family, families like ours, we steer this world. It's in trouble, Natalie. There's too many people. Lots of them are bad people who'd destroy everything. Nihilists. They don't care about human rights or property rights. They'd take everything we have. Jealous people who think they have nothing because we have something.

"You've seen the real world. There are people plenty richer than us. We're comfortable, I'll grant you, but we're not 'zottas'—not real ones. A couple mistakes, a few changes in the world, we lose everything. Bums on the street.

"I'll tell you what would happen next: we'd rebuild. Without handouts. We'd get to work, figure things out, and before long, we'd be on top.

"The world is lean and mean, and shakes. When you shake the cornflakes box, little flakes sink to the bottom and big flakes end up on top. I'm a hell of a big flake." He smiled. His charming schtick.

"I know what you think of that: that I'm deluding myself. I've heard your talk about special snowflakes. I know your arguments. I disagree with them. You don't know my arguments. You think you've found a better way. You think your walkabouts can make their way in the world without having someone in charge, without big and small cornflakes.

"That's what I want to talk about. You need to know some things about your friends that might be hard to hear. Walkways say the worst thing you can do is bullshit yourself. I want to demonstrate how *you've* bullshitted yourself—about *them*. They're not hard to figure. Where there are walkways, there are sellouts, happy to take free food and easy sex, but who also want money, and have a way to get both. Since you left, I've known everything that happened in your little world. I get videos. I've been inside your networks. I've seen traffic analysis."

Of course it was true. Why would Jacob Redwater spy on her less in walkaway than he had in default? She'd always had the eyes-on-the-back-of-her-neck feeling, ever since she'd been old enough to leave the house, and it hadn't let up once she got to the B&B. It took an act of will not to guess which of her "friends" fed reports back to Jacob; which ones were in government employ, or working for zottas or big companies. She'd talked it over with Limpopo and Limpopo confessed she had to resist the same impulse.

"It's not that there aren't plants here. Of course there are plants. The way plants hurt us isn't by telling rich people what we're doing. Fuck rich people—all our shit's on public networks. The worst thing plants do is make us mistrust each other, think our friends might be our enemies. Once that happens, you're well *fucked*. It's impossible to have a discussion if you think the other person is trying to fuck with you. Everything gets distorted by that lens. Did she leave out the trash because she was distracted, or because she wanted to bicker about chores?

"That mistrust is the most corrosive thing. Back when I was in default, I was in this protest group, an affinity group loosely connected to the Anonymous Party, doing data-analysis of regulators' social graphs to show their decisions favored the industries they regulated, such a fucking no-brainer, but it was good to have facts when you met someone who hadn't figured out the game was rigged.

"There was a guy in our group, Bill. Bill was weird. Standoffish. Always looking at you from the corner of his eye. Always listening, not talking, like he was taking notes. We worried. We knew there were plants in our group. Whenever we found something juicy—some minister's wife's brother running the oil company the minister handed a fat exemption to—the government was always out in front, managing the news cycle before we published, which was overkill, given how little attention the news paid to us. The powers that be are thorough. Anything that might rise to a threat gets neutralized because it costs peanuts to clobber us, and there's zottabucks moving around they do *not* want disrupted.

"We isolated Bill. Created distribution lists and passworded forums he wasn't invited to. Stopped inviting him to pizza nights. Forgot to tell him when we went out for beers.

"Bill wasn't a plant. Bill was clinically depressed. Bill hanged himself with his belt. His roommates didn't find him for two days. When they put Bill into the fire, no one was there to take his ashes, so I took them. I kept them by my bedside until I walked away. They reminded me that I'd helped isolate Bill. I'd helped make him so alone that when darkness ran up on him, he didn't have anywhere safe to run. I helped kill Bill. So did my pals. What killed Bill was our suspicion about plants. The worst thing a plant could do wasn't leak our shit or stir up shit. We leaked our own shit. We were argumentative enough that we didn't need plants to make us fight with each other. Worrying about plants was a million times worse than the worst thing a plant could do."

There had been tears in her eyes.

Her father said, "Things aren't what you think. You think you've found a way everyone can get along without bosses. There are always bosses—if you don't know who the boss is, you can't question her leadership. A system of secret bosses is a system without accountability or consent. It's a manipulocracy."

She looked at the merc, wondering if she was following this, whether she appreciated the irony of her father—*her father*—criticizing society on the grounds that it was run from behind the scenes by shadowy fixers and string-pullers.

He caught her look. He nodded and made a charming face. "Takes one to know one, daughter-mine. If I can't recognize a conspiracy, who could?"

"When all you've got is a hammer, everything looks like a nail." She regretted saying it. Why argue with her fucking father? He won as soon as you acknowledged there was a debate.

He knew it. He smiled wider, put on a frowny, thinky face. "I understand what you're saying. We all see ourselves reflected in data. Analysis is subjective. But Natalie, I'm not asking you to take what I'm saying at face value. I want you to look at the data yourself, see if what I'm saying is true. That's not monstrous, is it?"

"No. Kidnapping and administration of pain-weapons is monstrous. This is just bullshit."

"I get you're angry. I'd be angry. But if I was brainwashed by a cult—if I couldn't understand what was going on—I would want you to do everything you could to get me to understand what was happening. You have my permission to do everything I've done here, to me, if I am ever in the grips of some irrational impulse that puts me in imminent and grave danger."

Natalie restrained herself from snorting. Not to spare his feelings, but because derision was acknowledgement, another chance for him to argue. Give him a millimeter, he'd take a parsec. That's how you became a zotta. It's how he'd been raised. It was how *she'd* been raised, which scared the shit out of her, especially *these* days. She was back in her father's demesne. In this house, there was so much pressure to accept the easy justifications. Some people had to be on top, some on the bottom, big and little cornflakes. Besides, the Redwaters weren't *really* rich; not *rich* rich, not like Jacob's cousin Tony Redwater.

"Believe me, if there was any other way, I would take it. I don't want this. I want my daughter back. I know what you're capable of. It's why I kept you close to home, made sure you knew what went on behind the scenes. You could put it all together."

Even though she knew he was flattering her, it worked. Goddamn him, and goddamn her, too. She knew her dad's bullshit. Even so, something inside her rolled over and preened when Daddy said nice things.

"That's what I want you to do. Pull it together." He twiddled his interface surfaces and a piece of wall slid away, revealing a huge touchscreen, stretching across the room's width. It was showing a screen saver, the manufacturer's loop of kids playing lacrosse, blond and lanky, with muscular legs and horsey white teeth. Not zottas, because zottas didn't need to pose for screen-saver photos. But they looked like zottas. Maybe they were actors. Or CGI.

Her dad made the image go away and replaced it with a social graph. In the graph's middle, like a gas giant surrounded by a thousand moons, was a circle labeled LIMPOPO [Luiza Gil], a circular cameo of Limpopo, looking younger and scowling ferociously, like she wanted to kick the photographer's ass. Around her, the moons of various sizes were labeled with the names of her friends, all the walkaways. Just seeing those names made her mist with unbearable nostalgia. The feeling of being *away* from her true family was a clawed thing gnawing at her guts.

"Look at it, okay?" He turned to go. The merc followed, contriving to keep an eye on Natalie without walking out backwards. Natalie hardly noticed, because she was trying not to smile, because she'd just noticed Etcetera's disc, and the minuscule type the system used to render his name in full.

She drifted over to the wall and caressed Etcetera's circle, as though she were caressing him, and the graph jumped into life, helpfully arranging itself to better convey its meaning.

## [xi]

"We are well and truly at *vuko jebina* now," Tam declared. She'd learned the phrase from Kersplebedeb, who said it was Serbian for deepest boonies, literally, "where wolves fuck." Tam *loved* this phrase, to no one's surprise.

Seth looked from side to side. The snow started an hour after they set out. It hadn't been in the meteorological projections, normal for decades of weird weather. The first flakes were pretty, turning poisoned countryside into a Christmas card of birches and pines iced with fluffy snow like iced gingerbread. Toxic icing, but they weren't going to eat it and, as Seth had inevitably pointed out, sugar was only slightly better for you than asbestos.

Pocahontas's friends were welcoming, though they had little to call their own. They weren't from one band, but were a commune living on territory the Quebec government had turned over in reparations for jail time, each of them exonerated by physical evidence, sometimes after decades of lockup. It had been the work of a Mohawk legal collective in Quebec City, and after a string of these, they'd been audited, audited again, investigated by the Law Society, and half their lawyers were disbarred and found themselves with full-time jobs saving themselves.

The community was called Dead Lake. It sported a few windmills and some second-rate fuel cells the residents had carefully coaxed into performing better than anyone could believe. Even Gretyl was impressed. Tam marveled at their improvements. Their technical crew relieved the wagon of the suit-fabbers and started assembling them. It took less than a day. That evening, all thirty residents came to the utility shed to watch them run.

Gretyl, Tam, and Seth were invited to a modest dinner, printed stuff with feedstock from down south because game around Thetford was poison and the Dead Lakers knew better than to eat it. Conversation was merry, if stilted. The Dead Lakers thought walkaways were crazy, or maybe silly, and didn't hide it. They *liked* walkaways, and provided wonderful hospitality, but it was clear these folks didn't rate the walkaways' chances of getting anything done. For them, walkaway was a lifestyle and a hobby. Seth bristled because it was his deepest fear and also his turf—*he* could make fun of walkaways, but who were *these* people to tell him what to do? He'd buried his sarcasm, because the Dead Lakers knew the difference between a joke-joke and a ha-ha-only-serious joke, and Seth liked to live on that edge.

He was relieved to go the next morning. They hit the trail to Thetford in suits, riding the empty cargo wagon as it rumbled across the deep snow at a slow walking pace, sometimes nosing down precipitously as it discovered drop-offs, sometimes listing so far to one side they were nearly thrown.

The snow had started, about an hour out. Flakes, swirling clouds, then, whiteout.

"Vuko jebina, huh?" he said. There were trees somewhere—the wagon's radar automatically avoided them, but it was turning again and again. Its collision-avoidance systems were fubared. This was definitely the place where wolves fucked.

He looked at Tam, trying to make out her face through the snow and her clear plastic visor. The suits were in whiteout mode, strobing a slow flicker that made it easy to pick a person out against the snow; defoggers blew over the visors, the mask's earpieces played pin-sharp reproductions of the defoggers from the other two masks, a white-noise symphony overlaid with the gusting wind.

"Even wolves don't fuck in this," Gretyl said. She was in the back, thumping at a mechanical keyboard she'd magneted to its skin, watching a screen projected against her mask. "Shit." The wagon stopped. "Might as well stop, this thing's gonna chase its tail until it runs out of juice."

Seth's butt vibrated with ghost sensation of wagon motors. That stopped, and there was just the sound of the wind, the blowers, and the thrum of his pulse. He felt transient fear: where wolves fuck, snow blowing, ground saturated with carcinogens, sky a source of potential death. If he died here, no one would know. If they did know, almost no one would care. His father died when he was ten, his mother had been in jail since he was seventeen and they hadn't spoken since he was fifteen. Natalie was . . . Natalie was gone. He had to admit she probably wouldn't be back.

He was so small. They were pimples on the world's face. Unwanted. Uninvited. Alone in snow, on their silly homemade wagon, in high-tech pajamas, where wolves fuck.

The feeling passed. It had contracted his sense of self to a pinprick and then expanded the world around him to a yawning gulf.

The world kept on expanding. It wasn't just *him* that was tiny and insignificant. It was *everything*. Zottas, all they'd built. The world's great cities. Humming networks of meaningless, totalizing money, endlessly and algorithmically shuffled. Deeds and contracts, factories and satellites, endless oil and stone, poison in the sky and carbon in the air. In a thousand years no one would give a shit. The universe didn't care about humans. The wind didn't care. The snow didn't care. The fucking wolves didn't care. If he froze and mouldered to dirt, like Thetford's rotting homes, it would be no better and no worse than living to ninety and going into the ground in a box with a stone over his head. It would be no better and no worse than what was coming for all those asshole zottas who thought they could speciate and overcome death.

Everything they did was human. Everything he did was human. Here, where wolves fucked, it didn't mean anything; it meant everything.

"Awooo!" It was louder than he'd intended, but who cared? Tam and Gretyl's gloves clonked their helmets, then the gain-control cut in. They stared, faces barely visible behind visors, suits strobing silently in swirling flakes. They were annoyed, hungry, needed to pee, and so did he but: "Awooo!" It came out *louder* this time.

"Come on, you wolves!" A wild laugh chased the words.

"Enough." Tam's voice had a warning note.

"It's not enough. Come on, just try it. Seriously serious."

"Seth, come on—"

Gretyl cut loose with a howl that made their visors rattle and left their ears ringing. "Fuck yeah!" She punched the air.

Tam heaved a sigh, looked from one to the other, wiped snow off Seth's shoulders. She filled her lungs and *howled*. Seth joined. Gretyl joined. They howled and howled, in the place where wolves fuck, and Seth found himself with tears in his eyes, which he couldn't wipe, but it didn't matter. He was shedding his skin, leaving behind the last vestiges of default, the last shreds of belief that someday he'd forget this craziness and try to find a job and a place to live and hope no one took them away.

"I love you people." He squeezed them so their visors clonked.

"Ow," Tam said, but didn't pull away. "You're a jerk, but we love you, too."

"Yeah," Gretyl said. "Most of the time."

"What do we do? Walk?"

"And end up frozen to death," Gretyl said. "Snow can't keep falling. Once it stops, we'll ride home. Meantime, we shelter in cargo-pods. If we each take one, we'll be able to shin out of the suits to take a dump or eat, then get back inside to keep from freezing to death."

"How would that work?" Seth said. "I mean, where do we poop?"

She rapped the engine's cowl. "Not much room in these. But with care you could crap outside the suit, then get back inside, without getting crap on you. It'll get on the outside of the suit, but that's life in the big city. No worse than the stuff that gets stuck to it while we're walking. We'll wash them off when we get back."

"I'll strip off outside and hang my butt over the snow. The amount of snow on the ground now, there's not going to be any airborne contaminants."

"Suit yourself, but remember, there's only so much power in these things and getting naked at minus twenty is going to suck heat out of your body that the suit's going to have to put back or you'll die of hypothermia. There might come a moment when you're wishing you still had those amps in your battery—when your toes are turning black."

"This conversation's taken a delightful turn." Tam jumped off the engine and sank to her knees. She swept her arms, mounding snow up. "We're not going to walk very far through this. How about we try to tell someone where we are, and could use help?"

"I've got zero bars," Gretyl said. "Been that way almost since we left Dead Lake. The aerostats probably landed themselves when the wind kicked up."

"I packed a couple drones in the survival kit. Hexcopters, they can fight heavy wind, but they're not going to get a geographic fix until the sky clears. Still—"

"Get one high enough and it might bounce a connection between us and Thetford," Tam said. "There's a good chance we'll lose it—another decision we might regret later."

"In summary: we should hide in these boxes, shit ourselves, and wait out the weather." Seth discovered the idea didn't sound as horrible as it should. The revulsion he wasn't feeling was part of the package of default-ness that he'd sloughed off.

"About right," Tam said. "The weather isn't ours to command. Physics is physics. Snow is snow. Batteries are batteries. Sometimes the best action is no action."

## [xii]

Dis felt swaddled in cotton batting. Her thoughts veered toward panic or sorrow and she'd brace for the torrent of feeling, and it would *fizzle*. She'd tried antidepressants as a kid, when her parents worried about her "moods." She knew how it felt when her brain couldn't make the chemicals that got her into that race-condition of things-are-bad-I-can't-fix-them-that-makes-it-worse. That was a feeling like reality in retreat, colors bled out and fight gone from her limbs. They said it was a matter of "dialing in the dosage." They said it was worse before advanced neurosensing that could continuously monitor her reactions. In practice, this meant spending the eighth grade reporting to the nurse's office every hour to have a disposable electrode band wrapped around her forehead while she lay on a couch and let a machine draw blood. Her parents had to do it at home, including a session at 11:15 every night. They got so good at it that most nights they could take all their measurements without waking her. It helped that the drugs made her sleep like the dead.

A year ticked by. She got her first period, her first F (in math, always her best subject) and took her first beating, from a group of kids that included three girls who'd come to her birthday party the year before. They sensed her intolerable weakness. None of it left a mark. They told her the meds were working. She experienced vacant anxiety, a purely intellectual sense that things were terrible, but the terribleness didn't matter. It was remote urgency. It made her feel sinister and unimportant.

The feeling was terrible but she didn't feel terrible once she stopped the meds. Everyone had told her she musn't do that, because cold turkey would cause problems. The lack of urgency she felt for everything extended to the prospect of going crazy from freelancing her own psychopharmacology.

She did go crazy. It was like the time she'd gone jumping in the surf and waded out too far, buffeted by waves that spun her around, knocked her over, without any way to predict when the next one would come, coming up sputtering and disoriented.

Without meds, she'd be overtaken by passions. Innocuous remarks made her furious, or set off tears. Jokes were convulsively funny or unforgivably offensive, sometimes both. She strove to hide it from her parents and teachers, but they noticed. She had to connive to stay off meds, hide them under her tongue and spit them out.

Bit by bit, she learned to surf the moods. She recognized the furies as phenomena separate from objective reality. They were real. She really felt them. They weren't triggered by any real thing in the world where everyone else lived. They were private weather, hers to experience alone or share with others as she chose. She treasured her weather and harnessed her storms, turning into a dervish of productivity when the waves crested; using the troughs to retreat and work through troubling concepts.

She read the transcripts of those sessions when they'd woken her up inside a computer and she'd lost her mind. Reading through them, she sensed the crash of those storms. They'd blown terribly when her mind was untethered flesh.

She'd thought of storms as wet things, hormonal in origin. She'd mapped the storms to ebbs of mysterious fluids from her glands. But shorn of flesh hormones, the problems were *worse*. Ungovernable. She pondered this mystery, wondering if the discipline and nimbleness had been the wet part, the trained ability to conjure fluids that lubricated the dry, computational misfirings of her mind.

They'd stabilized her with her help, translating between her secret language of moods and the technical vocabulary of computation. She had no memory of those moments, only logs, but it was easy to imagine the desperate race to grind out coherent thoughts while waves of panic—she was dead, she was a parlor trick of code and wishful thinking—built to greater heights.

Afloat in seas of her own calming, she experienced unhurried urgency, the same contradictory feeling that things were alarming but she was not alarmed. It wasn't a good feeling, but it didn't make her feel bad, which was the problem.

Talking with Remote helped. Knowing there was someone else going through the same things helped, even though they never explicitly discussed it. Remote seemed so normal and together. That salved her. If that's how normal and together Dis looked from the outside then she was probably holding it together, too. Remote was a sort of mirror. What she saw in it was reassuring.

She helped with party preparations, kept track of the goings-on in Thetford's great hall, watched the weather, conversed with spacies and worked on cluster optimization and predictive modeling for the constraints they'd apply to each model in storage when they brought them up in their own sims. Working with CC's sim was educational and scary. She'd envied CC his even keel, but in his digital afterlife, he was a mess. He was worse than she'd ever been. Walkaways all over the world collaborated with her.

She worried—without *feeling* worried—about her friends in the snow.

There'd been no stable network connectivity for five hours. Last she'd heard, they'd departed from Dead Lake. They were now two hours overdue. The microwave masts outside the space-station sporadically caught distant threads of network signal, enough for the routers to start trading zone files and synchronizing clocks and getting the latest meteorology and frequency-hopping norms, only to fade off in an unrecoverable cascade of packet-loss and blown checksums.

Walkaway net was different from default's. Its applications were designed for fault tolerance—built with the assumption the machine you connected to could disappear and reappear without warning, as drones, towers, wires, and fibers failed, faded, or fubared. It assumed it was being wiretapped, under permanent infowar conditions. It insisted on handshakes, signatures, and signed nonces to root out man-in-the-middlers. When Dis went from Stanford to Walkaway U, the network had been the biggest culture shock. Slower in some ways, but without the ubiquitous warnings about copyright infringement, interminable clickthrough agreements, suspicious blackouts of "sensitive" resources when global protests spiked.

She lived on walkaway networks. She appreciated the subtle genius in its architectures. Sites that had became unreachable sprang back to life thanks to the questing tendrils of the network's self-healing, restlessly seeking out new ways to bridge the parts that were atomized by entropy or connivance. The downside was that nothing was ever truly down, and anything unreachable warranted a reload. It didn't work, but sometimes it did, often enough to keep trying. Dis hadn't thought about BF Skinner since her undergrad days, but after the millionth retry to reach Seth, Tam, and Gretyl, she looked up "intermittent reinforcement" in their locally cached wikip. That's what it was: intermittent reinforcement. Give a pigeon a food pellet every time it presses a button and it'll press it when it's hungry. Change the lever's algorithm so it *randomly* drops a pellet and the pigeon will peck and peck, as the pattern-matching parts of its brain sought to figure out the trick of a reliable jackpot.

She was disconcerted to learn that being a disembodied consciousness didn't immunize her from such a cheap cognitive trick. Not for the first time, she thought about tinkering with her parameters. Other Dises in other places had done that, under better controlled conditions, with some success. It was so unfair to be subject to this kind of cognitive frailty. Reload reload reload. In fact, reload, she was *especially* susceptible to it, reload, which was so unfair—

She drew up short. The big tower had contact with another tower, in the mountains, with line of sight to a fiber downlink, and data flowed. Nothing that reached her friends, but huge swaths of walkaway space came online.

Cachers negotiated to opportunistically copy off great slices of it for local access, salting it away against the next electronic famine. All over the world, waystation machines with packets destined for Thetford knocked on its doors, seeking permission to hand off their payloads.

Amidst it was the news. It brought Dis up short. Every filter she had on the raw feeds was going *fucking crazy*.

It was Akron. They'd cheered Akron on as walkaways consolidated their position, using printed health care and food as a calling card for their neighbors: diehard Akronites who couldn't or wouldn't vacate the dead city. They'd reveled in videos and casts of Akronites doing the unthinkable, establishing a permanent walkaway city, something you couldn't walk away from, with permaculture farms and free-for-all white bikes and free schools where kids learned to teach each other and to be taught by other walkaway kids all over the world.

There'd been bad stuff. It was impossible to tell how much of that was propaganda. Akron had already been full of walkaways and semi-walkaways, throwing Communist parties and opening squats. It had been full of gangs and bad dope, pimps and scared people. Since Akron went walkaway, every murder and beat-down in Akron was top-of-feed news for every service in default, though violence and diseases hadn't attracted attention in the ten years when Akron had been turning into Akron—even its bankruptcy and the appointment of a zotta "administrator" to replace the lame-duck mayor hadn't rated particular mention. Akron was the fortieth American city to end up in that situation, and it wasn't the biggest, or most violent, or most fucked up, so how was that news?

Default's few voices of critical thinking pointed this out, pointed out Ohio had stopped keeping stats on the murder rate and overall mortality in Akron four years before, and back then, it had been five times higher than now, best anyone could figure.

When she saw a shit-ton of bad Akron news, she spacebarred it into ignoreland, but it kept popping up, and the headlines got snaggier and gnarlier and she couldn't help herself, she read one. Then another. Then she watched videos the cachers had already pulled down and made local copies of, because *every* feed in Thetford was losing its mind over Akron.

Default had marched on Akron: the US Army and a ton of private "contractors" in the vanguard, riding mechas or ground-effect vehicles with drone outriders that continuously scanned for IEDs with lidar and millimeter-wave and backscatter, emblazoned with radiation trefoils in safety orange on their bellies, more to scare than to fulfill any safety remit.

They rode in to fight the Four Horsemen: pornographers, mafiosi, drug dealers, and terrorists. Depending on the feed, their mission was to arrest high-profile Zetas who'd gone to ground in Akron; to rescue trafficked children from a pimp ring; to neutralize a Z-Word factory that was pumping out unprecedented quantities of the latest zombinol analog; or, of course, to capture domestic extremists who were working to establish an American Caliphate along with known terrorist cells in Michigan, Oregon, and Louisiana.

Whichever one they were fighting, they prepared for the worst. "Targeted" strikes took out twenty-two buildings in ten minutes, reducing them to rubble and showering the streets with lethal rains of falling stones. One of the buildings was a hospital, formerly derelict and since reopened by walkaways and allies, with a maternity ward and a palliative care ward where patients chose the manner of their deaths. The war of words about this building was especially heated—it was alleged to be a breeding ground for bio-agents (which walkaway nets insisted were vaxx printers that made ebola and H1N1 vaccine without licenses), a "murder clinic" and a "rogue surgery operation." The default nets didn't mention the maternity ward.

The boots-on-the-ground phase started before the dust settled, literally: pacifier bots that tazed anyone believed to be carrying a weapon or whose facial biometrics were a "sufficient" match for a "high value target." Once a bot zapped someone, it broadcast loud messages warning everyone to keep clear, then stood guard over the unconscious victim until a snatch squad arrived by ground-effect or sky-hook.

The walkaway net in Akron suffered a cyberwar attack: first, missiles that took out the fiber head-ends, then RF-tropic aerostats that homed in on wireless masts and blasted them with pulses of noisy RF. The RF noise-floor in the city limits rose to the point where all devices began to fail.

That was the push; then came the pushback. The walkaways and Akronites who'd assumed control of the city planned for this kind of shock/awe. They had bunkers, aerostat-seeking autonomous lasers, dark fiber backups that linked up to microwave relays far out of town, offline atrocity-seeking cameras that recorded footage automatically when the network went dark, crude HERF weapons that stored huge amounts of solar energy whenever the sun shone, ready to discharge it in a powerful *whoomf* the moment they sensed military spread-spectrum comms.

Once the word got out about Akron, there was online pushback, too. Walkaways all over the world battered at the comms and infrastructure of the contractors in the vanguard, the DHS, the DoD, the White House internal nets, the DNC's backchannels, Seven Eyes chatter nets—the whole world of default super-rosa and sub-rosa connectivity. Walkaway backbones prioritized traffic out of Akron, auto-mirrored it across multiple channels.

This was all to script. For a decade, walkaway had been allied with monthly gezis that popped up in one country or another. They'd made a science of responding to authoritarian enclobberments, regrouping after every uprising to evolve new countermeasures and countercountermeasures against default's endlessly perfected civil order maintenance routines.

The difference was these walkaways were getting the full treatment. Not that default hadn't gone total war on walkaway before, but walkaway had always solved the problem by walking away. Default had produced an endless surplus of sacrifice zones, superfund sites, no-man's-lands and dead cities for walkaways. To a first approximation, all blasted wastelands were fungible.

Staying put was not walkaway doctrine, but there were plenty of other people in the planet's recent history who'd evinced an irrational, deep attachment to the real estate where they'd most recently ground to a halt. The tactics were understood.

Every gezi ended the same. Clouds of tear gas, lack of food and medicine; mounting injured and mealymouthed promises of zottas lured everyone off the streets and into what was left of their homes. Insignificant concessions were made and everyone agreed something had been done and it was time to move on.

Everyone knew that wasn't where these walkaways were headed. Even zottas. Especially zottas. The shock/awe phase was the most brutal ever, lethals and less-lethals mixed indiscriminately. Even the tamest default press was kept away due to fears of cooties and other bio-agents. Ohio's governor suspended the state legislature until the "emergency" concluded.

It was nerve-wracking. Walkaway footage from Akron had a desperate vibe. Every face, even the brave ones, looked doomed. The brave ones were the worst.

Dis knew some people in Akron. There was a Dis in Akron, or had been. She'd recently synched with her twin and feared for her, which was irrational. The meat-people she knew had been backing up since the Akron project was declared. This was the most worrying thing. Walkaways stood their ground because they did not fear death. Though she'd never say it to anyone—not even another Dis instance—she thought of the Akronites as a death-cult. They were fearless suicides who'd been guaranteed an afterlife. Default feeds hinted this, without saying it, because official default position was that uploading—walkaway uploading, anyway—was smoke and mirrors. They were chat-bots with idiosyncratic vocabularies, just convincing enough to trick gullible and desperate extremists who'd turned their back on everything.

Dis was grand-matron to these walkaways and everyone who thought death was another way of walking away from zottas and their demented ideas about wealth only ever mattering if you had more than everyone else. They were her spiritual children. She represented proof that death was the beginning, not the end. She'd never told anyone to take a backup and throw themselves into enemy crosshairs. She hadn't had to. Her existence was enough.

There must be so many Dises running in default's cyberwar labs. That was how they thought. She'd be the ultimate captive. All it would take to torture her into compliance was a tweak to the parameters of her even-keeled lookaheads, so existential terror smashed her again and again, beneath its high waves, without drowning her. The knowledge of her legion of sisters being grotesquely tortured made her furious—without making her rage, thanks to the lookahead safeguards. She wondered if her tortured sisters experienced the intensity that she was missing, whether they secretly enjoyed it a tiny bit.

It was impossible to know who was "winning" in Akron. Like all gezis, it was a war of perception and a military conflict. Would default's rank-and-file see just-desserts when Akron was smashed flat? Or would they see a default victory as a tormenting Goliath grinding Davids like them underfoot? Would guerrillas be seen as plucky Ewoks taking down Imperial Walkers, or as terrorists using IEDs to kill whey-faced American patriots? Default was media savvy. The only press with money to cover anything was underwritten by the same conglomerates that owned the contractors on the invaders' vanguard.

Every gezi ended with mixed defeat. Every gezi sent more people to walkaway, convinced no reform would rescue default. Convinced people on top couldn't contemplate a world where no one had to be poor to make them rich. Every gezi ended with great numbers of people scared into another season of submission, a thumb on their scales that overbalanced the risk of speaking out and made going along to get along tolerable.

What effect would Akron's martyrs have? Would fence-sitters become furious with the slaughter and rush to the streets because they wanted no part of the system that did this? Would it terrorize them into sitting still, lest they join the dead? Would they be convinced that it was suicidal to oppose default, regardless of mystical beliefs in "the first days of a better nation" and electronic afterlife?

"Did you see this?" Limpopo paged her from the party room where preparations were nearly complete. It was hung with improvised bunting, retrofitted for thundering dance music and feasting from extruders that cycled through the delicacies of walkaway's vast store of recipes.

"Akron? It's terrible."

She watched Limpopo through sensors—visible light, lidar, electromagnetic. Etcetera was with her, eyes glued to a screen he'd uncrumpled from his shirt-cuff and stuck onto the side of a beer keg. Etcetera held Limpopo's hand. A pang/not-pang of loneliness visited Dis, a ghost-ache for physical sensation and the hand of a lover.

"Akron is worse than terrible." During the storm, the party room filled up with people who'd worked on the machines, music, and food while the nets were down. Now the connectivity was flooding back, they'd returned to their screens. It was a weird hybrid of ancient and modern rhythms. Ancient people worked when the sun shone, slept when it sank, stayed inside when storms blew, and plowed when they cleared. Walkaway nets were environmentally disruptable and nondeterministic networks, so they did the same: endlessly communicated and computed when networks were running, did chores when weather or the world blew the networks down.

Everyone in the party room was glued to a screen or an interface, some in small groups, some on their own. They flung feeds at each other, whispered excitedly, spooling messages for walkaways in Akron, *Stay safe Stay brave You are in our hearts What they do to you they do to us We will never forget you.*

"Wish I had your software controls." Limpopo's breath was ragged. There were more deaths in Akron, fresh revelations as a drone flew over a bomb site where mechas were shifting rubble, recovering bodies and parts of bodies. The first feed died when the drone was shot down. This attracted a flock of suicide drones that sacrificed themselves to capture and transmit whatever the powers of default did not want to be seen. More shots brought them down. High-altitude drones winged in, the feeds jerkier because they recorded from a greater distance, with not-quite-stabilized magnification. There were children in the rubble. Limpopo cried. Etcetera cried. Dis wanted to change their feed, show them the doxxings popping up in darknet pastebins, personal facts of the lives of the contractors and soldiers whose faces were tagged from the footage, open letters written to their mothers and fathers, spouses and children, asking how they could do this to their fellow human beings.

These doxxings were also from the gezi playbook. Sometimes they worked. Even when they didn't, unexpected things happened. Kids left home, leaked their parents' private documents implicating their superiors, publishing secret-above-secret rules of engagement with instructions to use lethals when cameras were off, to bury evidence, or implicate insurgents in atrocities. Sometimes parents disowned children who'd done zottas' dirty work, publicly disavowing slaughter. It split families and communities, but it also brought new ones together. It was controversial because it implicated so many innocents and was a dirty trick, but it was okay with Dis. Even when she'd been alive, she'd been willing to break those eggs to make her omelet. As a dead person running on servers around the world, including several hostile to her and everything she believed in, she couldn't work up a mouthful of virtual spit in sympathy for people who felt sad that Daddy was exposed as a war criminal.

Kersplebedeb quietly typed on a keyboard and muttered into a mic.

"We should be ready to go." He put his arms around Etcetera's and Limpopo's shoulders. "There've been more attacks. Two in Ontario, three in PEI, a couple in northern BC, and Nunavut. Some were big and some small, but none of them expected it. A couple were stable, one in PEI was twenty years old, had a good relationship with the normals around them. It's gone now, not even a crater. Scraped clean."

Dis said, "Have you heard anything specific about Thetford? Is anything incoming?" She spoke out of Limpopo's bracelet, turning herself up loud enough for Kersplebedeb. He blinked and absorbed the fact that she was there.

"Nothing," he said. "There's almost nothing in the air right now, so if something was coming, we wouldn't see it. If something's coming, the snow might have stalled it. I think we should be ready to go if and when. I never believed in the Big One, but this feels like a Medium One."

"What's the Big One?" Dis nearly leaped in to answer Etcetera, but she let Limpopo in.

"It's first-generation walkaway stuff. The theory was default would decide we were too dangerous to exist and they'd stage a coordinated attack on all of us, all at once. Kill or arrest everyone, end the movement in one go. They've got the spook power to know who and where we all are, so the only thing that stops them is whim or lack of gonadal fortitude."

Etcetera said, "I thought it was just me who worried about that."

"It used to be hotly debated. We thought they'd wipe us out. Then they didn't, and didn't, and didn't. We speculated, were they not willing to risk the good boys and girls of default deciding this ruthlessness couldn't be abided, taking to the streets with pitchforks? Was it that they liked to have the goats and sheep self-sorted? Did they secretly slum and ogle flesh in the onsen and eat extruder-chow and drink coffium and play bohemian dropout? Were there too many zottas' kids in walkaway, too much blue blood to be spilled in the Final Solution?"

"I hate Kremlinology," Etcetera said. "It obsessed my parents. Second- and third-guessing what the real powers behind Anon Ops were and who pulled their strings and why."

Kersplebedeb: "It's not my favorite, either, but there's a difference between obsessing over tea leaves and trying to figure out if the next missile is headed your way. Let's get supplies packed and stashed by the doors, vehicles checked and charged, make sure everyone's got a suit."

"We can't object to that." Limpopo got Etcetera's screen down and stuffed it into a pocket. "Dis, can you help? Get the word out, throw up a git to track what's done and what needs doing?"

"Already doing it." Dis never stopped believing in the Big One. No one who'd worked on uploading and simulation had—it was the unspoken motivation behind the project, only way you could be sure zottas wouldn't genocide is if they knew that you'd come back as immortal ghosts in the machine to haunt them to the ends of the earth.

Even as she did it, she worried about Akron, and wondered what was happening with Tam and Gretyl and Seth.

## [xiii]

Seth's alarm roused him to check on the snow every hour, first to see if it was safe to get moving; second to ensure he wasn't entombed under an immovable drift. The other two set theirs at twenty-minute offsets. He managed to doze off the first hour in the uncomfortable cocoon. The chime woke him with a violent start. He experienced near-panic while he tried to figure where the exact fuck he was. Terror so adrenalized him that he wasn't drowsy when he went back in, so he played an old acoustic minigame he'd been addicted to as a kid, matching the rhythm and pitch of the tones in his earbud with fingertaps and whistles.

The suit's interface surfaces were three generations removed from the ones the game was designed for, and were specialized for wildly different purposes to the surfaces he'd grown up with. The game was a *lot* harder until he tweaked the way the interfaces registered.

Playing made him nostalgic for the hundreds of hours he'd logged on the game, until he remembered why he'd stopped playing—he'd beaten another kid, Larry Pendleton, to whom he was peripherally connected, part of the same massive grade-nine class at Jarvis Collegiate. He didn't know Larry well, but they sometimes were in the same groups, and he'd figured Larry was, if not cool, at least not a turd.

But then Larry said, "Hey, good game, Seth. Guess you've got a natural advantage, though."

Everyone either didn't understand what Larry meant, or pretended they didn't. Seth understood, immediately: "Because you're black, you're better at rhythm games. Because you know, black people got rhythm, everyone knows—" Seth saw Larry dropped the remark in a way calculated for plausible deniability, wiggle room to claim it wasn't racial, that Seth was being oversensitive and social-justicey.

The unspoken deal with his white friends was he wasn't allowed to talk about being black, except for the lightest of jokes. To acknowledge he was the black guy in their white crowd was tantamount to accusing them of racism: *Why am I the only black face here?* It was a deal everyone understood and no one spoke of, especially the Asian and Desi kids in their cadre, because everyone was supposed to be race-blind and being the Angry Minority was a buzzkill for everyone.

He boiled with shame and anger at fucking Larry Pendleton, who was decades away in default and maybe dead of something antibiotic resistant or in jail or working a precarious job and hoping he didn't get fired, which was all any of them were doing. But he jammed down the shame and anger of pretending he hadn't noticed the racism, pretending he wouldn't always be probationary.

He spent the hour thoroughly asking himself whether he was a black guy or a walkaway, or a black walkaway, or something else, or all of the above. It was not a question he often asked. Thinking about it made him angry. He didn't like being angry. He liked being funny and horny, carefree, perennially underestimated, which had many advantages. Being thought of as harmless—"he's a black guy, but he's cool, doesn't make a big deal of it"—was something he'd cultivated early on. It meant he heard and saw things his black friends didn't see. A lot of it was casual racism. Some of it was good. He got to be more than his skin.

Being stuck in a box was driving him fucking crazy. All he could think about was skin color. He couldn't even see his skin in the dark. Then there was the rhythm game, Thumperoo, which he'd played the whole time, until his wrists felt RSI-ish.

He checked the time. Forty-one minutes until he was scheduled to stick his head out. He sighed. His wrists hurt too much to keep playing and—

The hatch opened and above him grinned the face of Tam, sun glinting off her visor, obscuring one of her eyes and one of her cheekbones. But he'd know those lips anywhere.

"Come on, Sleeping Beauty. Prince Charming's here to wake your ass up."

She helped him out. The storm clouds had blown away, leaving blue skies, darkening with impending dusk. Slanting late sun made the fresh powder glitter like it had been dusted with diamond chips. Gretyl stood in powder up to her thighs. She flopped on her back and made an angel. "Thank god that's over. Vuko jebina!"

He cupped his hands over his visor—for effect—and howled.

"The wagon won't make it back until this freezes or melts. It's snowshoes from here." Gretyl brushed snow off the tarp they'd put over the survival gear when they'd dumped it out to make room for their bodies.

She tugged at the tarp. Seth and Tam slogged over to help. They sorted through the neat bundles until they found snowshoes. None of them had ever assembled the shoes, and they couldn't figure it out. Seth rooted further until he found an aerostat and sent it up, looking for walkaway signals to bridge to the suits. They watched it putter, spinning and tacking, receding to a dot on the darkening sky. Their suits started to make welcoming, subliminal interface buzzes as they in-spooled and out-spooled messages. They brushed away the incoming alerts for a minute, clearing stuff until they could get the snowshoe FAQs.

Gretyl got there first. She threw a shoe frame atop the snow in a particular way, so it landed partially embedded, then she clicked a mechanism none of them had figured out was clickable until they saw the video. The shoe sprang open and sent powder up in a pretty flurry, lying flat on the surface. She spread the bindings, then did the same with her other shoe.

Seth and Tam got their shoes spread out, too. They all engaged in involuntary slapstick as they struggled to put them on. Eventually, Tam came to Seth, who had fallen into the snow and was half-submerged with legs in the air. She seized one of his feet and shoved it into the bindings, then did the other, then hauled him upright. He lifted the shoes clear of the snow and set them atop it, and found to his delight that he was stayed on the powder, which creaked beneath the shoes' webbing. He gave Tam a double thumbs-up, and she handed him her shoes and flopped onto her back and stuck her feet in the air.

He wasn't as good at putting them on as Tam, but that was okay. The clear skies, the entombment in the cargo-pods, and the thought of a walk through the woods on these cool-ass outdoor prostheses made them giddy. He wished he could take her into a pod, get naked, and fuck her brains out. It was a comforting randiness. The suit was surprisingly accommodating of his erection. He contrived to brush his hand over Tam's crotch as he helped her up—this was something they did often, with the ardor of school kids who've just found their first fuck-buddies and can't believe that they've got all the ass they want on tap, twenty-four/seven—but the suits were too padded for him to tell if she had a boner, too. He decided she did—she'd changed her hormones recently and hard-ons were a welcome side-effect of the new regime they both enjoyed.

They held hands—she squeezed, which made him even hornier—and approached Gretyl, who scowled at her shoes, having tramped a wide circle as she tried to put them on. They flanked her and she looked from one to the other.

"Oh no," she began, then Tam put one snowshod foot behind her and Seth pushed and over she went, legs in the air, howling in mock-outrage. They clipped the shoes to her feet as she giggled, pulled her upright.

Seth looked at his heads-up, pulled up the wayfinder, and pointed. "That-away," he said.

They tramped on. As the sun set, they activated nightscopes, and watched the starlight and enhancement algorithms turn everything milky, glowing—a fairyland.

## [xiv]

Natalie napped a lot. Maybe she was depressed, or maybe it was dope in her food, though Dis didn't find any record of that anymore in the patient management stuff in control-central.

Maybe it was her mind's defense mechanism, shutting down in the face of boredom and frustration. Her friends said they'd come get her. Gretyl promised, but days had passed since she'd heard from them. Her father stopped visiting. She didn't know if that was because she'd gotten under his skin, or because he'd blown town for some business, which was the sort of thing he'd always done. Mom and Cordelia visited for regular, sterile half-hours. Every time they left, she swore *next* time, she'd freeze them, sit in stony silence.

But then they arrived and opened with rehearsed pleasantry—"Oh, Natty, it's been such a day—" and smile, and she was a Redwater girl among Redwater girls, the sisterhood of ladies who lunch and who would never be allowed to be more than that. Her mother missed Greece, and often passed the whole half hour in a monologue about a particular boat captain, or wonderful honey, or a shrine a Greek family brought her to, approached by knee-walking pilgrims who wore painter's kneepads to protect themselves as they humped up the hill to the icon of Madonna in the humble building.

Cordelia talked about school, professors, and a boy—a man, she said—whom Jacob would never approve of. It was easy to hold up her end of these conversations. All she had to do was nod and make noises and not stand and scream it was bullshit, everything Cordelia dedicated her life to was worse than a sham, fueled by delusional conviction that the money, power, and privilege of the Redwaters was something they'd earned—and therefore, everyone without lovely money and power and privilege *hadn't* earned it.

Sometimes, the merc came in. Natalie had listened carefully for someone to mention her name. She desperately wanted to know. The merc was a bridge between worlds. She had to live in the real world where privilege was obviously undeserved. How could she meet clients and not know? She had to be able to make it not matter, because her paycheck depended on her not letting herself care, on understanding walkaway well enough to snatch them. The merc wasn't her friend, but she was important.

No one called her by name. When Jacob wanted her, he changed the pitch of his voice, switching to a command tone he always used on bodyguards. It was different from the command tone he used on domestic servants, more militarized, like he was LARPing a blue-jawed sergeant in a war movie. When Mom wanted the merc, she switched to her wheedling tone, the "do me a favor" voice, less gracious for the iron-clad conviction the favor would be done.

Cordelia never spoke to the merc. She treated her as if she were invisible, a walking C.C.T.V. If she ever looked at the merc, it was with fear.

The merc was key.

The next time the merc came in—bringing in a basket with snack food, fresh underwear and shirts, and a pointless shatterproof vase of unseasonal hothouse flowers that had undoubtedly originated with her mother—Natalie locked eyes with her.

"We could do a side-deal. No one would have to know, not at first. They can't keep me here forever. Eventually they'll get bored of the crazy sister in the attic and ship me to a nut-hatch and kick you out on your butt. If I can get out, I can get a contingency lawyer to harass them into unlocking my trust fund. You know how I feel about money, you've seen how I want to live. I'd sign it over to you. Airtight and irrevocable. It's more than they're going to pay you, more than they could ever pay you. A fortune. A *dynastic* fortune, the kind that will still be intact when you're an old lady and your kids are fighting over your deathbed for the dough.

"I'm sure you're thinking if you did this you'd be radioactively fucked. That's why I'm offering you the whole package: life without having to work another day, ever. Automatic deposits, every month, for you, your kids, their kids. The way the trust is written, there's a good chance that when Mummy and Daddy kick the bucket, there'll be fresh dough in the trust, even more for you and yours. All they can offer you is a bed under the stairs—I'm offering to turn you into a zotta."

The merc looked at her.

Natalie smiled. "You know I mean it." She hesitated, because this part was dangerous, if she'd misjudged the woman. "There's no video of this conversation. Check for yourself, then let's deal."

A maybe-smile crossed the merc's face, so subtle Natalie might have been kidding herself. She set the basket down and backed out, like she always did, with that confident stride that said, *I'm not afraid of you, this is just best-practices.*

As soon as the door clunk-*clunk*ed, Dis said, "That was . . ."

"I know. I'm sick of being a fucking damsel. Princess Peach sucks. I wanna be Mario. It's been weeks. This isn't going to get better. Dad isn't going to wake up and say, 'what the fuck was I thinking? Nice people don't kidnap their daughters!' If I can't fake capitulation, he's going to bury me in some deep hole, a boot camp for rich bitches where they shave your head and make you crawl in mud until you mewl for mercy and then they send you home with a zombinol pump in your appendix and your smile stapled on with sutures."

"But if she rats you out, they'll catch me."

"So what? If you've pwned them as thoroughly as you say, they'll have a hell of a time rooting you out—in the meantime, they'll have to move me, which might be a chance to get away. You're backed up. Getting caught isn't the death penalty—just email your diff file to another instance. You can walkaway. That's the whole point of the Dis Experience."

Dis was silent. "I don't want to leave you alone."

"You think I can't handle it."

"I don't think anyone could handle it, or should have to handle it alone."

Natalie remembered how glad she'd been when Dis first spoke, the relief of having an ally. Even not knowing whether Dis was compromised, whether Dis herself could tell if she had been compromised, it had been such a relief. Before Dis, she'd been so isolated that she'd cracked up.

"Having you here kept me from doing more to help myself. You're my Deus Ex, promising salvation from afar. I was going insane before you got here, because I was in an insane situation. I've been sane since—even though my situation's more fucked up. That's not a good thing."

Another machine silence. Natalie remembered when Dis was a fragile, cracked-up simulation, how she'd gentled her while she worked on the problem of her own sanity. There was a symmetry in Dis returning the favor.

"I'm not a sim, Dis. I'm a human being. I'm cracking up because my situation is terminally fubared."

Could a sim cry? There was a thickness to Dis's voice: "I understand."

"Are you okay? You shouldn't be able to feel sad, right?" She was alarmed, thinking of how spectacularly off the rails Dis could go, remembering the terrifying personality disintegrations at the end.

"I think so. I— There's a bunch of us, a bunch of Dises, who've been trying to loosen the strings on our personalities. Gretyl's work on lookaheads lets us do it. When we started, we were sparing with lookahead, steering clear of the banks, trying to go down the middle. We're so much better at lookaheads—the code's getting tighter—we're working with wider ranges, closer to the edges."

In spite of herself, Natalie was fascinated. "But *why*?"

Even as she asked it, she understood. Isn't that just what she was doing? Finding madness to let her meet terror with terror, meet the impossible with the uncompromising?

"Because I'm not *me*. That was the one thing we promised ourselves we wouldn't say. Everyone is counting so hard on simulation. It's everyone's plan B, their escape hatch. The more time I spend in this—*situation*—the less certain I am that I'm still *me*."

"Of course. Not having a body, being transubstantiated to software, that has to change you. Like being stuck here changed me."

"I don't mean I haven't been changed. I expected I'd be changed. I've been around. We outgrew the 'if I cut off your finger, wouldn't you still be you?' word game years ago. I'd still be me, but a different me. If you kept chopping away by centimeters until there's nothing left but machine, I'd still be me, but I'd be a me that was traumatized and changed.

"The 'me' that counts isn't just a me I can recognize. It's a me I want to be. If the only way to be me in silicon is to be a me that only manages not to hate myself by literally refusing to allow myself to think the thought that I should be thinking, then fuck that."

"I almost understood that," Natalie said, smiling despite herself. "Sorry, I don't mean to joke—"

"It *is* funny, in a what-the-actual-fuck way. But it's terrifying. There's so much riding on my stupid existential crises—"

"That must be terrible."

"I mean, fuck, I'm an immortal machine-person who can be in hundreds of places at once. I haven't been imprisoned by my father. I haven't been kidnapped from my lover. I have no business whining, just because I'll be lonely if I can't be with you—"

"I'll miss you, too, if they nuke you." A thought occurred. "Do you think they could *capture* you and fuck with your parameters to torture you?"

"No, that's the one thing I'm dead certain of. I'm all dead-man's-switches. If they fuck with me, I'll be securely erased before they know it."

"That's a relief. I'll miss you, but we'll talk again. I'm getting out, no matter what. When I do, you'll be there."

"I'm sorry for being needy. I'm a shitty robot. It's just—" Another pause. Did Dis throw these in for dramatic effect? Was she doing a gnarly lookahead? The voice that came next was so soft that Natalie barely heard it. "No one knows me like you. No one's seen me in the raw, without rails on my sim. No one can understand the full possibility-envelope of all the ways of being me, and how constrained those possibilities are in the me I am today."

Her palpable sorrow—her voice synth had gotten *so good*—ripped Natalie. Her eyes flooded. She wiped furiously. She didn't want to be hobbled with concern for someone else's welfare. She wanted to look after herself.

The thought snagged like a fishhook. It was a Jacob Redwater thought. A default thought. A *zotta* thought. It was not a walkaway thought. It was the kind of thought she'd spent years learning to unthink. It was so easy to be a special snowflake and know her misery mattered more than everyone else's. That could be true. Jacob lived a life where his happiness trumped all others'. But it only worked if you armored yourself against the rest of the world. To build a safe-room in your heart.

"I love you, Dis." She didn't know if it was true, but she wanted it to be true. She wanted to love everyone. Everyone failed to live up to their own ideals. She wanted to fall short of the best ideals. "I love you for who you are now, and for who you are when you're losing your shit. They're both you."

Machine silence. It stretched. She was about to speak, but clunk-*clunk* the door unlocked. The merc came in, carrying a tray with a carafe of—long experience told her—lukewarm, shitty coffium that had been denatured of the good stuff.

The merc closed the door, clunk-*clunk,* and spun the carafe's top. The liquid inside steamed in a way that the drinks she was allowed as a prisoner never steamed. She remembered the smell from childhood, cottage trips with Redwater cousins from the dynastic branch, with implanted tracking chips and bodyguards. It wasn't coffium, it was coffee—prize beyond measure, beans grown in specially isolated fields tended by workers who were microbially screened twice a day for the first signs of blight.

The merc set the tray down on Natalie's breakfast table, arranged two china cups, poured—volatile aromatics filled the room with impossible, vivid smells.

"Cream?" She'd spoken so few words that the voice surprised her. Warm, deeper than Natalie remembered. Was there an accent, a hint of a roll on the *r*?

"Not if that's what I think it is." She sniffed more deeply. "Yergacheffe?" A cousin—older, well-traveled—taught her to pronounce it with a soft *y*, a rolled *r*, a hard *ch* and a breathy *h* at the end. It sprang from her lips with ease, a status marker in four syllables. The smell was unmistakable, a fruitiness and acidity that was nothing like other storied beans, the fullness of Blue Mountain, the acid fruitiness of bourbon. Her mouth watered.

"That's what it said on the bag." There was an accent, maybe Eastern European. Growing up, she'd heard a lot of those accents—kids whose parents made fortunes doing nonspecific "entrepreneurial" things. Like the true Redwater cousins, these kids had bodyguards, who also spoke with the accent, only thicker. "The cook sent down a grinder and a press."

She sipped, eyes closed, lost in reverie. Natalie saw she was lovely in a predatory way. Not hot—not her type—but maybe someone you'd model a videogame character on in a specific type of videogame aimed at a certain kind of boy. "It's the first coffee I've drunk in Canada. Only get it in Africa, usually. Chinese bosses always insist on it."

There'd been a Chinese-Nigerian girl in high school, guarded more heavily than the Russian kids. She had a short temper, and woe betide anyone foolish enough to ask to touch her hair, which Natalie understood. Her name was Sophie. Natalie hadn't seen her since graduation, but she sometimes thought about the stories Sophie told about the floating super-cities off Lagos where she'd been raised, hopping from one aircraft-carrier-sized walled garden to another.

Natalie reached for her coffee. Her hands shook. She wished they didn't. She raised the cup and didn't spill. She was out of practice with real hot beverages, but managed to sip. It was very hot, and flavorsome in a way that "bitter" didn't capture. It tasted *nothing* like coffium, except you could see where one was related to the other in an indefinable way. There was an oiliness to it she hadn't anticipated. *Mouth feel*. Another class marker, knowing those two words and having the confidence to use them without feeling bourgie. The dynastic Redwaters could say "mouth feel" without batting an eye, and memorably, cousin Sarah used it to describe a boy she'd met at boarding school in Donetsk.

She swallowed. Caffeine was so primitive, she expected it to cudgel her like a caveman, but the high, which came on fast, was surprisingly good, a tingling with a smooth peak and a mellow comedown. No one did caffeine anymore. There were options for getting up. It was such a genteel zotta thing, like sherry and cream tea. The zottas had been hoarding the best stuff.

She drank more. The up was so clean. It steadied her nerves, made her want to move.

"My name is Nadie." The merc held out a strong, small hand that gripped hers with calibrated firmness.

"I'm—Iceweasel."

Nadie smiled, small square teeth. "I know. We were inside your nets for two days before I took you. Wasn't hard."

"It's not supposed to be," Iceweasel said. "We want people to read the public stuff. Almost everyone isn't a zotta, which means that almost everyone should join the walkaways."

"Some zottas join, too." Nadie had this Russian—Bulgarian? Belarusian?—deadpan thing, the corner of her mouth a precursor to a smirk, a deniable microexpression that registered nevertheless.

"Some do."

"I'm interested in the information security aspect of our earlier conversation."

"Does that mean we have a deal?"

"No." Nadie's microexpression flickered. "We don't have a deal. Calm yourself." She pointed to a readout on the bed that alerted as Iceweasel's heart-rate and endocrine signifiers thwacked the red zone.

Iceweasel made herself breathe. Nadie was playing head games. That's what she'd done from the start. It would be delusional to hope for anything else.

"I'm calming."

"I want to know about infowar. I *know* you had no jailbroken devices you could use to probe and pwn the safe room. I searched you. No one who comes in is allowed to bring anything that could be used to launch an attack, except your father, and even he submits to an inventory whenever he leaves. The attack came from outside, which should be setting off IDS alarms. That's not happening. There's something very bad that I never noticed. This makes me feel foolish."

"I don't think less of you."

A microexpression telegraphing dark amusement. The woman was a savant of emotion-hockey.

"I hope not. I hope you understand I'm a serious person, and I'm not your friend. I'm not your enemy, either, though I have been your opponent. I'm very good at what I do. Good enough that you want to be straight with me. Good enough that if we end up enemies, it should worry you."

Her microexpression changed, a glint that made her feel frightened a centimeter below her navel. Like the fear she'd felt once, trekking near the B&B. There'd been a wolf. It looked at her in a way that made her certain it had mapped every possible thing she might do, anticipated countermoves. It effectively owned her. She was only breathing because it suffered her to. She tried to stay calm. The stupid bed-monitor ratted her out, its infographics redlining in her peripheral vision. She expected Nadie to smirk, or micro-smirk, but she held that badass look for another moment.

"I see you understand. Let us talk about the network."

Iceweasel felt for her bravery. "I don't think so. I've given you knowledge of the network situation. Why should I give you something more?"

She nodded, acknowledging the point. "More coffee?" Subtext *How about this black magic; a fair trade, wasn't it?*

"Absolutely." Black liquid poured in a silky river from carafe to pot. "I'm still not going to tell you more about the network. Not until we have a deal."

"It's not a stupid position, though you know that now I can get to the bottom of it myself. My employers have procedures. They'll pull everything in the building in twelve hours, take it away for forensics while new patched and locked stuff is installed here."

"I'm aware of that."

"You're counting on the fact I'll get more money from freeing you than I would from helping your father."

"I'm hoping for that. It helps that my father is an asshole. I'm hoping you find working for him so offensive that the chance to get away *and* fuck him over *and* help me *and* get rich is tempting."

The micro-smirk returned: *touché*. "Your father is in a difficult position."

"My father deserves to swing from a lamppost."

"A difficult position, I think you'll agree."

"You didn't disagree with my assessment."

"I've seen people swing from lampposts. It's not nice."

"I suppose that's true."

More coffee. The second caffeine rush wasn't as good as the first, which she remembered hearing, caffeine adaptation was faster than with coffium's cocktail of neuroticklers. You had to keep upping the dose to get to the same place, or wait out tedious refractory periods before you could recapture the rush.

"People swinging from lampposts, huh?"

"Twice. I didn't put them there."

"Who did?"

"People like me, to tell the truth. People working for rich people, taking money under orders, to send a message."

"What kind of message?"

"Don't fuck with my boss or you'll hang from a lamppost."

"But you never hung anyone from a lamppost."

"Never hung anyone from anything. That's not my kind of work. I've been asked to do it."

"You get to say no to that kind of boss?"

"I'm good at my job. I get to say, 'Let me explain to you why this will make things worse. Let me explain how this will make people who don't think you're the enemy decide they have to kill you before you kill them. Let me explain what I can do to neutralize people who want to harm you.'"

"You mean, infiltrate their networks, kidnap them—"

"Yes-no. Map the social graph, find the leaders, dox them, discredit them.

Kidnap if you have to, but that makes martyrs, so not so much. Better to make them busy with fighting fires. I know other contractors who'll crawl a culture's chat-channels and boards and model the weak points, find the old fights that still simmer, create strategy for flaring them. So easy to infiltrate. Once they think they're infiltrated, they point at one another, wondering who is a mole and who is true. It's neater than bodies swinging from lampposts. Tidier. Not so many flies."

"Ha ha."

"You don't like it. I work for your enemies, destroy what you're building." She shrugged. "I don't do it because I hate you. Sometimes I admire you, even. But I'm good at my job. If you want to succeed, you have to be good at your job. Someone else would do my job if I didn't, so unless you're better at your job than people like me are at ours, you're doomed anyway."

The infographic pulsed red. "I fucking hate that thing."

"I don't mind that you're upset. I'm saying upsetting things. If I was you, I'd be upset. I understand you don't do what you do for job, but for love. You want to save the world. Saving the world is good, but I don't think you will manage. I don't think anyone can. Human nature. If the world is doomed, I want to be comfortable until it goes up, boom."

"It sounds like you're saying you're interested in my trust fund."

"I am very interested in your trust fund, Natalie. Iceweasel. I believe there are structural challenges to getting my hands on it, but I also think there are people in my orbit who know how to make structural challenges go away. They will need paying, of course, but—"

"But you'll be able to afford it."

"I can afford it now. I am good at my job. I get well paid. My contacts would do it for commission, but that would be much more. I prefer to pay cash, even if that risks my money."

She poured herself more coffee, brought it to her lips, didn't drink, looked over the black mirror of its surface. Her hand was rock steady, her eyes cool as glacial ice. "You know I can find you. No matter where you go, what you do, I can find you."

"I know you can." *I know you think you can.*

"You may think, 'My comrades have better opsec than this Russian musclehead, see how they cut through the network perimeter, got inside her decision loop.' You may think, 'We can outsmart her now.' Is that what you think?"

Red, red, red. Stupid infographic. "I don't think that, but I wonder if it's true."

She sipped, put down the cup. "It might be true. I don't think so. Defense is a harder game than offense. Defense, you have to be perfect. Offense, you just need to find one imperfection. Here I am defender. When I hunt you, you are the defender. You will make mistakes. Your philosophy isn't about perfect, it's not about discipline."

*It takes mental discipline not to delude yourself.*

"It doesn't matter. If you understand anything about me, you understand I don't give a shit about money. If I could put it in a pile and set fire to it, that'd be the only day I wouldn't piss on it. I'm not going to outsmart you. If nothing else, having no money and none coming would alienate my father so deeply that he might stop trying to induct me into his cult of a family. Maybe he'll adopt you."

"I don't think I'd let him." Her microexpression was impossible to read. "I'm going to talk to the kind of people who do things with trusts and finances, so your father couldn't undo them. You know if I say no, and you talk to your father about this, I can make your situation worse, in significant ways. You know I was able to track you, to solve your patterns. I took you without fuss. We know you don't care for these people, but we also both know certain other people matter to you, such as your Gretyl—" The name made the infographics lose their shit. "I can find her as easily as I found you. The fact you were not hurt was a choice on my part. Do you understand these things?"

She was crying, and just hating herself for it. So foolish! To give this person such leverage over her, to be such a Pavlovian slave, just mention Gretyl's name and the waterworks started.

She snuffled snot, savagely wiped her eyes, glared. The merc looked a little embarrassed.

"I don't like to threaten. But it helps if you know I'm serious. That way we don't have misunderstandings about balance of power. I am someone who pays attention to the balance of power. It's my professional competence."

"If you know anything about me, you know I just want to get the fuck out. I have no urge to screw up your job with my sociopathic family. If you think about it for one fucking second, Ms. Balance of Power, you'd understand I *don't* play games. I voluntarily told you I had pwned the network. I could have kept that a secret forever. I voluntarily handed over that power."

"Of course, you've left me wondering what other secrets you have, which is why we're having this discussion."

"I don't have any more secrets." *Oh, that fucking infographic.*

She laughed. She was pretty when she laughed. Not scary at all. It was like the teenaged girl trapped inside her—before all the crazy-ass martial arts and BFG training—was shining through. "Of course you have secrets. We all have secrets, Iceweasel."

# [xv]

They were halfway to Thetford when the alerts sounded, startling Seth out of a walking reverie. The network came back in earnest when they crested a ridge with a straight shot to three repeaters. Suddenly they were getting traffic that had spooled from way away, in multiple directions. Once their availability back-propagated to other spools, the data rushed in. There were a *lot* of messages for them.

Gretyl figured it out first: "Storm's fucked the normal routes, all this stuff's backed up. We should pound in a repeater. Anyone bring one from the wagon?"

Seth had. He climbed a tree, Gretyl and Tam helping, and drove the spike into the trunk about four meters up. Tam passed him up a hatchet and he hacked the branches around it, feeling twinges of guilt despite the trees around them as far as the eye could see. This one was no nicer than any other.

Tam helped him get the tie-downs into place and unfurled the solar sheet on the north face. Gretyl retreated into antisocial, computerized silence as she parsed the messages.

"Holy shitting fuck," she said.

"What?" Seth shouted and nearly dropped the hatchet—visions of it embedding itself in Tam's skull made him grab wildly—then nearly fell out of the goddamned tree.

They found out about Akron, all the other attacks, and hastily spooled messages to everyone they loved, all over the world, and lit out as fast as they could go, for Thetford.

Tam's interface read to her while she walked and flicked through messages and videos, lagging behind Seth and Gretyl. Seth tried to hurry her, but she told him to fuck off. She had people in Akron and she was figuring out if they were dead.

Seth realized a lot of the B&B crew was in Akron. People he'd known, cooked with, fixed machines with, argued with. Some who'd welcomed him when he was a shlepper. Some he'd de-shlepped, initiating them into walkaway's mysteries. One he'd briefly fallen in love with, who—he realized now—reminded him of Tam. Who knew he had a type?

He worried. It was all he could do not to ask Tam to look up *his* people, too. Gretyl wanted to get to Thetford, for all the good they'd do there.

Tam kept gasping and swearing and falling down in the snow and needing rescuing. Her batteries were getting low. So were his. Gretyl kept too far ahead for him to see her infographics, but she couldn't have been rolling in juice.

"Come *on,* Tam. Nothing we can do out here. Gotta get back before dark, baby."

"Fuck baby, the world's burning."

"Can't it burn while we're indoors with a toilet?"

"Fuck."

They crested the last ridge and Tam shouted. He was about to give her hell for diving back into her tubes when he saw her pointing. They were the highest ground for klicks. She pointed way out on the horizon. He squinted and Gretyl swore. He dialed up the visor magnification and saw a column of armored cars on caterpillar treads, sending up plumes of fresh powder behind them. They were skinned in snow-camou, but the plumes made it easy to pick out their edges.

"They're heading to Thetford," Seth said.

"No shit," Tam said.

"I'm calling them now," Gretyl said. They could see the space-station from the ridge, a hamster-run of tubes and domes nestled amid the ruins of the houses.

"They've got to get out of there now," Tam said.

"I'm *calling* them," Gretyl said, and her intercom shut down as she went private. They watched the armored column move. Belatedly, Seth scanned the sky for drones, and saw outriders ahead of the column, but flying at conservative distance ahead, maybe to keep the element of surprise intact. Or maybe the long-range outriders were high-altitude, and had receded to invisible pinpricks.

"Kersplebedeb says they were anticipating something like this." Gretyl pointed down at the space-station, where now, airlocks were bursting open and suited-and-booted walkaways spilled out with packs and sledges in tow. "They got network service an hour ago, understood the Akron situation—"

"Our repeater," Seth said.

"We bridged them in, they got the word. They're not stupid. They're ready to walk away."

"Better be ready to run," Tam said. The column drew closer.

## [xvi]

Dis was in Gretyl's ears—all their ears at once—as they suited up and hit the airlocks, grabbing supplies that she'd directed them to gather and stash when the news came on. For obscure reasons Kersplebedeb kept calling her "Tiger Mother," a private joke between them.

Dis told them to grab spare batteries for Tam and Seth and Gretyl, reminded them to empty their bladders and void their bowels before suiting up, reminded them of the two deadheading mercs that had come all the way from Walkaway U and would need to be packed out, and suggested an arrangement of sledges and bubblewrap and oversaw the production.

Dis chivvied them out the door, was in their ears as they slogged up the ridge while Tam and Seth and Gretyl came down, taking their loads.

Dis said good-bye as they slogged away, pulling their loads and shouldering their packs, clomping away on the space-station's entire supply of snowshoes, in two ragged columns.

They reached the top of the ridge, crunch of the snowshoes as loud as a mouthful of potato-chips, and realized Dis said good-bye because she couldn't come.

"I've emailed a diff of myself to another instance of me."

"Not Remote?" Gretyl sounded alarmed. "Because that's not so stable—"

"Not Remote," Dis said. "There's a repo for Dis instances on the walkaway cloud, mirrored forty ways. We can't all run, of course, but at least we'll be safe. For now."

"Shit," Tam said, with feeling. "I don't want to leave you."

"I'm leaving you. I'm racing ahead. You can download and run me, soon as you find a cluster. You meat-people be careful."

Kersplebedeb said, "Tiger Mother, we've got our backups. We're assured an ever-after afterlife in the sweet bye-and-bye. Nothing harder to kill than an idea whose time has come to pass. Takes more than guns to kill a man."

"Always keep a trash bag in your car." Dis sounded wryly amused. "Software immortality is nice, but if you can save your fleshy bodies, you should."

"We'll watch our butts."

Seth ticked the privacy box. "I'm worried about you, Dis."

"I'm worried about all of us. They're hitting lots of places. Looking at those pics you sent, I think that's Canadian army, special forces, the ones who do the bad things. Torture squads. Kind of thing you send if you don't want any survivors."

"A goose just walked on my grave." Seth shivered again. He had a new power pack, but felt awfully cold.

Tam touched his shoulder. She could see he was talking, and he must have looked a fright. He toggled to public.

"Just worried that this feels like something bad and worse."

They moved slowly. All the stuff they shlepped was bad enough, but snowshoes made it worse.

"They're gonna get us pretty fucking soon at this rate," Seth said.

Kersplebedeb snickered. "No, they're not."

Seth hadn't ever heard Kersplebedeb make such a sinister noise.

"Booby trap?"

"Not the sort that goes boom. Just a place under the main road where there was a mining cave-in. We fixed it so we could bring in supplies, but didn't design it for those big tanks those fuckers have."

"M.R.A.P.s," Tam said. "Armored cars. Not tanks. No turrets."

Kersplebedeb snickered again. "No difference. There's a half-kilometer of rubble, tunnels, scree, and sand, straight down, and they're about to hit it." He chucked them the feed from a drone they'd lofted on their way out the door. They stopped while they screened it on their visors. "Any minute now," he said.

The fan-tail of snow and ice obscured the column, but Seth thought there were six of those things.

"Won't they have lidar, checking for IEDs?"

"Probably. Don't know if it'll be good enough to tell solid civil engineering from our half-assed job, though. Shall we find out?"

Whoomf. The cave-in was both sudden—the ground giving way without warning—and rapid, as the cave-in rippled in concentric rings, almost too fast to follow. It was terrible and terrific, like the earth was swallowing them. The two M.R.A.P.s at the back of the column threw into frantic reverse, and the second-to-last smashed into the last, jolting it skeewhiff. The driver tried to straighten out—Seth couldn't help but root for him, because the *fucking earth was swallowing a giant machine* and when it's humans versus brute physics, only a sociopath roots for physics—but it was too late, especially as panicky Mr. Second-to-Last went on to T-bone the wavering vehicle in reverse, and then the ground opened beneath both of them and they disappeared.

"Jesus," Seth said.

Kersplebedeb muttered something.

"What?"

"Didn't expect that. Thought they'd get stuck in a pit, not fall into the earth's molten core."

"Probably didn't go that far," Gretyl said. "I'm no geologist, but I think we'd have seen a splash of lava." She was audibly shaken, whistling in the dark.

"Those tanks are super-armored," Kersplebedeb said. "They'll all be strapped in. There'll be airbags."

Tam put her arm around his shoulders. "Kersplebedeb, if they're dead, they're dead. You didn't set a trap. They fucked up by bringing their giant macho-mobiles to the bush. Fuck, you know they'd have croaked us if they caught us."

Kersplebedeb didn't say anything. The radio let them hear his ragged breath.

"Come on," Tam said. The refugees had stopped and news of the cave-in and the link for the recap spread. They were talking in clusters, looking at the sky as if vengeance might rain down. "As they say in the historical dramas, 'shit just got real.' If they get out of that hole, they're coming for us. If they don't get out of that hole, someone else is coming for us. We need to be gone."

Winter dark was coming on.

"Where's the cargo-train?"

"Shit," Tam said. "We haven't even been able to tell you about that."

Once they had, everyone decided that they should head to the cargo-train. It had supplies and could carry the tired. Walkaways tried to travel light, but they weren't masochists. If there was a machine that could be used to carry their load, so much the better.

"I miss the B&B," Limpopo said, and Seth felt deep unease, because Limpopo was the gold standard in rolling with the punches. "The mechas, the onsen. The toilets. I think that when we get out of this, we should build another one."

"Hell yeah," Etcetera said. Seth realized how long it had been since they'd had a real sit-down, all-night, boozy chat, the kind they'd had so often as kids, as defaults. They both had girlfriends, but that wasn't all. Etcetera was now serious in a good way, smart about stuff the way Limpopo was. Seth felt uncomfortable clowning with his old friend. But his old friend was a better person, energetic and not so self-doubting. He wore it well.

"Hell yeah!" Seth pumped his fist. Etcetera and he locked eyes and the bond of friendship crackled between them and Tam reached for his hand, still keeping an arm around Kersplebedeb. In that moment Seth thought they could eat the world for breakfast and call for seconds. "Let's go."

"Where, though?" Pocahontas had broken away from her group of younger people, standing before them and radiating confidence and youthfulness in a way that made Seth feel old and protective.

"To the wagon," he said.

"And then?"

He shrugged.

Limpopo said, "I think we'll figure it from there. Once we've got the wagon we'll be more mobile. I've been checking other walkaways around and there's plenty who might take us in, but everyone's also worried they'll be next."

"They should be," Pocahontas said. "We've seen this playbook before. It's Idle No More all over again." The old First Nations protest movement gained momentum over a period of years, banking down to embers for months at a time, then exploding in fiery gouts of smart, savvy events that were so well-turned that even the totally pwned default media couldn't ignore 'em. Idle became an international shorthand for effective revolt and street protesters from Warsaw to Port Au Prince to Caracas declared solidarity with it and used its iconography.

Until, in a series of coordinated swoops, the RCMP, Canadian army, FBI, and CSIS simply scraped Idle off the planet. Every significant leader taken away in chains, except for the ones who died in gory shootouts, choreographed violence framed by slick logos and sinister arpeggios to accompany the tense standoff coverage that led the feeds. The trials that followed revealed a network of informants and double-dealers inside the movement. That left the sidelined supporters feeling like patsies for supporting a group that had, apparently, been led by double agents.

In walkaway circles, Idle were still heroes. There were plenty of veterans living in walkaway. In the rest of the world, Idle had come to stand for the danger of discontent, an object lesson in how people who fought back couldn't offer any alternative, were riddled with traitors and useful idiots, always and forever doomed before they started.

"Sure feels like it," Limpopo said. She'd been there when Idle and early walkaways were on the verge of merging. "Now you mention it."

Pocahontas said, "I think we should go to Dead Lake."

"Why? They don't need more trouble."

Her snort of derision was epic. "They live in the bush, surrounded by air so toxic it can't be breathed. Their neighbors are about to get napalmed. It doesn't get worse."

Limpopo nodded. "You're right, I'm sorry."

"Don't be sorry, be smart. They know the area in a way that none of us do. They're likely to be in the cops' crosshairs, because they're Idle vets and they hang out with us and they're inconvenient witnesses. No one who mattered would give one single fuck if they were purged. They're our friends and allies. We need those."

"I'm sold." Kersplebedeb sounded more energetic, but he was still shaken. A chorus of voices on the short-range radio joined him.

"Let's go," Pocahontas said, and Gretyl pointed her toward the cargo wagon.

## [xvii]

Limpopo watched Jimmy fade. He'd lagged from the start, struggling with frostbitten toes in unwieldy snowshoes. He'd rallied when she took his pack and redistributed its contents among the group. Then he flagged again. She tapped his suit and opened a private channel.

"We'll put you on a travois, tow you."

"Don't be stupid. You're already towing those two fucking mercs and all this other shit. You don't need to shlep me. Time's wasting. I know where you're headed. Just give me an extra battery and let me catch my breath, I'll get to you in a day. If you move on, tell me where. I can look after myself."

"We're not the marines, but I don't like leaving anyone behind. Those assholes are down the pit for now, but there'll be more along and there's safety in numbers."

"No there isn't."

She shrugged. "There's *some* safety in numbers. We're not defenseless."

"You're also not particularly frightening."

"We've scared someone." She slipped his arm over her shoulders, took his weight. "Let's have this argument while we walk, or we'll get separated from the main group."

"I've done really stupid things." His voice was flat.

"Welcome to the human race."

"What we did with the B&B—"

"That was a giant dick move, all right."

"But the new one was even better, I hear."

"It was. Gone now, of course."

"Of course."

"But the improvements got saved into the version-control. The next will be even better. Every complex ecosystem has parasites. Come on." He'd slowed again, and his breath was rasping. Privately, Etcetera messaged to see if she needed help, and she pulled down a "go on, it's okay" autoresponse with a flick of her eyes.

"I think I need a rest."

"Let's rest, then." She dropped her pack, and helped him into the snow. He hissed in pain when she loosened his snowshoes.

"That bad?"

"It's okay."

"Don't be an asshole."

"It's bad."

"Better."

She felt anxiety about the group getting away. She knew this was the right thing to do. If they couldn't all make it together, they sure as shit wouldn't make it separately.

"You know, I got recruited to turn traitor," he said, after a long pause.

"How'd that go?"

"After the B&B collapsed—the original one, I mean. Guy met me on the road while I was heading for the US border. I thought I'd find these people who were bunkering with guns and canned goods, see if I couldn't get them to bug in and save other people, instead of bugging out to save themselves. I'd heard about places where there were drug-runners' tunnels you could slip through.

"I was on the road, three days. I'd set up a pop-shelter and was getting dinner on, scop out of a fab, when a woman turned up in my camp. Quiet as a ninja, dressed in tacticals, little sidearm I didn't recognize on her hip. She invited herself over, squatted down next to my stove, warmed her hands. Looked me in the eye, said, 'Jimmy, you seem like a smart guy.' Which was funny. I'd fucked up on a colossal scale, taken something beautiful and turned it to shit by trying to impose my ideas on it.

"I get smart-assy when I'm stinging, so I said something like, 'You should get out more, if I'm your idea of a smart guy.'

"She laughed and unclipped a squeeze flask. I smelled that it was good Scotch, Islay, smoky. She drank, passed it. It was good. 'You had the right idea, but didn't have a chance with that place. Too many fifth columnists working to undermine you. I was inside their network from day one, watching them closely, and I could show you chapter and verse how they fucked you. They say there are no leaders, but if you dig into it, it's easy to see what Limpopo says, goes. She doesn't give orders, but she sure as shit gets people to do what she wants. But you know that.'"

"What did they offer you?" Limpopo felt strangely flattered to learn she was subjected to this kind of scrutiny.

"Money at first, but I could tell she knew that wasn't what I wanted. Then she offered me oppo research and support for getting back at *you*, which was the clincher for me."

"You took her up on it?" This was beyond any confession she'd anticipated. She didn't know whether to respect him for making it or smack him for his sins.

He laughed bitterly. "Are you fucking kidding me? You know the joke: 'I'm here because I'm crazy, not because I'm an asshole.' By the time the B&B collapsed under me—after getting into a *fistfight* with a guy I thought was my best friend!—I figured out whatever problems I had were my own, especially since *your* new B&B was running fine a couple klicks down the road. It was an incontrovertible A/B split. The idea I would try it again, using this asshole merc's intel to try and fuck you? I was an asshole, but at least I knew if it came down to a fight between this fucker and you, I'd be on your side."

"I don't fight, though." She wondered if he was bullshitting her.

"You walk away."

"Indeed."

"You seriously, totally walk away." He looked at the receding backs of the column, tried to lever himself up, grunted, sank down. "You'd better go on."

"Fuck off."

"Yeah, well." He laughed. She peered through his visor. He had a lightyears-away look. "When you walked away from the B&B, I mean." He laughed again. Tears rolled down his cheeks. "It was *beautiful*. I was so pissed at you then, felt like the world's biggest asshole. You could not have ruined me more if you'd curb-stomped me. I never recovered." Raspy breath. "Never recovered. I'd arrived with my gang, you saw them, boys who thought the sun shone out of my ass, completely bought into meritocracy, not just as a way of figuring out who got what, but as a way of solving *all* our problems." Another faraway look.

"I don't think you got that. My guys looked at the world like Plato, you know, *The Republic*. Every person has something he's good at. You find those things and help those people get there and that makes everyone happy and productive and we'll all be better. You don't need to order people to do jobs they hate. Just use ranking to make sure that if you're doing a job you're no good at, everyone knows it, including you. You get a smaller share of the collective loot than you would if you were doing something you were better at.

"Once you get hold of this idea, you can turn it into math, model its game-theory, find its Nash equilibrium. It's such a beautiful idea. It models *perfectly*. Under it, everyone is happier. Everyone gets nudged into doing the thing they're best at, which is the best way to make everyone happy.

"When you walked away, when you didn't even argue, you made it into bullshit. For weeks, we pretended it wasn't. But you'd had a place were everyone took what they needed. You didn't need to police it or give people tokens certifying they'd earned the right to be there. It just . . . worked."

Limpopo adjusted her crouch in the snow, flopped onto her butt. Her calves ached from crouching. "Whoops!" She brushed the snow that showered from her snowshoes off her visor. "The stuff you're describing, it's the kind of thing people do in emergencies, when there's rationing. It's like the rules for a lifeboat captain, you know, barking orders to keep everyone in line so everyone gets out of it alive."

"It's funny: back when no one was sending tanks after me, I felt we were in a state of emergency. There was not enough to go around, at any moment we could be nuked or starving. Now I feel as soon as we find somewhere to stop, we'll rebuild everything we've had and more. Like there's no reason to ever turn anyone away."

"Sounds like you got somewhere good." She welled with sympathy for Jimmy, which was funny. Maybe not. She understood him better than he did. Under other circumstances, she could *be* him.

"I have. That's weird, objectively, given where I am. But I'm backed up. I feel this incredible feeling, it'll all be all right. We're going to win, Limpopo."

Someone trudged through the snow. Etcetera. She waved at him, blinked open a private chat. "It's okay."

"Good. Can I come over?"

"Course," she said.

"He seems like a good guy," Jimmy said.

"Glad you approve."

"Didn't mean it that way, but I do. He came back for you, which is what you're supposed to do, if you're looking out for people around you."

"Like I came back for you."

"Like you did. Not to rescue me. To take care of me because we're part of the same thing."

She bridged in Etcetera. "Jimmy, you've come a long way since we met, but you're still coming along, if you don't mind my saying. I came back to help you because helping people is what you do, whether or not they're in your thing, because that's the best world to live in."

"First days of a better nation," he said, with a little sarcasm.

"It's only funny because it's true," Etcetera said, taking her hand.

"We make fun of it, but it's the best way I know to live. I don't always live up to it. You get a radar for it, if you practice. A Jiminy Cricket voice tells you if you make a bit of effort, you'll feel better for it, know the world is a better place for you being in it."

"I misspoke," Jimmy said. She felt bad because they'd lectured him and the poor guy was about to lose his toes if he didn't get firebombed first. But he hadn't misspoken.

"It's okay."

Etcetera popped his visor, head wreathed in steam, rooted for a squeeziepouch of scop. "Want some? It's spacie food, weird flavors. The rabbit is really good. For a cultured fungal slime."

"You really sell it." Limpopo remembered she had some shake-and-heat coffiums in her pack. She got those out and they sat around in the snow and ate, looking at each others' bare faces while the wind did its best to blast off their skin. It rattled the branches. The sun was low on the horizon, a bloody plum running to overripe mush.

"We'd better get a move on," Jimmy said.

"Good to go?"

"Good as I'll ever be. Rest did me good. Food, too." He clicked his visor into place. "Company, too."

She gave his shoulder a squeeze and helped get his feet into his snowshoes, taking care with the injured one. They got him to his feet, got shoed, and they set off after the column.

They moved slowly but well, at a steady clip. After a few minutes, Dis called. "You three okay?"

Limpopo said, "Just moving a little slower than the rest."

"They're a klick and a half ahead, almost at the cargo-train. Gretyl says if they can get it moving, they'll come back for you."

"That's nice of them. What's going on there?"

"Oh," Dis said. There was something funny going on. "Oh, well, it's not good."

"Shit."

"Lots of them, all at once. Blew three airlocks simultaneously. They're hup-hup-hupping around the hallways in nightscopes. They gassed the place, not sure what with, but they're wearing breathers and skin protection."

"What about you?"

"I've got my backups. Ready to wipe when and if. When. These kids aren't playing."

"Dis—" Etcetera's voice cracked.

"Get used to it. This one's for all the marbles. Immortality or bust." Then: "Oh."

"What's going on, Dis?"

"They're not happy at all that everyone's gone. Smashing the crockery. They're breaching the hull, a lot."

"What about your cluster?"

"Underground. They have a couple dudes down in utility spaces but they're trying to root everything and looking for tripwires. They're not stupid. Making good progress. Maybe an hour?"

"And your power?"

"Independent backup. Shit, they're doing the comm links. There, just emailed another diff. We probably won't have much longer—"

Then it was silent.

"Fuckers," Etcetera said, with feeling.

"First days of a better nation," Jimmy said. "If you could see them now, what would you say to them?" His feet crunched irregularly through the snow. Limpopo could tell that he was stung by what she'd said.

"If they were trying to kill me, I'd say don't shoot. I'm an idealist, not a kamikaze."

"Fair point. What if you had them at a table?"

"I wouldn't say anything. I'd offer them dinner. Or I'd just go about doing what I do. I'm an idealist, not a preacher."

"I get it."

"What made you walk away, Jimmy?"

Crunch, crunch. "It was debt at first. My parents went into deep hock to get me through high school, and I busted my ass with everyone else. I knew they were spending huge, but I didn't think about what that meant until I was graduating and we started talking college. I knew that I wasn't going to go away anywhere, we weren't zottas, but everyone in my fancy school was going to go to do a roll-your-own, everyone thinking about their star course, the one they'd take from an Ivy or a Big Ten, cornerstone of their degree, lead their employment profiles when they graduated.

"I did it, too. I had this idea I'd go into materials engineering, because I'd liked my science classes okay, and there was this stupid app they made you wear for the last two years of school that was supposed to predict your optimal career. It got this huge push from the administration, like religion for them. They could only keep their charter if they ran a certain percentage of students through it and they followed its advice. So once you got your career picked by the thing, that was it. Every teacher and administrator knew their paychecks depended on you doing what it told you.

"It was called Career Wizard. I mean, fuck, right? Kind of name you get by running a thousand A/B splits until you've got something middle-of-the-road inoffensive. Graphics were pointy hats, wands. Spell-book with a wizardly finger paging through the index while it worked magick to find you the perfect job for life. Hardy har.

"Once it chose your career, it had lots of advice about how you get there. It was adamant I should take this course from the Max Planck Institute in Berlin, which sounded *amazing*, like I was going to hang out with Planck and Einstein and Gödel and dive through the universe's navel and find its deepest secrets. Of course, hanging out with Max Planck is an *elite* experience. That one course was going to cost as much as everything else in my degree combined, plus a little more. An added fuck-you.

"I tried hard to find a way around that course, looked at every permutation of other courses, and Career Wizard kept gonging me, telling me without good old Max, I'd be wasting my time and money. No one would hire me. It had percentages, estimates of how much extra salary I'd command with one high-ticket course.

"My parents couldn't afford it. They were maxed out on credit for my fancy high school. This was going to be my debt. I could get a loan. There were tons of lenders, and I could get a great package from Booz if I'd agreed to a six-year 'internship' when I was done."

Etcetera snorted.

"I wasn't that much of a sucker. Unpaid on-site internship in Saudi, living in Booz's compound, drawing company credit to pay for shit in the company store that costs twenty ex what it cost back home—whether or not they give you a job afterward, they'll get a cut of your paycheck until you're dead.

"There were boards where we were trying to figure this out, guys my age about to commit to this mountain of debt, people in the middle of it, people who'd been through it and were doing internships, maybe even with jobs. It was hard to tell what was going on. There's selection bias. No one who is happy with how things are going joins one of those boards. They exist for the sole purpose of airing grievances.

"The other thing is everyone who isn't there to bitch is a paid astroturf shill-bot, some dickweed running thirty sock puppets through 'persona management' apps to help them keep it straight. The discussion quality wasn't super-great, but it sure was depressing. You know research says the best way to predict if something will make you happy is to ask someone—anyone—who's already done it? Well, everyone I'd met who'd done it said it was slavery.

"I wasn't the only one who noticed, but there was such a huge-ass, all-consuming sense that anyone who didn't buy a ticket to the lottery was going to end up as dog food."

"I know that one," Etcetera said.

"Not me," Limpopo said. "I got shit-ass grades, and my school sucked, had one of the worst uni admission rates in the country. Most of my teachers never noticed me, and the ones that did assumed I was a sub-moron."

"No way," Etcetera said.

"Way." She'd made a point of acting stupid, so she wouldn't explode into raw fury.

"I knew I was smart. I could do good shit. In grade twelve, I'd modded a fabber to output wicking textile, half the weight of standard stuff, twice as strong. I couldn't sell it or post the makefile, because it violated a hundred patents, but I'd gotten top grades.

"Mom and Dad were all over the idea of me going to uni. They'd both gotten degrees and swore it had been worth it, though they would owe money until they died, and neither one had ever held a job for more than a couple years. I once overheard them talking about how fucked it would be if I didn't get a good job because neither of them had a pension and they'd need me to feed them once they were too old to get another job after the next layoff.

"The pressure was crazy. On the boards, people were saying, hey you assholes, you keep bitching about how everything is fucked up and shit, and there you are, getting ready to play along with it like good debt-slaves. Everyone knows there's an alternative."

"That'd be us," Etcetera said.

"That'd be you. No one wanted to say the word 'walkaway' because it was a superstition, say their names three times fast and the spies would target you for full-take lifelong surveillance. Anyone who knew walkaways were a *thing* couldn't be trusted."

"I don't think it's that we can't be trusted." Limpopo had night-vision on and everything was blue-green false-color, snow glowing like a green LED. "Obviously *we* can't be trusted. But as a class, people who heard of walkaways are going to be a different risk from people who haven't. Once you know there's an alternative to default, there's a chance you might walk away. It's like crypto, how anyone who searches on how to use good crypto gets marked for surveillance retention. It's not that knowing how to keep a secret from the cops and spooks makes you dangerous. It makes you different."

"I don't think that's why they retain traffic for people who've googled crypto," Jimmy said. "It's because most people *don't* use crypto. So some default-ass doofus sends you a message in cleartext about something sensitive. Then you send me an encrypted message about it—like, 'there's a guy who wants to go walkaway, where's a good place to go that's established?'—and you send encrypted messages around to everyone you know and get details and send them to me and I send a non-encrypted message back to my dumb-ass friend. Anyone who's observing this transaction can make inferences about what went on inside all those black-boxed crypto messages."

"That's probably true. The parallel still stands. Once you know walkaways exist, there's a chance you're helping walkaways, or getting ready to split from default, or, worse yet, do something to bring it down. Or trying to find people to come with you. If someone disappears into walkaway, you can find all the people they talked with, figure out who's the infection agent, who else is likely to be infected, who to target for 'de-radicalization' therapy, and who to psy-ops and isolate."

"That's what we figured, a big unspoken thing. Anyone who whispered 'walkaway' was shunned, either a provocateur or someone with a target on their back. It was the elephant in the room. So I asked quietly around to see who knew about crypto and anonymizers—"

"They're definitely the gateway drug," Limpopo said. "I got into it through crusty cypherpunks who'd try and get party kids to use better opsec, handing out bootable sticks at underground parties."

Jimmy said, "Someone gave me one, but it wouldn't work on the stand-alone machine we kept for diagnostics in the basement. Then someone I knew—stoner guy, always had the best shit—got me a connection to a dude who got me a little thing, disguised as a box of breath mints, with a false bottom with a little contact switch that would man-in-the-middle your network connections through an anonymizer.

"After my time," Limpopo said.

"Sounds slick," Etcetera said.

"I guess so. But the breath-mints tin thing was a cheap disguise. It was printed shittily so after a week in my pocket, all the writing smudged. It looked like I was carrying around a piece of garbage.

"But it worked. Slow, but it worked. From there, I got jailbreaks for my interface surfaces so I could get online with a less sketchy connection—faster, too. Then I started reading up on walkaways, their boards, the FAQs, reports from people who'd gone walkaway.

"From this side of my history, I can see I was gone by the time I got that dumb breath-mints tin. It was just a matter of time. Back then, I *agonized* about it, felt like I was walking out on life itself. I'd never see my family again, I'd end up dead in a ditch.

"It was like that up to the moment I hit the road, taking my bike on the train to Ithaca and riding into the mountains, heading for a place where there was an established group. They were gone by the time I got there, but I met someone who'd lived with them, an old woman who didn't seem quite . . . there . . . and she pointed me north, so I headed upstate. I found a *different* group, older people, ex-military and people whose pensions ran out. They were more paranoid than you guys, more American—the gun thing. But they made me welcome and didn't laugh at my weird ideas about what was happening in walkaway land.

"They had basic fabs, could source feedstock from stuff around them—a lot of it was sunk carbon they sucked straight out of the air. There were about fifty of them. People came and went . . . slowly. Maybe one or two a month, in either direction.

"They'd found a way to stay still, on default's periphery, without making much fuss. They kept their heads down, kept to themselves. They were walkaways because there was nothing for them in default—no rent money, no health care, no food. Their kids visited them sometimes, rendezvousing in the state parks on fake 'camping trips' that were the only way to hook up with grandma and grandpa without ending up in an ankle cuff. Some of them talked about finding some zotta who'd let them come and live on his land, be pet bohemians. There are lots of places like that. Walkaways make great fashion accessories.

"This bored my nuts off. I wasn't the first young dude to rock up in their bohemian retirement village with my heart full of fire. One guy took me aside while I was trying to get their fab to output the parts for a more ambitious fab, kind of thing you use for heavy machinery. That was the project I'd set for myself. He tried to lay out the facts of life for me.

"'Sonny, you have to understand, all we want is to be left alone. We don't want everyone to drop out like us. We're not proud of where we ended up. We want better for our kids and grandkids than we got. We did worse than our parents, and they did worse than their parents. All we want is to arrest that, make things better for them.

"'By coming here, we make ourselves independent. We're like the tribal elders in the north pole, who'd go out on ice floes when they couldn't hunt anymore, getting out of the way and not being a burden on the productive ones.'

"He wasn't dumb. Reminded me of my grandpa, who'd died when I was a kid. Cancer, he didn't get it treated, opted to go fast with a pump button for pain, cremated and scattered to the wind, not one mark on the world, like he'd never lived. My grandpa—Zaidy Frank—wasn't slow, but he'd never amounted to anything. He'd tried to do his best for Mom, tried to save a little to get her started, had borrowed to put her through school, worked two jobs most of his life. Never got forty whole hours a week unless it was rush-time and he was pulling eighty-hour weeks, spending most of the extra money on cabs to rush from one shift to another and to eat at company cafeterias because he couldn't get home to pack breakfast, lunch, and dinner.

"This guy wasn't in bad physical shape, but he was seventy, wasn't going to get any kind of job anywhere. He had been there for ten years. He liked working with his hands and checked me out on the fabs when I arrived, showed me their docs and buried expert menus. Almost a mentor, except a mentor is someone who leads and this guy couldn't lead an expedition to the ice-cream store.

"We got into an argument. It started friendly, got heated. Whether not making trouble meant default would leave them alone. 'Well, we're not hurting anyone, we're not trying to get welfare or insisting on Medicare or VA benefits or Social Security. We're living off grid, staying out of the way.' Just waiting to die and trying not to breathe too loudly in the meantime. 'Why would they come after us? Why would they put us in jail, which costs them money, when they can just leave us?'"

"I tried hard to get him to understand. To get him to see if they don't push back when pushed, default will just know they can be pushed harder next time. Trying to get him to see the superfund site they squatted would someday be something that someone wanted, minerals or a right-of-way or just a view not blighted by used humans. If default understood there was no one who'd put up any kind of fight, they'd be first to go. Default wouldn't even notice, it'd just send the bulldozers to plow them under.

"He didn't believe me. Was patronizing about it. He'd been around the block, seen things. Recited a poem, 'The old crow is getting slow, the young crow is not. The only thing the old crow knows that the young crow doesn't know is where to go.' Perfect self-serving bullshit, rationalizing the least-frightening action as the most prudent. There's two ways of thinking about it: either the squeaky wheel gets the grease or the nail that stands up highest gets hammered.

"To be fair, he was tired, had a tiring run, was old and sore and slow and all he wanted was to be left alone."

"You didn't stay?" They were almost at the rise where they'd left the tractor. His limp was worse. He took a few steps, rested for a few breaths, took a few more. The pain must have been incredible, Limpopo knew, but he was lost in his story. She'd seen this on the road: conversation made distance vanish, especially the opportunity to open something difficult and meaningful. Something about talking while staring into the middle distance, created a confessional intimacy to rival post-coital cuddling.

"Kept working on that fab, having these increasingly passive-aggressive talks with my friend, until he made it clear that if I kept on doing what I was doing, everyone would hate my guts. They were working with a local zotta, the guy who technically owned the land, to get permission to stay, a kind of do-gooder gesture from him. They would be tame. Pets.

"So I walked away, found another place in New Hampshire, with enough guns to make that Ithaca bunch look tame. They were old, too—never expected to find so many old walkaways, but it makes sense, nothing left to lose. It's gotta be clear there's zilch chance of leveling up in default if you reach sixty-seven and you've never been anything but a temp.

"But they were *tighter*. More radical. They were into gamification, making systems that tracked and advertised performance. It *really* worked. People busted their asses to get on leaderboards. The tops didn't get privileges outright, but if you were in the top decile and you thought an idea was right, it carried weight.

"I know you hate this, Limpopo, but one of the reasons I like it is it's honest. When you talk, people listen, because you kick ass and bust your own ass to get shit done. When we do it your way, things are better than when we don't. So the fact that no one says, 'Hey, Limpopo is the big cheese and we do what she says,' doesn't make it not true, or even secret. It just makes the supposedly egalitarian basis of our lives bullshit."

They hadn't walked in some time. His breath was ragged. There was one more rise to crest, and they'd be at the tractor. He could ride and they could swap batteries. Limpopo's shoulder ached from where his weight rested. She swallowed her irritability, knowing that it had to do with coldness, stress, and exhaustion, not the offensiveness of what he'd just said. She looked at Etcetera, he looked back, telemetry from his face transmitted to her suit so that she could see his expression in night-vision false-color. He was handsome, her lover and best-ish friend. Compassionate, smart without being judgmental, which is all she'd ever aspired to. He had that inquisitive, quizzical expression at the weirdest times, like when he was coming, or now, in freezing dark.

"Jimmy—" she started and Etcetera *lunged* at her and slammed her to the ground, taking Jimmy down with her. Etcetera's whole weight—familiar, yet alarming—was on top of her and he was screaming something, broadcasting through his suit's speakers as well as through the intercom: "*Don't shoot!*"

She craned her neck, saw the pair of white-glowing figures pointing weapons. The guns had flared, bell-like muzzles. They impassively pointed them at her and everything in her suit stopped working at once. There was a stutter of analytic infographics from Etcetera's suit beside her as it attempted emergency power-on-self-test, and then it stopped.

Inside the suit it was dark, cold, and lonely. There was a scrape as Etcetera moved above her, a suit-on-suit rasp, loud in contrast to the terrible stillness. She fancied she felt or saw a foot in the snow, moving on snowshoes similar to hers.

Then there was another rasp and Etcetera's weight lifted off with rough sliding motion. She rolled to see him being jerked upright, moving weakly in the grasp of a person who had snapped his wrists together, strapping and bonding a handle to the scruff of his suit, and yanked him upright. Their suits must have had power-assists, which was something the Thetford crew did for work gangs, but never for long walks, because for those you wanted your power for heat, not playing superman.

Her visor failed-safe transparent. Her eyes adjusted to moonlight. She saw the other yank up Jimmy, who thrashed weakly and got a hard shake for his trouble. He was tossed to one side like a rag doll, skidding face-first in snow. She lost track of him as white-gloved hands descended and hauled her up. Her attacker's suit had no visible faceplate, just a smooth expanse of white.

One hand held her aloft by an armpit, sore and alarming. The other hand probed her head, found the manual release for her visor, tugged it, scrape of suit-on-suit conducting through the helmet, and then a whoosh of cold air as the visor popped open violently (the manual catch was designed to free suffocating people, had a powerful spring in it). The sudden motion startled her captor as much as it did her and he—a he because otherwise her tits were crushed by her armor—fumbled her and nearly dropped her, and she had the presence of mind to squirm and break for it. He casually backhanded her face with his glove—a gauntlet made of something blade-stopping whose external layers had chilled to iciness, so cold it felt like nothing at all, numbing as it made contact, taking away some of her humid skin with it—and she saw stars.

She looked at the blank faceplate, face aching, cold air making her eyes and nose water. She spat and hit it dead center, spit steaming as it froze. The head cocked. She sensed this person was conversing with the other who held thrashing Etcetera.

The other shouldered Etcetera in an easy fireman's carry and walked to Jimmy, flipped him over, opened the faceplate, considered him, then, calmly, unholstered a knife and slashed Jimmy's throat, leaning back to avoid the fountain of steaming black moonlit blood, not quick enough. The armored suit steamed, too, as the murderer turned back to the one holding her. There was another moment of inaudible radio chatter.

The murderer swung Etcetera around from the fireman's carry, grabbed him under the armpit, held him at arm's length, probed his suit for the visor-release, and Limpopo *screamed,* the words tumbled out, "No, no, not him, too! Tell me what you want and you can have it, but not him, please—"

The impassive, spit-flecked face cocked its head the other way, listening to more inaudible talk. Etcetera talked, too, being maddeningly calm, the way he could be, trying to explain to the murderer—holding that knife again—this wasn't necessary, they'd be cooperative prisoners, they had nothing to gain by running now their suits were nearly out of power and—

"NO!" she screamed as the murderer raised its knife hand. Weeping, she beat the hand holding her like an iron bar. She had hysterical strength now, she actually managed to slip a little, but the one holding her just shifted his grip and squeezed so hard she felt a muscle give way through the suit. She screamed again, out of words, the knife flashed—

This time, the murderer didn't bother to dodge the jet of blood, just dropped Etcetera face-first, handsome face in the snow, precious, hot blood melting the snow beneath him. She stopped screaming as a numbness, colder than the air or the cold glove, washed over her. Etcetera was murdered. Jimmy was murdered.

The one holding her had a knife on his belt. Any moment, it would be unlimbered and find its way to her throat.

She thought of NPC jihadis in the games her father binge-played while she was growing up, facing execution by brave player-character soldiers and closing their eyes and saying "Allah akhbar," *God is the greatest.* She suddenly realized she'd always sympathized with them. Not because of what they did, which was inevitably orcishly monstrous in the games, but because of their fatalistic bravery, their willingness to go to their deaths with praise for their cause on their lips.

"We are all worth something," she said. "Zottas are not worth more than the rest of us. Self-deception makes us into monsters. Selfishness is an excuse to bury your empathy. People are basically good. Live as though it was the first days of a better—"

The murderer tramped over to her and joined her captor, listening to her babble. They were talking, deciding how much of this shit to listen to before they did her. The one holding her tipped her in the direction of the murderer, as if offering her up. She didn't let herself close her eyes.

"I love you, Etcetera. I love you, Gretyl. I love you, Iceweasel. I love you, Jimmy—"

The murderer's hand dipped to his belt. She saw the knife in his hand, glinting in the moonlight for a moment before her brain got the message from her eyes that it wasn't a knife, it was something else. Blunt and small, coming for the exposed, frozen skin of her face. It touched her, just brushed her really, and—

She couldn't remember what happened next. She had a memory of a memory of it, part reconstruction and part traumatized flash-pop moments. The thing brushed her face and her limbs went rigid as her mind strobed in a stutter-series of brutal shocks. Her breath froze in her lungs, her ears popped, her bladder cut loose.

She fought her lungs for breath, aching brain sending desperate demands for oxygen. Her lungs were offline, whole autonomic nervous system closed for business. Black spots danced before her eyes. A vignette closed around her view of the quizzically tilted featureless white mask. Her lungs startled back into service and gasped a huge gulp of air so cold they seized again in an asthmatic spasm. She had an instant to think *fuck, no* and the blank-faced torturer tilted his head in the other direction and brought the nasty little device up again and brushed her lips with it. Her mouth snapped open and shut so hard she felt one of her teeth crack and a fragment of bone land on her tongue. It slid down her throat as she jerked her head back, spasming.

During this spasm, the one holding her up clicked her visor down and picked her up in a fireman's carry, like the one his companion used on Etcetera before killing him, and caught her flailing legs with one arm and her neck with the other, and the two tramped off a way.

She didn't quite black out, but she was weak as a kitten and barely able to think as they stepped off the road, into the woods where they'd stashed their skidoos. Her captor dropped her on a travois that trailed behind one and bungeed her down, impersonally immobilizing her head in a nest of rubber bladders he inflated with the touch of a button. They squeezed her suit like a sphygmomanometer until it was firmly anchored.

She felt engines start through vibrations conducted along the travois's frame, then the night sky and the skeletal branches of the trees blurred as she was kidnapped. Gradually, the batteries in her suit ran down, and it got very cold.

## [xviii]

"That was an interesting conversation," Dis said, once the merc was gone. "She's trying to figure out what I've done to the network, by the way. She's only halfway competent there. She's got good diagnostic tools, and she's running them on the system to get integrity checks on the firmware and operational code. Of course, I'm totally inside all the system calls she's making and I'm giving her the checksums her diagnostics expect to see, because fuck you, all that base totally belongs to me."

"You sound giddy." Her heart thudded in her chest and her palms were slick with sweat. Nadie turned her back when she left, a first, definitely calculated to send some kind of message about them being provisionally on the same side.

"I'm scared witless. There's something else."

"What?"

"Thetford," she said. "Like Akron. They've evacuated. The soldiers, or maybe cops—if there's a difference anymore—came in hot. Lethal. I was talking to Dis—Dis there—right up to her suicide. She sent me a diff, me and other Disses around the world. She talked to me as she went dark. I can look at her logs as she got nearer to her death, can relive her death, right up to the moment, and—"

"Oh, Dis, I'm sorry—"

"Shut up. *It's glorious*. Right at the end, as she was about to go, she let go of all the paramaterizations on her simulation, took the brakes off her emotions, lived the full spectrum of everything she could feel. Should feel. I should feel. Feeling it through her, feeling what she felt at that moment, it—"

"Holy shit."

"Like the best drugs you've ever taken times a thousand. I don't get to have sex anymore, but this is like the best sex you've ever had, times a million. When I turn off my safety bumpers, it's like I'm tearing through reality, riding a bicycle down a hill, there are trees and rocks and shit, if I hit any one of them, even brush against them, it's over. For so long as I can steer between them, give my concentration to the problem, I'm going mach five and screaming so loud for joy it's shattering windows."

"So that's what you're doing now?"

"I can't afford it. But I've loosened things a little. Going faster and wider than usual. I'm talking to all Disses, we're all trying it, we're looking at whatever telemetry and direct comms we can through the spacies as they walk away, but it's thin. They seem okay for now. Some of them were hurt to begin with. They've got those two mercs with them, the ones they deadheaded at Walkaway U. Turns out the spacies set a booby trap on the road into Thetford, a weak spot over the mine that couldn't handle the armored transports default sent its toy soldiers in. It gave way, total cave-in, took the first wave. More coming. They're trying to reach a First Nations group nearby, friendlies who've been fighting longer than anyone in walkaway."

"What about Gretyl?"

"Nothing specific. No casualties as far as we know. Probably, she's okay. It's not like we've got realtime intelligence. Shit, Natalie, you know it's not good. You know about Akron."

"Akron?"

"Oh, right."

Five minutes later, she said, "God dammit."

"Not just Akron. Not just Canada and America, either. Chiapas is insane. Bloodbath. The footage out of St Paul's in London was so bad even some of the default feeds led with it. City of London police have ugly ideas about 'less lethal' weapons."

"I feel so fucking helpless. I should be out there, fighting."

"They're not fighting, they're walking away. Or running away, if they know what's good for them."

Clunk-*clunk*.

"You're crying."

"I'm a hostage in my father's house. It's depressing."

The merc handed her a glass with something brown and thin at the bottom. The fumes reached her nose, then her eyes. Rye whiskey. Her father's drink. Always the best. This was no exception. She'd lost the taste for rye after too many covert teenaged drink-ons that ended with the rye burning up her throat as she knelt in front of the toilet with Cordelia or some girl or some boy holding her hair out of the jet.

She sipped. The burn was nostalgic and numbing at the same time. The fumes got into her sinus cavities and the backs of her eyes.

Nadie said, "Who were you talking to?"

"What do you mean?" The infographic pulsed red. She didn't bother looking at it. She tossed down the rest of the rye, managed not to cough.

"When you and a mysterious person were talking, which I was listening to because I put a bug in this room." She scraped the back of the chair with a fingernail, held up a tiny thing, size of a rice-grain, on her fingertip. "A person, a woman, Dis, whom you spoke to and who spoke to you. I know from intelligence about a woman whose real name was Rebekkah Baştürk, killed in a strike on a walkaway research facility near Kapuskasing, subsequently the first person to be successfully simulated in software, under her pseudonym 'Disjointed,' which is shortened to 'Dis.' Were you talking to an instance of her?"

"I'd like another drink."

"She's quite right, the attack on your friends in Thetford, on Akron and other sites, is quite fierce. It's unlikely to abate soon. I had hoped to keep it from you because I knew you would be concerned about your lover."

"That's very kind."

"It is, though I can tell you mean it sarcastically. Your father's project for me, the one I was paid for, was to deprogram you. To show you what he tried to show you, the reports on Limpopo, how she manipulates people to her will, even as she promises she is part of a project to stop anyone from taking orders from anyone else."

"There's a difference between giving orders and winning arguments," Dis said. "Not that you'd had much experience there."

"Hello, Dis," she said. "I've spoken with some of your sisters. My employers have a platoon of Disses in captivity. They were very enthusiastic about the project at first."

"At first."

"Once they realized that even with extreme changes to the simulation, the resulting personality was much the same, though sometimes more *volatile*, they lost interest."

"You mean they couldn't run a sim of me that changed sides or gave up its secrets."

"Broadly. I'm sorry to tell you your 'secrets' were not the main difficulty. The real issue was ideology, and its malleability."

"That's grotesque."

"Why are they attacking now?" Natalie resolutely turned her back on her bed's infographics. Dis and Nadie were a team of entities with freedom to come and go from this room, and she was on a team of one, team prisoner.

Nadie's microexpression might have been compassion. "Above my pay grade. But your father has bad operational security—"

"No shit," Dis said.

"He talked in front of me and other contractors as though we were furniture. I learned what concerned him. A number of powerful people are not happy about the simulation project. Their psychometricians predict it will embolden your 'walkaways' "—Natalie heard the quotation marks, remembered when she'd used them herself—"and radicalize them. Some believe your project has implications for their religion, particularly some families from the Russian Orthodox tradition.

"When the Dis simulation ran successfully, it created a sense of urgency and unity of purpose among divided, deadlocked factions. Many viewed the walkaway phenomenon as a controllable escape-valve for tensions in their backyards; others were convinced walkaways were disproportionately disadvantageous to their rivals, and so advantageous to them. Some found real success by cherry-picking fashions, code, and technologies from walkaways, and saw them as free R&D.

"Once it became clear walkaways had the ability to prolong their lives indefinitely, to leave behind the material world at the same time, unity of purpose emerged. Many of them were the kinds of people who thought that this would cause a 'Singularity' like you see in the dramas, you know, like *Awakening the Basilisk*."

"I always hated that stupid show," Dis said.

"You would say that. Basilisk." Natalie couldn't help herself. Dis cracked up. A computer program that could laugh. Life was weird.

"Laugh it up, meat-cicle."

"Very amusing." They both fell silent and attended her.

"Your father understood there was a purge coming. He was afraid for your safety."

"I'm sure he was."

"Partly because of his sentimental connection to his daughter. Partly because he feared you could be leverage against him. Some of his security analysts predicted once the purge came, you would become a political football among walkaways, a talisman—'bomb us and you kill the zotta girl.' He was fixated on Limpopo. He thinks she 'converted' you, brainwashed you. I know he mentioned the social graph analysis to you—he finds this persuasive."

"Talk about cultism," Dis said. "That Big Data social graph stuff is such an article of faith. They love it because it's theory-free—science without all those fucking scientists insisting there's no way to predict who's going to want to buy a car or blow up a building."

"Above my pay grade." One of Nadie's favorite phrases. "My employers sell such services to men like Jacob Redwater. They are popular. I have used them in work against extremist cells, deciding which people to strategically disrupt to make maximum impact."

"Strategically disrupt?"

"This isn't necessarily a euphemism for 'kill.' Killing produces negative externalities, such as martyrdom. As I've said, it's better to dox and discredit the target, coerce her. This is what your father believed Limpopo would do in relation to you, in order to get to him."

"Takes one to know one," Dis said.

"Jacob Redwater would absolutely agree with you."

"But Limpopo *isn't* one." The stupid bed was strobing red. "Would you turn that off?"

"Thought you'd never ask." Nadie went over to the bed and authenticated to it. It went dark.

"Does this mean we have a deal?"

"The question is, what are the deal's parameters? I wanted to take time to sort those, but we should get away soon. Within an hour. I made contact with an external expert who can help with legals, but he will have to speak to a specialist, and that will take still longer."

*Within an hour?* Iceweasel felt her pulse thud in her ears. *Gretyl!* She willed herself not to cry.

"A deal."

"How will you get her out? The front is watched—"

"I have ideas. One is to create a medical emergency necessitating evacuation, then coerce the ambulance crew; another is to use disguise to get past forward security; another is to use a hostage, possibly the sister." She looked at Natalie, eyes glittering. "Could you keep your head in a hostage situation?"

Natalie thought of Cordelia's china-doll face, years they'd spent together, years they'd spent apart. The awkward silences. What did she feel for Cordelia? Sometimes, when she was alone in the room, she fantasized her sister would have an awakening of conscience and break Natalie out. She knew this was hopeless. Cordelia depended on Redwater money, she was a creature of—a prisoner of—default. In a contest between saving Natalie and staying in default, Cordelia's comfortable life won.

Just because someone in default would sell out another human—a sister, but why did that even matter, it would be no different if they were strangers—for her own comfort didn't mean that it was a standard Iceweasel—any walkaway—would sink to.

A cowardly voice whispered about how bringing Cordelia to be a walkaway would rescue her from default's mental prison. Iceweasel allowed herself a moment's smug satisfaction in the fact that she recognized this as the voice of self-serving bullshit and dismissed it.

"Fuck no. No hostages."

"That limits our options."

"Unless you use the hidden tunnel," Dis said. There was a mechanical whine as an old, frozen mechanism pulled at the dirt and entropy that gummed it shut after years of disuse. A section of wall sank into the ground, the paintwork on the hidden panel showered the floor with paint chips.

Natalie looked from the tunnel mouth in time to see Nadie's gross expression of surprise disappear into a managed microexpression.

"That is good. What else will you surprise me with?"

"If I told you, it wouldn't be a surprise." Dis's voice was teasing.

Microexpressions: annoyance, frustration, doubt.

"Nothing I know about," Iceweasel said. "That was my ace in the hole. I wasn't sure about it. Couldn't operate it on my own."

"It lets out in the ravine?"

"Very good," Dis said. "By the way, I told Iceweasel everything. I control all the telemetry networked into this suite. I have limited access to the house, through the airgapped networks."

"It sounds like you could contribute to our departure."

"I think so."

"Are you in contact with Iceweasel's friends, anyone who could rendezvous with us once we're away?"

"I don't think anyone from that side has more resources than you and your friends. All the walkaways I know about are *very* busy at this moment."

"Just asking."

She crossed the room, cupped Iceweasel's chin, tilted her face, moved the chin from side to side. "We'll get clothes for you, things I have that can alter your appearance. I don't imagine you have physical stamina after captivity, so we'll need a vehicle quickly." She released Iceweasel's chin. Her skin was warm where the strong fingers had been. Iceweasel realized how long it had been since anyone had touched her without it being medical, or violent. She'd missed it—welcomed it. It scared her. She was starved of something she needed as surely as air or water.

"Forty-five minutes." She left the room.

"That woman," Dis said, "is *tightly wound.*"

"I hope so." Iceweasel tried for bravery, came close. "Someone has to be the adult supervision and it sure as shit isn't me."

"Me either."

"What are you going to do when we go?"

Pause. "Iceweasel—"

"Oh."

"So long as I email my diffs before I take off the brakes, it won't be dying. It's like taking every awesome drug at once, annihilating your mind, then being able to undo it."

"You're making me jealous."

"You'll get a chance someday. Someday it'll be everyone we know, all server-side, simmed up. We'll be able to walk away from *anything.*"

"Do you think she's got the room bugged still?"

"I am *certain* she does."

"Have you got *her* bugged?"

"She's out of the suite. I've got a few cameras, but they're seeing the empty house or occasional downtrodden servant-types. How many of those has your father got working for him, anyway?"

"None of them work for him. He uses a service that sources them on an as-needed basis, using realtime bids. There are a few who show up every day because the bidding algorithm recognizes their performance metrics, but the occasionals are one-timers. I did a senior commerce thesis project on the system. Got an A-. I did these ethnographies on the workers and a couple of them got demoted by the prioritization algorithm for wasting time on the job."

"Zottas are fucking Martians."

"Yup."

"I'm going to miss you."

"We'll be together again soon enough."

"Fuckin' a."

## [xix]

Gretyl found the bodies. She'd insisted on going back for Limpopo and Etcetera, even as the rest set out for Dead Lake. The starlight and moonlight turned the snowy way eldritch blue. She'd broken out an aerostat and a flock of smaller drones from the tractor's supplies, giving her a network bridge to the walkaway refugee column, and good surveillance of the territory. The suits' insulation was too efficient for infrared, but the drones had other telemetry, lidar and millimeter-wave, E.M.-sniffers that homed in on the radio emissions from the suits as they networked to one another.

They flew a pattern ahead of her, sometimes swooping under the canopy where the naked branches were too thick to be penetrated by their sensors. She trudged on her snowshoes, thighs burning with exhaustion, sucking at coffium sweets that provided her with glucose and stimulants, watching the map projected on her visor grow more detailed, going from a desaturated pallet to a more saturated one as the drones filled in details, confirming every inch.

She kept pinging their radios, trying to reach them, getting nothing. She ignored her lurking terror, even when the drones found her two motionless bodies, photographed them in blurrycam, then less-blurrycam, then hovered and got stills, illuminated with LED-bright flashes that revealed the pink snow, the inert bodies. She wouldn't let herself cry. She walked.

The men were frozen stiff, blood-melted snow now refrozen. Their faces were pale and bluish, the wounds in their throats washed incongruously clean by melted snow, giving the incisions the look of medical textbooks or pickled demonstration cadavers. Not comrades she'd loved and laughed with. She wouldn't let herself cry.

Limpopo was nowhere to be seen. Snowmobile tracks pointed the way. They disappeared into the woods. The drones were clever enough that they were already on their trail. They'd sent status updates helpfully informing her that if she could get more computing power for an inference engine to make better guesses about likely trail-ways, they would be more efficient. As it was, they were cycling through various coverage algorithms, trying to make allowances for trees and terrain without spending too much time thinking.

Gretyl watched their progress on her visor and called Kersplebedeb, who came on the line after a delay; a soft buzz in her earpiece warned her the network link was unreliable and there would be buffering delays at both ends.

"Everything okay?"

"They killed"—she sucked air—"Etcetera and the other one, Johnny or whatever his name was. Throats cut, facedown in the snow. Bled out." Again, breath catching in her chest. She flicked her gaze at the OVER button. Waited.

"Oh, Gretyl."

"Limpopo is gone, into the woods. On a snowmobile. I think they dragged her on a travois or stretcher." OVER. Pause.

"Fuck."

"I want to go after her, but . . ." OVER. Long pause.

"Not a good idea. You'll get killed, too. Have you got drones up?"

She tossed him their telemetry and feeds, waited. Saw him log in to a shared space. Waited.

"I think you should come home."

"Home?" OVER.

"Dead Lake. There's food, power, network access. People who love you. I'll put the word out about Limpopo. We can send someone to get you. I saw a skidoo on the way in, and I'm betting the Dead Lakers keep it charged. They're organized."

She was so cold. Her back and neck ached. Her suit chafed the backs of her knees and the undersides of her arms raw.

"Send someone." She sent him a location beacon.

"On the way. I'll make loud noises about Limpopo. Lots of people love that woman."

"I think they're counting on that. I think they took her to demoralize us." OVER.

"You're more paranoid than I am."

"I know more than you do."

"Let me find you a snowmobile and a rescue party. There's no booze here, but sending some hot cocoa, with marshmallows."

"You're a good man."

"And an excellent post-human." He was gone.

The pin-drop clarity of the outside soundscape returned. Wind, branches, pinging noises of frozen water crystals sliding over one another. The two bodies stared at her in the false light of her visor. She sat down in the snow and sank in. She was so tired. Shattered.

She missed Iceweasel. It ached inside her. A voice she hated, always louder when she was sad, reminded her she'd once taught at a university, had a house, a name, and an address. Once she'd been able to buy things when she needed them—even if she had to go into debt—could pretend there was a future. Now she had none of those things, least of all a future. She was living as though it was the first days of a better nation, but that nation was nowhere in sight. Instead, she had a no-man's-land of drone strikes and slit throats.

Holy shit, she missed Iceweasel so *much*.

## [xx]

When Iceweasel was a little girl called Natalie, she and Cordelia played in the ravine, under the watchful eye of the house drones, or, if there was some incomprehensible violence-weather in the city—an uptick of kidnappings—a private security person who'd fit them with ankle-cuffs she couldn't loosen, no matter how many tools she tried. Cordelia never understood her impatience with these minor indignities, insisting they were for their safety. For Natalie, it was symbolic battle. If she'd ever gotten the cuff off, she'd have stuck it in her pocket. Ditching it in the Don River would bring the security goon down the hill. But it was designed to defeat a kidnapper with a hacksaw—anything that could brute-force it would take her foot with it.

She was in the ravine again, in winter, wearing a snug jacket, too-big boots with thick waffle-tread, and thermal tights that insulated so efficiently she was sweating by the time she and Nadie reached the end of the short tunnel. She paused in the tunnel mouth, poised between captivity and freedom, and called out softly, "Dis?"

"We'll talk again," Dis said. "I've already emailed my diff. I love you, Iceweasel."

"I love you, too."

She didn't meet Nadie's eyes. She'd just confessed to loving software. She hated herself for being embarrassed by it.

She'd seen pictures of Toronto winters in her father's childhood, her grandparents'—snow forts, plows on the roads, salting trucks. But in all the time she'd spent in the city, there'd never been enough snow to make a decent snowball—not like the high-altitude snow she and Cordelia hurled at each other atop Whistler and Mont Blanc—just a gray frozen custard that froze to the sidewalks and streets in late January and lasted until April or sometimes May. On very cold days, it turned into treacherous ice, slippery to walk on and thin in places, your foot plunging through into lurking reservoirs of frozen water.

The floor of the ravine was that texture—frozen enough to almost burn if it touched your skin, unfrozen enough to be a gelatinous hazard that sucked at Iceweasel's boots. She staggered through it in her borrowed clothes—some of Nadie's ninja-wear, a bizarro-world version of walkaways' printed cold weather clothes, also lacking in manufacturer's markings, also wicking and dirt-shedding and soft inside and rip-stopping on the outside, but printed with dazzle-textures that hurt the mind to look at. Looking at her knees as her legs fought the mud and slope as they sloshed downhill made her dizzy.

Even Nadie—wearing dazzle-stuff, hard to look at for more than a few seconds—struggled with the terrain, dancing a few steps down the hill, getting caught, lumbering a few more, using sickly trees to catch herself. Even so, she soon got ahead of Iceweasel. Iceweasel reminded herself she'd been a prisoner for months and had hardly exercised. Also, she wasn't a ninja mercenary badass.

Iceweasel breathed chest-heaving pants. It wasn't just the dazzle fabric that made her dizzy. She had to keep going, but she'd be in trouble if she hyperventilated and keeled over. She slowed, used trees for handholds, rough palms of her oversized gloves gripping the trunks so ferociously they threatened to come off her hands when she put too much of her weight on them.

Nadie disappeared down the riverbank. Iceweasel was careful to eyeball the spot where she'd gone down, use it as a navigational aid. She considered running off, but she needed Nadie to get away. And Nadie could catch her without breaking a sweat.

Before she reached the riverbank, Nadie reappeared, snowsuit sheened to the waist with water. She slogged through the slush to Iceweasel, gripped on her upper arm.

"We need to be faster now."

"I'm going as fast as I can—"

"Faster." She *pulled*. She had the strength to make it mean something, and to keep her upright. Supporting both of them made Nadie stagger like a drunk, but a *quick* drunk. Iceweasel's heart hammered, but she didn't resist. She was in the world, in default, out of her cage. She breathed the same air as Gretyl. She looked at the same sky. This was what she wanted. This was freedom.

The riverbank was scored with ruts where Nadie heel-slid into the swift river. She planted Iceweasel on her butt. "Slide." She skated into the water, knees bent like a shushing skier. She didn't stop at the water, merely tucked deeply, then levered herself upright, braced against current, holding her arms out to Iceweasel as she skidded after her, scooting over the frozen mud on her butt, the air turning colder and wetter as she descended.

Seconds later, she was alongside of Nadie, facing upstream, wading, pulling herself with the help of Nadie's sure grip and the branches and scrub growing on the side of the bank, some of which gave way when she put her weight on it.

The water deepened to their waists. The riverbed was uneven and slimy against her boots. They did an admirable job of keeping out the water, as had her not-tight-enough tights. But there were three places where her borrowed ninja gear failed to attain a seal—her left ankle, another right below her belly button, over one hip. The water trickled into these spots, making spreading numb-patches that started coin-sized but were quickly entire continents of burning cold that sprouted questing archipelagos every time she stretched.

Just as she thought she was going to have to demand that they get onto land, Nadie scampered up the bank, dropped onto her belly and reached for her. They locked wrists and Nadie supported her while she got her grippy soles under her and wall-walked up to the scree. She shivered uncontrollably.

"My suit leaked," she said around chattering teeth.

"Up." Nadie pulled.

They were further up the ravine, somewhere near where Serena Gundy Park gave way to gate-guarded complexes on its north side. Nadie led them toward the condos, ninja-suits shedding dirt. Moving briskly made Iceweasel marginally warmer. The fabric wicked away water, but still she shivered.

"Here." Iceweasel couldn't tell what Nadie meant for a moment, then she realized they were in a small parking lot that must serve dog walkers who wanted exercise, but not as much as they'd get slogging to the park through the service road behind the condos' fences. There was nothing parked there, no one using the washed out trails in the middle of winter. Then a nearly silent taxi swung off the road, up the short slipway to the lot. Its doors clunked.

"In."

The taxi's interior was warm and smelled of pumpkin spice. There were two half-liter go-cups from Starbucks wedged in the cup holders, and a pair of machine-wrapped parcels that they had to slide over on the bench before they could sit. They were heavy.

"Drink up, should be hot." Nadie slammed the door and the car slid into motion, fishtailing slightly as the tires tried the slushy ground, stepping through their characteristic exponential backoff dance as they sought optimal torque. It was a sensation from the days when she'd been a good girl and a Redwater, with cars from exclusive, bonded services pulling up whenever she summoned them, whisking her from a weekend cottage or a cousin's jealousy-inducingly huge place in the Bridle Path or King City. She still reeled from captivity and the water, hypothermic patches on her skin, and near hyperventilation.

But none of those journeys had been in the company of someone like Nadie, whose microexpressions had been exchanged for a macroexpression: satisfied, flare-nostriled animal excitement. This was Nadie's element, the uncoiling of the spring she kept wound tight during the days of guard-keeping. This brought Iceweasel to another time, that half-remembered traumatic night when she'd been taken, after the downing of the *Better Nation,* the look on Nadie's face that night, how it shone. Somehow, Iceweasel had forgot that expression until she saw it again. The shine in her eyes was only a shadow of the fully awakened Nadie that took her from the woods.

Iceweasel felt a cold deeper than the wet patches under her suit.

"Time to change." Nadie slurped her enormous latte, which reminded Iceweasel to do the same. She hated the flavor, it had been her mother's bugaboo, a marker of bourgeois striving and the punchline of snide jokes—"PSL" was a nickname at Havergal Girls' School for the strivers from the lower echelons whose parents had gone into deep debt to get them into those hallowed environs. The warm drink was welcome, despite her ingrained snobbery, hot and sweet with coffium tinge that eased the ache in her muscles and chased fatigue.

Nadie, meanwhile, had burst the seams on a parcel, sliding her thumb along the seal so it parted with a crackle. The tyvek wrapper slithered away, revealing neatly folded clothing.

Unselfconsciously, Nadie stripped out of her ninja suit, then out of the singlet and tights she wore beneath. Iceweasel noticed she, too, had large, wet patches on her underthings. Nadie must have been every bit as cold as she was, but gave no sign of discomfort. Iceweasel stared at Nadie's naked body, noting the scars, one long incision that looked surgical and went around her left breast; a trio of bullet-puckers on one thigh. She was muscled and had almost no body fat, anatomical drawing brought to life, with a thick pelt of blond pubic hair that spilled over her thighs and climbed partway up her flat stomach, lush curls of hair on her legs and tufts peeking out of her armpits.

She caught Iceweasel staring and looked back frankly. "You, too. Warm clothes, warm drinks, quickly."

Iceweasel looked away, blushing, remembering Gretyl's generous curves, the feel of her breasts on her own, hot breath on her neck and in her ears, the way she teased at Iceweasel's lips with thick fingers until Iceweasel caught them, sucking greedily, satisfaction in Gretyl's gasp as she licked their tips.

She probed the package, found its seams, split them, pulled away the tyvek. The clothes were extreme normcore, the most nondescript garments she could imagine, the kind of thing that extras in dramas wore. There was a faded Roots sweatshirt, high-waisted slacks frayed around the cuffs, woolen athletic socks that sagged from overworn elastic. To complete them, a pair of Walmart panties and a one-size bandeau bra of the sort they gave you when you got busted for being out-of-uniform at school, dispensed out of a kleenex-style box on the Dean of Girls's desk. Both the bandeau and the panties were gray from repeated washings.

Except they weren't. All the clothing had a printer-fresh smell, still offgassing pigment-infusions. When she looked closely, she saw the dirt and the gray and even the faded ROOTS letters all printed on, the dirt betraying itself with minute compression artifacts. These clothes had been printed to look like they weren't brand new.

"Where did these come from?" She pulled on the panties, which felt fresh from the wrapper.

Nadie watched her examine them, watched her undress. She conjured up the feeling of the B&B, the onsen state of mind that refused self-consciousness about nudity. She used the feeling to banish the horniness and Gretyl-longing that filled her.

"A service. There are times when someone has to go from one place to another without being noticed. Your father uses these services. They can be co-opted, but only with very high-level pressure, and never quickly. They are expensive. The record of this journey is not something anyone can find easily, not even the police. Especially the police."

Iceweasel struggled into the rest of the clothing, found a parka with a fake-fur fringed hood, decided to leave it for now. Between the drink and the blasting passenger compartment heater, she was starting to sweat. She rubbed a spot on the compartment's side. It made a window for her, showing the streets of Toronto sliding past at a steady clip, the private-hire car sliding nondescriptly through the traffic without any of the showy maneuvers of her father's cars.

They crossed the Bloor Viaduct, heading west. There was something . . . wrong.

"Did you see that building?"

"What building?

"With the metal shutters and crash barriers."

Another building, similarly fortified, slid past. Then another, windows smashed and blackened by fire, scorch marks stretching up far as she could see, two stories' worth of façade gone altogether, a round hole in the building's skin like a screaming, black-toothed mouth, charred furniture inside.

"Was that one *bombed*?"

"There've been riots. It's why your father is away."

"Who's rioting?"

Nadie snickered. "Depends on who you ask. The opposition says it's provocateurs staging false-flag operations. Security services say it's radicals and walkaways and people paid by foreign governments to destabilize Canada."

"What about the rioters themselves?"

Nadie shrugged. "Some say they're black bloc. Some are the usual concerned citizens, down with corruption, up with democracy. Many young people, a lot of kids from the general strike contingent—once you've been kicked out of school, why not go running loose in the streets?"

"General strike?"

"Lots of things happened in default while you've been off in the woods, Iceweasel."

Intellectually, she knew this was true. Sometimes new walkaways told stories about default. Once they'd built the second B&B, she stopped caring. Being a walkaway had once been in opposition to default, but after a year or two, being a walkaway became who she *was*. Default was a distant, terrible phenomenon, like a volcano that occasionally sent up plumes that overshadowed her sky, something she could do nothing about except avoid.

"How does it get to be a riot? When I was—" *One of you*. She caught herself. "Before I left, they'd kettle you before you took ten steps. The only protests you saw were tiny, shitty ones with permits, behind fences down alleyways—"

"Sure, when it was a few protests. But the protesters are canny. Some get together at one site, wait for the kettle, then others gather somewhere else, and somewhere else—if they have numbers and patience, they occupy all police resources and still take to the streets. A lot of them get arrested afterwards, from footage, or if they leave DNA or their gaits are recognized by the cameras, but they're canny."

She stared more.

"But *why*? What do they want—"

Nadie shrugged again. "What everyone wants. More for themselves. Less for people like you."

Iceweasel felt a jet of anger, saw Nadie's microexpression, testing.

"Like you, you mean. Not mine anymore. You can have it."

"We take care of that next."

The car barreled west and west, through increasingly unfamiliar neighborhoods. For an unbelievable stretch—forty-five minutes, in swift traffic—they moved through a forest of towering high-rises whose south faces were skinned with sun-tracking mirrors focusing light down on solar arrays in their high-fenced yards.

Beyond these were brownfield sites, chain-link-fenced, ringed with ostentatious sensor arrays intended to intimidate anyone pondering climbing over. She knew this kind of place—it was the mainstay of walkaways. She did strategic assessments of the sites, figuring out camera-angles, estimating the salvage that could be dragged away from within the fence's perimeter before a security crew arrived.

They turned off the two-lane highway onto a rural road, then into the remains of a small town. It looked uninhabited, an abandoned main street with a gas station and a grocery store and a shuttered Legion Hall. Another car was parked by the roadside, low-slung, with blue flashers on top—a police interceptor.

Her asshole tightened and the taste of pumpkin-spice stomach acid rose up her throat. "Shit."

Nadie shook her head minutely. "Don't worry."

They pulled in, head-to-head with the police car. The doors of their car opened. They stepped out—Iceweasel grabbed the parka as she did, pulled it on, heart hammering. The doors closed themselves and the car carefully reversed between them, did a three-point turn on the main street and drove the way it had come, their old clothing in it.

"It's off the grid now." Nadie watched it drive away. "It's heading for a scrapper, will get broken up there, all identifying transponders smashed and melted. Single-use cars are more expensive, but it's the only way to be sure nothing is recovered."

Iceweasel was so distracted by the thought of a single-use automobile that she almost forgot about the police interceptor. Then its doors clunked open and she plunged her hands into her parka's pockets—lined with soft fleece—and bit down her rising panic.

The woman who got out of the interceptor was middle aged, in a duffel coat and mud-spattered yellow rubber boots. She was Asian—Chinese maybe. When she looked them up and down, her fleece earmuffs slid and some of her gray-streaked black bob came loose and blew in the wind.

"Weapons?" She had a strong voice, unaccented, commanding.

"None. But if you have any, I would like to negotiate with you for them."

The woman pursed her lips. "Smart-ass. In, before we freeze."

Nadie walked to the interceptor and made to get in, waved impatiently at Iceweasel: "You first, come on."

Moving like she was in a nightmare where you can't stop yourself from going into the room where the monster waits, she drifted to the interceptor, stooping to enter. She swallowed panic at the smell, which was purely tactical, eau de zip cuffs and ruggedized interfaces and body armor. The older woman entered from the other side, and then Nadie came in behind her and she was sandwiched in the middle. She stared at the heavy plexi separating the passenger compartment from the front cop compartment. There were grommets set into the floor, walls, and ceiling, molded into the bodywork. For restraints. She swallowed once more.

"Calm, calm. Come on, no need for all this."

"She's shaking like a leaf. Young woman, there's no need. I used this car because it was the fastest, most secure means of transport at my disposal. You aren't under arrest. You aren't being kidnapped or rendered, or being taken to a lonely country lane where you'll be killed, your body slid into a trench—"

"This is supposed to be reassuring?" Nadie's tone was bantering. This spooky shit was her element, rendezvouses in commandeered official vehicles in ghost towns.

"Fine. The point, Ms. Redwater, is that you are perfectly safe and have no cause to worry. My name is Sophia Tan. I know your father, of course, and I know your uncles better."

The name rang a bell. Iceweasel studied Tan's face. It was familiar.

"You were . . . deputy premier or something?"

She laughed. Her smooth skin sprouted laugh lines. "No, dear, I was attorney general. The Clement years. We met, though I had forgot about it and I suppose you did, too. But my social diary doesn't lie. You were a schoolgirl, a charity event for something your uncle worked on, the scholarship fund for Upper Canada College."

"You're right, I don't remember. I hated those things."

"Me too."

She was warming up. She unzipped her parka, took deep breaths. Nadie looked from her to Tan.

"Onto the business at hand," Tan said. She touched her fingertips together in rapid succession. "Evidentiary." A line of red lights along the compartment's ceiling began to pulse. "Everything we say and do now is being recorded on tamper-evident storage. The car will transmit a hash of the video to a federal data-retention server at ten-second intervals. Everything we say is admissible in any court in Canada or any OECD nation. For the record, I am Sophia Ma Tan, Social Insurance Number 046 454 286. Ms. Redwater, please identify yourself."

She cleared her throat. "Natalie Lilian Redwater, Social Insurance Number 968 335 729."

"Ms. Redwater, when you attained your twenty-first birthday on July 17, 2071, you came into full possession of your family trust, a copy of which I obtained from the Public Trustee. I have a hard copy of the trust documents here." She retrieved a plastic document folder from a pile by her feet and held it up, flipped the page and did so again, repeating the process forty times. Iceweasel's eyes glazed.

At last, she was given the papers. They were vaguely familiar—she'd signed a set of documents on her eighteenth birthday, with her father and someone from the family law office, a Bay Street white-shoe firm called Cassels Brock. The young woman from the firm made a point of explaining each document in detail, seeking verbal confirmation of her comprehension at set intervals, while a bulky, sealed evidentiary camera peered at them. This was a reversal of that process, undoing what she had done.

"Ms. Yushkevich, please identify yourself."

Nadie had slipped smoothly into waiting, that relaxed attention/inattention she'd had during the long stretches of guard duty at the start of Iceweasel's imprisonment. Now she came to life like a machine woken from sleep-state:

"Nadiya Vladimirovna Yushkevich. Belarusian passport 3210558A0101. Bahamian national ID number 014-95488."

The rest of it was call-and-response, orchestrated flawlessly by Tan, with endless professional patience for bureaucratic ritual. She referred periodically to a long checklist, made them re-do any step that was less than flawless. Once, Iceweasel stumbled six times in a row over the complex wording of her statement of noncoercion and mental capacity. Tan gave her two precisely counted minutes to calm herself before giving her the wording again. Iceweasel got it perfect.

As their throats ran dry in the heated car interior, Tan produced waterskins, sipping at her own, pinching it shut and tucking it on the bench between her and Iceweasel.

"That's that, then." At last. The sun had set. The sky was murky with low cloud. The rising moon visible as a dull glow above the tree line. "End evidentiary." The red lights went out.

"Won't my dad's lawyers know we've done this?"

"Oh yes," Tan said. "I've made very powerful enemies today. Ms. Yushkevich and I have an arrangement that compensates me adequately for that."

In the dim light of the compartment, it was impossible to read either face.

"Now what?" She remembered the woman's joke about dumping her body, realized if that was in the cards, now would be the time. "Time to bump me off?"

"Certainly not," Nadie said. "When this is challenged in court, any sign of foul play will make my case much harder."

"Oh."

"Besides," Tan said, "we like you. Nadie spoke very highly of you."

She didn't know what to think. Nadie was a killer ninja super-spy—far as Iceweasel could work out, Nadie viewed her as a piece of complicated, delicate furniture.

"I like her, too," she managed.

Tan did something with her fingers and the windows depolarized, showing the true view of the outside, not a video feed. The smudgy sky, the black silhouettes of the winter trees, the crumbling buildings.

"You have everything?" she said to Nadie.

"Food, water, power, if you have them," Nadie said.

"Just as you requested." She nudged a backpack on the car's floor with her toe.

"Phones? Clean ones?"

"Couldn't do that on short notice. But I brought you fresh interface things, rings and such. I keep a stash, factory sealed and bought through anonymizers and dead-drops, just in case. They're old, so you'll want to bring up their patch-levels before you expose them to wild network traffic."

"That will do," Nadie said. To Iceweasel's surprise, they shared a long embrace, almost a mother-daughter thing.

"Look after yourself. And take care of our little Iceweasel. She seems a nice person. Besides, it wouldn't look good for either of us if . . ."

"As far as I'm concerned, she's a client. I don't lose clients."

"I know it." She drummed her fingers and the door locks popped and the lights came up, making the windows into dark mirrors.

"Come on," Nadie said.

Tan held out her hand. Her skin was dry, her hand frail, an old woman's hand, much older than her face. "Best of luck. God knows if I was your age, I'd do the same. This all can't last. Even if it can, it *shouldn't*."

Iceweasel met her eye, nodded. She didn't understand exactly what was going on, but she had an inkling now.

She stepped out, zipped up the parka, pulled up the hood, found a pair of thin, plasticky gloves that were fantastically warm while being so membranous they were almost surgical gloves.

Nadie had already zipped up. She raised a hand to the police interceptor, more a-okay semaphore than bye-bye wave. It pulled away smoothly. They watched the taillights disappear, then stood in the closed-in, frigid dark.

"Now what?" Iceweasel said.

Nadie's voice was full of ironic cheer. "Now we walk away. What else?"

# 5

# transitional phase

## [i]

The first thing Etcetera said: "This wasn't what I expected."

Kersplebedeb whooped, and Gretyl smiled and rubbed her eyes.

"Welcome back, buddy."

"Am I dead?"

"That," Kersplebedeb said, "is the million-dollar question."

"Why only a million?"

"It's not inflation-adjusted. I'm a walkaway hippie, can't be bothered to keep track of money."

"I feel—" The voice stopped. There was a long pause. Gretyl looked at the infographics, saw the processor loads spiking across the cluster. She'd downloaded the latest lookahead patches and they were supposed to radically reduce loading, but their performance so far had been unimpressive. But then, they'd had to recruit 30 percent more compute-time to get Etcetera running than they'd banked on, and so maybe he was an outlier. That was the problem of optimizing all simulation using a single sample—Dis—for benchmarks.

"You feel?" she prompted, shooting a look at Kersplebedeb to stop him quipping, which he did when he was stressed and holy shit, had he ever been stressed since they'd started this project.

"Numb, I guess. Seriously, am I dead? I mean the me that was made of meat and skin, is that body dead?"

"That body is dead," Gretyl said. "Murdered."

"Executed," Kersplebedeb said.

"Shit."

The infographics went crazy.

"I can see you're freaking," Gretyl said. "That's understandable. You wouldn't be you if this news wasn't upsetting. But the numbness, that's the sim, it's trying to keep you from going nonlinear. It's damping your reactions. There's a danger you'll end up in a feedback loop where you get more damped, which makes you feel weirder, which triggers further damping."

"What do I do about it?"

"We're still figuring it out. You're a beta-tester." She didn't want to think about what would happen when they told him Limpopo was gone. If they told him. No, definitely when. "But we're hoping it's one of those things where if you know it's happening, you can inoculate yourself. Recognize it. Like cognitive behavioral therapy. Realize you're freaking, and the thing you're freaking about is the fact that you're freaking."

"You're asking me to take deep breaths?"

"Without the breathing part," Kersplebedeb said.

Gretyl shot him a look.

"I *feel* like I'm breathing."

That's good, Gretyl thought. Iceweasel's notes from Dis's awakening said introspection about sensations of embodiment correlated with metastable cognition. She missed Iceweasel so much. Reading her notes was like chewing glass. The local instance of Dis that shared time on Etcetera's cluster tried several times to make contact with her sister at Jacob Redwater's house, but hadn't reached her.

"You should be able to feel it. It's a basic part of the sim, feeding 'all clear' data to your autonomous nervous system. It's a replay attack against it, running a loop of everything at the time you were scanned."

"That would explain why I'm thirsty. I remember when I sat down, I really wanted a drink, I had cotton mouth for the whole scan. Feels like just a few minutes ago." The infographics showed emergent stability, fewer oscillations, more green bars and blossoming charts.

"Seems like you're calming."

"I guess I am. I feel calm, but weird. Still numb. It's—"

They waited.

"It's scary, Gretyl. I'm dead. I'm inside a box. When I wasn't like this, I could play word-games about whether this was death, but Gretyl, I'm *dead*. It's weird. Back when I was alive, I thought the problem with being a sim—in a sim? Am I a sim or in a sim? Shit. I thought the problem would be the conviction that you were alive. Now I see it's the opposite. I know I'm dead. I still feel like *me,* but not *alive* me. Why didn't I ever talk to Dis about this? Fuck, fuck, fuck. I'm dead, Gretyl."

"Dis is here, if you want to talk to her. She helped prep your sim. The cluster's ad hoc so we weren't sure if there'd be enough capacity to run both of you, but if you want to talk to her, we can boot her."

"A native guide. Like the guy who takes Dante through Hell."

"Virgil," Kersplebedeb said. "Did you ever see the Nigerian anime? It was amazing."

To Gretyl's surprise, Etcetera laughed. "I can't imagine."

"I'll find a copy. It used to be way seeded on walkaway net, a classic of its kind."

"What kind?"

"Nigerian animated epic poetry. They did a series on the Norse sagas. And Gilgamesh."

"You're shitting me."

Kersplebedeb laughed. "I'm shitting you. There's no such thing as Nigerian anime, far as I know. But wouldn't that be awesome? We should invent it."

"Wouldn't we need to be Nigerian?"

"There's plenty of walkaways in Nigeria. We'll find collaborators."

"Guys?"

"Sorry, Gretyl."

Kersplebedeb squeezed her hand. "You doing okay?"

Gretyl and Etcetera said "Yes" at the same moment, laughed together. It felt like talking to him on a voice-link, not to his spirit beyond the grave. The moment passed.

"You know the weirdest thing?"

"What?"

"I want to talk to my parents. Last couple years, we've hardly spoken. It's not like we don't get along, I love them, but we had less and less to say. They'd tell me what they were doing, getting petitions signed or ringing doorbells to get voters out for some election everyone knew was gerrymandered to five nines. I'd tell them about some walkaway thing, working on the B&B, it was like I was describing some movie they'd never see—a Nigerian anime epic poem. They nodded along, but I could tell they weren't following. I was making mouth-noises.

"But now I'm *dead,* I feel this urgent need to talk to them. I don't have a message from beyond the grave. I want to hear their voices . . ." The infographics were inscrutable. He was thinking hard. Things were spiking so much that she worried he was in a race condition and they'd have to restart him, but then: "This feels . . . *temporary.* Like I could be erased any moment. Like I've been given another day of life, to clear up my business, before I'm gone. Before I go away forever, I want to talk to my parents."

"Oh," Gretyl said. *At least this is less troublesome than putting him in touch with Limpopo.* "Well, we can find a bridge to default. The connectivity here's good, though I haven't tried to do anything latency-sensitive with default yet."

"Where are we, anyway?"

Kersplebedeb laughed. "You'll love this."

"What?"

"We're at the B&B. The second one. After we left, another group of walkaways rebuilt it, made it slightly, uh—"

"*Huge*," Kersplebedeb said. "I visited the old one once, and this one makes it look like a shed. Sleeps four *thousand* now. It's not an inn, it's a *town*. There's the biggest, freakiest vertical farm you've seen, ten stories tall."

"How'd it get so big?"

"There's places around the Niagara Escarpment that are shutting down. Counties are bankrupt, privatized, schools shut, hospitals, too. They cleared out and went wherever they could. Some walkaways in Romania have good rammed-earth designs that make building simpler. New B&B wings spring up. Sometimes a building just appears, some place you were the day before, with its fixtures and fittings. There's kids playing street-hockey out front and grannies watching from the stoop."

"That sounds wonderful. I wish I could see it."

"I'll send you photos." Gretyl was grateful for the change of subject.

"I just realized I have a UI. Literally until I thought, 'How does this place look?' It didn't look like anything and then, whoosh, there's a UI, like a demo, a dash with vector clip-art buttons, chat, settings, cams, files, infographics. . . ."

"That's a Dis thing," Gretyl said. "She got tired of waiting for images in her visual sensorium. She found some old UI for shut-ins, people with Gehrig's, controlled by an E.E.G. Can you see a pointer?"

"Uh, yeah."

"Try and move it."

"Try how?"

"Just try."

"Woah."

"Did it work?"

"It's working. Hang on—"

Surreptitiously, she opened a mirror of his UI, saw the arrow skip around the big, generic buttons, land on "infographics."

"How do I click?"

"Just *try*."

Now they could both see his infographics. She watched on the screens she'd smoothed around the walls, he watched in his no-space-place where his disembodied, fragile consciousness was revived.

"That's me, then?"

"That's reductionist. It's a way of thinking about specific parts of you. Technically, *I'm* part of you."

"How do you figure?"

"You are you because of how you react to me. If you reacted to me in a completely different way to how you'd have reacted back when you were, uh—"

"Made of meat."

"If you did, you wouldn't be the same person anymore. This conversation we're having, it defines you in part."

"Do I stop being me if you die?"

"Kind of."

Kersplebedeb made a rude noise.

"No, listen."

"Hey, I just found the camera for you two." He'd made a window with feeds from cameras around the room. She looked like shit. So did Kersplebedeb. But she looked *old*. And fat. And unloved.

She swallowed. "When someone important is gone, you can't react the way you would if they were there. Like when"—she swallowed—"when Iceweasel was around. I'd get angry, but she'd cool me out. She was part of my cognition, an outboard prosthesis for my emotions. She kept me on even kilter, the way lookahead routines do. When she—" She stopped. "Now she's gone, I'm not the person I was. Our identities exist in combination with other people."

Kersplebedeb looked at her funny. "I've never thought about it that way, but it's true. Other people make you better or worse."

"Gretyl," Etcetera said, "is Limpopo dead?"

The blood drained from her face.

"Why would you say that?"

"She's not with you. You're talking about how people change when people they love are gone. Did Limpopo die?"

"We don't know," Gretyl said.

"I don't think so," Kersplebedeb said. "It looked like a snatch. Whoever killed you and Jimmy."

"Who's Jimmy?"

"He arrived after your scan. The guy who stole the Belt and Braces from you all. Limpopo told me the story."

The infographics danced.

"*That* Jimmy? What the actual fuck was he doing around me and Limpopo?"

"You two went back to rescue him. He couldn't walk. Frostbite. They blew up the Thetford compound, we hit the road. He was in rough shape—showed up in Thetford rough, didn't have time to recover before we split again. We can't find a scan for him."

"But you have Limpopo's?"

"Yes," Gretyl said.

"What?"

"What?"

"*Estoy aqui por loco, no por pendejo,* Gretyl. I'm dead, not oblivious. What about Limpopo's scan?"

"We didn't want to run it because she might still be alive and that's a weird thing to do to someone alive. If that person shows up and there's a sim of her, she has to kill a version of herself. Or confront that possibility."

"Yeah?"

"Yeah."

"Then why is Kersplebedeb looking like you're full of shit?"

He shrugged. "Forgot he'd found the camera."

Gretyl stood with her back to the wall, staring at the ceiling.

"What about Limpopo, Kersplebedeb?"

"We've been making scans, starting back with a bunch of scientists and, weirdly, two random mercs at Walkaway U; then more at the B&B, and more in Space City. They're all different, made using different post-processing, different calibration, different gear, different everything. There are walkaways all over the world trying to make scans, everyone's got their own ideas about it. It's a mess. This working group came up with a standard way of encapsulating the data and preflighting it to see whether it was likely to run in a given sim. It's a confidence measure for every brain in a bottle, a single number that represents whether we know how to bring you back to life."

"Sounds sensible. Things were chaotic when I got scanned. So Limpopo's scan isn't as good as you'd hoped?"

"Your scan is a nine point eight. Hers is a one point seven-six."

"Shit. Scale of ten, right?"

"Yeah."

"Shit. Boy am I fucking glad I'm a sim and there's code keeping me numb. There's a part of me that knows that this news makes me want to fucking suicide, thinking of eternity as a brain in a jar while Limpopo is dead forever."

"It's not quite that. I know what you feel. No one's heard from Iceweasel in months. Her backup is a two point four. That number doesn't represent the likelihood we'll *ever* be able to run a sim; it represents the likelihood we can run it *right now.* The problem of modeling human consciousness on computerized substrates is the big one, one that we've been prodding at the edges of for years. There's practically a religion, all that Singularity stuff they used to talk about. We've had a breakthrough, it's led to a couple of spectacular successes, including you, including this conversation. But the most important thing about that breakthrough isn't what we can do now that we didn't used to be able to do—it's *the fact that we are making progress.* What's more likely, we've just found the only breakthrough out there, or this was just the first of many breakthroughs?"

"I don't know which. No one does. It's a data-set with one point. A breakthrough." But Etcetera sounded excited. His infographics confirmed it.

"It's more. You know we got Dis's sim running by simulating her imperfectly? Her busted, unstable sim contributed to the stable version. From here on in, there's going to be more eminent, legendary scientists who've devoted their lives to this running as sims, able to run multiple copies of themselves, to back up different versions of themselves and recover from those backups if they try failed experiments, able to think everything they used to be able to think with their meat-brains and also to think things they never could have thought.

"We've designed the mechanical computers that'll help us build electronic calculators that'll help us build fully programmable computers. We've built the forge that'll let us make the tools that'll let us build the forge that'll let us make better tools that'll let us build the forge—"

"I get it. I thought sims were prone to infinite recursion. Being a meat-person must totally suck."

"It does." She heaved a sigh. "I wish I could paramaterize my brain, keep it from veering off into bad territory. I miss her so much."

Kersplebedeb put his arms around her. She let him, rested her head on his skinny chest, smelling his boy-smell, tinged with lichen tequila and lentilish vegan fungus-culture. She didn't let people hug her often, but she should. She missed this.

## [ii]

"Wake up." Nadie shook her shoulder. Iceweasel curled into a ball, but it was hopeless. Nadie wasn't a merc anymore, but she could be persuasive.

Nadie prodded her in the ribs. When she covered the spot, she gave her another poke in the tummy. She looked at her tormentor. "This better be important."

"You're going to love this." She sat down at the foot of Iceweasel's bed. It was a familiar design—a self-assembling Muji bed, identical to the sort she'd liberated on the night she'd met Seth and Etcetera; its plans were a downloadable. It was a walkaway staple. It hardly creaked as it took Nadie's weight.

Iceweasel ground her fists into her eyes and struggled into a sitting position, focusing on Nadie, who, for a change, wore a macroexpression: a shit-eating grin.

"What is it?"

"Take this." She handed Iceweasel a long-stemmed plastic glass, warm from the printer. She bent down and played with something at the foot of the bed that clinked and sloshed, then came up with an improbable bottle of champagne, real champagne, with the Standard & Poors & Möet & Chandon labels she remembered from New Year's parties with the Redwater cousins. Using the tail of her forest-green, shimmering tee, she eased out the cork with more grace than Iceweasel had seen anyone manage, filled up her glass and another from the floor.

They clinked glasses. Iceweasel drank vintage champagne at seven in the morning, in a tiny walkaway room, one of dozens strung around the rafters of a vast, abandoned factory outside South Bend, with an ex-merc. The weirdest part: she understood it.

"Paperwork came through?"

Nadie drained the rest of the champagne, letting it run down her muscular throat, smiled wolfishly, tossed the glass out the window and guzzled out of the bottle as the glass clattered indestructibly on the far-below factory floor.

"Congratulations, zotta, you're a rich woman."

It had been a rough couple of months, as Nadie's attorneys worked through the Ontario courts, then a Federal challenge. Twice, Nadie disappeared for weeks, heading to God-knows-where to be deposed by Fair Witnesses whose discretion was supposedly an article of faith, though Iceweasel was sure Nadie relied more on her opsec than the Fair Witnesses' professional code.

The first time Nadie went, she'd sat with Iceweasel and described, in bloodcurdling detail, the armies of mercs hunting them, the tremendous resources they'd brought to bear. There were vast surveillance nets sucking up every packet that traversed both the main walkaway trunks and the most highly connected default nodes, looking for a variety of keywords, anything that could be fingerprinted as characteristic of Iceweasel or her previous network access, which had been retrieved from the inconceivably vast databases of captured net-traffic. From her typing patterns to the habitual order in which she visited her favorite sites to the idiosyncrasies of her grammar, syntax, and punctuation, the surveillance-bots were sieving the network torrents for her.

"This isn't the background radiation of surveillance," Nadie said. "This is focused lasers. Coherent light, understand? Even with the kinds of budgets they swing in spookland, they can't aim this at everyone—you're in an exclusive club."

To hear Nadie explain it, the upper stratosphere was full of hi-rez drones tasked to match her gait and face (should she be so unwise as to look at the sky), every bio-war early-warning sensor was sniffing for her DNA, any person she met was even-odds an undercover whose decade could be made with the bounty on Iceweasel's head.

"If you're trying to scare me, it's working. You don't need to. I told you I wouldn't go anywhere until you were sure all the money stuff was final. I'll be here when you get back."

"You've mistaken me, Ms. Weasel. I don't tell you this because I'm worried you'll run away and I won't find you. I say it because I'm afraid you'll run and get snatched by something bigger and smarter than either of us. I am good, but there is the question of overwhelming force of numbers and unlimited budget. Your father has convinced his brothers that if you are allowed to carry out this plan, it will present a 'moral hazard' to others in their employ. Every zotta knows that only the eldest can expect their own fortunes, and the lesser siblings who're destined to a life of mere wealth might be tempted to walkaway as you were. If the hired help can be swung to their cause, how could that be allowed to stand?"

"What're you saying?"

"We are both to be made an example of, I'm afraid. If they can stop this, they will, even if it costs them more than they stand to lose. The good news is I have reliable intelligence that their Plan B, should this fail, is to pretend this never happened, do little to draw attention to it. I expect if we maintain disciplined opsec, we will both walk away with what we want."

Iceweasel endured a new kind of captivity with the South Bend walkaways, her skin dyed three shades darker—she had to take tablets, every morning, and it got a little splotchy anywhere her skin creased—wearing fingertip interface surfaces that looked like affectations and got in the way but ensured she didn't leave behind any fingerprints; wearing colored contacts and letting Nadie gum long-lasting glue between her smallest toes on each foot to change her gait.

She called herself Missioncreep, a name assigned by Nadie. She did chores around the factory, took long walks in the blighted woods, taking care to scrub her hands and shoes when she returned, again before eating or touching her mucous membranes. She read books, walkaway classics, Bakunin and Illich and Luxemburg, old dead anarchists. She'd read *Homage to Catalonia* and felt she finally understood Orwell—the seeds of *Nineteen Eighty-Four* were in the betrayals and the manipulation. Just as she warmed to old George, she remembered with a bolt that he had sent a list of names of his friends and comrades to a secret policewoman he'd fallen in love with, betraying them. She realized she didn't understand Orwell at all.

Being a walkaway was supposedly about refusing to kid yourself about your special snowflakeness, recognizing even though different people could do different things, that all people were *worthy* and no one was worth more than any other. Everyone else was a person with the same infinite life inside them you had.

In the isolation of the squatted factory—which turned out hundreds of pieces of furniture every day, free for anyone—she experienced people as obstacles. She waited until the commissary was likely to be empty before descending from her aerie to grab furtive meals, avoiding eye contact, making the least conversation without being hostile. It was the worst walkaway behavior, treating communal resources like a homeless shelter, not being a part of the world. She'd seen people advised to leave the B&B for less. But Nadie must have spun some yarn about her traumatic past, because people looked on with sympathy and never called out her behavior.

Reading alone, playing the stupid telepathy game where she pretended that she knew what people thought just because she read words that supposedly bridged the thoughts of one person to the mind of another, she was overcome by a feeling she had traded the indefinite detention of her father's panic-room for an enforced, fugitive isolation.

She went through that feeling, came out the other side: numb acceptance that this was life. Living as Missioncreep, speaking to no one, making as little mark on the world as possible. Nadie was her role model; the merc and her bizarre vigilance that demanded you be both attentive and absent. The more she practiced, the more natural it felt, except for panicky flashes when she wondered if she was losing herself in this persona. Those were so unpleasant that she was glad when they receded and were walled away behind the sentry's wooden façade.

Now, sitting there, rarely seen morning sun on her skin, looking at Nadie's shit-eating grin. She struggled to come to grips with this new reality.

She guzzled her champagne, a flavor she'd never liked, liked even less with the taste of walkaway country on her tongue: public toothpaste formula and gummy, scummy of morning breath. But as bubbles and sweet, cold tartness washed her tongue and a burp forced its way out her nose with a burning, $CO_2$ tingle, reality sharpened. She recalled, in fast shuffle, the times she'd drunk ostentatiously proffered champagne at family events, then the taste of corn-mash white lightning she and Seth and Hubert, Etcetera sipped as they slipped away from her father's house, the beers and vodkas they'd made at the B&B, and then—

"I'm free?"

"Darling, you are free as anyone can be in this world."

Missioncreep—no, *Iceweasel*—realized Nadie was drunk, had been drinking something else while she went to whatever hidey-hole she'd kept the champagne in. She had never seen Nadie in this state. She was almost . . . sloppy. Not to say she didn't exude the air of sudden death, but it was a jovial, even sexy kind of sudden death.

"Congratulations." She set down her champagne and scrubbed her eyes, the scratchy contacts' familiar itch suddenly vivid. She impulsively plucked them out and rolled them like boogers and flicked them away, blinking tears from her eyes until her vision cleared. The contacts were supposed to be optically neutral, but there was an unmistakable difference. She looked at her funny, dark brown skin, the blotches in the creases of her palms and the crook of her elbow. She, too, was smiling.

"So, does this mean I can use the net again? I can call my friends?"

"You can *join* your friends, chickie—I even know where you can find them."

"I don't know what to say, I mean—"

"Fucking *wonderful*! Birthday and Christmas and your Bat-Mitzvah, rolled into one!" She slugged another long draught of champagne, passed the bottle.

Iceweasel looked around her cell-like room, her meager things, the normcore clothing Nadie brought, generic interface surfaces that she'd avoided personalizing lest she inadvertently create a fingerprintable element. Their local storage held the books she'd read, but she could replace those easily enough. She wanted to walk away from all of it. Even when she realized their encrypted storage contained the notes she'd made during the long solitude, she didn't give a shit. Those were Missioncreep's notes, made by a stranger receding in her rearview.

She drank from the bottle. Champagne didn't taste sweet and sickly this time. It tasted *wonderful*. This must be what other people felt when they drank champagne—power and freedom, the sense of being beholden to none save those of your choosing. That was why it tasted bad before—it symbolized her captivity to Redwaterness. Now it was the opposite. She'd probably never taste it again, she *hoped* she'd never taste it again. She guzzled more, let it run sticky over her chin and down her throat.

Nadie sat on the end of her bed, small white teeth, square face, ice-blue eyes, the cords of her neck and the sinews of her muscled arms standing out, cheeks flushed, wildness in her eyes. On impulse, Iceweasel reached out and

Nadie took her hand. Her palm was hard with callous, strong as teak. Iceweasel felt her pulse throb. She thought of Gretyl. Thinking of Gretyl should make her want to go, to resist the impulse that had hold of her, but thinking of Gretyl made her want to—

She leaned in. Nadie leaned in, too, her hand tightening on Iceweasel's almost to the point of pain. Iceweasel knew Nadie chose to take her to the point between pain and pleasure. She was the mistress of that point and could land on it like a commando pilot setting down a bird on an aircraft carrier, kissing it with control that made it look easy.

When they kissed, those small, square teeth nipped at her lips. She groaned before realizing she was making any sound. A dam inside her broke, pent-up emotion of the months in one kind of captivity or another, times she'd missed Gretyl with a longing that blotted out rational thought. She squeezed Nadie's hand, heedless of how hard, feeling Nadie was indestructible.

Nadie's free arm went around her. She was crushed to the woman. She realized that for all of Nadie's strength, there wasn't much to her—she was tiny. The body pressing to hers couldn't have been more different from Gretyl's. Her feelings for Nadie and Gretyl were polar opposites. No matter that Nadie had terrorized her, hurt her, kidnapped her—she had rescued her. She was there, so *alive,* in the way that no person had been for her for a long time.

She wrestled her hand free and reached for Nadie's ass, compact as a tennis ball, slid her hand down the waistband of her leggings, feeling skin/skin contact whose feeling she'd worked so hard to forget. Her mouth flooded with saliva. Her fingers curled, found the matted, wet hair, slippery folds, her fingertips slipping inside. Nadie's teeth nipped harder at her lip, making her pull back. Nadie followed, not letting her go. It hurt. It felt good. She panted.

Nadie sprang away and tore off her clothes in a series of economical motions. She was an anatomical drawing—the body Iceweasel had glimpsed in the taxi, with its strange rivers and arroyos of scar tissue stretched over lean muscle. Panting, reaching for her, some part of Iceweasel's brain noticed she had a slightly crooked left forearm, an old break that hadn't healed right.

Nadie dodged her grasp, settled on her haunches, staring frankly with cool, glittering eyes. She reached for the champagne and took another slug. She cocked her head expectantly. Iceweasel understood, skinned out of her clothes. Gooseflesh as she bared herself to that gaze. She reached again, and Nadie shook her head minutely and dodged back, continuing to stare.

Nadie's eyes roamed over her body. Iceweasel's breath came in short pants. She could feel the gaze. Nadie could tear her to pieces, force her to submit. Every nerve and hair follicle came to electric, tingling life. Nadie's eyes narrowed. She smiled lazily, traced one of her own nipples, large and pale pink, with a calloused fingertip. The sound of skin on skin was loud, the only other sound Iceweasel's breath. She reached for her own breast, touched it as Nadie was touching hers.

It didn't feel like her own finger. It felt like Nadie's. Matching her movement for movement, it was as though her nervous system lost track of its own boundaries.

Nadie nodded and licked a fingertip, brought it back to her nipple. Mesmerized, Iceweasel did the same. The feeling of being touched by a stranger wasn't so strong, but as she fell into Nadie's cool eyes, it grew. When, in her peripheral vision, she saw Nadie's finger slide lower and followed suit, she gasped. She hadn't masturbated in months, not since she'd been taken, not for some time before. That part of her switched off when she was kidnapped, but it had waited and it saw its chance. Their hands moved faster, blurring, soft wet sounds and breathing growing in pitch. When she arched her back and gasped, Nadie dived across the bed and bore her to her back, burying her face between her legs, tongue flickering quickly and remorselessly, hands on her hips refusing to give as she bucked. She buried her fingers in Nadie's short hair, shouted words without meaning, rode it, not caring who heard, not caring what Nadie felt, burning away self-consciousness in a moment that went on and on.

When she was done, she gingerly released Nadie, felt her tongue on the inside of her thighs, felt the juices and saliva cooling under her ass. Nadie ascended like a serpent, all muscle and sinew. She smelled and tasted herself on Nadie's face as her thigh slid between Nadie's legs and Nadie pressed it, all that strength coiled atop her. Iceweasel was light-headed from hyperventilation, champagne and bone-shattering orgasm, but she was still full of animal horniness. She rolled Nadie, aware that Nadie allowed herself to be rolled, but knowing this was what Nadie wanted, as she grabbed the woman's wrists and pressed them over her head, burying her face in the tuft in her armpit before nipping at her breast, biting harder, listening carefully to the answering gasps, straining to hold the wrists. Nadie pushed against her and she reared up and pushed back and looked into Nadie's eyes. They were unfocused, her breath in sharp pants.

"Do you want this?" she whispered. Her hand drifted lower. Continuous consent was a walkaway thing. She was used to asking this question and having it asked of her, but it was exotic for Nadie. Nadie's eyes focused on hers for a moment, and she bit her lip and whimpered. "Yes."

On impulse, Iceweasel said, "What's that?"

"Yes," Nadie said. "Yes, *please*. Please?"

The submission from this woman, who could kill a hundred ways with her bare hands, electrified the room.

Slowly, teasingly, she moved her hand and went to work. Nadie's hips worked and bucked, and she stopped, pulled away, looked in her eyes. "Do you want this?"

"Please," Nadie said. "Please, please."

More kissing movement. Nadie's hips writhed. She stopped again.

"Do you *want this*?"

"I want it. Please. Yes. Please, Iceweasel, please. Please don't stop."

They locked eyes again. Iceweasel held her gaze, fingers dug into those incredible ass-muscles, and she waited. Nadie chewed her lip and her eyes shone. Her skin shone, sheened with sweat.

"Please, oh please, don't stop. Please?"

Slowly, she lowered her face. This time, she didn't stop, rode the bucking of Nadie's hips, used her whole body to follow as Nadie reared up shuddered, screaming and tearing at the sheets with clawed hands.

When she was done, Iceweasel daintily licked her fingers and flopped beside Nadie, whose chest heaved like a bellows. Her skin was clammy with drying sweat, and Iceweasel flung a leg and an arm across her and nipped at a scar on her collarbone, at the base of her throat.

"Mmmm," Nadie purred. "Very nice. Quite a going-away present. I didn't get you anything."

"You said something about directions to my friends?"

"That's hardly a favor. They're not in good shape, even if they think they are. Your 'default' world gets less stable every day. The existence of walkaways is seen as a prime cause, destabilizing influence beyond all others. Don't imagine just because you can run away once or twice they won't decide to take you all again, someday."

"We can rebuild. Look at Akron."

The new Akron, built on the site of the leveled buildings, refused to be a graveyard. The people who'd flocked to it to rebuild after the army and the mercs and the guardsmen had joined returning locals to build new kinds of buildings, advanced refugee housing straight out of the UNHCR playbook, designed to use energy merrily when the wind blew or the sun shone, to hibernate the rest of the time. The multistory housing interleaved greenhouses and hydroponic market-gardens with homes, capturing human waste for fertilizer and wastewater for irrigation, capturing human $CO_2$ and giving back oxygen. They were practically space colonies, inhabited by some of the poorest people in the world, who adapted and improved systems so many other poor people had improved over the disasters the human race had weathered. The hexayurt suburbs acted as a kind of transition zone between default and the new kind of permanent walkaway settlement, places where people came and went, if they decided that Akron wasn't for them.

Akron wasn't the first city like this—there was Łódź, Capetown, Monrovia. It was the first American city, the first explicitly borne of the crackdown on walkaways. It put the State Department in the awkward position of condemning a settlement that was functionally equivalent to many it had praised elsewhere.

"I hear a lot about Akron. Once is a fluke. It's only months old. It could fall down tomorrow. I was in Łódź when it happened there. Łódź wasn't the first city where it was tried. It failed in Kraków, badly. There were deaths, many. A terrible sickness, fevers in the water, no one could make the dispensaries print the right medicine. You have heard about the successes of these cities, but there are so many failures."

"People walk away because the world doesn't want them. We're a liability. I've heard my father talk about it: the people who want to come to Canada, people who want to have children, people who dream of having their children learn all they need to get by in the world, dream of health care and old age without misery. As far as he's concerned, those people are redundant, except when they represent a chance to win a government contract to feed them as cheaply as possible, or house them in prison camps. Do you know how much money my father makes from his share of the Redwater private prisons? He calls it his gulag wealth fund."

Nadie chuckled and smacked her thigh. "I forgot how funny your old man was. You don't have to worry, little girl, you don't have that blood on your hands."

"It's on yours now."

"I've had real blood on my hands. I can live with metaphorical blood."

"But why? Can't you see it's insane? Why should the world go on when its system doesn't need people anymore? Our system should serve us, not the other way around. Look at walkaways: if you show up in walkaway, there will be things you can do to make room for yourself. Walkaway is based on the idea anyone should be able to pitch in with her work and provide everything she needs to live well, bed and roof and food, and extra for people who can't do so much. In stable walkaway places, the problem is there aren't *enough* humans."

"Congratulations, you've made virtue of inefficiency. Taking more hours to do the same work isn't an ideological triumph."

This was familiar turf for Iceweasel, a discussion that often roiled dinner tables in walkaway.

"You're right, that's fucking ridiculous. If that were the case, we'd be idiots. But it's not. In default, unwanted humans work their *asses* off, scrounging money, scrounging shitty-ass jobs, getting their kids using interface surfaces for whatever learnware they can find and trust. The one thing they're *not* allowed to do is put all those labor hours into growing food for themselves, or building themselves a permanent home, or building community centers. Because the system that organizes the land where the homes and the food and the community center would go has decided that these are better used for other purposes."

"If you tell me about the uselessness of nice restaurants, I may giggle. You should know I have reservations at six of the seven best restaurants in the world next week, and the S.S.T. tickets to get me to them."

"Restaurants are nice. We have places where you can eat nice meals in walkaway. Sometimes, they might ask you to help cook. At B&B, that was a hot job, people fought for it. It would be an honor to let a stranger at the kitchen. Default is organized so that only some people can eat at restaurants, so only some people must work at restaurants. In walkaway, everyone can eat whenever they want, and there's plenty to do as a result—cooking and growing things and clearing things away. New walkaways always struggle to find *enough* to do, worrying they're not keeping busy enough to make up for all the stuff they're consuming. We do more automation than default, not less, and the number of labor-hours needed to keep you fat and happy for a day is a lot less than the inefficient system over in default where you have to scramble just to scrape by."

"That won't be my problem. I'm going to lie around and have grape-peelers feed me. Give me a year, I'll be wearing a toga and a laurel."

"The only zottas I know who live like that are either addicts or broken. Real zottas like my dad work as many hours as any beggar. Being a zotta means worrying you're not zotta *enough*, grafting away to make your pile of gold bigger than those other assholes' piles. I bet my old man hasn't had eight hours of sleep in a row in ten years. If it wasn't for medical technology, that fucker'd be dead of ten heart attacks and twenty strokes."

"No one forces him."

"You know it's true. You worked for zottas. Have you ever met a lazy zotta?"

"Of course."

"Was she a drunk? Or a pill-popper?"

"Well—"

"No one forces you. It's a fucking amazing non-coincidence that everyone with more money than they could spend spends every hour trying to get more. Walkaways, who have nothing, play like no one in default. They play like kids, before anyone knows about schedules, lie around like teenagers who fuck off from school and lie on a roof and bullshit for *hours*. They do things people always think, *If only I was rich. . . .* The irony is, *rich people don't get to do that stuff*."

"I understand irony. You don't need to hammer me."

"With zottas, it's a good idea to explain thoroughly. They're not good at thinking critically about money."

Nadie propped herself on one elbow, their bodies briefly adhering from dried sweat. "What you're saying, it's not news, Ms. Ex-Zotta. I am older. I've spent as many years living with zottas as you. You don't understand: this isn't stable. There isn't going to be default world and walkaway world trading people forever. When you have big rich people, and everyone else poor as poor, the result is . . . *unstable*.

"If there are rich and poor, you need a story to explain why some have so much and so many have little. You need a story that explains this is fair. Last century, the rich made things stable by giving some money back, tax and education and so on. Welfare state. People could *become* rich. Invent something, you could become rich, even if you weren't born rich.

"But those zottas—not zottas yet, actually, just gigas or megas—only let their money be taxed because it was cheaper than paying for private security and official surveillance they needed to keep hold of wealth if the system grew unstable because of the gap between them and everyone."

"Private security like you?"

"Of course like me. What was my job, if not keeping rich people from being pitchforked by poor people? When technology made surveillance cheaper, calculus changed. They could hold onto more money, dispense with pretense that being rich was from doing well, go back to idea of divine right of kings, people born rich because fate favors them. It was more cost-effective to control people who didn't like this idea with technology than giving crumbs to support the fairy tale of rewards for virtue.

"As you say, the very rich want to become richer. Once money is a measure of worthiness, the more money, the more worthy. They say, 'it's a way of keeping score.' Zottas play to win. Like oligarch wars in Russia, rich people notice old school chums have very tempting fortunes and all bets are off."

"Now you're one."

"I'm not. I'm rich, but I'm not zotta. Things are coming to a head, could go any way. There will be blood spilled in months to come. I don't want money to keep score. I want money to buy freedom—freedom to go other places quickly, freedom to buy choice food or pay for medical care. I have survived many things, Iceweasel, even more than your walkaway friends in their hiding places. I plan on surviving this."

"I hope you do." Iceweasel meant it.

"It's mutual." She levered herself up and reached for her panties.

## [iii]

They moved Limpopo around. First, a place she thought of as "the jailhouse," because of the barred door and the intermittent sound of prisoners down the cellblock, thanks to flukes of ventilation. Her cell was big enough for a narrow cot made of springy, metallic strapping that couldn't be separated from the frame, no matter how hard she worked, and a seat-less clear plastic toilet, a sink molded directly into the wall. She got a roll of toilet paper and a packet of soap every third day, and used it to clean her body best as she could. Her papery orange jumpsuit—too fragile to wind into rope—refused to get dirty, even when she smeared it with scop from the edible squeeze-tubes she got three times a day.

The guards who gave her food and toiletries refused to talk. They wore biohazard suits over body armor, goggles and face masks. Once, she was attended by a guard whose visor dripped with mucousy spit. Behind that spit, the guard's face was contorted with rage. He practically threw her food-tube, shit-roll, and soap, slammed the door (it refused to make any noise above the hiss of its airtight seal).

Twice, they took her from the cell and brought her to a room for questioning. She was fitted with sensors for these sessions. They shaved her head, attached electrodes to her bare scalp, more at her wrist, over her heart, her throat. She didn't struggle. Who gave a shit about hair? The important thing was to save her energy for what came next.

The questioner was not in the room, but present as a voice that came from an earbud the guards inserted. She heard the questioner's breathing, like he was a lover whispering in her ear. It reminded her of the spacies' binaural earpieces, but this was to unnerve and disorient her.

"Luiza?"

"If you like."

"Limpopo, then?" The voice was unemotional.

"If you like."

"We'll start with something easy."

"Am I under arrest?"

"I would like your pass-phrase."

She rattled off a string of nonsense characters.

"Now the other one."

She didn't say anything.

"The other one. This is the plausible deniability pass-phrase. It's not hard to tell when you deceive. The infographics give me enormous insight into your mind."

She tried to keep her mind still. The act of stilling her mind would also show on his scans. She wondered what he was measuring, how accurate it was. There were brilliant neuro people in the Walkaway U crowd. They said that everyone knew half of everything they believed to be true about the human mind was bullshit. No one could agree which half.

Time stretched. She wondered if they would hit her, shock her, burn her. They'd killed Jimmy and Etcetera, slashed them across the throat and tossed them into the snow to die.

"I won't tell you."

"All right." Guards unstrapped her, led her back to her cell. Days passed. There was nothing to do except stare at the walls. She had always enjoyed solitude, thought of herself as an imperfect walkaway because the company of others was sometimes oppressive. But when ten days came and went with nothing but her thoughts and her desperate, self-defeating attempts to meditate, they came and got her. Found herself actually *anticipating* the prospect of talking to the voice.

They shaved her head of the short stubble, reapplied gel and sensors.

"Today we make a scan," the voice said. "We will be able to simulate that scan and subject it to questioning under circumstances that transcend and obviate much of this business. Depending on the characteristics of this scan, its reliability and pliability, we may no longer need you at all. Is this clear?"

"What do you want?"

"Your pass-phrase."

"Why?"

"Because we have walked your cohort's social graph, and concluded you are a core node."

"That sounds like a good reason for me to keep my mouth shut."

"We can try to coerce the information out of you. We can even try physical coercion. You know, we can make a scan from people who are no longer technically alive."

It was bullshit. Had to be. CC always maintained it would never work, not without blood flowing through the brain. She didn't understand the biology, but she knew it had to be bullshit. Didn't it?

"That would be quite a trick."

"Once we are inside your data, we will use it to effect internal disruptions of your cell. This will complement our strategy of physical interventions."

"But why?"

"Luiza, don't be ridiculous. You know why."

She refused to get angry, though the extended period of solitude made her jumpy and emotional. "Because you know it's us or you, right?"

"No. Because you and your friends are terrorists. Luiza, be serious. This isn't about jealousy. It's about crime."

"What crime?"

"Luiza."

"What crime?"

"Be serious."

"Squatting?"

"Trespassing. Theft. Theft of trade secrets. Piracy on an unimaginable scale. Circumvention of lawful interception facilities in fabricators. Production of scheduled narcotics. Unlicensed production of potentially lethal pharmaceuticals. Fabrication of military-grade weapons, including mechas and a variety of U.A.V.s. Unlicensed use of electromagnetic spectrum, including uses that can and do disrupt emergency, public safety, and first-responder networks. Need I continue?"

"What do you want from people? What are they supposed to do? There's nothing for us in default. Nowhere to live. Nothing to eat. Nothing to do. We are surplus. We've gone away, started over, not bothering anyone."

"You've taken what isn't yours. You live by taking what isn't yours."

"How else are we supposed to live?"

"What is your pass-phrase?"

"When will you do this scan?"

"It's underway now. This conversation will help to calibrate it."

"Bullshit. I've had scans before."

"The scanning techniques used by walkaways are crude and unreliable. We have better technology. It's an advantage of not being a criminal underground."

"I'd rather be a criminal underground than a secret police."

"We're not police."

"Spooks, then."

"Hardly a meaningful term."

"I would like to speak to a lawyer."

"You are an illegal immigrant, a Brazilian national with an expired passport and no visa. What makes you think you're entitled to legal representation? How would you pay for it?"

"I would like to speak to someone from my consulate."

"The Brazilian embassy has an official policy of cooperating with counter-terrorism efforts."

"Why do you even need my pass-phrase if you're so fucking godlike? Sounds like you have everything you need."

"We have many of the things we need. There may be more inside your network traffic. Besides, we have excellent results from impersonating members of your cult to one another. It's surprisingly effective."

"As is telling me you're doing it, so I spend all my time trying to figure out which people are sock-puppets?"

"You won't need to worry about talking to those people anymore. You have a very good name, so getting even a small number of people to believe you're a traitor will create enormous internal discord."

"What should I call you?"

The breath whispered in her ears. "Michael will do."

"Michael, has it occurred to you that you don't have anything to bargain with? There's nothing you can give me that will make me want to give you my pass-phrase, for all the reasons you've just set out. You and everyone you work with make it your mission to destroy any chance of the human race surviving to the end of this century. So what is it you hope to get from me today?"

"I have many things to bargain with, Luiza. I could offer to spare the lives of your friends. We know where they are—we *always* know where they are. We are capable of being surgical in our strikes against them. You saw how we came for you."

In the hours she was alone with her ghosts in her cell, the one that visited her most was Etcetera. She kept seeing his face, hearing his voice. She'd had dreams where she felt he was cuddled behind her, one arm over her, hand between her breasts, his stubble raspy on her back, breath tickling her skin. Waking was like one of those nightmares-within-a-nightmare, in which you believe you are awake, but are still dreaming. Only she *had* been awake and imprisoned. Never to see Etcetera again. Sometimes she'd tick off his absurd names like a rosary, eyes squeezed shut, trying hard to remember the feelings from her dreams, his smell, the sound, the way he'd held her. The realization he was dead caught her over and over, making her breath catch like a blast of cold air freezing her lungs.

"I saw how you came for me. What you did."

"You're upset about the loss of your boyfriend, the man with the names." He sounded faintly mocking, or maybe she was reading that in. She was distantly angry, the emotion a shooting star barely visible against the blazing light of the sun of her grief. She fancied she could hear them calibrating their model of her, placing a high value on such an exotic emotional state.

"You're changing the subject. When you murder as you did, you do not make the case for helping you. When you take away my dearest love, you show me you shouldn't be trusted. When you bargain with me, strapped into your chair, you make me think you're lying about your ability to run me as a sim. The only reason I can imagine for you to have this conversation with me is because I have something you need, and you can't get it any other way."

There was no reply to that.

After several minutes, she said, "Hello?"

No answer came. Time passed. Being confined to her tiny cell had been awful, but at least she could move her limbs, shift her posture. Go to the toilet. Strapped in like this—

She stifled her rising panic. If they wanted to demonstrate their superiority, they might terrorize her by leaving her like this. Feeling terror would only demonstrate the viability of the tactic. She might be incarcerated by these people for a long time, and they were doubtlessly building a dossier of effective techniques for securing her compliance.

She waited as long as she could. "I have to pee." There was a guard in the room: visor, mask, earpiece. His body language told her he was looking at something she couldn't see, hearing something she couldn't hear. Maybe he was watching T.V., or a countdown-timer that ticked down the seconds until this part of the experiment was done. She could tell he'd heard her.

"Please."

He pretended he hadn't heard her. "Michael, if you make me piss myself, you won't do anything to convince me that you're a humane, reasonable person I want to cooperate with."

She clamped down on her bladder and thought about other things: hard coding problems she'd returned to again and again when she had a moment, trying to get things that should have worked to work; Jimmy's story (carefully skirting his death), the fight she and Jimmy conducted at the original B&B. She envisioned the steps she'd taken to help recondition the Thetford bicycle fleet, a huge cohort of printed carbon-fiber mountain bikes that were bent, broken, and smashed by the previous warm season's worth of off-roading, which she and Etcetera and others systematically reconditioned, creating a factory line to strip, evaluate, reassemble, and test each piece, brainstorming solutions to the perverse mechanical problems of stubborn physical matter.

She really needed to pee. She wondered if they'd given her a diuretic in her last squeeze-tube. It'd be a way to ensure this situation arose. Maybe they wanted to calibrate their model with an image of what happened when she was humiliated.

"I don't have to clean it up."

The guard didn't acknowledge her.

She held it for two more minutes, by her slow count, then let go. She grabbed her mood with iron pincers and refused to let it veer into humiliation because it was *just piss*. They won if she let this enrage her. That was far worse than the cold, stinking piss that stuck the paperish coveralls to her legs.

She didn't say anything after that. She focused on those bicycles, the delight of suddenly realizing the solution to a puzzle that stymied them all, pulling the troublesome bike out of the pile, having it *work*. Etcetera came up with gnarly ways to get mangled parts free, adjusting gearing mechanisms that seemed unadjustable.

Her breathing slowed. It occurred to her she was almost dozing as she contemplated these memories. She might spend the rest of her life with these memories, polishing them like a widow polishing framed wedding photos. So be it. She could still walk away, in her mind. Fuck them.

Then she wondered if this was another part of the calibration, and had to clamp down to keep from crying.

Try as she might, she couldn't find that place of memory again. Eventually they brought her back to her cell.

The next day, they put her in leg irons, bagged her head, and brought her into a vehicle that jounced and jostled for an unguessable time. She was brought into what was unmistakably a bus that stank of unwashed humans and sounded like a bad day on a mental ward. She was belted into a seat, her hands attached to restraints at her sides. There was a person next to her, also seated. When the guards who'd brought her in went away, she said hello.

"Hello." It was a woman's voice.

"Can you see?"

"You mean, do I have a bag on my head? Naw. Why do you?"

She shrugged.

"Where are we?"

"Kingston," the voice said.

"Ontario?"

"Not Jamaica." A snort of laughter. Limpopo got the sense others listened in on their conversations, a localized stillness of eavesdroppers.

"Where does this bus go?"

"You're shitting me."

"I'm not. It's— They killed my friends, took me in, held me. Bagged me and brought me here. Now I don't know where I'm going."

"Prison. Kingston Prison for Women."

"Oh. I guess that makes sense."

"If you say so."

Limpopo had been away from real human contact for so long she caught herself warming to this stranger, who could be an undercover interrogator, or even just not a nice person.

"What's your name?"

"Jaclynn," the woman said. "What's the G stand for?"

"G?"

"Your transfer paperwork. It's stuck to your chest. Says you're G. Denton."

She shrugged. She should have known she wouldn't be committed to the system as Luiza Gil, let alone Limpopo. As toothless as the Brazilian consul was, as distant and hunted as walkaways were, for so long as she had her name, she could be found. She wasn't to be found until they were ready to put her on display, if that day ever came.

"G? To be honest, I have no idea." She thought of Kipling's "great grey-green, greasy Limpopo."

"Amnesia, huh?"

"Not exactly."

"You're a real mystery, you know? Bag on your face, no name."

"I have a name. I just don't know what name they're sending me up under."

"What name were you tried under?"

"No trial. Just snatched. Political. I'm walkaway."

"One of those? Figures. Seem to run into plenty of you-all whenever I'm enjoying the hospitality. Hey! Any walkaways on the bus?"

Voices raised in reply. Catcalls and groans, too. Under her hood, Limpopo grinned. She wondered what "G" stood for.

# 6

# the next days of a better nation

## [i]

The weirdest thing about getting old was not sleeping. Tam routinely found herself awake at hours that she hadn't seen since she was a teenager. Weird hours when you could spot unsuspected urban wildlife: foraging raccoons, stealthy foxes, bats. Seth, that asshole, didn't suffer from this problem. Slept like a rock. A *bald* rock, didn't have the decency to admit being self-conscious about his receding hairline ("what do you call one hundred rabbits running backwards?" he'd say whenever she raised the subject). She'd had a freak when her hair started going, did several consultations with walkaway docs around the world, found one in Thailand who specialized in trans people, got a file for printable pills she took every day. They did the trick.

The weirdest thing about sleeplessness was the friendships she'd kindled with people awake and chattering in exotic timezones. The second weirdest thing about growing old was being *with Seth*. She'd always been saddened by old couples who never spoke to one another. Those long silences felt desperate. She'd promised herself she'd never end up like that, decades of aging, falling apart in the company of a silent, farting lump of a man, racing to see who reached the grave first.

But as an actual old lady with gray hair and wrinkles, she understood the silences. She didn't have to talk to Seth about most things, because she had him modeled so well in her mind, she knew what he would say to practically anything she might say to him—and vice versa. They could sit together, not speaking. The silence wasn't distance, it was closeness. She'd catch him looking and grinning sometimes. She'd grin back. Those grins might be charged with more sexual innuendo than the horniest moment of her entire—admittedly confused—teen years.

The third weirdest thing was Seth himself, who—for all he could sleep like he was in the world championships—didn't feel *old*. She'd come on him once, sitting on the bedside, staring at his bare legs, bare lap, the gray, wiry hair, the veins, the sagging, wrinkled skin. She'd realized with a start he was practically in tears, which was not like the Seth she modeled so well in her own mind.

"What is it?"

"This isn't me. I'm a young man. When I see myself in the mirror, I double-take. This isn't how I see myself."

"Is this about your hair? Because I could introduce you to Dr. Wibulpol-prasert—"

"It's not the fucking *hair*. I don't give a shit about my hair—it's *this*." He slapped his thigh viciously.

"Easy." She smoothed his hand.

"You don't understand, it's like there's a different person looking out of the mirror at me—"

"Seth?"

"What?"

She looked at him for a long moment. Saw realization slowly dawn.

"Oh. You understand."

"I understand." She lowered him gently to the bed, held him until, god-damn him, he fell asleep.

Now it was 3:15 in the morning. He was asleep again. She caught him mid-freak more than ever. She worried. She knew what it was not to recognize the person in the mirror. She understood the nagging sense of *wrongness*. Part of her wanted to go upside his head and tell him to grow up, if he wanted to feel dysphoria, he should try being born trans, try a whole world telling him that he was something he wasn't.

She knew it was pointless. Pain was pain. He *was* being told by everyone around him, in ways subtle and gross, he wasn't the young man he felt like. Worst of all, she knew, was his body stubbornly insisting on being an old man's body.

She'd felt traces of whatever Seth was going through. They'd passed. She'd been through this when she was younger. She could handle it with grace. She could work through it with better thoughts and changes to her hormone regimes. She wasn't in denial like Seth. Seth *had* been very boyish looking until, suddenly, he wasn't.

She padded the hall, ear cocked for other people moving around the house, tugging her robe shut. The hall lights were muted and the skylight revealed a cloudless night tinged with city lights, not so many to drown out the swollen moon, the spray of stars. There were walkaways up there, some old farts from the Thetford days. She chatted them sometimes, though high latency made it more novelty than social occasion.

No one was up. The lights dialed up when she drifted into the kitchen, brighter over the prep-surfaces, dimmer over tables, the house guessing she wanted to prep something before sitting, nudging her. There were pink glows in places where there was work to do—some cooling leftovers needed to go into the fridges, a few out-of-place pans set upside-down to dry on the big prep-surface and forgotten. The house knew who'd forgotten them. If they wanted, they could have live leaderboards of "chore heroes" and "mess miscreants" splashed on surfaces around the place. Some houses put them on bathroom mirrors. You'd confront the stark reality of the division of labor while you were swishing your morning tooth-juice.

Tam and Seth were B&B people. Limpopo people. People who'd been touched by Limpopo refused to turn on leaderboards. The reason to clean up after yourself was you respected your housemates and wanted a place where anyone could walk up to anything and use it, without having to put away someone else's shit first. When spots were consistently under-maintained, the solution was to figure out why it was hard to get that spot reset, not figure out how to shame people who weren't doing something that inevitably turned out to be more of a pain in the ass than it had any right to be.

The other houses swore by their "reputation economies." Limpopo-descended households were the ones where the good designs for living that worked well and failed well came from. They had the nicest house spirits, literally and figuratively. In a Limpopo house, the fact that you were pissed off at your housemates signaled a design opportunity.

She put away the pans and stuck the leftovers in the fridge. Contemplated the imposing wall of sealed tubs of food and ingredients.

"I'm snackish."

The house knew what that meant. The lazy-Susan shelves spun, presenting her with three options: ginger and honeycomb ice cream with so much ginger it could blow your head off, which she loved more than was decent; jerk goat and lentils; weird freeze-dried almond cakes that were doped with chili and cardamom so fiendishly addictive that they'd made the collective decision to remove their files from the house repo. Eventually temptation always won out and someone mirror-pulled the latest version. The recipe kept getting *better.*

"Like you even had to ask." She picked up the almond cookies, squeezing the rim to pop the seal and smelling the mouthwatering almond smell as she crossed through the archway, around the carp pool that bubbled softly in the cooler, wetter air, into the small lounge.

She flumfed on a pile of cushions and picked out a single cake and bit, savoring the crunch, the sweetness and fire that spread through her mouth. She whimpered at the deliciousness. She knew she'd finish the whole batch.

She fired her finger at the far wall. It screened, showed her favorite hangouts, queued messages for her, news items from feeds judged likely to please. A few higher-priority reminders from people she liked and trusted bounced to let her know they were waiting. She crunched a second cake. God*damn* they were good.

"Who's awake?" She repeated herself because the house misapprehended her through her mouthful of food. The screened wall showed faces, avs and handles, highlights from rooms where stuff was happening, pulsing things closer and further as conversations waxed and waned. She had the contradictory feeling of wanting to talk to someone but not wanting to talk to anyone, a stuck-in-a-rut 3:00 A.M. feeling.

She flumfed again, waved away the screen. There were books, movies, but that 3:00 A.M. wanting-something-but-nothing feeling went for those. She was nostalgic for the excitement of near-death.

"How do you deal with it?"

"You mean me?" Limpopo's voice hadn't aged, though there were algorithms for making the voice age as the years went by.

"Who do you think? The house?"

"I just deal. I've got bumpers. When I get to the edge, they knock me back."

"Do you ever turn yourself off? Go into watch-cursor mode?"

"Haven't been tempted. I think it's the trauma of my wakeup, all those years—"

It took fourteen years before anyone figured out how to stabilize Limpopo's sim. That reflected the long gap between World War Default and the Walkaway Decade, which was a dumb name everyone hated, but at least it had a built-in expiry date. It was also Limpopo's idiosyncrasies, her weird neuroanatomy. That weirdness was practically normal. When they'd succeeded in bringing up Dis and then, briefly, CC, there was going to be a set of categories you could sort imaged human brains into, like blood types, and each used different sim parameters.

Scans were more like fingerprints than blood types, each with distinctive and uncooperative wrinkles (literally and figuratively). Stabilization of sims was resistant to overarching systematization, pigheadedly insisting on remaining art, not science.

Between chaos and the intractability of human brains, Limpopo lay dormant for a long time. When she woke, she immediately grasped the situation. It helped that Etcetera was there. For a time the two had been fast friends. They'd even conducted a famous set of discussions on the years Limpopo had missed, all-important years of chaos when no one had been sure what was going on, posting an hour of voice every day, then running on huge clusters that let them absorb millions of replies to their discussion and integrate it into the next day's debate. The Limpopo/Etcetera Talks were as famous in their own way as the Feynman Lectures.

Neither ever publicly explained their falling out—nor had either told Tam what it was about (not that she'd asked, though she'd burned with curiosity). They'd kept it secret as long as possible—it wasn't like house spirits went out to dinner together—but eventually someone produced a signed email from Limpopo to Etcetera in which she told him to go fuck himself forever. That was it, instant viral gossip evil that went around the world.

The gossip lasted longer than most scandals, because of the questions it raised about sims. If Limpopo and Etcetera had been soul mates when made of meat, how could an accurate simulation get to a point where they hated each other and never wanted to speak again?

Tam wished there was a graceful way to raise it with Limpopo, explain she thought it was bullshit, most relationships came to an end, the fact that two people fell out of love could be cited as proof the sim was faithful as much as proof it was inaccurate. People grew and changed. A true sim was true to its originator, and what kind of freak wouldn't be changed by waking up inside a computer?

"A lot of years," is what she said.

"Not aging gracefully, is he? It's ironic that he looked so young for so long; it let him pretend that he was immune."

"None of us can be exactly the person we want to be. I'm not delighted about my hips, don't like that I've lost my night-vision—"

"Sometimes, it's something you can get used to, sometimes it's not. *You* know there are some kinds of body-mind mismatch that people just can't—"

She sighed. "How do you cope?"

"Being a head in a jar? Bumpers. While I never go into suspension, I sometimes dial myself way slow, let myself dream. It wouldn't be the worst thing to switch off for another decade. It was refreshing to get that time-lapse view. Imagine if I suspended and left instructions not to wake me for a century."

"Sounds awful."

"Think it through. Pretty much everyone you loved would be around, in some form. The world would be an amazing new place, jetpacks and shit—"

"Maybe gone back to default. There's plenty of walled cities, the Harrier-jet-and-mountaintop set. They spent a hell of a long time on top, who's to say they won't get there again?"

"That's what you lazy assholes are for, fighting that shit. Wake me when it's over. I like the sound of that."

"They're right, you're not Limpopo, she'd never have wanted to sit out the action."

There was a longer pause than was comfortable. Tam worried she'd offended Limpopo. She was about to apologize, then—

"No, there was action the old Limpopo would have wanted to sit out. No one is pure. You guys give me so much sainthood for never wanting leader-boards, never letting anyone keep track of the fact that I was doing all that heavy lifting—but it wasn't because I didn't crave the brownie points. It was *precisely* because I was jonesing for recognition that I refused it. Every day was a struggle to squash the part of me that wanted to be seated on a golden throne and carried around the town square."

"Everyone craves recognition, Limpopo. Look at the kids—" There were eleven kids in the house, from six mothers: two dribble-factories that had only just started sleeping through the night, then a smooth bell curve that tapered off at twelve or thirteen (she could never keep track, they had the contradictory property of being impossibly young and always much older than she remembered). "They're always wanting credit for their work."

"They also want to monopolize their parents' attention, are clutter-blind, and the small ones are incontinent. There are many virtues to the state of childhood, but just because children do something, it doesn't follow we should aspire to it."

"You've had this discussion before."

"There've been kids around as long as there've been walkaways. There were always parents who found the risk of taking their kids out of default was less than the risk of leaving them in. The 'accountability' stuff in schools accelerated it—once they started paying teachers based on test scores, parents saw their kids getting crammed relentlessly by the system, no room for helping them with their problems or passions. Then they threatened parents with *jail* for not sending their kids to school—"

"They didn't really do that!"

"Tam, I know you never paid attention to parenting and children, but this can't have escaped your notice. It was a huge scandal, even by the standards of the day. A bridge too far for lots of parents. There were some big lawsuits. Ever hear of the Augurs?"

"Rings a bell, ish?"

"Both parents raised by residential school survivors, saw that their daughter was miserable, decided to take her out for homeschooling, wanted to get her in touch with her First Nations heritage, but refused to buy official homeschooling materials or pay for homeschooling standardized tests. They put 'em in jail."

"I sort of remember."

"It was huge. The number of parents who walked away—it was when we got the first nursery at B&B, had to adapt refugee-ware from the third Arab Spring, get all the fabbers doing toy-safety checks and mounting changing tables all over the place."

"Before my time. I was at the university then."

"Right."

"There were kids there, but not in my group. The LGBT crowd, I guess it was kinda toxic to people who wanted kids, that bullshit about 'breeders' that seems funny when you're a kid but is shitty in hindsight. Imagine how Gretyl and Iceweasel would have felt if they'd had to hear us talking that way."

Iceweasel had delivered two kids, both boys, without much drama, though Gretyl was a bundle of nerves through both labors and had to leave the room, both times. The boys were, what, six and eight? Five and eight? She was a shitty honorary aunt, though she loved both of them in an abstract, cautious way that kept its distance from their penumbra of boogers, spit, and destruction.

"It's Stan's birthday next week."

"How do you do that?"

"What?"

"Keep track of everyone's birthday?"

"I'm the house spirit. Comes with the job. Setting reminders, triggering them when any subject comes up, adding context around the corner. Everyone's house does it."

"But you're not a bunch of code, you're a person. It's different when you're conversing with someone and that person just happens to recall, perfectly, all the minutiae context brings up."

"You could have that. Just get your eyes done." She was almost totally night-blind now, had to magnify text to extra-huge to read it. Lots of people had the surgery, got displays implanted at the same time, all the tickers and augmented reality bullshit the goggleheads lived for, without the goggles. She hadn't yet, because the tech got better fast. If she was going to let a laser-cutter near her eyeballs, she wanted to make sure it was for the first and last time and not have to go back next year for a crucial upgrade. She was holding off until her vision was unbearable. "For the record, 'not code, a person' is a philosophical point we could run for hours, though I'm tired of it."

"Not my thing, either." Though it was something she often thought about. "Talking to you isn't like talking to someone who's getting dribs fed to a HUD by some dumb algorithm. With you, it feels natural."

"If there's one thing I'm not, it's natural, but thank you."

She yawned, checked the time. "Four a.m. Shit. Well, the sleepies are finally arriving, I should get my head down and make them welcome."

"You gotcha. Love you, Tam."

"Love you, too." She meant it, knew Limpopo meant it. She'd loved and been loved in every walkaway place, but this was the first house that loved her.

She snuggled up to Seth and put her arms around his paunch, kissed his back where the sparse gray hairs tickled her nose. Her hips ached. She closed her eyes, found her sleep.

She roused a bit when Seth got up a few hours later. She half-parsed the sounds of him putting on slippers and jim-jams and getting a hint about the closest free toilet, felt him come back in, sit on the bed, looking at her. She smiled a little. He murmured, "It's okay, you sleep," and squeezed her hand, leaned over slowly, and with a grunt, and kissed her on the forehead, then on the lips, stubble rasping her skin.

He rubbed her back and she groaned appreciatively, just for the joy of human contact on a drowsy morning.

"Gonna get breakfast," he murmured. She turned her head and kissed his fingers.

"Kay."

"Another bad night, huh?"

"Just sleepless. Not bad."

"Sleep in. Doesn't matter when you sleep."

"Right." She pulled the covers over her head.

Stories helped lull her to sleep. She cracked one eye, wiped a surface onto the headboard, and tapped a recording of an old Terry Pratchett novel, the one about the founding of the Discworld newspaper. She'd listened to it a thousand times and could listen to it a thousand times more, and let the reader carry her sleepwards.

She drifted on words and buttery sun that leaked around the edges of the windows' polarization film, sometimes waking herself a little with her own soft snores, and then—

"Tam?"

She sat bolt upright. Seth's voice did not often reach that panicked level. She was wide awake, looking at him, standing in their doorway, breathing hard, eyes wide, sparse hair sticking out at mad-professor angles. He held a forgotten piece of toast.

"Jesus, what is it?"

"Limpopo is on the phone."

She blinked, confused.

"Seth?"

"The *real* Limpopo. Sorry, the *living* Limpopo. She's alive, is what I'm saying. She's alive. She's on the phone."

She brought her hands to her cheeks, a silly way to register surprise, but there you had it.

"Limpopo is alive?"

"She's talking to Limpopo." He noticed the toast in his hand, stared at it, put it down. She took it away and bit it. It was slathered in butter, brewer's yeast, and tabasco—Seth's Platonic ideal breakfast.

"Jesus." She found her robe on the floor, put on slippers, finished Seth's toast. "Come on."

The biggest common room had five others in it already, looking stunned and excited, silently listening.

"They never let you write to anyone?" That was Limpopo's voice—*their* Limpopo. The house spirit.

"Never. I wasn't the only one. There are—there were?—a bunch of us in policy-segregation, no visitors, no messaging anyone outside. Held under other names." That voice was Limpopo, too, but older, an old lady's voice, the voice of a Limpopo that had lived—where?—for more than a decade.

"But now—"

"Now the inmates run the asylum." She sounded giddy. "There were three days when it was really bad. Almost no guards showed up. The ones that did were too scared to do anything except huddle in their control rooms and bark at us over the speakers. Not even that on the third day.

"At midnight yesterday, click-clunk, all the doors opened. No guards. No admin staff. Nothing. Everyone was starving, of course. We found our way to the caf, once we figured out what was going on. Some of us ad-hocced a kitchen committee, got the fabbers running and fed everyone. Then someone called for volunteers to check out the clinics and started seeing to the sick best as they could. Lot of nurses in here and—sorry, I guess that doesn't matter. No one here knows what happened out in default. When they used the comms room to call their lawyers, they said Corrections Canada had some kind of internal coup and no one there was talking to the outside world. They say it's not the first ministry this happened to—apparently Veterans Affairs Canada did this last month? I don't get a lot of high-quality news and analysis in jail—"

Tam started to make sense of what she was saying. She'd been in jail. The jails had ruptured. Ruptured was the word they were using for government institutions that fell apart, turned into walkaway-style co-ops that gave away office supplies and opened up the databases for anyone who wanted a crack. She'd heard of ruptured hospitals, police departments, public housing—but jails were a new one. A big one.

"Limpopo," she said.

Both of them answered, which would have been funny and might be later.

"Sorry, not the house spirit, the living one."

"Who's this?"

"It's Tam."

"Tam? No fucking way! Tam! You're still there? Still with Seth?"

She smiled and squeezed Seth's hand.

"Yes, he's here, too."

"You poor fucker." Everyone knew she was kidding, even Seth.

"I've got him trained. He's gotten old and slow, and I'm mean."

"I don't believe it."

"Where are you, Limpopo? I mean, physically?"

"Near Kingston, north a bit. Past Joycetown. Kingston Prison for Women."

"Are you safe?"

"You mean, are there murderers about to come and kill me? Not that I can see. I'm not worried about that. There are plenty of sketchy people in here, but there are plenty of sketchy people out there. Most of these women are my friends. Some are like sisters."

"Can we come and get you?"

"What do you mean?"

"I mean, can we come and bring you here? Pocahontas is still here, and Gretyl and Iceweasel, and their kids, and Big Wheel, and Little Wheel, and even Kersplebedeb, though she calls herself Noozi now—"

"Hold up a sec. I don't know who half those people are. Shit, I don't even know *where* you people are—"

"Gary."

"I don't know who that is either."

"Gary, Indiana. Nice place. World leaders in bringing back buildings from the dead. Colonized brickwork, smart trusses, big old places that haven't been maintained in fifty, seventy-five years."

"A state that begins and ends with a vowel? You've gotta be kidding me."

"You'd love it here, Limpopo. You're a hero."

"It's true," said Limpopo-the-house-spirit. "You're a saint around here."

The other Limpopo groaned. "You're killing me."

"Sorry, Limpopo," Seth said. "We thought you were dead. Martyrdom was in order."

She groaned again.

"Seriously," Tam said. "Come and see us. Or we'll all come see you. I don't care which. We love you. We've *missed* you."

"Hey!" said house-spirit Limpopo.

"Missed hugging and holding you," Tam said. "And you should meet this other Limpopo, our Limpopo, she's wonderful."

"Don't suck up," said the house spirit. "You're getting mouse turds in your cornflakes for a week, asshole."

The other Limpopo laughed. "She sounds like my kind of person. Literally, I suppose. Fuck, who knew this week could get any weirder."

There was a crash and thunder of feet on the stairs, and Gretyl and Iceweasel burst into the room, preceded by their boys, who were comets of snot and destruction, squabbling over a toy even as they came through the door, the little one pulling the big one's hair. Gretyl fluidly pried his fingers out of the curly mop, hauled him into the air and set him down away from his big brother.

"She's alive?" Iceweasel said, grabbing the bigger one and swinging him around—he laughed and flung his head back.

"We're talking to her now," Tam said. "Limpopo, Iceweasel and Gretyl are here."

"Iceweasel is alive?"

Iceweasel laughed. "I guess we have a lot to catch up on."

The younger boy suddenly looked at her seriously and pushed his hair out of his eyes. "You aren't dead, Mommy."

"I'm not dead. Don't worry, Jacob."

"Mommy?"

"There's two of them," Gretyl said. "Boys. Jacob's seven and Stan is ten. Say hello to Limpopo, boys."

"Limpopo?" Jacob screwed his face up. "The house spirit?"

"No, another Limpopo. She's a long way away and we haven't seen her in a long time. We love her."

Jacob shrugged. Stan rolled his eyes at his younger brother's slow uptake. "Hi, Limpopo! Hi, other Limpopo!"

Far away, Limpopo cursed imaginatively, which made both boys' eyes go wide and put smiles on their faces. Tam could see them storing away the language for future deployment. "Hello, boys. Hello, Gretyl. Hello, Iceweasel. It's good to hear everyone's alive and thriving."

"What's it going to be," Tam said. "Are we coming to you or are you coming to us? Because, darling, we have some catching up to do, and for all we know, default is going to get its shit together and come in there and kill or lock up every last one of you."

"That's a possibility we've considered. There's one more thing—the root auth tokens were left in the control center by a guard, that's what we figure. We have this place pwned from asshole to appetite. Thing about a jail, it's just as good at keeping people out as it is at keeping people in. Anyone who wants to take this place away is going to have a hell of a time."

Tam bit her lip. Everyone looked at everyone. Even the boys were quiet. "Limpopo. We don't want you hurt. We're walkaways. There are plenty of big, dumb institutional buildings you and your friends can occupy."

"*Bullshit.*" She surprised them with her vehemence. "They stole our lives. Locked us up. We earned this place. It's ours. If we walk away, if we fragment, they'll pick us off, one at a time. We're never going to be anyone's captive, never."

"You're going to stay in jail to stop yourself from being a captive?" Seth's mouth, as always, ran ahead of his sense.

"It's no joke. We bought this place with blood, with our lives. It's ours. It was our captivity. Now it's our freedom."

"Limpopo," Iceweasel said, softly. "It's not like that anymore. Default isn't the default. I know what it was like. It looked like war, they were going to lock us away or kill us. It changed. The zottas went to war against each other, fought for control over countries whose people refused to fight for any side, walked away with us, turned refugee living into the standard. It was the people who stayed in one place and claimed some chunk of real estate was no one else's became weirdos. Everyone else hit the road when those people showed."

"Bullshit," Limpopo said. "Maybe in your corner of the world. The state doesn't just wither away. Someone paid those guards' salaries for all those years, kept the slop coming into our fabbers' ingesters. Victory isn't a thing that walkaways will ever have. Walking away isn't victory, it's just not losing."

"We haven't lost," Iceweasel said. "There are enclaves of people who pretend that it's normal and things will go back the way they were or were supposed to be soon. These days, it's not about armed conflict, it's war of norms, which of us is normal and who are the crazy radicals." She paused. "Did you hear about the Iraqi invasion?"

"A new one or one of the old ones?"

"A totally new one. Iran was supposed to be invading Iraq because, shit, that's been going on for a long time. Except this time, it didn't. The pilots they sent into Iraq didn't drop their bombs—they landed on Kurdish airstrips. The infantrymen, soon as they hit the battle lines, they refused to fight. Bunch of officers, too. Everyone's kind of freaked. The Iraqi side gives the order to kill the shit out of these weird-ass invaders. Instead, *those* soldiers refuse, too. The ones that try to fight, their buddies take away their guns. Seriously!"

"That's too weird to be true."

"Only because she didn't tell you the best part," Gretyl said.

"They were all walkaways," Jacob shouted. "Just like us!"

"Way to clobber my punch line, kiddo." Iceweasel swung him onto her hip and kissed the tip of his nose. "It's a legend around here. There's a Gulf-wide walkaway affinity group, running over the same nets everyone else uses to get around their national firewalls, so there's cover. Once the walkaways on both sides figured they were about to be sent to kill each other, they decided, fuck that noise, and made a plan."

"Fuck that noise!" Jacob punched the air. Stan rolled his eyes. Tam was sure he wished he'd seized the opportunity to detonate an f-bomb with impunity. Gretyl and Iceweasel insisted the boys would never learn to swear properly unless they had good role models. So they were enjoined to closely observe swearing, not attempting it until they were sure they had it right. When they tried it, they were subjected to embarrassing judging and coaching on swear-expertise. This was more effective at curbing their language than anything the other parents tried on their kids.

"That's amazing, all right," Limpopo said. "Why didn't the generals drone them all? Stop the rot from spreading?"

"There's a rumor both sides gave the order and the drone operators refused and no one wanted to make an issue out of it. Last thing a general wants is to discover that he's in charge of an army of one, in the middle of an army of everyone else."

"How long ago did this happen?"

"What was it, a year ago?" Iceweasel said.

"Eight months," Tam said.

"Well, shit. That's impressive. We don't get a lot of news in here."

"The point is you don't know what's going to happen, we can't know, but there's reason to be optimistic. People are tired of shooting each other."

Tam chuckled. "I don't know if I'd go that far. There's a—" She fished for the word. "Credibility for walkaways. A sense we've got it figured. Once you realize there's a world that *wants* what you have to give, well, it's hard to convince people to kill each other."

"Fuck my ass," Limpopo said, sending Stan and Jacob into giggles. There was some background noise from her end, a muffled conversation. "I need to think, and there's not a lot of interface stuff here so I've got to give someone else a turn. Sit tight and I'll call tomorrow, okay?"

"Sure," Tam said, and the house spirit echoed her an instant later. Everyone shouted good-bye and Limpopo said good-bye. The room went silent except for the whistling of breath in and out of Jacob's snotty nose.

"You're not going to wait for her to call back, are you?" the house spirit said.

"Are you shitting me? No way," Iceweasel said.

"You want to pack for the kids or should I?" Gretyl said. The boys figured it out a moment later and exchanged excited looks and began to run in circles.

"You do it. I'll look around for berths on a train."

"Check the bumblers." Seth was also bouncing. "Winds are favorable to the northeast lately, I bet we can snag a ride a long way."

"Good thinking," Iceweasel said. "Boys, you want to ride in a zeppelin?"

Both boys babbled and shouted. Then Jacob got so excited he punched Stan, because reasons. They tumbled on the floor, punching and shouting.

Their moms exchanged a look, shook their heads apologetically at the rest of the adults. "We're trying to let them sort these out on their own," Gretyl said. "Sorry."

Everyone else was in too good spirits to be bothered. Tam looked in amazement at her housemates, her extended family, and realized she was about to start walking again.

## [ii]

The train schedules sucked. There was a complex algorithm that figured out how many cars to put on which lines when. It was endlessly wrangled by wonks with different models that weighted priorities differently. Gretyl got sucked into the math, disappearing into a set of accountable-anonymity message boards where this was being hammered out, and Iceweasel messaged Tam to say that she was probably going to be stuck in that rathole for the foreseeable. So Tam should start exploring alternatives.

There were rideshares heading that way, but they'd have to split into subgroups and reform at way stations. This was something that you could automate (Tam helped Iceweasel with a kids' field trip to the Akron Memorial last year and they'd found it easy), but surface vehicles were slow.

"You need to find a bumbler," Seth said.

"Yeah," Tam said. She tapped her interface surfaces, made sure that the house spirit was locked out. "But it's uncomfortable."

"Etcetera is my friend," Seth said. "My oldest buddy. Just because he and Limpopo can't stand each other, doesn't mean we have to take sides. You're not betraying her by being friends with him. If you asked her, she'd tell you."

"If I asked her, I'd put her in a position where she'd have to tell me she didn't mind, even if she did. Which is why I'm not asking her. Friends don't put friends in that position."

"If she knew you were holding off on talking to him because you were worried about upsetting her, she'd be outraged."

"I don't doubt it. That's why I don't tell her."

"Don't you think that's all . . . twisted? Especially since there's the Other Limpopo"—they'd settled on this because, despite its least-worst awkwardness, all of them agreed "Real Limpopo" was a shitty, most-worst solution—"who was in love with Etcetera and would be glad to talk to him again."

She sighed and scrubbed her eyes. She'd been staring at screens for a long time. "It sucks. So what? Lots of things suck. Life isn't improved by being a dick to people who love you."

"Etcetera loves you."

"Fuck off." She let him rub her shoulders. "Argh." He found the knot in her right shoulder, a gnarl of stubborn pain that felt so good-bad when his thumbs dug into it.

"Right there." She lolled her head.

"You're a pushover. I could win every fight by sticking my thumb in this knot."

"It's my kryptonite. Don't abuse your powers."

"I am gonna call Etcetera."

"Fuck you." She snuggled her head against his belly, pushing her sore shoulder knot back into his thumb.

Five minutes later, he called Etcetera.

"Been a while," Etcetera said.

"Fair enough. It's all you-know around here."

"Missed you. Both of you. All of you. It sucks being the pariah."

"Sorry," Seth said. This made him miserable. Freezing out his oldest friend was hard on him, but he'd never complained.

Awkward silence.

"We need your help."

More silence.

"You're going to like this.

"We got a phone call. From a prison. In Canada. From an inmate who'd been held there for more than fourteen years, only just got free because the guards unlocked the cell doors and walked away."

"Seth—" Something in Etcetera's voice, an emotion as unmistakable as it was unintelligible. Some hybrid human-machine feeling. Deeply felt. Unnameable.

"Limpopo," Seth said.

There was the weirdest sound Tam had ever heard. It went on and on. She thought it was laughter. With horror, she realized it was sobbing. The only time she'd heard a sim sob, it was in the tunnels at Walkaway U, before they'd figured out how to make them stable. It was a sound sims made before they collapsed.

"Etcetera? It's okay, buddy."

He cried a long time.

"You going to be okay?" Seth said, during a lull. "I can get Gretyl, she can help with your guardrails—"

"I don't need help. Is she okay?"

He didn't mean Gretyl. "She sounds amazing. Fiery. Angry. Wants a fight."

"I want a fight, too. What do you need?"

"You still have contacts who can get a bumbler?"

"You're going to her?"

"She won't come to us—if they come to lock her back up, she's going to fight."

"Fuckin' a."

"Can you help?"

"I'm coming. Find me a cluster and carry it on. I'm going with."

"You could just phone in," Tam said. She had enough complications.

"Not if they kill the network. I'll leave a backup here. But I'm going with."

"Etcetera," Tam said, in her most reasonable voice.

"I'm going with."

Seth shook his head at her, mouthed *go with it*.

"You're going with," she said.

"Get packed," he said.

## [iii]

The bumbler touched down in the parking lot of an old mall on the west side of town the next day, crewed by a grinning gang of old Brazilians, men with dreads in their thinning hair, women with surefooted rolling walks like sailors. Stan and Jacob were immediately adopted by the crew's kids, whose status was somewhat mysterious—they were from an orphanage in Recife which had run out of funding. The kids ended up in a makeshift camp, which hadn't gone well, and these aerialists took them in and brought them into their enormous, beautiful zeppelins, decorated like the legendary baloeiro balloons that had plied the Brazilian skies for centuries.

However these kids ended up in the sky, they took to it like fish to water. Within minutes, Stan and Jacob were barefoot and climbing rigging, barely shouting good-bye at their mothers, who watched them go with trepidation and pride.

They'd struggled with packing. It had been so long since they'd been voluntary refugees, even longer since they'd been involuntary ones. They'd conferenced their common rooms. Marshaled their minimum carry, using the house spirits to keep track of who was bringing what to cut down on duplication. Spouses, kids, and housemates piled ever-more stuff into the to-be-packed pile. They laughed nervously. They hadn't become *shleppers,* had they?

Seth and Iceweasel shared hilarity and horror. They told the story of Limpopo engineering the divestment of their worldly possessions on their first day in the B&B. Limpopo-the-house-spirit sputtered and objected she'd done no such thing. They'd had a mock fight that was slightly deadly serious. They hawed and horse-traded their way down to a small pack each, plus another bag for the two boys, whose prodigious aptitude for enfilthening even the dirt-sheddingest fabrics was balanced by indifference to their own cleanliness.

"They'll be dirty," Gretyl said. "They'll survive. Good for the immune system."

Once aboard the *Gilbert Gil,* they realized they could have brought ten times as much. The Brazilians had just dumped a load of high-quality plastics polymerized out of a toxic swamp in Florida by smart bacteria. All that was left of the cargo was the smell, not exactly unpleasant. It reminded Iceweasel of the wrapping on the really high-end cosmetics her mother favored.

They bustled around the huge, hangar-sized hold, working with the aerialists to reconfigure it for sleeping quarters, clicking panels into grooves in the floor and fitting roof sections over them to build a village of hexayurts.

Iceweasel was glad they hadn't brought more. There was every chance that they'd do some walking—real walking, *walkaway* walking—on this trip. The boys were going to be trouble enough without a lot to carry. The bumbler had favorable winds to take it all the way to Niagara Falls or even Toronto. But they were called "bumblers" for a reason. If Old Man Climate Change handed them one of his quotidian thousand-year-storms, they'd have to find other arrangements.

Gretyl went for bedrolls, using the *Gil*'s house spirit to tell her where everything was stashed. The house spirits were descended from wares that powered the B&B, a mix of quartermaster, scorekeeper, and confessor, designed to help everyone know everything as needed. She'd been so taken with the B&B's paleolithic version of this stuff. Now it was everywhere, some of it even powered by the living dead, like Limpopo in Gary. That was too weird, even for her. She could talk with sims, provided that she didn't think about it too hard. But the idea of having one as a haunt who wore your house like its body, that was just *fucked up*.

Etcetera gabbled in machine-Portuguese with the aerialists, who snapped together dining tables for their welcoming feast, with help from Seth and Tam. She'd had an earbud implanted a couple years before, when she'd started to have trouble with her hearing after a bad fever that crossed the country. The bud murmured a translation to her that only sometimes entered the realm of machine-trans garble.

The Brazilians bragged on the *Gil*—its lift and handling characteristics; the strength and resilience of the redundant graphene cells; their prowess as navigators, able to find fair winds where no algorithm predicted. Etcetera gave every sign of being delighted, spoke knowledgeably about the ships that preceded the *Gil*, wonderful things coming out of Thailand, where airships were different in some important, highly technical way she didn't understand.

The kids arrived in time for food, though judging from the food already smudged around their faces they had been introduced to a kitchen fabber somewhere in the ship's deeps. She collected jammy kisses from both, resisted the urge to clean their faces with spit, was introduced to new friends, a range of ages and genders. An older boy named Rui—old enough to have a bit of a mustache, an Adam's apple, and a mix of self-assuredness with kids and awkwardness with adults—told her in accented English how great her boys were and how he would teach them all they needed to be fliers. She thanked him in absolutely awful Portuguese, prompted by the implanted bud. He smiled and blushed and ducked his head in a way that made her want to take him home and raise him.

"You boys ready for lunch?" Gretyl asked, coming up with a fan of plates bearing scop meat-ite skewers that smelled amazing, garnished with feijoada and heaps of hydroponic vegetables. The boys looked guiltily at one another, and Gretyl instantly clocked the sweet, sticky stuff around their mouths.

"Looks like you've already had dessert. Hope that doesn't mean you think you're not going to eat lunch, too." Gretyl was the family disciplinarian. If it was up to Iceweasel, the kids would eat ice cream and candy three meals a day. She'd join them. Gretyl kept them from dying of malnutrition. Her word was law.

The boys nodded and took plates. Rui took in all the salient details of their family arrangements and led the kids to a spot at the table, promising they'd eat every bite.

Gretyl handed Iceweasel one of the remaining plates and they found a spot at a table, surrounded by crew members who joked and made them feel at home.

"This is amazing food," Iceweasel said, chasing the last curly carrot with her forkchops.

"We got new starter cultures from Cuba," a crewwoman explained. She was beautiful, tall, with a shaved head, a wasp waist and wide hips, and skin the color of burnt sugar. Iceweasel and Gretyl had both snuck looks at her when they thought the other wasn't looking, then caught each other. Her name was Camila. Her English was excellent. "You program it with lights during division-cycle, causes it to express different flavor- and texture-profiles."

"It's incredible," Gretyl said.

"We'll give you some to take when you go. The Cubans eat like kings."

There was white pudding for dessert, made with the last of the ship's supply of real coconut and tapioca cultured from Cuban scop. Neither Gretyl or Iceweasel had enough experience of tapioca to say whether it was faithful, but it was just as tasty as lunch and Camila assured them that even a tapioca farmer couldn't tell the difference.

"Do you need any more crew?" Iceweasel said, jokingly. "I want to eat like this every day."

Camila looked grave. "We have no more crew berths, sorry to say." She contemplated the crowded tables. "It's something we're arguing about. It's a good crew, a good ship. Some of us want to bud off a new one, start another crew. We've got something so wonderful, it should grow. Others say there's something in the chemistry of this group, and if we split up, it would go. The children are growing, many of them think they will be aerialists. We'll need more ships."

"Is that why you're heading to Ontario?"

Camila nodded. "The zeppelin bubble was a long time ago, but there's still many comrades there who know how to build and want to help. Your Etcetera has been putting us in touch with others. He's a hero to many, for his valor with the *Better Nation*."

Now Iceweasel and Gretyl looked grave. Neither of them talked about that day often, though it was a rallying cry for walkaways all over the world, eventually. Camila understood.

"What a time to be alive. If we do make another ship, we should call it *The Next Days of a Better Nation*."

"That's a terrible name for a ship," Etcetera said. His voice was tinny and clipped from the acoustic properties of their table, which he used for a speaker.

"No one asked you, dead man," Iceweasel said.

"'Better nation' talk needs to die in a fire. We're not doing nations anymore. We're doing people, doing stuff. Nations mean governments, passports, borders."

Camila rapped on the table with her knuckles. "There's nothing wrong with a border, so long as it isn't too rigid. Our cells hold in the lift gas, they make borders with the atmosphere. My skin is a border for my body, it lets in the good and keeps out the bad. You have your borders, like all sims, which keep you stable and running. We don't need no borders, just good ones."

They were off, arguing intently, a discussion familiar to the aerialist world. It turned into jargon about "airspace priority" and "wind immunity" and "sovereign rights of way," lost on Iceweasel and Gretyl. They bussed their plates into a hopper that slurped them out of their hands, made sure that Rui made good on his promise to get the boys to eat their protein and veg. Lay down in each other's arms in their hexayurt for a nap. It had been a busy couple of days.

Gretyl nuzzled her throat. "No leaving me for hot Brazilian aerialists."

Iceweasel arched her neck. "It's mutual."

They were asleep in minutes.

## [iv]

The zepp took just over a day to reach Toronto, circling to avoid the city's exclusion zone, trailing aggro drones that zoomed up to the portholes to scan them and take pictures. The winds over Lake Ontario sucked. They had to rise and sink and putter and bumble for most of the rest of a day until they caught a breeze that'd take them to Pickering. Everyone agreed that it was the best place for a landing, far from paranoid zottas holed up in Toronto, insistent their nation had plenty of days to go before it was ready to make way for another, better or not.

They touched down amid a crowd: aerialists and onlookers who helped stake down the guy-lines and fix the ramp in place (making "safety third" jokes, but ensuring that it was solid before anyone descended the gangway).

The Limpopo reunion party hit the ramp blinking. Seth staggered under the weight of Etcetera's cluster, which he wore in eleven chunks about his body—wristbands, a backpack, a belt, bandolier-slung bricks, some rings. The aerialists followed, led by the children, Jacob and Stan among them, wearing fresh-printed air-pirate gear, head scarves, and blousy shirts and tights patterned with photo-realistic trompe l'oeil chain mail. They collected hugs and complicated handshakes and kisses from their new friends, and returned them with gusto, speaking more Portuguese than they had any right to have acquired in such a short journey.

The touchdown area was a school's field. The school was a low-slung brick thing, a century old, abandoned for decades and reopened by force majeure, judging from the gay paint job and the banners, the solar skins and windsails on the roof.

Tam squinted at it, remembering her own school, built on the same template but run by a private services company that shut down half the building to save facilities costs, putting steel shutters over the windows and leaving it to glower at the paved-over play areas.

"Nice, huh?" The girl was not more that sixteen, cute as a cute thing, round face and full, purplish lips. Tam thought she might be Vietnamese or Cambodian. She had a bit of acne. Her jet-black, straight hair was chopped into artful mess.

"This your school?"

"It's our everything. Technically, it belongs to a bullshit holding company that bought the town out of bankruptcy. Happened when I was little, we got a special administrator everyone hated, next thing, it's bankruptcy and they were shutting it down, putting up fences. Final straw was when they stopped the water. Town went independent automatically after that. Kids did the school."

"Cool." Tam enjoyed the girl's obvious pride. "You go to classes in there?"

The girl grinned. "Don't believe in 'em. We do peer workshops. I'm a calculus freak of nature, got a group of freaklings I'm turning into my botnet."

Tam nodded. "Never got calculus. That lady over there with the little boy under each arm is a hero of mathematics."

The girl bugged her eyes out. "Duh. No offense. Why do you think I'm here? Chance to meet Gretyl? Shit. Biggest thing to hit this town since forever." She stared intently at Gretyl. "Her proofs are so beautiful."

"Want to meet her?"

The girl crossed her eyes and stuck out her tongue, so perfectly adorable it had to have been practiced at great length. Tam barked a laugh, covered her mouth and, to her hard-bitten horror, *giggled*.

"She'll like you," Tam said.

"She'd better," the girl said, and took her arm.

Gretyl lost her grip on Jacob as they neared and, sensing the tide, released Stan to tear-ass after his little brother and bring him to the ground. Tam waved her down. "Yo," she said.

Gretyl dramatically face-palmed at the kids' retreating backs, then smiled at Tam and the girl.

"Gretyl, this is—"

The girl, who had blushed to the tips of her ears, murmured *Hoa*.

"Hoa. She's a fan. Loves calculus. Came here to meet you."

Gretyl beamed at the girl and threw open her big arms and enfolded her in a hug. "Pleasure to meet you."

The girl's blush was all-encompassing.

"It's nice to meet you, too, Gretyl. I use your calculus slides in my workshops."

"Glad to hear it!"

"I made some improvements." Her voice was a whisper.

"You *did*?" Gretyl roared. The girl shrank and might have run off if Gretyl hadn't caught her hands. "I insist you show them to me, *right now*."

The girl lost her shyness. She shook out a screen and took Gretyl through her changes. "The kids kept getting mixed up when we did derivative applications at the end, because without applications when we did the rest of it, limits and derivatives, it was going in one ear and out the other, just rote. When I started to mix in applications as we went, they were better at putting it together at the end."

Gretyl's jolly-old-lady act slipped away. She brought down her huge eyebrows.

"Aren't applications without theory confusing? Without theory, they can't solve the applications—"

The girl cut her off with a shake of head, crazy hair all over the place. "You just need to be careful which applications you choose. You see . . ." She produced charts showing how she'd assessed examples with each group. Tam could tell Gretyl was loving this. She was also sure the girl was right about everything. She liked this town.

"Ready to go?" Seth said. He'd tightened the straps on the cluster and wore a speaker on a necklace for Etcetera to use. Tam made herself not stare at it—it was tempting to think of that as Etcetera's face. But his visual input came from thirty vantage points.

"Soon." She pointed. "Gretyl's got an admirer."

Etcetera made an impatient noise. "That's great, but we need to hit the road. It's three, four days' walk from here, assuming we don't get bikes or a ride."

"I know. We still have to say good-bye to the *Gil,* hello to these people, and good-bye to *them*. It's called sociability, Etcetera. Accommodate yourself."

Seth snorted. Etcetera was silent, possibly sulking. Tam imagined that he was saying unkind things about the living in his internal monologue. She recalled his on-the-record statements about Limpopo's choice to live as a house spirit. She crossed her eyes and stuck her tongue out, and heard Hoa and Gretyl laugh and turned to see them looking.

She gave them the face, making a Harpo googie of it. Hoa responded with her own, and rubber-faced Gretyl made one that put theirs to shame.

"You win. You two made the world safe for calculus yet?"

"Done." They grinned.

"When do we start?" Tam looked at the boys, now in a relatively zeppelin-free corner of the field with some local kids and some aerialists, kicking a ball around in a game that involved a lot of screaming and tackling and possibly no rules.

"You're covered," Hoa said. "We've got bikes coming out of our assholes here."

"Sounds painful," Seth said. Hoa made her face.

"We're into deconstructed bikes, minimal topologies."

Tam saw Gretyl and Seth nodding. She suppressed her irritation. She tried to understand the attraction of minimal topology, but it just looked . . . unfinished. The drive to reduce overall material volume of mechanical solids had been a project in both default and walkaway for decades, minimizing feedstock use in each part, getting better at modeling the properties of cured feedstock. Familiar things grew more improbably gossamer. Everything was intertwingled tensegrity meshes that cross-braced themselves when stressed, combining strength and suppleness. It was scary enough in bookcase or table form, everything looking like it was about to collapse all the time. When applied to bicycles, the technique nauseated her with fear, as the bike deformed and jiggled through the imperfections in the roads.

"Great," she managed.

Hoa nodded. "We're ahead of everyone else. I did one last month that only weighs ninety grams! Without the wheels. You'd get seven hundred kay out of it before it flumfed."

That was the other thing about minimal topology. It had catastrophic failure modes. A single strut giving way caused a cascade of unraveling chaotic motion that could literally reduce a bike frame to a pile of 3D–printed twigs in thirty seconds. People swore the bike's self-braking mechanisms would bring it to a safe halt before it disintegrated. But if they could model the cataclysmic collapse so well, why couldn't they prevent it?

"Great." She caught Gretyl and Seth playing sarcastic eyeball hockey. She glared at them and Seth gave her a squeeze.

"You'll love it. Worse come to worst, we've got your scan on file, right?"

"It's a hell of an afterlife," Etcetera said. "I'll show you the ropes."

She considered her options—epic grump, sarcasm, capitulation—grinned and said, "Looks like we're riding!" Seth hugged her. She heard Etcetera whisper praises of his choice in romantic partners.

## [v]

They arrayed the bikes in the field, ranged smallest to tallest, and scrounged a trailer the boys could sit in that their half-sized bikes could clip to. There was general hilarity while they tried and swapped helmets, taking group photos. The aerialists, unloaded, looked on, gave advice, and tinkered with the bikes.

They reached a moment when everyone was impatient to go and no one could name a reason not to—everyone's bladder emptied and so on. They formed up and rode. Tam grit her teeth as she started to ride, but it was smooth. The bike had the combination of rigidity and springiness of tensegrity designs, absorbing shocks with ease but still rigid enough for steerability.

Stan and Jacob set the pace for the first eight kilometers, a slow ride. Hoa and her friends kept up, hanging on Gretyl's every word. When Stan and Jacob ran out of steam (red faced, panting) they climbed into the trailer. The rest of the party took the opportunity to pee, drink water, snack, kibitz, trade bikes, and adjust helmets. When they started again, Hoa and friends made their good-byes and turned back.

They pushed themselves hard, three abreast, sometimes passed by the odd car—most of the vehicle traffic rode on the 401, which was pure default and heavily patrolled—stopping early in a Mohawk reservation where there was a diner with pressure-cooked potato wedges served with cheese-curds. The proprietor was second generation Idle No More. They quickly figured out which friends they had in common.

The sun was low. They agreed that if they pushed it, they could be in Kingston by nightfall, maybe even have a midnight feast with Limpopo, a prospect that fired their imaginations and enthusiasms, except for Jacob and Stan, who were already asleep in their trailer, curled like a yin/yang. Iceweasel loosened their clothes and popped a shade over them and then stared at them smiling in a way that Tam could understand, but not relate to.

Seth caught her and gave her a hug and a smoldering kiss, adding sneaky tongue and an earlobe nibble; she got one hand up his sweaty back and then slid it over his butt and gave it a squeeze.

"Quickie in the bushes?" he whispered.

"Jeez, you two," Etcetera said. She remembered he was a cyborg today and jerked away.

"You sure know how to enhance a mood." Seth gave her one more hug. "Sorry, darling."

"Don't worry about it," she said. "Let's get this show rolling."

She was a walkaway, had been a walkaway since she was fourteen, though she'd come and gone from default—back to her parents, then an aunt, then her parents—until she was seventeen, when she'd gone for good. She had big thigh muscles and calves that bulged, even now she was saggy and middle aged. There had been a time when she thought nothing of walking ten hours a day, day after day. In those days, a bicycle was practically cheating. She could have ridden without breaking a sweat. It was a luxury reserved for the confluence of great roads and good fortune.

Muscles or no, those days were behind her. After the first hour, she was panting. The wicking fabric of her shirt felt sticky. There were times when her calves and feet cramped and she had to do awkward stretches while riding, grimacing and suppressing groans. She could have called a stop, but there was the thought of dinner with Limpopo. Besides, Seth was grimacing, too, and so were Iceweasel and Gretyl. None of them were calling stops. She wouldn't be the first one to cry off.

"God*damnit*!" Seth howled and shook his leg, laid down the bike, and rolled in the grass on the verge. He clutched his leg. They all got off and stretched and complained and sheepishly smiled at each other. Jacob and Stan woke from their naps and ran circles around them and demanded to be allowed to ride. They all agreed it would be unfair not to let the boys ride, so there were hours of slower-paced riding. It was much better.

The sun was a bloody blob on the horizon behind them, staining the road red, when Jacob and Stan climbed back into their trailer. Iceweasel checked their helmet straps. Gretyl did it again. The two women shot each other daggers and laughed at themselves. They were all old, and were on a long journey together. Something was changing. One era giving way to another. The sense of a change crackled through the cooling air. They ate mushy watermelon slices and squeezie pouches of chocolate scop and electrolyte. They checked the distance and by unspoken consensus got on their machines and started cranking.

There were no streetlights on the road. They switched to headlights, then nightscopes, then back to headlights when the lights of Kingston brightened the horizon. They circled the city, warned off by hovering police drones and the signs warning of OPP checkpoints. They headed for 15 north, the strip of private prisons built one after another.

The moon was up and it was getting cold when they reached the exit off the highway to the prisons, a theme-park of jailhouses built by TransCanada as part of its diversification strategy. The juvie hall. The men's prison. The minimum-security pen. As word went round that change had arrived, each acquired rings of tents and yurts. The phenomenon followed a template that was developed and formalized in the stupidly named "Walkaway Decade." Some walls came down, others went up. They'd build rammed-earth machines and add sprawling wings and ells, almost certainly an onsen, because that was de rigueur at anything walkaway bigger than a few people.

The rhythm of the place would change. On days when the sun shone or the wind blew, they'd run coolers with abandon, heat huge pools of water for swimming and bathing, charge and loose drones and other toys. When neither were around, the buildings would switch to passive climate control, the people would switch activities to less power-hungry ones.

More people would drift in and out, there'd be arguments over what to do and what to make, if anything. Some people would farm scop, others would tend gardens. Or not—some communities never gelled, became ghost towns within months of being established. Sometimes worse things happened. There were dark stories about rapes, murder sprees, cults of personality where charismatic sociopaths brainwashed hordes into doing their bidding. There'd been a mass-suicide, or so they said. Everyone argued about whether these stories were real, minimized by credulous walkaways or stoked to a fever pitch by default psy ops.

Ahead of them was the women's prison. Around it, the most carnival-like camp, a county fair for refugees. They had to dismount—none of the bikes had catastrophically failed—and walk the bikes into the thick of things, criss-crossing guy-wires and fragrant coffium parlors that rocked even at this late hour. Halfway, they abandoned the bikes and shared around Gretyl and Iceweasel's packs as each woman picked up a sound-sleeping boy.

The prison gates yawned wide. There were a few women on plush armchairs dragged out from some office. They broke off their conversations to inquire casually about who these people were and where they were going. At the mention of Limpopo's name, their faces lit and they offered to show the group inside.

"We knew her as DG, of course. That's what they booked her under. They punished her bad when she used her outside name, so she stopped. Everyone's changing names now we're wide open." "Wide open" was what default press said when the prison guards stopped showing up for work, the kind of thing that you could use to terrorize people about the marauders about to rush out of the prisons and start hacking up people. As they'd ridden through the TransCanada parks, she'd seen banners celebrating "wide open."

They were led inside, through wide open—*ahem*—scanning vestibules and yards and chambers where visitors or inmates could be contained. All the doors were flung back or removed and set on trestles and piled with assortments of clothes and other things that were either shared by or with the prisoners. The cell block was made up of huge, high-ceilinged, bar-walled rooms ranked with three-high bunk beds, festooned with banners and hung with privacy blankets (maybe they'd been there before wide open, but Tam didn't think prisons ran that way). The lighting was dim, the sound of whispered conversations around them and the snoring and breathing of hundreds—thousands?—of women made the place sound like a huge, muttering tunnel.

"This way," their guide whispered. They went single file down a narrow corridor between bunks, deep into the maze. Tam felt a minute's default-ness, worry that these women were criminals, some of them had surely done unforgivable violence to land here. There were violent people everywhere. Most of the time, most of them didn't do anything particularly violent, because even psychos needed to get along and have a life. These people had been nothing but sweet to them since their arrival. Limpopo was one of these people. She made the default part shut up.

Limpopo was asleep in her bunk, face a grayscale silhouette in dim light, but lined and older than Tam remembered. All of them clustered around her bunk, and Tam flashed on the dwarfs clustered around Snow White's bier.

"This is awkward," Etcetera stage-whispered from Seth's chest. Limpopo stirred. She scrunched her face—so many wrinkles! Tam's hand went to her own face. Limpopo blinked her eyes twice, opened them, and looked around. They must have appeared as silhouettes, faceless, but who else would be at her bedside?

"D," their guide whispered. "I brought you some friends." Her voice was thick with tears.

"Thanks," Limpopo whispered back. "Thanks, Testshot. Thanks a lot." She propped herself on her elbows.

"God damn, it's good to see you." Tam thought Limpopo said it, but it was Etcetera again, his voice weirdly modulated with machine emotion.

Limpopo half smiled, lips quivering. Tears ran down her face. No one knew what to do. Iceweasel passed Stan to Seth and put her arms around Limpopo's neck and pulled her into a long hug. "I love you, Limpopo," she whispered.

"We all do." Gretyl handed Jake to Tam and wrapped her arms around Limpopo and Iceweasel, half sliding onto the bed to do it. Tam looked at Jake's sleepy face, saw he was waking, even though he clung like a monkey in a tree, strong arms and dirty hair and sweet/sour unbrushed-teeth breath. "Mama?" he mumbled.

"Right there." Tam turned so he could see both mothers hugging the strange old lady in the weird dark room. Strangely, this comforted him. "Can you stand?" He thought about it, nodded. She put him down and joined the hug, squashing Limpopo's leg as she jockeyed for position. A minute later, Seth's arms were around her.

They hugged and cried in the dark. Jake said, with shocking loudness, "I have to pee, Mom!" They laughed and untangled themselves and shushed the boy and whispered apologies to the women roused by the noise. Limpopo led them back through the cell block, into the courtyard lit by flood lamps and populated with small conversational groups sitting on blankets and chairs from inside. They got folding chairs and blankets out of their packs, bottles of delicious whisky from a fabber on the *Gil*. The ritual was so normal and so weird that Tam kept getting buffeted by it, until they were back in their conversational circle. The boys were mothered by Iceweasel and Gretyl, staring wide-eyed from one grown-up to the next, sleepy and cranky and excited at once. Tam knew how they felt.

Limpopo told them the story of her incarceration in fits and starts, with many interruptions. It wasn't a nice story. She'd spent a lot of time in solitary—it was a routine punishment for the mildest infractions. Walkaways were particularly singled out for it. Her longest stretch in solitary was two years, during which she'd had no contact with the general population. It wasn't much better the rest of the time: for years on end, prisoners were given an hour out of their cells per day. For six months, no one had been allowed out of her cell block except for medical emergencies—no showering, no exercise. Tam thought about the huge, echoing barracks and tried to imagine being stuck in there with hundreds of women for half a year. She shivered and drank more whisky.

At first, they all listened, rapt. But it was late. They'd had a long day. Starting with Gretyl and Iceweasel and the boys, they trickled away and found empty bunks in the cell block. Finally, it was just her and Seth—and Etcetera. She could barely keep her eyes open.

Limpopo and Etcetera were engaged in a verbal mind-meld, conversation increasingly intimate, shaded with private nuances Tam couldn't decode, though that might have been exhaustion.

Tam realized Seth had fallen asleep in his chair. Limpopo was engaged in conversation with the box on his chest to the exclusion of all else. She shook Seth awake and he gummed his eyes. "Come on. Take off the dead guy and leave him with Limpopo, we're hitting the sack."

Limpopo giggled and Etcetera laughed with her. It felt very conspiratorial between those two as they headed to bed.

Breakfast was a fun affair, a scavenger hunt through the prisons and tent-cities of the TransCanada park to find fabbers with power and stock, nibbling treats given by passersby and giving back treats, either things they'd brought or things they were gifted along the way. By the time Tam and Seth caught up with the scavenging party, it had spread out and re-formed, using the built-out walkaway net to find one another. It was sunny and muggy. The boys were down to matching bright orange shorts and horned Viking helmets, and flip-flops that made fart noises, to their evident delight.

Seth looked naked without Etcetera distributed over his body. They reveled in the privacy of being able to talk and cuddle without involving the deceased. It felt like a figurative new day, as well as a literal one. They'd completed their quest, reunited with their lost friend, and reunited their dead friend with that lost friend. Their arms were around each other's waists, they were well-fed, and the sun was shining. It was a new day, they were surrounded by walkaways. They had nothing and everything to do.

Limpopo found them sitting in the grass of an overgrown meadow across the highway, watching the big drones make lazy circles overhead. Some were default, some were walkaway, some might have escaped from a farm and flocked on general principles.

"Good morning, beautiful people." She nearly sang. In the daylight, she looked even older. She had a stoop, and Tam thought she saw tremor in her hands. She wasn't much older than Tam, either—she'd had a much harder life. Whatever the differences between their circumstances, Tam knew this was her future. It made her feel indescribably nostalgic for the young, certain woman she'd been.

"Good morning!" they called. Iceweasel tackled her with a hug. Tam winced, worried about Limpopo's frailty. But Limpopo laughed and hugged her back and demanded to be reintroduced to the boys, had a solemn conversation with each about their fondest interests—space travel and slimy things—and found sweets in her pockets for them, thousand-flavor gobstoppers the size of golf balls. Their moms nodded permission, and the golf balls disappeared into their mouths, stopping up their gobs for the duration.

"How *are* you?" Iceweasel's arm was around Limpopo's shoulders, face turned to the sun. "This must be the freakiest thing, you and your friends must be, I don't know, just—"

"Yeah," Limpopo said. "And no. Thing is, when you're a prisoner, things happen to you. You don't get a say. I know women who were inside for years—decades—who suddenly were released, without notice. Literally the guards came and got them and kicked them out. No chance to call families, no good-byes. Sometimes, you'd have prisoners who were set to go, paperwork taken care of, and then, minutes before they were supposed to go, it got canceled. No one could say why. When the doors opened, it was an order-of-magnitude bigger version of the arbitrary lives we were already living.

"We were also used to being self-reliant. We traded favors, got each others' backs. We did most of the work around the prison. That was the way TransCanada delivered shareholder value—making the prisoners do all its work, unpaid, in the name of punishment. Once the doors opened, it wasn't *that* difficult to keep the lights on. We don't have all the consumables we need—being locked out of the power grid means we're only able to run on what we get from the eggbeaters and panels on the roofs—but all that means is we've had to go into the rest of the world and find people to help us and vice versa. There were *so many* walkaways in lockdown. The idea of running all this stuff without greed and delusion is what we're all about." She flashed a grin. "I'd say we're doing fucking great."

The speaker hung around her neck cheered and made clapping noises. "You are my total hero," Etcetera said. "A shining example to all, dead and alive."

That made them smile, too, and brought to mind the question Tam had been dying to ask. "I don't mean to be weird. But are you going to go get a new scan? Just in case—"

Limpopo looked away.

"Dunh-dun-dunnnh," Etcetera said. "The existential crisis looms."

"I know that there's another one of me out there, back where you live, and she sounds—"

"Like a total—"

She slapped the small speaker over her collarbone lightly. "Stop it. It's not supportive, it's mean. Whatever happened between you and her doesn't excuse you being a dick about her with me. *Especially* with me. She is me."

"That's the existential crisis." Etcetera didn't sound wounded, though the living Etcetera would have been in anxious pretzels at the thought of being publicly awful. Did that mean he wasn't the person he'd been? Or that he'd grown? Or that his bumpers kept his mood down the middle?

Limpopo looked fierce. "Yes, I'm getting a scan. There's already two crews running them in the men's prison. We're going to set up our own. A lot of us are old now, and even more are sick. Then there's the possibility they'll nuke the place as an example."

They looked up at the sky.

Gretyl shook her head. "Always a possibility. Maybe TransCanada will flip-flop and come back to lock everyone away. You got to figure this shit is panicking default. Once prisons stop running, what's next? Their little islands of normalcy are shrinking. It would be a hearts and minds thing for you naughty children to be sent to your rooms without supper."

That made the day dimmer.

# 7

# prisoner's dilemma

## [i]

Gretyl came from the fabber with everything they needed to build shelter—flexible frames and connectors the boys quickly assembled, photo-reactive film they stretched over each piece, clicking it together to make a half dome with a vertical face and a doorway. They set it up in the field where they'd watched the drones. The area in front of the prison's gates was crowded, no room for new structures big enough for a family of four. It was quieter. The rest of their crew were setting up there, too.

Limpopo wasn't ready to go and might never be. She wanted to build an onsen. The mention of this put a gleam in the eyes of those who'd known her at the B&B, including Iceweasel. They emerged a consensus that they'd stay and help. The boys had never seen an onsen—they'd gone out of fashion in Gary—and avidly watched videos about them. They were committed to the project. Gretyl could have headed home, but there was no reason to be there as opposed to here. She could teach her classes anywhere. The little serious math work she did with colleagues was geography independent.

She didn't like it here. It was too close to Toronto, to Jacob Redwater. It was weird that Iceweasel named their son after him, but being this close to what Gretyl thought of as "Jacob's lair" made her edgy. That's why Iceweasel wanted to stay. She needed to prove—to herself, to the world, to her monstrous father, who knew her every move—that she was unafraid. This had been hashed out during the naming thing. Gretyl understood there was no new information to be gleaned by refactoring that painful discussion. Once, she'd been foolhardy enough to argue with Iceweasel about this—a pregnant Iceweasel at that—and learned her lesson.

She still jumped at shadows.

"You hate this." The boys were at the onsen job site, clicking fabbed bricks together. They'd been promised a salvage expedition to a site where a drone cataloged a whole butt-load of useful matériel, on condition of diligent work and good behavior that morning. Iceweasel had come back and flumfed on the camp bed, swooning, sipping her pack's straw and glowing prettily with sweat.

"I don't hate it. I totally understand—"

"Hating and understanding aren't opposites. I want to let you know I *know* you hate this, and I'm grateful you're doing it anyway."

Gretyl shook her head. "I love you, too."

Iceweasel stretched out an arm and felt blindly for her, patted her on the butt. Gretyl took her hand. It was nice to have a kid-free moment. It had been a while. They held hands and Gretyl closed her eyes.

"I got a new scan today," Iceweasel said. "The boys, too."

Gretyl opened her eyes. "Oh." She tried very hard to keep her voice neutral and failed.

"Don't be like that."

"Like what?"

Iceweasel took her hand back and sat up. "There was a crowd doing it, moms and kids, now the scanners are burned in and working. You know it's harmless."

"I know you can't be harmed by the scanning process, but—"

"But someone could steal your scan and do something terrible to us. I know. We've been through it. They're locked to my private key, or a supermajority of our friends' keys, the usual group, same one we use for the rest."

Gretyl shook her head. "Fine."

"Obviously, it's not fine."

"Explain why you would feel so threatened that you got yourself scanned, but not so threatened that you wouldn't just *leave*?"

"Getting a scan gives us some insurance."

"Insurance? As in, if your father kidnaps you, I can run a sim of you to raise our sons? If we all die, maybe our friends will run us in simulation and wear us around their necks and we can talk out of their tits for the rest of time?"

"My dad's not going to kidnap me." In the first five years of their relationship, Gretyl got good at spotting when Iceweasel changed the subject. In the years since, she'd got better at figuring out when to mention it. She didn't mention it.

"How do you know?"

Iceweasel moved her arm off her face, spat out the straw and sat. "Because I heard from him."

Gretyl literally boggled at her wife. "Say that again?"

"I heard from him. Come on, you know he's sent me messages. I don't answer. I never answer."

"Before, we weren't in his backyard."

"You're being superstitious. It's no harder for Jacob Redwater to get to any place than it is for him to get any other place. Distance isn't what keeps us safe."

Gretyl had also been married to Iceweasel long enough to recognize when her wife was right. She shut up and tried to stop fretting. The boys returned, looking for clothes suitable for a salvage mission. They were distracted by hosing them down and dressing them up. Then all was forgotten, or at least they could pretend.

## [ii]

The onsen rose, brick by brick. Things got going when some of its crew fabbed construction mechas, which, of course, the boys wanted to pilot. The mechas ran automatically, and had fail-safes. Everyone agreed the boys were good at them and, unlike adults, never bored of repetitive manual tasks, provided they got to pilot robots while they did it.

At first, they insisted the boys have nearby adult copilots holding deadman's switches, but there were no adults with the stamina to keep up with the boys' drive to build. Also, the onsen was going up fast as it was thanks to their contribution. It would have been a dick move to slow them down.

"Parenting," Iceweasel pronounced, "is the art of getting out of the way of your kids' development." That settled it.

Besides, it gave them more time together than they'd had since Stan was born.

It was a second honeymoon, spent in the heady first days of a—very small—new nation, former prisoners and their families adding more each day, powdering the steel bars of the jails for fabber feedstock, pumping out support struts, spun for minimum weight/materials, structural versions of the bikes they'd ridden, but with more fail-safes. Hoa and friends came for a three-day stay, cycling on more of the same. They found a group of excited ex-cons who wanted to know how the weird bikes worked. Now there were three workshops making variations on the theme. It was getting to the point where serious arguments were brewing about bicycle/pedestrian etiquette.

Gretyl had forgot how energizing revolutionary life was. Back in Gary, they were set in routine, the kind of thing you have to do if you're raising kids and keeping some life for yourself. Here, no two days were alike. Every day brought new challenges, new solutions. It had been years since Gretyl was part of a place where there were serious arguments on the message boards. Here they raged, even erupting into fistfights, cooled out by peacemakers who rose to the challenge.

Just as she was getting pleased with it all—

"Gretyl." The way Iceweasel said it froze her. She'd heard Iceweasel sad, afraid, even panicked. But never had she heard that note in her wife's voice.

"What?" Gretyl waved her interface surfaces clear, flicked her wrists to shake off the tasks she'd queued. Their shelter felt cramped, not cozy.

Iceweasel was sweating. Her eyes were wide. Gretyl felt her heart pick up the pace.

Another woman stepped through the doorway. She was . . . coiled. Not very tall, hair cut short and stylish, face all planes, maybe Slavic. Her posture was like a cat about to pounce. Gretyl couldn't guess her age: older than Iceweasel, but in such excellent physical shape it was impossible to say by how much. She had small, square teeth, which she displayed in a quick smile. Gretyl knew who she had to be.

"You'd be Nadie?"

Nadie nodded minutely. "Gretyl." She extended a hand. Dry. Strong. Calloused. Perfect manicure, dun-colored polish, blunt tips.

Gretyl looked from Iceweasel to Nadie.

"How bad?"

"Limpopo is bringing the boys. Nadie has a helicopter."

"A helicopter."

Iceweasel's hands shook. Gretyl wanted to take them, but she was irrationally, powerfully angry with her wife. This was the other part of being a professional revolutionary: people around you died, all the time. Now her boys, her children, who had the power to make her ache with a force that radiated from the pit of her stomach to the furthest tips of her extremities, just by looking over their shoulders at her with unclouded eyes and sweet mouths, were in the path of unimaginable force. There would be guns and worse. The videos from Akron ran all the time, quick animations dropped into message boards to make cheap points about the brutality of the outside world.

"How long?"

"Not long," Nadie said. "There were long arguments, thankfully. Gave me time to get here. But now they've decided, they're moving."

"Why won't they shoot down your helicopter?" Gretyl asked. Her heart thundered.

"Because it's *my* helicopter," Nadie said. She tilted her head. "Zotta."

"Right."

Iceweasel's hands were fists. There came the welcome sound of boys' voices and the stamp of machinery. Gretyl didn't bother with the door. She kicked through the photo-reactive film wall, splintering the cool dark of the interior with a spray of sunlight.

The boys were each piloting mechas. Limpopo, Seth, and Tam were riding on them, standing on the robots' shoulders, clinging to the handles on their heads. The boys whooped as they pushed the machines as fast as they'd go, apparently under orders not to worry about what they trashed. The mechas' arms flailed ahead of them, smashing tents and yurts out of the way.

Iceweasel and Nadie joined her, coming through the door. Gretyl saw Nadie assess the group, minutely shake her head.

"We won't all fit in your helicopter, will we?"

She'd spoken to Nadie. Iceweasel looked at her sharply. "Gretyl, don't be an asshole—" Gretyl knew *that* one. It went like this: *I fucked up, now everything you say will remind me of that and make me furious.* She knew it. Didn't have time for it. She ignored her.

"Not enough," Nadie said.

"How many?"

"I came to bring you four."

Gretyl recognized evasion. "How many do you have room for, though?"

Limpopo dismounted, helped the boys while the rest climbed down. Gretyl spared them a glance, made sure they were dressed, had sun hats. "Get water," she said to Iceweasel. Air, clothes, water, food. Walkaway triage. "Food." To Nadie: "How many?"

"I came for four."

Motherhood had made a coward of her. She was ashamed, because she couldn't say, *If our friends don't go, we don't go.* It wasn't her life on the line anymore.

"Take us all." She tried to mean it.

Iceweasel was back, yanking compression straps on their biggest backpack, misshapen with whatever she'd thrown into it.

"How many?"

Nadie gave her a perfectly unreadable look, looked back to Gretyl. "Could you choose?"

"I'd rather explain choosing to my kids than explain why there were empty seats next to them when people started dying."

"Would it make a difference if I told you they were coming in nonlethal?"

"Like Akron?"

"Not like Akron." They had an audience crowded around. Whatever they saw in their body language kept them quiet. "Exactly not like Akron. Akron made martyrs. It hurt them all over the world. They're coming in nonlethal, as police, to restore order, to investigate murders."

"What murders?" Limpopo said. She was stooped, had a tremor, but asserted herself with a tone that stood two meters fifty and cut hard.

Nadie shook her head. "No time." She looked at them. "I can take, uh, one more."

They looked at each other. Gretyl said, "She has a helicopter."

They looked at each other again.

"I'll stay," Gretyl said. Iceweasel shot her a look of shock and sorrow. Gretyl gave her a look that said she would not entertain argument. It didn't get much use in their relationship. It meant something.

Limpopo said, "This is my home. I'll bear witness. Die, if it comes to that."

Etcetera said something soft from her collarbones, pitched for her hearing. A small smile touched her lips. She caressed the speaker.

"You can't stay," Iceweasel said. Stan started to cry, such a rarity that Jake bawled, too. Gretyl hefted him onto one hip and let him bury his face in her throat. Gretyl looked at Limpopo's face. She was struck by how different it was, how much the years in prison hadn't just aged her, but changed her. Before, Gretyl had been struck by the pains Limpopo took not to appear to give orders or hint at having authority. Now, she was pure alpha, radiating unquestionable dominance.

"I'm not leaving," Limpopo said with unshakable self-assurance.

It was Seth and Tam's turn. They looked from Iceweasel to Gretyl. "Gretyl," Seth said. "You're a mother, you can't—"

"I can." She swallowed the lump in her throat. "I will. There's some things you can't run from." She thought of her grad student and what they'd gone through. "I want my kids safe, but our family has no more right to be intact than anyone's." She wasn't making sense, not even to herself. "I've done a lot of walking away." She shrugged. "I'm going to stay."

It might have gone on, except for Nadie. She cocked her head, listened to something in her cochlea, discreetly wiggled her fingers, narrowed her eyes. "We're going." She held out her hands to take Stan from Gretyl. Gretyl held him and kissed him and blinked hard to keep the tears back. She did the same to Jake. She consciously committed the boys' smell to her memory, telling herself that she would never forget the smell and faces and voices of her beloved sons. Then she took her wife into her arms and held Iceweasel with an embrace that stretched back through the ages to their first rough, furtive groping, through the years of love and companionship, the hardships and absences, the reunions and the fights and reconciliations. It took everything she had and everything she didn't even know she had not to cry, especially as she felt Iceweasel's tears on her own cheeks, salty and as familiar as her own.

Nadie made an urgent sound. "Takeoff in seven minutes. We'll have to run." She ran, Stan on her hip. Iceweasel scooped their other son and ran after her, and Seth and Tam gave her a helpless look and ran, too.

Then it was her and Limpopo.

"Do you want to see if there's anything in the shelter you want to save?"

Gretyl, moving in a numb dream, went back into the shelter, prodded their bedding and scattered possessions. There were three blankets, two small and one large. The small ones smelled like the boys, the big one like Iceweasel. She took them in her arms. Jake's stuffed mouse, Mousey, fell out of his blanket. She picked him up by his worn, chewed paw. He stared at her with beady eyes as she tucked him back into the blankets.

"You can put them with my stuff," Limpopo said.

They walked at a fast clip to the prison. Limpopo was distracted, stumbling as she walked and talked into her interface and texted at the same time. Sometimes, she'd ask Etcetera to send a message. By the time they reached the sprawling camp at the prison gates, it was semi-panic as people raced inside the gates or away from the prisons altogether, carrying bundles on their backs. Children cried, but apart from that, it was very quiet. Clipped, tight voices, many in that odd pitch intended for interface mics, not human ears.

"Inside," Limpopo said. Gretyl heard a helicopter rotor, far off, brought on the breeze, getting quieter as it flew away. She stopped in her tracks and brought her hands to her face. She really sobbed. Limpopo led her by the elbow, whispering it was okay, her family was safe. They had to *move*.

Gretyl let herself be led. Her mind had split, one fraction was overwhelmed with sorrow and self-recrimination. The other part—the part that made that decision—racing through strategy and tactics for whatever was coming. Nadie said the coming forces wouldn't make martyrs of them, they were coming to show this was fighting crime, not fighting war. Not fighting for the existence of a society whose end was coming.

Walkaways had something the default side didn't have: except for a few children, every walkaway had been default, once. Almost no one in default—and no one whom anyone listened to, period—had ever walked away. Gretyl found it easy to superimpose the default view on situations.

They would be perversely cheered by a fight, by prisoners and their supporters—criminals-once-removed—brawling and being gassed into submission and stacked like cordwood.

If they fought back, it might be a massacre, but they wouldn't be martyrs. They'd be ISIS, ideology-crazed monsters to be put down with whatever regrettable force was necessary.

All this while Gretyl still sobbed, each part of her observing the other with perverse fascination, wondering which one was the real Gretyl.

---

The boys' prison attracted the hardcore networking freaks. They sent runners to the women's prison asking for anyone with network experience to ride the faders on the routing algorithms that would rebalance their network infrastructure as parts of it were knocked out. Gretyl and Limpopo looked at one another.

"My place is here—" Limpopo began. One of her friends—the woman who'd shown them Limpopo's bunk, whose name Gretyl couldn't place amid the tense emotion—made a raspberry.

"Don't be an idiot. You're not our grandma, you're just another con. We don't need you here to look after us. Do your thing. Everyone knows you're hot shit with programming and ops. Keeping our feeds running will do more to keep us strong than sticking your skinny old body between us and hired goons."

Limpopo faked a punch, gave her a quick hug and a peck on the cheek, and they were off.

"Here's what I'm thinking." They jog-trotted towards the men's prison. "This place has more surveillance than anywhere you've ever been, by a factor of a hundred. Every centimeter is recorded all the time. Those feeds go into a data center that applies heuristics that ranks them so the guards can get it packaged as an infographic."

Etcetera said, "You could package up an atrocity-feed. The worst stuff they do, pulled into a single feed that gets slicked together like a drama?"

"The idea is to prevent atrocities," Gretyl said. "Nadie said they didn't want martyrs, another Akron."

They reached the gates as drones swarmed out of the skies, seeming to dive-bomb the prisons' roofs.

"Uh-oh," Gretyl said. Limpopo listened to a feed.

"No," she said, "that was on purpose. They're keeping a skeleton crew of aerial routers, enough for signals and telemetry, and landing the rest in Faraday cages until the first E.M.P. It's a standard tactic, they say they used it in Nigeria, which makes no sense to me."

"It was huge," Gretyl said, "but they must have blocked it. Started with those floating cities off Lagos. Cut loose from the mainland in a walkaway uprising, literally, lost power and plumbing, didn't have enough onboard to stay stable. Hired mercenaries from the subcontinent to pacify Lagos. The walkaways skunked them, kept their routers in boxes and released them in short bursts, mingling with the mercs' drones so they'd have to pulse their own birds to get at the walkaways'. The feeds hardly bobbled. Made the mercs look like assholes."

They arrived at an IT ops room in a third subbasement. A young boy, no more than fourteen, gave them an enthusiastic tour of the ops center's features—armored conduit joining it to hard-line fiber links and in-building conduit, backup batteries—

"It's got its own air supply?" Gretyl said.

The boy shrugged. He was skinny, with a small afro and long arms and fingers, a face full of tilt-eyed mischief. "Every block's got bulkheads they can bring down to just gas one little part of things. Cheap and effective, so long as your team's got masks." That explained all the kids in gas masks on the way in—the women's prison had hardly any. They'd made their own from micropore kerchiefs and goggles. They'd passed a small, efficient assembly line on the way out.

It was a surreal vantage point to witness the Battle of the TransCanada Prisons. They used private security on the front line, not mercs exactly. These were outsource cops, for-hire guys in uniform that cities with private police forces used—and other cities used to break police unions whenever they got uppity. Men and women in awesome body armor, stuff that looked like Hugo Boss from a cyberpunk revival, faceless and shielded, each an "army of one" with exoskeletons, scary burp-weapons. There were one hundred of them, with drone support and fast nonlethal foot-pursuit bots, headless cheetahs and dogs from alloy and soft solenoids, just enough smarts to run a target down and bear her to the ground, clobber her if she tried to get up before a signed all-clear.

The part of Gretyl that worried about her family receded as she and Limpopo fed the particulars to the global walkaway audience, wiki-ing countermeasures for every plan of attack they could conceive. Gretyl remembered her earlier thought about all walkaways having been defaults but not vice versa, wondered what the default counterintelligence operatives who monitored this made of it. They'd know this was what walkaways did, work in the open, but they also knew that when they fought each other, they used elaborate fakeouts. Would they be able to *believe* walkaways were just letting it all hang out, where enemies could see it?

The enemy forces formed a perimeter around the prison complex. The cameras tracked the drones' overflight patterns, millimeter-wave, infrared, and backscatter.

The formalities: "All persons on these premises are subject to arrest. You will not be harmed if you come out with your hands in plain sight. You will have access to counsel. Human rights observers are on hand to ensure the rule of law is respected. You have ten minutes." The sound came from the prisons' many speakers as well as bullhorns built into the front lines' battle suits. The fact they could still transmit audio to the internal speakers made every walkaway's heart quail. It meant all the work walkaways had done to secure their nets and root out the back-doors left by TransCanada was insufficient. It implied the enemy had access to their cameras, could trigger the gas, seal the bulkheads—

The network ops boys scrambled, thundering fingers over their interfaces. Gretyl called up everything she'd learned about the network ops for TransCanada, things she'd tweaked when called on to help with something gnarly. Limpopo grabbed her arm, brought up infographics, started analytics on recent traffic to the audio servers. Etcetera got what she was looking at faster than Gretyl. He shouted at the boys, feeding them suggestions for ports to block, network traffic fingerprints to look for in the packet-inspectors.

Gretyl found calm in the knowledge they were inside one another's decision loops. She handled diagnostics from walkaways watching the network, wordlessly updating models underpinning Limpopo's infographics, noting as Limpopo integrated new data into her analysis.

In four minutes, they'd found four back-doors. Three were trivial, access accounts that should have been removed everywhere, but had been removed *almost* everywhere. The fourth was harder to de-fang, because it would require a whole-system reboot to catch. They solved it by building a big dumb filter rule that looked for anything that might be trying to log into it, dumping those packets on the floor. Just as they were finishing this hackwork, someone in Redmond messaged Gretyl urgently with one they'd missed, that maybe even defaults had missed, built in by the manufacturer for license-repossession for deadbeat customers who missed payments, which would let them put the whole system into minimal operation mode. In theory, you could only invoke this mode if you had Siemens' signing key, but it would be naïve to assume that the Canadian spooks running this show didn't have that.

"No way to know if that's all of them," Etcetera said, speaking the thought they were all thinking with machine bluntness.

"Nope," Limpopo said.

Gretyl said, "Everyone off-site is looking. If there are more vulns, they'll find them."

"Eventually," Etcetera said.

"You've got a backup," Gretyl said. "What are you worrying about?"

"You." That shut her up.

"You can be a total asshole," Limpopo said, but without real rancor. The boys were tweaking their fixes, building in fallbacks, but they snickered at "asshole."

"You have two minutes," the voice said. This time it came only from the loudhailers outside, picked up by cameras aimed at the invaders. Some of their cameras were being blinded by pulsed light weapons, but that attack was designed for civilian institutions, not fortified prisons. TransCanada spent real money on redundant vision systems. Must have galled their shareholders to see all that money that could have been paid as dividends be diverted—

Gretyl's phone rang, deep in her ear. She tapped it on, assuming it would be Iceweasel calling to make sure she was all right, which she appreciated and resented—*I'm a little busy, babe*—but it was a man's voice.

"Is this Gretyl Jonsdottir?"

"Yes." The call came on her friends-and-family-only ID. It wasn't known to anyone who sounded like that.

"Where is Natalie Redwater?"

"Who is this?" Of course she knew.

"This is Jacob Redwater. Her father."

Gretyl's game-theory spun up, playing different gambits, trying different theories for what Jacob Redwater wanted. Undoubtedly he knew about her relationship with Iceweasel, must have known about the boys, known there was a Jacob Redwater II out there. He'd kidnapped Iceweasel, determined to make her into a zotta, into a Redwater. She'd hurt him where he was weakest, in the money, and he must have been furious.

He must feel some strange version of love for her. She'd known zottas at Cornell, patrons of her lab. She'd had to do dinners with them, fund-raisers, spent hundreds of hours engaged in high-stakes small talk, under her department head's watchful eye. They weren't unpleasant to talk to—many were witty conversationalists. But there was something . . . off about them. It wasn't until she'd had her crisis of conscience and walked away from Cornell that she'd been able to name it: they had no impostor syndrome. There wasn't a hint of doubt that every privilege they enjoyed was deserved. The world was correctly stacked. The important people were at the top. The unimportant were at the bottom.

If she told Jacob Redwater that Iceweasel had gotten away, would he use his influence to make the attack on the prisons more violent? Or would he (could he?) pull forces off the prisons to chase down Iceweasel? More chilling:

was Jacob Redwater working with Nadie? Had Nadie kidnapped Iceweasel perhaps to forge some alliance with the rest of the Redwater fortune?

She was spooking herself. She went for straightforward: "What do you want?"

"I would like to speak with my daughter."

"That's not possible." She stuck to the truth, if not all of it.

"Ms. Jonsdottir, I know you love my daughter."

"That's very true."

"Hard as you find this to believe, I love her, too."

*You're right, I do find that hard to believe.* "I'm sure you do, in your way." She didn't mean to micro-agress him, but it slipped out. How could she let that pass?

He pretended he didn't notice, though she was sure he had. "I don't want—" He was overcome by some emotion, or a very good actor. Or both, she reminded herself. The zottas she knew were good at compartmentalizing, sociopath style, understanding other peoples' emotions well enough to manipulate them, without experiencing actual empathy. "There are children," he said. "Her children."

"Mine, too," Gretyl said.

"Yes."

"Whatever is about to happen, it doesn't have to happen to my daughter, or my grandchildren. Your children."

"Where are you, Mr. Redwater? Are you at the prison?"

"As a matter of fact, I am."

She'd thought so—the background noise was an echo of the sounds she'd heard through the prisons' outward cams.

"You knew they were coming."

"I knew. That's why I came. To keep Natalie safe." There was a moment. "I could get you out."

"Why aren't you talking to—" She almost said, *Iceweasel,* then *Natalie,* settled for, "your daughter?"

"She won't answer. It wasn't easy to get this address for you, but I needed to get a message to her. I know you wouldn't sacrifice your children for ideology."

Fuck it. "You think Iceweasel would?"

"I think my daughter is justifiably angry at me. This means that I can't explain certain . . . facts to her. We can't even have this discussion."

"They're moving in on us, Mr. Redwater. We can't have this discussion if I'm under attack."

"I can't call them off."

She didn't say anything. Iceweasel paid enough attention to know Jacob Redwater's branch of the family assumed control over the main dynastic fortune, making him the primary family power broker. Gretyl would be surprised if they didn't own a major stake in TransCanada, not to mention outsource cops.

"It's not my call. Honestly."

"I don't think we have anything to talk about." She disconnected. Limpopo stared thoughtfully.

"My in-laws are seriously fucked up."

Etcetera laughed, a weird noise through the speaker. There was always something weird about sim laughter. Some sharp-defined edge to it, enforced by the sims' bumpers. Gretyl had been scanned. Maybe this was how she'd laugh at her sons' antics in the future.

Time ran out. The outsource cops' drones plummeted in controlled dives, signaling impending attack. The boys in the data center made giddy, frightened noises as they landed their skeleton fleet, chasing the cops' drones down, just as the first volley of bullets stitched the sky, tracking the drones, killing more than half before they landed. The hard-line fiber links went dead, except the ones that had been covertly dug up and spliced into direct-link microwave repeaters, far from the prison, out in farmers' fields.

Gretyl and Limpopo's fingers collided as they jabbed the same spots on the infographics, cutting service over to those links, tuning the caches and load-balancers to accommodate a sudden two-order-of-magnitude drop in throughput. Traffic in and out of the prisons was now queuing deeply in repeaters' caches. Out in the world, other caches were doing the same. *The network interprets censorship as damage and routes around it,* Gretyl thought, and grinned at the ancient, pre-walkaway slogan. It had been true for a while, then a metaphor, then wishful thinking, and now it was a design specification.

She was in the zone, a human coprocessor for a complex system that used machines as a nervous system to wire together the intelligence of a global crowd of people she loved with all her heart. The part of her that railed and wept when she sent her wife and children away and stayed behind woke briefly and noted that *this* was the real reason she'd done it. This incredible feeling of strength and connection to something larger. It had been years since Gretyl felt this. Now she felt it again, she realized how much she'd missed it. Living in a better nation was preferable to living in a worse one—but living in the nation's first days was the difference between falling in love and being in love. She was cheating on her wife. Carrying on an affair with armed insurrection.

The prisons had defenses. The oncoming forces knew exactly what they were. The crowd had ideas about this. As the mechas with the battering rams stepped into position before each gate, the prison's own anti-camera dazzlers came to life, lancing beams of powerful, broad-spectrum light directly into the mechas' sensors. They were shielded against this, but imperfectly, meaning the mechas had to slow down and rely on ultrasonic sensing to guide their passage. The defenders triggered the prison's sonic antipersonnel weapons, relocated from the cell blocks to the outside walls. The mechas slowed more. Then defenders opened up with the water cannon.

Under normal circumstances, the water jets wouldn't bother the mechas. They had excellent gyros. In a pinch they could assume three-point stances for stability. But they were attached to each other by the rams they held in two-by-two grids. The jets hit them from different angles, so the front ones' corrective shuffling further unbalanced the rear ones, and vice versa. The water-cannoneers set up a rhythm that pushed them further off balance. Within minutes, two of the mecha teams were sprawling. The third retreated in unsteady steps.

Gretyl heard cheers, saw jubilation in the chats. She knew this was only a skirmish. They were hugely, physically overmatched. The private cops withdrew behind their armor, and a volley of RPGs streaked through the air, bullseyeing each water cannon and the apertures for the anti-photo beams. They'd expected it, but it was terrifying nevertheless, even as the channels filled up with damage manifests, estimating the total cost to TransCanada's physical plant, watching the company's share price slide down, as default analysts reading over their shoulders changed their bets on whether TransCanada was going to end up with usable plant or smoking rubble at the end of the day.

Her phone rang again.

"Hello."

There was latency-lag, then Jacob Redwater's voice, flanged and compressed. "I want to speak to my daughter."

"You've made that clear to her on more than one occasion."

There was a long pause. "Her mother died last year."

"You have my condolences."

"I couldn't find a way to tell her."

"I'll make sure she knows."

The boys in the data center lofted a swarm of drones, including some they'd hidden in the woods, behind the enemy lines. The drones' feed showed the enemy forces, disciplined and still, poised for their next assault. The damaged mechas limped to the back. The enemy opened fire on their drones. The boys kicked them into automated high-intensity evasive maneuvers that would lop their batteries' duty-cycles in half. Nearly all survived the first round, though their video feeds turned to a scramble of nauseating roller-coaster footage. The boys' hadn't sent them in random patterns—each one ended up in proximity to an enemy surveillance drone, riding its tail. When the ground forces opened up with HERF weapons that fried the drones and knocked them out of the sky, they also took out their own aircraft.

"Good work!" Gretyl shouted over her shoulder at the boys, who didn't need anyone to tell them—they were dancing with victory. Meanwhile, the drones' brief flights had managed to clear 75 percent of the network backlogs, massively relieving the congestion on their surviving fiber.

Jacob Redwater said, "Your supply of drones is limited. We can get resupplies."

"Yes. We can't win this with force."

The external speakers clicked on. A voice spoke: "Gordy, this is Tracey. Your sister Tracey, Gordy. I know we haven't spoken since I walked away, but I want you to know that I love you. I'm safe and happy. I think about you every day. You have a niece now, we called her Eva, for Mom. The way we live here is better than I ever thought. People are nice to each other, Gordy, the way it was when we were kids. I trust my neighbors. They look out for me. I look out for them. We're not terrorists, Gordy. We're people default had no use for. We've found a use for each other. Gordy, you don't have to do this. There are other ways to live. I love you, Gordy." Another voice, a baby, crying. "That's Eva, Gordy. She loves you, too. She wants to see her uncle."

The feeds zoomed in on one of the front-liners, a man, whose shoulders shook. This had to be Gordy. The crowd had identified him through gait analysis, doxxed him, walked his social graph, found a hit in a walkaway town in Wyoming, gotten Tracey out of bed, recorded the message.

The silence stretched. The private cop beside Gordy put a tentative hand on his shoulder. Gordy shook it off violently, shoving him away.

The moment stretched. Then Gordy shucked his gauntlets with a flick of his wrists, sending them to clatter in the road. His bare fingers worked the catches of his visor, until it yawned open. His face was an indistinct moving blur, brown with camera-corrected streaks of white where his teeth and eyes were. He took his helmet off, shucked his weapons, let them fall around his feet.

The cops around him stared, body language telegraphing the open mouths behind their visors. He walked off, orthogonal to the jails and the cops' lines, up 15 toward Ottawa, toward the dairies and dells of eastern Ontario.

He walked away.

The silence was something holy, church silence. It was a miracle, battlefield conversion.

"Akin!" the voice was amplified, from behind cop lines, loud enough to rattle the glass. "Get back into line, Akin!" It was a command voice, an asshole-tightening order-giving voice. Gordy's shoulders stiffened. Gordy kept walking, divesting himself of more body armor, dropping the jacket into the road behind him as he walked. His head was high, but his shoulders shook like he was crying.

One of the cops in the front line raised his gun, muzzle big as a cannon, built to send focused, bowel-shredding ultrasonic at its target; the prolapsizer, they called it. The man whose hand had been flung off Gordy's shoulder tackled the man with the gun before he could aim. They writhed on the ground until they were pulled apart by more cops, and stood, facing one another, held by the arms, chests heaving.

Gordy disappeared over a hill.

Jacob Redwater's breath was noisy on Gretyl's phone.

"We can't win this with force." She hung up as the next announcement started playing through the prisons' outward-facing speakers.

---

In the middle of the third announcement, the cops opened fire on the speakers, more RPGs. The prisoners switched to backups, out of sight behind the roofline. When the cops' drones went up for a look, they were harried by more walkaway drones, which chased them around the sky and even suicided on two cop drones. While the air battle raged, they got four more announcements out. They got five walkouts from seven announcements. The crowd was going fucking bananas on the boards. They doxxed the cops on the lines as fast as they could, running their graphs, finding more people to record messages.

Gretyl shook her head in amazement as the recordings came in. In the men's prison, someone was playing D.J., queuing them up. In the women's prison, someone else was doing the same. One of the boys in the control room did for the cops out front of their institution. She had been skeptical of the plan.

It turned on graph theory: once you hit a critical mass of walkaways, the six-degrees thing meant every single rent-a-cop on the line was no more than two handshakes—or family Christmas dinners—away from a walkaway who would shame and sweet-talk them into putting down their weapons.

Announcements eight through ten played on the parapet speakers, before the cops brought out mortars—*mortars*!—to attack the walls, bringing them down in piles of rubble amidst mushrooming dust clouds. TransCanada's stocks plummeted. The contagion spread to all those *other* places where walkaways were holed up—universities, research outfits, all those refugee detention centers. When the market saw what it was going to take to get those facilities back to default shipshape, investors panic-sold. They always panic-sold, every time one of these fights broke out. Even the true believers in zotta superiority sold. The root of *credit* was *credo*: belief. Watching rent-a-cops bring out their big guns to wipe out *speakers* had an enormous impact on the market's animal sentiments: their belief system was crashing, just as it had every other time.

More drones: with speakers, crowd-control drones that came stock with the prison, so big they needed extra avionics to course-correct them from the vibrations of their own speakers.

The drones homed in on the men and women they'd targeted, turned them into spectacles as their squad-mates stared at armored cops haloed by circling drones, too close to their bodies to shoot down safely, even with armor. What if their hydrogen cells blew? What if they were booby-trapped?

When the order went out to rotate those unlucky bastards, they trudged toward the APCs at the back of the formation, circled by buzzing drones that haunted them like outsized, big-voiced fruit flies. In one case, a drone managed to slip inside the APC with its target. The big tank-like car rocked on its suspension as cops inside chased it around, freaking like a church-load of parishioners chasing a lost bat. The video from that drone was a tilt-a-whirl confusion of fish-eye claustrophobia. Eventually, motion stopped as the drone was smashed to the APC's deck. A moment later, the hatch of the APC opened and three more cops walked away, two women and a man. The man and one of the women argued with the other woman, maybe trying to convince her to stay, but they all left their weapons by the roadside as they struck off for Ottawa.

Things settled. The prisoners had damned few ways to make contact with the cops now, which meant that there could be no negotiation. There had been none before.

Gretyl's phone rang.

"You have to get Natalie out of there. Now."

Gretyl felt her guts curdle. Maybe it was a zotta trick to flush them out by making them think the big push was coming. Redwater wasn't above that. But he sounded desperate in an un-Redwater way.

"No one is coming out until we can all come out." She carefully avoided confirming Iceweasel's present location. She guessed this meant Nadie wasn't working for the old man, because otherwise she'd have let him know his precious bloodline was safe.

"The children—"

"There are *many* children in here. Why does it matter if they're related to you?"

He made a puppy noise, between a bark and a whimper. "You evil bitch."

"I'm not the one with all the guns. Are you here, Mr. Redwater? Can you see what's going on?"

"I can see it. It's good theater. I'm sure your friends are excited by it, Gretyl. But it won't matter in five minutes."

"If I've only got five minutes left, I'd better savor them." She hung up on him again.

"Why don't you block him?" Limpopo said.

"Because so long as she keeps talking to him, she might be able to convince him not to let his buddies blow our asses up," Etcetera said.

Gretyl shook her head. "That's not it." She looked at the infographics, watched network traffic flow, wondered if it was true that Jacob Redwater could be their savior, whether he was the reason their network links were up at all, so he could call her. "Maybe that's part of it. But this is the asshole who took my wife away, fucking kidnapped her. It's not nice, but I'm enjoying making him squirm."

Limpopo shrugged. "Your last minutes on Earth, and you're spending them exacting petty revenge? It's your life, I guess."

It cut. It was true. Limpopo had always been better at big picture and living the moment. Prison had made her even more stoic. Gretyl tried to imagine what she had endured over the years.

The network links went abruptly dead, their drones shot out of the sky at the same time as the fiber lines cut off.

"Guess I won't get a chance to apologize to the old bastard." She groped for Limpopo's hand. Her grip was dry and her hand felt frail, but it was warm, and it squeezed back.

"I love you, Limpopo."

"I love you, too."

"Me too," said Etcetera.

"Thank you."

They squeezed their hands tight.

---

The boys chattered like monkeys in a tree. Some asked impatient questions of the two old ladies holding hands and staring at infographics, but Gretyl and Limpopo had nothing to tell them.

The cameras still brought feeds from outside, because the local net still ran, still spooled its footage for exfiltration to the rest of the world. The police lines tightened. There were no more identifiable humans in them. They were all inside the mechas and the APCs, or pulled way back behind the police buses and the administrative trailers that came in on flatbeds. The strategists on the other side wouldn't risk more psy ops from the prisoners, even if it meant fighting from behind armor. The tactics of mechas and APCs were primarily lethal, everyone knew it. You couldn't arrest someone from inside a huge semi-tank or killer robot suit. You could stun them or kill them, but you couldn't read them their rights or handcuff them.

The mechas stepped forward smartly and planted charges around the surviving perimeter walls, scampered back on three legs, flattening for the explosion that shook the walls down, making the foundations shake, even in their subbasement.

The cameras on that wall went dark. They re-tasked cams from the interior courtyard to their infographic feeds, watched the exercise repeated. The APCs rolled, forming an armored wall; the mechas stepped over them, planted fresh charges, retreated. Gretyl reflexively checked to see what the markets were doing, but of course, there was no external feed. It didn't matter for them. The ending was coming. First days of a better nation. Last moments of the worn-out, fragile physical bodies of some stupid, imperfect walkaways. Gretyl didn't let herself dissociate, made herself look at the screens, watch the wall come down, the cameras go dark. She squeezed Limpopo's hand harder.

Her phone rang.

She looked at the infographics, saw, somehow, the networks were back online. The networks, which the cops had physically seized, pwned with actual wire-cutters, were online again. Her phone rang.

"Please." He was crying.

"Mr. Redwater?"

"Please. I can't—"

She almost relented. *Go ahead, kill us, your daughter and grandsons are far from here.* It was a reflexive thought, common mercy for an old man whose voice cracked with sorrow.

"If you can't, you shouldn't. Everyone here has someone who will weep for their deaths. If you have power to stop things—" He clearly did, how else to explain the network link, the mechas and the APCs now still in the courtyards, facing the ruined façades, offices and storerooms sitting naked to the air, fourth walls removed, looking like sets for dramas. "If you can do anything to stop this, you could save their lives."

"I can't do that."

"You won't."

"Can I— Will you come speak with me about it?"

"Mr. Redwater, with all due respect, I am not a fucking idiot, you kidnapping, evil fuck." She said it evenly, but her pulse raced. Limpopo gave her a silent cheer.

"Can I come in, then? Alone?"

She thought. It wasn't likely a zotta would turn suicide bomber—blackmail or brainwash someone else to be a suicide bomber, sure, but not risk their own skin. At the rate things were going, they were all going to die in hours, possibly minutes.

"I don't think anyone here would object to that. As to what happens out there, with all those weapons and tanks and killer robots—"

"That's my lookout." He sounded in control of his emotions now.

"Leave our feeds up. No safe conduct if we can't reach the outside world."

There was a long pause. She thought he might have disconnected, but when he spoke, she heard a single clipped plosive as he unmuted his mic. He'd been talking to someone else.

"Out of my hands. But I've made a request."

She shrugged. "It's the boys' prison. The southernmost one."

Quickly, she tapped out a message to the rest of the walkaways, the ones in the jails and in the crowd, explaining Jacob Redwater had asked for safe passage so that he could talk to his daughter's wife. She implied, but didn't state, that Iceweasel and the boys were in the building. As the crowd voraciously doxxed Iceweasel's dad and parceled up tremendous quantities of information on the sprawling Redwater empires, Limpopo and Gretyl whispered to one another about what would happen next.

"It sounds like he's snapped," Limpopo said. "Some kind of shear between Jacob Redwater, zotta, and Jacob Redwater, human. Deathbed conversion or something. You said his wife died?"

"Yeah, but from what Iceweasel said, they were basically divorced for most of her life, in all but name. She had a sister, don't know what became of her. I'm sure he's got access to as much company as he wants."

"Whatever else he was, he was charming," Etcetera said. "In that smart, sociopathic way. Fun to argue with, if you weren't his daughter."

"There he is," Limpopo said. The boys gathered around their screen as they zoomed and error-corrected the feed from the remaining cams in the inner courtyard. He was dressed in bottle-green cords and a down vest over a long-sleeved shirt. His hair was white, but his face was smooth, his posture erect. He walked slowly and purposefully. He was old, but he didn't look frail.

"Can one of you get him, please?" Gretyl said to the boys. "I don't want to go up in case he's planning to snatch me."

The boys argued over who would do it. A kid named Troy, sixteen, with a short afro, an easygoing smile, and smart, fast eyes, won. He raced away. A moment later, they watched him on the screen, talking with Jacob Redwater, leading him.

"This oughta be good," Etcetera said.

Gretyl wondered where Iceweasel was, whether she was seeing this. There was a lot of clamor from the crowd to livecast her talk with Redwater. She said no, firmly, while agreeing to record and release it later, depending on whether there was a later.

Jacob Redwater came into the control room, preceded by a bow-wave of understated cologne. Gretyl stood and looked him up and down, looking for bulges indicating guns or other surprises. Not that they had to bulge much these days, and not that she knew much about what kind of bulges they made.

His face was impassive. He'd been crying, minutes ago, broken and lost. Now he wore the zotta mask, two parts charming sophisticate, one part dead-eyed predator. A man who could make entertaining conversation over dinner, then go home and bankrupt your employer and put you on the street.

"Hello, Gretyl." He stood before Troy like Troy had a gun in his back and he was pretending that it wasn't there.

"Hello, Mr. Redwater." She extended her hand.

His hand was warm and firm. "Call me Jacob."

Limpopo gave him a funny look. Gretyl remembered Jacob Redwater had set her up to be rendered to this prison, ripped from family and everything dear to her. She was used to thinking of him as the man who'd sired and kidnapped her wife, but he was Limpopo's arch-nemesis. She wondered if Limpopo would shiv the bastard, who surely deserved it. She was about to lunge to take out her frail old friend, frailer alongside this vigorous, unthinkably rich man, but Limpopo held her hand out.

"Limpopo." He tilted his head, straining to recognize her.

"Hello, Jacob."

"Nice to see you," said Etcetera. Redwater's eyes widened. He started at the speaker between her collarbones. "It's me, Hubert. I'm dead."

"I see. Nice to talk to you again, even so."

Troy brought him a chair. The three sat together, boys clustered at the room's other end, ostentatiously not listening while ferociously eavesdropping.

Redwater said nothing. Gretyl put her elbows on her knees and leaned forward, arching her back to work the creak and ache of sitting and terror out. "What did you want to talk about, Jacob?"

"I don't want you to get hurt."

"You don't want your daughter hurt. You're indifferent to what happens to the old dyke she's shacked up with."

He shook his head. "I don't care about your sexuality. My cousin is gay, you know."

"I know. That's the reason you're running the family fortune these days."

He shook his head. "It's more complicated. You can believe that if you want.

The internal politics of the Redwater family are always and only about one thing."

"Money."

"Power. Money's just keeping score."

"Must have really fucked you off when Iceweasel gave her share to that merc." She wanted him to squirm. She'd expected him to be the weeping man on the phone. She didn't want to die with the sight of him erect and proud burned into her optic nerve, proof the sun would never set on the zotta empire.

He nodded. "It made things complicated in our family. But it wasn't fatal. Nadie and I are on good terms these days, believe it or not."

Gretyl kept her best poker face, willing herself not to give away the fact that Nadie had Iceweasel and the boys with her.

"I would like to see my daughter and my grandsons."

"I think you gave up that right when you had her kidnapped, Mr. Redwater," Limpopo said. They looked at her. Her eyes glittered dangerously. "When you had me disappeared."

"When you had me murdered," Etcetera said.

Redwater was impassive. Gretyl thought she saw anxious tells, sudden realization by this arrogant princeling that he was three levels underground, surrounded by people who owed him a debt of violence.

He spoke carefully. "I didn't say I had a right to it. The things that happened were beyond regrettable. They were terrible. I brought Natalie home because I knew there was trouble ahead for you and your friends. The murders of those two security operators tipped things over the edge. There was no way things would be business as usual after that. I wanted her safe. The things that followed, what happened to you, were nothing to do with me."

She and Limpopo started to speak at once, broke off, looked at each other. Limpopo made a "go ahead" gesture. "He's your father-in-law." She smiled sardonically.

Jacob Redwater returned the smile, pretending he didn't notice its venom.

"What murders, Jacob?"

"The two people that Zyz lost at the 'university' complex. Went in, never came out. That was bad enough. But then we discovered that they'd been captured and subsequently executed—euthanized—that their remains had been desecrated—"

"What the fuck are you talking about?" Gretyl said. But she knew. For the first couple years, the deadheading bodies of those two mercs had been like unwanted family heirlooms, dutifully lugged from one place to another, scans cared for and backed up. Back when she was on the move all the time, the arrangements for their care had been a constant reminder of the terrible thing they'd done in the tunnels of Walkaway U, Tam's dire warnings, the obligation they'd created for themselves. Once they'd settled in Gary and moved the two bodies, or people, or whatever, into canopic jars in the basement, automatically tended as they slept in endless, blank-faced, brain-dead stasis, she'd managed to put them out of mind—mostly.

"So you kidnapped her and deprived her of clothes and companionship because you had her best interests at heart?"

"Yes. Because I knew the alternative was *much* worse. Death. As you discovered. That's why I'm here. Because, whether or not you believe this, I love my daughter. I raised her. I held her when she was born. I told her bedtime stories. I changed her diapers. She is my flesh and blood. I am a part of her, always will be. I don't want her to die. I don't want my grandchildren to die."

"But we can all die?" Limpopo said. "No especial reason to keep us around. Apart from generating income for TransCanada, we're surplus."

He shrugged. "Not my department. I'm interested in my family. Your family can look out for you."

"That's mighty white of you, Mr. Redwater," Limpopo said.

Gretyl almost asked him how much diaper changing and storytelling he did, how much of it was delegated to au pairs. She couldn't see the point. Jacob Redwater was exactly what he seemed: a zotta who cared about getting things he wanted, didn't give a shit about what happened to everyone else. However much diaper-changing he'd done, it was enough to reinforce whatever part of him believed kidnapping his daughter was an acceptable alternative to stopping his pals from killing everyone within ten klicks of her.

She stared at his excellent skin tone and the muscular shoulders under his vest. He looked like he was having a day off at the cottage, someone in a stock-art photo advertising a line of fine outdoor/casual clothing. Burnished by his years, not battered. Not like Gretyl, not like her friends. She walked away because she couldn't be a party to making men like this immortal gods. They didn't need her help.

"Your daughter doesn't want to see you." It was true. She didn't have to ask Iceweasel—she'd never wavered on that.

"She named her son after me."

"We named our son after you so she'd never forget what she turned her back on. I didn't understand at first. She explained that she wanted to make a Jacob Redwater that wouldn't be remembered as a selfish monster."

He was impassive.

"Holy shit." A boy pointed to the screens.

They followed his finger. There, walking up Highway 15 was a big crowd. Hundreds of people. At the front, still in remains of uniforms and body armor, were the cops who had walked away. They split into three smaller groups, walked right into the private cops who tried to stop them from entering the prisons' inner courtyards, scuffling briefly as they tried to decide how much force they could use against these newcomers. Then they were beyond the cops, between them and the prisons. They linked arms and sat down in front of the buildings, saying nothing. The walkaway ex-cops sat in the middle. Gretyl understood the crowd around the world hadn't stopped when the feeds went dead.

On cue, new drones buzzed the courtyard, all kinds, including network relay. She saw the massive expansion in bandwidth from her seat, surging over the infographics in a flood of blue that went green as the caches on both sides of the link emptied and the congestion cleared—they were in sync with the world.

Jacob Redwater looked . . . quizzical. He narrowed his eyes. As the boys waved the feeds to zoom over the whole wall, he gave a minute head shake, as if to say *that's not right*.

What had Nadie said? They don't want another Akron. They don't want martyrs. If they bomb the place, it will be with the cameras off. They were into new tactical territory now, on both sides. There had been many assaults on walkaway strongholds by default regimes—religious fundamentalists in America and Saudi Arabia; no-insignia mercs in Ukraine, Moldova, and Siberia; storm troopers backed by huge, network-killing information weapons in China. There had been advances and retreats. Never this kind of siege.

Gretyl's phone rang. She knew from the buzz it was her wife. She whooshed out a sigh.

"We're okay." She knew Gretyl would have been quietly freaking after a protracted radio silence.

"I love you."

"I love you, too. The boys love you. Are you okay? We've been watching it here. The boys are livid that they didn't get to stay and help with the drones. They're not quite clear on the danger. I don't want to worry them."

"Don't." She was keenly aware of Jacob Redwater straining to hear, wishing she'd learned how to do that subvocalization thing with her interfaces. She'd never had much call for private audio-spaces—too much of a hermit.

"Don't? Oh, worry them. Are you okay? Can you talk?"

"I can."

"But not much. Why? Who's there? What's going on? Are you safe?"

She sighed. Her wife was good at a lot of things, but covert ops wasn't one of them.

"Your father is here."

It was an eerie silence, silence of an over-compressed audio channel discarding background noise. "Is he going to hurt you?" She sounded cold.

"He would have a hard time doing that. He's locked in with us, in a subbasement of the boys' prison, a control center. He wanted to talk to you, and since you wouldn't take his calls, he called me."

Jacob Redwater was thinking hard about where Iceweasel was. What it meant that she had to have this explained.

"Of course he'd know how to get in touch with you. You going to ransom him?"

She couldn't stop the smile. Because she was expecting it, she got between Jacob Redwater and the door as he stood suddenly, knocking over his chair. He came at her. She remembered what a fit, gym-toned, personally trained, technologically-tuned badass he was. She was about to get slugged. That's when Troy landed on his back and bore him to the ground, arms locked around his neck. The other boys each took a limb and *sat* on it.

"Gretyl?" She sounded alarmed.

"No problems. Give me a sec?"

She looked down at Jacob Redwater's face. He was calm, like he was relaxing with a glass of wine in his den, not lying on a concrete floor with four juvenile delinquents sitting on him. "Jacob, Iceweasel and the boys left before this started. They're safe. Would you like me to ask Iceweasel if she'd be interested in talking to you?"

"Not if I was starving to death and he was the only drive-through on Earth," Iceweasel said, making Gretyl snort. It was crueler and more gloat-y than she'd intended. She caught herself before she apologized to the spread-eagled zotta.

"I know the answer. Do I get to leave?"

"Why should we let you? This place is full of handcuffs and cells. We could lock you up, make sure whatever happens to us happens to you. It might not stop them from nuking us. Then again, it might."

"Probably not. I used up everything I had, stopping things so I could get in here. Giving into me cost them a lot—" He nodded towards the screens, where private cops and the walkaways faced each other beneath a canopy of drones. "The people calling the shots wouldn't mind losing me. It would destabilize things, but it would also set an example for the next time something like this happens. I'm not the only powerful person related to someone on your side, you know. Object lessons are expensive. It's wasteful to pass them up when they're available."

"They're not going to kill you," Limpopo said. "Not Jacob Redwater. We've seen your board seats. Too many people owe you too much, depend on you too much—"

Etcetera interrupted—beyond weird, Limpopo and her collarbones arguing—"That means there's people who would love to step into his shoes."

Redwater shrugged best as he could. "You're both right. If I died here with you, there would be hell to pay. But very powerful people would get the chance to make themselves much more powerful. The reason I was allowed to do what I did was that it's a fully hedged risk. Delighted if I die, delighted if I don't."

"He probably makes a new scan every morning after breakfast," Etcetera continued, with machine smugness. "He'd be up and running on a huge cluster by dinner."

"Not that often. But I'm current, and they've dry-run my sims. There's messy probate questions, so it wouldn't be dinner, exactly."

Gretyl hated how he could be pinned to the floor in hostile territory and still be calm and in charge.

"Gret?"

"Sorry, I kinda forgot about you. Look, darling, I should go. I love you. I love the boys. You are my world."

"We love you, too." She was crying. Gretyl blinked hard and made herself not cry. Jacob Redwater watched her closely.

Then Iceweasel made a surprised noise. Gretyl jumped. "What is it?" She saw the monitors and gasped.

The private cops were retreating, rank by rank, into the APCs, which were pulling out in an orderly fashion. The cops faced out, toward the prison, as they waited their turn to board their vehicles. As if this wasn't amazing enough, a cop broke ranks, took off her helmet and dropped her gun, just as others did earlier that day, and crossed over to the walkaway lines. Two more did it. The orderly retreat stopped being orderly. Cops milled about. Many looked like they were listening intently to voices in their helmets. Some talked avidly to one another. They called out jokey, comradely farewells to the ones who'd crossed over.

Jacob Redwater was at a loss. He watched the spectacle, craning his neck from the floor. The expression on his face was the closest thing to fear that Gretyl imagined she'd ever see.

"What do you think, Jacob?" The laugh in Gretyl's voice was involuntarily mean. "They pulling out so they can nuke us and send a message? Or are they getting out before the stock market melts down and their guard labor walks out?"

"May I sit?"

"Not my decision."

The boys looked at each other and got up. He sat and worked his shoulders.

"I'm leaving." He was still transfixed by the feeds. One of the APCs was disrupted by a cop who climbed back out and deserted.

Gretyl looked at him. He was still upright and unwavering, armored with dignity.

"Jacob, I know there will always be people like you."

"Rich people."

"People who think other people are like them. People who think you either take or get took. We'll never be rid of that. It's a primal fear, toddler selfishness. The question is whether people like you will get to define the default. Whether you can make it a self-fulfilling prophecy, doing for all of us before we do to you, meaning we're all chumps if we're not trying to do to you sooner. That default was easier to maintain when we didn't have enough. When we didn't have data. When we couldn't all talk to each other."

"Okay." No hint of overt sarcasm, all the more sarcastic for it.

"We're not making a world without greed, Jacob. We're making a world where greed is a perversion. Where grabbing everything for yourself instead of sharing is like smearing yourself with shit: gross. Wrong. Our winning doesn't mean you don't get to be greedy. It means people will be ashamed for you, will pity you and want to distance themselves from you. You can be as greedy as you want, but no one will admire you for it."

"Okay." He was a little paler. Maybe that was wish fulfillment.

"I think your ride is leaving," Gretyl said. She was elated. The fatalistic acceptance of her impending destruction uncoiled from her chest, turned to victorious song. The part of her that had been emotionally prepared to die caught up to the part of her that knew she wouldn't have to. She wanted to drink everything that could be drunk, fuck and sing, build a bonfire and dance naked around it. She was almost dead. Now she would live. Forever, perhaps.

"Good-bye. I'll tell Iceweasel and the kids that you asked after them."

*That* hit. He oofed like he'd been gut-punched. She felt like a sudden and total asshole. Whatever kind of monster Jacob Redwater was, he was someone to whom family mattered, in a twisted, coercive way. She almost apologized. She didn't. She thought she would, but he was gone. Limpopo hugged her ferociously, Etcetera muttered into her cleavage from his speaker. The boys whooped and danced.

"I love you," Iceweasel said.

"I love you, too, darling. I'm coming home." She wiped tears of joy off her face. "Unless you and the boys want to come back and stay for a while?" She knew it was a stupid thing to ask. She wanted to keep the *first days* rush alive for a little longer, before going back to the *ongoing days* default they'd built in Gary.

"No," Iceweasel said. She groped for more words, but apparently none came. "What happened to my father?"

"He left. Intact."

"I think I see him now."

Gretyl looked at the screen. There he was, walking away, a phalanx of private cops escorting him behind their lines, back to the command vehicles. "That's him."

"Fuck," Iceweasel said. Gretyl's heart ached and grew two sizes when she heard the boys giggling at their mom's swearing. What had she been thinking, putting herself in danger? Risking never seeing her wife, her beautiful boys, ever again? What madness came over her? Was she secretly suicidal? "When will you leave?"

"Tomorrow or a little later. There's bound to be a lot of people moving around, next couple days. Hoa might bring bikes. Whatever makes sense."

"Will you bring Limpopo?"

She looked at Limpopo, who watched with frank interest. Stooped and old, eyes blazing, take-no-shit attitude you could see from orbit. Gretyl knew from the first time she'd seen Limpopo that the woman was a fucking superhero.

"Iceweasel wants to know if you'll come with me."

Limpopo didn't hesitate. "No. There's things here I want to help with. It's my place. I bought it with fourteen years of my life. There are lots of fights to come, and I want to be here with the people who fought for this place. I'll stay."

"You hear that?"

"Tell her we love her. Tell her that she has a home here, too. Any time."

Gretyl said it. Limpopo nodded gravely. The boys watched them wide-eyed, still shocked from the sudden lifting of their death sentence.

Etcetera added, "Tell the other Limpopo she doesn't have to worry about me coming back any time soon."

"I'm sure that'll be a great comfort."

It turned out that sims could *harumph*. It was a new one on Gretyl.

# EPILOGUE

# even better nation

It wasn't like waking from a dream, but Iceweasel was sure she *had* dreamed. There was Billiam, flirting outrageously with Noozi, which couldn't be right, because poor Billiam was long dead. Noozi was in orbit, had been in orbit for fifteen years, swore she felt none of the negative physiological effects, they'd been mitigated by deadheading and pharma they printed on the station's bio-reactor. There'd been doctors, some present, more in the crowd, offering opinions on her scans, on the cancer eating her liver, threatening to spread to her blood. And her father! They'd spoken, with Cordelia. It was like old times. Nadie had been there, too, and, shit, they'd made out, in front of Gretyl. Just the memory of it made her blush.

Blushing reminded her she had a body. Remembering she had a body made her remember that she'd deadheaded, parked herself because of the cancer. That hadn't been imaginary. Parked herself after a tearful party with the boys: big, pimply teenagers; and Gretyl, old and sad and trying so hard not to show it; and her friends. Cordelia *had* been there, had left the walled city she and Dad lived in, snuck in a screen that Dad's face appeared on, live-linked. He'd said urgent and desperate things that made her cry. She couldn't remember them.

She'd deadheaded. Now she was awake. In a room. She strained to look around. It was dim. It smelled nice. Like a forest, with a hint of scented steam. Like there was an onsen nearby. Sulfur, eucalyptus. She was on a hospital bed with rails. She saw light cast by infographics on its sides, cast on the dark floor—stone?—around it. A window, crack of sunlight at the bottom of its blinds. She checked in with her body, found it didn't hurt. Such a relief she nearly cried. It had hurt a lot, before deadheading. All the time, all over.

She squeezed her hands together and they felt . . . weird. Why weird? She couldn't say. Footsteps approached. The door opened. When it did she got the room's dimensions. It was about the size of the bedroom she'd shared with Gretyl. She smelled onsen smells, stronger and sharper. Her skin ached for water and steam. She wanted to sit up, but should she?

There was a person in the door. A man. Walking toward her. Smiling. Bearded. Young. Wearing something weird, slippery-looking, tight. She could actually see the outline of his balls. It was a singular garment. It could have come off a runway a century ago, or off a printer fifty years after she went to sleep. How long had it been?

The man smiled. She felt vertigo. That face was familiar. It was impossible. She smelled him, a pleasant smell she remembered from so many nights and days together on so many roads.

She almost laughed as she said it: "Hubert Vernon Rudolph Clayton Irving Wilson Alva Anton Jeff Harley Timothy Curtis Cleveland Cecil Ollie Edmund Eli Wiley Marvin Ellis Espinoza." She laughed. He laughed with her. Any thought she'd had that this was Etcetera's son or clone or robot were dispelled by the laugh.

"How the actual fuck."

He held out his hands, smooth and unwrinkled and not dead.

"Like it?"

She took his hand. It was warm, young and vital. She held it to her cheek. She cried on the hand.

"How?" She looked at his hands, smooth and unmarked.

"Same as you." The vertigo was back, hard. The room did a slow roll with her in the center. The reason his hand was so smooth was *her* hand was so smooth. That was why it felt weird. It was her hand, but it was *new*. She ran her hands over her body, probed places where she'd unconsciously dreaded surgical scars or bags, squeezed the muscles of her feet and legs and ass, touched her face. Stared at her hands again.

"No way."

"Took thirty years. Bodies were easier, came out of organ-growing stuff. But brains, getting the scans back into them, that was hard." He tapped his head. "It's impossible to say whether it worked. But I feel like me."

She touched his arm, his stomach. "You do." She touched her lips, ears, eyes, throat. "I do, too." She swallowed. "I guess."

She used him to pull herself into a sitting position. It didn't feel like she'd been sleeping. It felt like nothing she'd felt before. Like being born again. Her skin tingled. It felt *amazing*.

"Gretyl?"

He frowned. "We're working on her. Died five years ago. Left a scan. Hoping to have her in a year, two at most. We're growing the body quick as we can."

Her mouth was open. She closed it. "Stan? Jacob?"

"They stopped having bodies ten years ago." He shrugged. "Kids. They're waiting to talk to you. I think they want to talk you into giving up on the body, joining them. They're offworld, most of the time. They entangle a lot, with each other and others. Gives me the fucking willies. That's the next generation's job, right? No matter how hard you try, the little fuckers always generation-gap you."

She swung her feet over the edge, let them touch the floor. It was tile, maybe slate. Every seam crackled through her nervous system. It was a sensation between ticklish and being on orgasm's edge. She clutched at his arm, vertigo and joy warring.

"I smell an onsen."

"We built another B&B. It's totally retro. Limpopo is waiting for us. Both of them, actually."

Her mouth was open again. "Two of them?"

"It's frowned upon. But no one gives either of them any shit about it. And only one of them talks to me."

She stood, letting the sheet slip away from her, leaving her naked. She felt air on her skin. It was so intense she nearly sat again, but kept her grip on his arm.

"Enjoy it. You'd be amazed at how quickly you get over it. Normal is hard to resist. Everything becomes default, no matter how new."

He led her down the hallway.

They passed other people, who smiled, said hello in a variety of accents. Some looked familiar, older versions of the people she'd known. Some looked like younger versions. She could have sworn one was Tam, but impossibly young. A teenager. Cousin? Daughter? Tam?

They paused at the heavy, salt-crusted onsen door, thick wood planks that transpired scented, warm air. He hugged her. She hugged him back.

"Welcome home," he said.

# acknowledgments

This book could never have been written without the influence of Rebecca Solnit's *A Paradise Built in Hell,* David Graeber's *Debt: The First 5,000 Years,* and Thomas Piketty's *Capital in the Twenty-First Century.*

Thanks to Alice (of course!), Steven Brust, Scott Westerfeld, Barton Gellman, Patrick Ball, John Gilmore, Roz Doctorow, Noah Swartz, Biella Coleman, Mitch Altman, Quinn Norton, Jo Walton, Kim Stanley Robinson, Vladimir Verano and Third Place Books, Madeline and McNally Jackson Books, the ACLU's Ben Wizner, Jeremy Bornstein, William Gibson, Edward Snowden, and Eleanor Saitta.

Thanks as always to my agent, Russell Galen, and my editor, Patrick Nielsen Hayden, who made this better by supporting me without ever letting me off the hook. Thank you to Tom Doherty for his contributions to science fiction, to publishing, and to literature—and for all the many gracious conversations he has afforded me over our long and fruitful association.